THE RETIRED ASSASSIN'S GUIDE TO COUNTRY GARDENING

ASSASSIN'S GUIDE

NAOMI KUTTNER

Copyright © 2025 by Naomi Kuttner

All rights reserved.

No part of this book may be reproduced in any form or by any electronic or mechanical means, including information storage and retrieval systems, without written permission from the author, except for the use of brief quotations in a book review.

PROLOGUE

This is a story about murder, and the lengths people will go to secure what they believe is rightfully theirs.

But it is also a story about a small New Zealand town by the sea, with its forests, rivers, and people who love gardening, gossiping, and good coffee.

Lastly, it's a story about ghosts and how they are part of our world, visible only in rare circumstances, and to unlikely people.

Now all these elements have gathered to dance around a central point that could be a life, but is in this case, a death.

POSTSCRIPT

1

In which we meet our unlikely heroes

Dante's watch buzzed against his wrist, notifying him that someone had entered his front yard. He tapped the screen and checked the hidden camera he'd mounted in the Victorian filigree above the porch.

A young man was making his way up the garden path.

Dante glared at the image on his watch. He'd come to this small coastal town on the assumption that everyone would leave him the hell alone. But he'd learned that this was not to be.

The villagers treated a foreigner moving into their digs like an invitation to be friendly. He'd had neighbours coming over with lamington cakes, people stopping him on the sidewalk to talk about the weather. One lady with a perm and leopard print leggings had even asked him to join her for a coffee at one of the village's two cafes.

He hadn't known what to say.

And now someone was about to knock on his door.

With a growl, he started tidying away the disassembled Glock he'd been cleaning. He wasn't going to allow anyone inside his house, but it paid never to leave things to chance.

The doorbell rang. It was a real bell — its copper gone green with age — not the electronic simulated bell most houses had.

Dante put the last piece of his sidearm in its padded metal box, closed it, and locked the lid.

He checked the camera again. The young man didn't appear to be armed, but he made sure his favourite Luger was in its underarm holster. Because old habits died hard, and Dante wanted to buck the statistic about people dying soon after retirement.

He padded down the wide hallway, the golden timber floor smooth underneath his sock-clad feet. The front door was solid oak, painted a dark green, with a wavy glass panel showing an indistinct outline outside.

Dante unlocked the door's original deadbolt. He then deactivated the second deadbolt he'd installed with a touch of his index finger and swung the door open.

The fresh-faced young man standing on his porch looked surprised at the silent arrival of the house's owner. He was about nineteen or twenty, with curly brown hair just shy of being auburn. Hazel eyes with long lashes completed the image of country wholesomeness. He even had rosy cheeks for god's sake.

"Er, hi." The young man gave Dante an uncertain smile.

"What do you want?" Dante winced internally. He tried to remember what his therapist had told him about meeting people for the first time. Eye contact, but not too much. Relaxed stance. Smile on the inside, that will show up in your voice. That last one made no sense to Dante. He'd seen plenty of people's insides in his line of work, and not one internal smile.

"Ah, my name's Charlie. Charlie Wilson."

The young man swallowed. Since Dante was six foot two with a street fighter physique, hair cut military style, piercing grey eyes and scarred knuckles, he was used to people being nervous around him. Being nearly forty had done nothing to mellow his features.

"Alright. Charlie Wilson." Dante tried to smile on the inside. "What do you want?"

Charlie swallowed, his Adam's apple jumping up and down. "Mr Reid—"

"Call me Dante."

"Mr Dante. My name's Charlie Wilson."

"You said that already."

"Um... Mr Dante, I'm here to do your garden."

"My what?" Dante looked around front yard of the 1920s villa he'd purchased six weeks ago, sight unseen. There were a lot of plants in it. Trees too. And other plants in pots. There was even a glass greenhouse out the back — an elegant wrought iron affair that must have been built around the same time as the house.

Dante supposed a garden like this would need looking after. That was what gardeners did.

"Are you a gardener?"

"Yes." Charlie nodded enthusiastically. "I've been doing this garden for the last five years. Mrs Davison - she owned the house before you — had me come in every Thursday to do it."

Was it Dante's imagination, or did Charlie's eyes flick sideways to the shadows under a purple flowered tree growing by the side of the verandah? Dante was sure he had. He scowled at the young man. He didn't like things that made no sense.

"You can't come on a Thursday." Thursday was when Dante tuned in to his AA meeting - 5pm EST, 9am New Zealand time. Things were discussed in these meetings that were not for gardeners to overhear.

Charlie looked crestfallen. "But Mr Dante, it's important the garden is looked after. It's one of the finest in the region. There's rare Chatham Island Lilies, native orchids, and an Amorphophallus Titanum."

"I don't know what an Amorphophallus Titanum is."

"It's a corpse flower."

"Oh." Dante wondered if burying bodies under a corpse flower would be too obvious. Then he remembered he was no longer responsible for burying bodies.

"Mrs Davison never got to see the corpse flower bloom while she was alive. They only bloom every seven to ten years, so it's bound to happen any time now. It's in the glasshouse, and the temperature needs to be kept just right for it."

"I'm sure it'll be fine." Dante stepped back, preparing to shut the door.

Charlie shot another look at the purple flowered tree, then stepped forward, his face flushed a cherry pink. "I'll work for free!"

"You will?"

Charlie managed to look both sheepish and grumpy. "Yes. The corpse plant is extremely rare. There's only two in the southern hemisphere. She — Mrs Davison would want to know it's being looked after."

Dante studied the young man. There was definitely something odd going on here. "Is it customary around here for the gardener to come with the house?"

"Yes?" Charlie looked hopeful.

Dante sighed. "You're going to keep on about this dead flower, aren't you?"

Charlie nodded. "It's unique. And it'd be much appreciated by the Te Kohe Botanical Society—"

"Fine, fine." Dante rubbed at his temples. "I get it." Who knew the local yokels would be so hardcore about gardening? "I should have bought that house by the harbour with the fully concreted front and back yard," he muttered. The guy who'd owned the house had painted the concrete green. To Dante, that seemed like a sensible type of garden.

"You won't regret it, Mr Dante," bubbled Charlie. "You'll get to see the corpse flower bloom, and—"

"You can't come Thursdays."

"Friday?"

"Ok." Dante considered. "I'll pay you whatever Mrs Davison paid you. Plus ten percent for inflation."

"Thank you!" Charlie's face shone like a lighthouse beacon.

"No problem." Dante wondered briefly if Charlie had hidden a body in the garden. Why else would someone be so keen to continue digging around in a bunch of plants? Perhaps there was something hidden under the purple flowered tree? He tuned in again to hear Charlie still effusing.

"—and Mrs Davison will be so relieved. She was worried about who would take care of everything when she passed. So I'll be here every Friday morning, half past seven sharp, is that alright?"

"Yeah, sure." Dante.

"And I can teach you all about gardening if you'd like. Since this is your garden now, not Mrs Davison's."

The last words came out slightly more emphatically than was necessary, almost as if said to someone listening in on their conversation.

Dante raised an eyebrow. "Correct."

"Right. Er, good morning then." Charlie raised a hand in an awkward wave. "See you on Friday!"

Dante watched Charlie leave, then shut the door thoughtfully. Was gardening something people did once they were retired? It seemed like he was going to find out.

2

In which Dante receives an unwelcome proposal

Dante Reid carefully picked up his coffee and sipped it. Enjoy the small things in life. Take each day as it comes. He repeated the mantra his therapist had given him last month.

Across the wrought iron table, his unwanted visitor, Ted Andrews, drummed thick fingers on the white tablecloth.

They were seated on the ground floor balcony of the Pepper Tree Hotel — a rambling three storey mansion where Dante had planned to enjoy a leisurely morning coffee followed by eggs on toast. The small things in life.

Then Ted Andrews' driver had parked his hummer on the grass verge, quite spoiling Dante's view of the sleepy village street. And Ted Andrews himself had crabbed his way up the stairs and onto the verandah to plonk himself down in the chair facing Dante.

"It's good to finally meet you," said Ted, baring bleached teeth in a smile. Ted's face was lined from years of gritty living, overlaid with luxury spa treatments.

"Whatever you're selling, I don't want it."

"Oh, but I think you might." Ted's smile spread like artificial butter as he spooned five teaspoons of sugar into his coffee, poured without invitation from the dainty bone china kettle sitting in the middle of the table.

Dante caught the eye of Libby, the sole waitress on for the early breakfast shift. "More coffee, please?" The words came out flat, and Dante felt a twinge of disappointment. He sounded like the British Terminator, not the personable manner he'd practised during his last therapy session. Perhaps she'd put it down to him not having had enough coffee?

Ted leaned back in the faded wicker chair. "You see, Mr Reid—"

"Call me Dante."

"Well, if we're on a first-name basis already." Another flash of too-white teeth. "I make it my business to get to know people in this town. You could say I'm a bit of a godfather figure around here."

Dante could imagine Ted putting severed horses' heads in people's beds. He nodded thanks as Libby placed another vintage kettle on the table, the small metal sieve inside filled with freshly ground coffee, steaming into the morning air.

"Nobody knows much about you, Mr Dante."

"I'm an introvert."

"So you say, so you say. However, I have well-connected friends from my time in London."

Dante said nothing, but his attention sharpened to a pinpoint focus. Within a heartbeat, he could trace every micro-expression in the muscles around Ted's mouth, every tiny dilation of the man's pupils.

Calm it, he told himself. Take each day as it comes. Enjoy the small things. He deliberately relaxed his shoulders and breathed out. Don't kill anybody.

"I'm a man of the world, Dante. Like you." Ted rested his free hand comfortably on his generous pot belly. "It's hard to believe there's anything going on in this hick town, but then a stranger moves in. And I make enquiries about him."

Dante swirled his coffee cup to gather up the dregs and tossed the last bit of coffee back. "I wouldn't know about that. I was an accountant in Kent."

"Of course, of course. And I wouldn't normally disturb your retirement. Only, I fired my bodyguard last week, you see. Turns out he had a nasal problem," Ted mimed snorting a line of cocaine. "Easily compromised, you understand?"

Dante did understand. It was the kind of knowledge he'd found useful to dig up back when he had been gainfully employed.

"And I find myself in need of a bit of extra protection. Nothing much. Just an added... security. Until I can find a suitable replacement. A little bird told me you would be quite the man for the job."

"I'm retired." Dante directed what his therapist called a 'warm and natural smile' at Ted, and the older man shifted uncomfortably in his chair.

"It's just a small job," Ted assured him. "Nothing to it. And you'll find I'm a generous employer."

Dante thought about the contents of a safe in Hong Kong, another in Switzerland, and various crypto wallets hidden in safety deposit boxes around the globe.

"Money's not an issue."

"You've lived here for how long? A couple of months. Surely you could do with a change of pace."

"I'm retired." Sometimes just repeating the same phrase over and over again made people go away. In this case, Dante wasn't sure Ted would get the message.

"This is a nice town. Good people. A nice, peaceful place to retire."

"That was my plan."

"It would be unfortunate for nasty rumours to spread about you," said Ted. "People will believe anything these days."

Dante considered the implied threat. A few rumours - true or false - expertly planted by someone like Ted could make this town quite an unpleasant place for him to live.

He mentally added an item to his to-do list, just above 'make sure the weapons cache under the kitchen sink is rat proof' and 'restock protein powder.' Find out what Ted knows about my past. And who told him. Without killing anyone. Preferably.

The trail leading from Dante's former employment to this small town was well disguised. Dante was sure of it. Both he and his former employer had insisted on it. He couldn't recall who was keener - them to see him out to pasture, or him to get away from it all. He remembered wanting to feel like he had a beating human heart in his chest again. To feel anything other than bleakness, punctuated by clinically directed violence.

Dealing with Ted was going to be difficult if Dante couldn't employ his usual methods. It was just that killing people solved so many problems, so easily. At least, it did if you were a moving target, working in unstable regimes around the globe. Not so much if you were planning to settle down in a small town where everyone knew everyone's business.

Dante looked up to see Ted waiting for a reply to something he hadn't heard. He gave a non-committal 'hmm' and swirled the kettle.

"So, what do you say, Dante?"

"About what?"

"Security and surveillance. Just one evening - next Saturday. I'm having a small, exclusive party at this hotel. With exclusive, important guests. We'll be watching the Jubilee fireworks. And I feel in need of extra security." For an instant, a flicker in Ted's eyes betrayed something that interested Dante intensely - fear. Genuine fear, the kind that would keep a man up at night, counting the hours until dawn.

"Hmm."

"And then I guarantee no one in this town will ever wonder about your past."

"I'll think about it." Dante slid twenty dollars under his coffee cup.

"Wait—"

But Dante was already striding down the stairs from the Pepper Tree verandah. He stepped onto the close-cut grass verge that passed for a sidewalk at this end of town. The sun was evaporating the morning dew. It was going to be a hot summer's day.

Enjoy the small things. Don't take the easy way out. One kill would be one too many. Dante's gaze rested on the leather band around his left wrist as he walked away. Eighty-nine days straight, no bodies. Don't break the chain. He breathed in for the count of five, out for ten, just like his therapist had recommended.

Near the end of his career, the distance between thought and instinct, analysis and action had narrowed to a razor edge.

That was why he'd been given the option of early retirement. It turned out too many bodies (even ones that vanished without a trace) looked bad on one's quarterly review.

It was why he had a weekly zoom call with his therapist, and spent the first thirty minutes of each day doing yoga, followed by slow breathing and a guided meditation. Zen Buddhist talks were currently a favourite.

Would the Buddha's inscrutable smile slip if Dante used Ted's face to smash the hotel's Queen Anne coffee set into tiny pieces?

On the balance of things, the Buddha would probably not approve.

A walk along the waterfront would diffuse his tension. And then Dante could think about what to do next. Also, there was a cafe halfway around the harbour. If he wasn't allowed to kill anyone, then at least he could indulge in a second breakfast.

3

In which Dante discovers the finer points of corpse plants

"So that's the corpse flower." Dante stared at a clay planter large enough to be used as a cannibal cook pot.

"It will be," said Charlie enthusiastically. "The flower tuber is lying dormant right now."

They were standing in what Dante's estate agent had called 'a gracious Victorian glasshouse, the focal point of the garden and a stately remnant of a bygone era.'

Dante acknowledged it was quite...nice. Delicate palms brushed the glass roof, while a banana tree spread luminous green leaves across the slanting rays of sun.

Above him, vines with ponderous white and purple blossoms trailed from the wrought iron arches, and orchids branched out from bark-wrapped perches.

Dante recognised the flowers because of a sting he'd orchestrated in the surprisingly cutthroat world of orchid smuggling. Some of Mrs Davison's specimens looked good enough to kill for.

"When will it do something?" The corpse plant pot was an uninspiring brown colour - the same as the dirt which filled it. There could be anything buried there. Although probably not a body. Not unless it had been well packed in.

"I don't know exactly, Mr Dante, but when it sprouts, it will grow fifteen centimetres per day, to a height of two and a half to three metres. It's quite something."

"Oh," said Dante. He shifted his shoulders, relaxing in the sunlight while Charlie extolled the virtues of corpse plants.

Dante realised Charlie was waiting expectantly for a response. He ran his mind back over what the youth had been telling him.

"You want me to buy a new glasshouse heating unit to keep the corpse flower alive through winter?"

"Mrs Davison wanted to get it — we did all the research, and it's the best one out there. But she couldn't buy it straight away on her pension. She was saving up for it when..." Charlie shrugged, as if to say even the best gardening plans can be disrupted by the grim reaper.

"Fine, fine. Just send me the details and I'll buy it," said Dante. Charlie had been working for less than half an hour, and already he was proving to be expensive. "You can install it?"

"Yes, sir."

"And this corpse flower," Dante eyed the clay pot doubtfully, "you say it'll reach three meters?"

"In just a couple of weeks." Charlie's face glowed. "The Te Kohe Botanical Society will be so excited to see it. And the local newspaper will want to take a picture."

"Do they have to see it?"

"Oh yes," Charlie nodded emphatically.

"I'd rather not have visitors."

Charlie poked his tongue into the side of his cheek. Dante guessed this was his thinking face.

"If you don't invite them, they'll be twice as curious. They'll probably pop by anyway, at all different times, and gossip even more."

Dante watched a Venus fly trap, disturbed by their presence, close its claws around thin air. "How will they even know it's blooming? If I don't tell them and you don't tell them."

"They'll know." Charlie's certainty was absolute. "Never underestimate the Te Kohe Botanical Society. They always find out."

Dante sighed. "Is there anyone else who'll want to see this dead flower?"

"The Wiri Flower Arranging Society, The Friends of the Cemetery, The Rotary Club, The Lions Foundation..." Charlie ticked off names on his fingers.

"That's basically the whole town!"

Charlie looked apologetic. "Not a lot goes on around here. People take an interest in local events."

Dante thought about the weapon stashes in each room of his house, as well as the larger one in the cellar. "They'll stay outside, right?"

"Um. It's usual to offer light refreshments. Tea and biscuits should do it."

"No way." Dante considered setting fire to the glasshouse.

"You value your privacy, Mr. Dante."

"I could give the corpse flower away. Would you like it?"

Charlie looked horrified. "Mrs Davison would be so upset. Her whole legacy—"

"You know she's dead, right? She wouldn't even know."

"Um..." Charlie's eyes flicked away to a space behind Dante and he made a quelling movement with his hand.

Dante resisted the urge to look behind him. No one had entered the glasshouse — he would have heard them. Maybe the boy wasn't all there. He seemed harmless enough, though. And hopefully a good gardener. "My house is off limits."

Charlie's face cleared. "I know what — I'll ask Mrs Eleanor Graham to organise an outdoor tea. She'll make sure everyone behaves themselves."

"Who's Eleanor Graham?"

Charlie beamed. "She's wonderful. You'll see. She'll sort everything."

"I don't want more people—"

"I'll ask her when I do her garden tomorrow," said Charlie. "Do you like pavlova?"

He looked so hopeful Dante couldn't bring himself to say no. It would be like kicking a puppy, something Dante had never done.

"Fine. Just... don't spring anything on me. I don't like surprises."

"Yes, Mr. D."

"Call me Dante."

"Dante..." Charlie was giving him a thinking look again. "I have a question for you. A non-gardening question."

"Oh." Dante tried not to look too relieved.

"What would you do if someone you knew had done something wrong, something bad, but you couldn't prove it?"

Visit them in the middle of the night and force a pre-mortem confession, was what Dante didn't say. What he did say was: "What kind of wrong?"

"Like, proper bad." Now Charlie looked like he wished he hadn't said anything. "But a long time ago."

"If it was a long time ago, that makes it harder." Dante watched a brilliant orange and black butterfly land on a pitcher plant. He wondered if he should intervene to save it. "Was it a matter of life and death?"

"Yes." Charlie looked sad.

"Everything's a matter of life and death, eventually." Dante wondered if he should offer to kill whoever had wronged Charlie. It could be part of his employee benefit plan. Perhaps he could offer it as an incentive for Charlie to keep the Botanical Society away.

Then he remembered the band around his wrist. Ninety days, no bodies. *Don't take the easy path.* "If you want to prove a crime, you need to get the evidence." Or fabricate it professionally, he thought.

Charlie let out a long breath. "That's a good place to start. Thanks Mr. D."

"Dante."

Charlie mimed tipping his hat with a grin. "Sweet as."

"Sweet as what?"

Charlie stared at him, then laughed with a delight Dante knew he would never, ever, be able to replicate, even if he practised for a lifetime. "It's not sweet as anything — it's a saying. Just 'sweet as.' Try it." He smiled encouragingly.

"Sweet as." Dante frowned. He preferred sentences that made sense.

Charlie beamed. "Hey, if it's alright with you, I'll go trim the camelia hedge out back now."

Dante watched the door swing shut behind Charlie, wondering how he'd agreed to a new glasshouse heater, a crowd of visitors, tea, biscuits, pavlova, and the mysterious Mrs Eleanor Graham. For all his fresh-faced innocence, Charlie would have done well as a hostage negotiator.

That was the trouble with settling down, thought Dante as he brushed orchid pollen off his shoulder. You let one person in, and it was like puncturing an artery - you couldn't stop the flow without major surgery.

Charlie Wilson opened the shed at the back of Dante's garden and tried to ignore his ghostly audience. At this time of morning, before the sun grew hot, there were always spirits hanging around. Later, as the day warmed, they would retreat into the shadows and dark, cool places in town. That suited Charlie just fine.

Hanging up on the wall was an array of gardening tools: rakes, spades, shovels, pitchforks, pruning shears and assorted trowels. He tossed the heavy canvas garden waste bag outside and began choosing his weapons for a surgical pruning of the camelias. A small ladder joined the bag outside, then pruning shears of two different sizes.

A shiver of cold swept from the back of his neck down his spine, heralding the presence of more ghosts. It was as if they were waiting for something.

Charlie listened, but heard nothing but the sleepy hum of cicadas. The dead did not always speak - especially the most recently dead. It was as if they bled into the real world from their spirit domain silently, the sound turned down like a TV with a broken speaker. It took an older ghost, well settled into its realm, to talk with Charlie.

And unless the spirit was exceptionally stubborn, it faded slowly over time. The oldest ghosts were like photographs left too long in the sun, barely visible in daylight, only fully present under the full moon.

When newly arrived ghosts did manage to communicate with Charlie, the message wasn't always that exciting. For instance, one deceased lady wanted to pass on a long forgotten sponge cake recipe. Another spirit clung to this world with the stubborn insistence that his family continue the feud over a contested cattle watering hole. They were not messages that Charlie was enthused to pass on. However, the cake recipe had been delicious.

There was a susurrus in the air. Charlie wondered what the collective noun for a group of ghosts was. A haunting? A whispering? There was probably a book somewhere that would answer his question.

One thing Charlie did know — a gathering of spirits like this usually heralded a change. Perhaps ghosts were gifted with special knowledge of the future. Or maybe they sensed the ripples caused by distant events as they made their way towards the little town of Te Kohe.

Whatever the reason, Charlie had never known them to be wrong.

4

In which Dante experiences a home invasion

Dante awakened from an unpleasant dream, where invisible hands pulled him under a black river.

It was morning, and sunlight filtered through a small crack in the curtains that covered the long sash window opposite his bed. He took a moment to orientate himself. He was in the master bedroom of the house he'd bought, in the village of Te Kohe, on the West Coast of New Zealand.

That was correct. He wasn't in Los Cabos, Minsk, or any of the other places he used to work. Places where information was gathered from dangerous people, and you were forever checking that no one had followed you back to your anonymous rented room in a soulless hotel.

He had been sleeping in this room for several weeks now, but he always woke the same way — disorientated and on edge.

In one swift movement, Dante rose out of bed. His clothes from the night before were neatly folded on the chair. He donned them, checking the secret pockets for his utility knife and flashlight out of habit.

The corridor outside his room was hushed, the deep quiet of an old house with only one silent occupant.

Feet bare, Dante paced towards the kitchen. Most of the people he knew craved morning coffee, but Dante had never needed an extra catalyst to come awake. The most he would concede to the change from sleep to waking was to drink tea with a few drops of lemon in it.

Times past, the lemon would have come out of a bottle. In some countries, the bottle contained no actual lemon juice in it.

But here, with Mrs Davison's well tended garden extending all around his house, Dante had begun to go au natural with his tea seasoning.

He opened the pantry to find the fruit bowl empty of lemons. No matter. The lemon tree was in the back garden, a gnarled specimen that could easily have been planted when the house was first built, making it a centenarian that had lived through two world wars and one moon landing.

It was the fashion these days to keep old villas traditional at the front, and create an open plan living and kitchen area at the back, with large ranch sliders giving it that 'indoor-outdoor flow' so popular with glossy magazines.

Mrs Davison had not embraced this trend. The kitchen led into the laundry, and from there a single solid wooden door opened to the backyard.

Dante swung the door open and something small and black flashed inside. He dropped into a combat crouch, every sense on high alert.

The thing had brushed past him, lithe and light, its paws soundless on the wooden floor. It had moved so fast he wasn't even sure what it was.

He'd been warned against opossums, a beloved Australian marsupial that had become a destructive pest in New Zealand.

He was fairly sure this was not an opossum. They were meant to be wild, after all, and their chief threat was in eating your fruit trees.

Dante carefully shut the door and retreated to the kitchen. It was unoccupied.

As stealthy as a fox, he stole into the corridor. Still nothing.

The front sitting room door was cracked open a foot. Dante pushed it wide and looked inside.

A luxurious cream rug covered the centre of the room, with couches arranged around it. A small coffee table was placed on the carpet, with an empty wooden bowl positioned precisely in the centre of it.

These were all things Dante felt it was his duty to provide. It was like bringing an umbrella - if the sitting room was set up to receive guests, then hopefully none would ever come to visit.

But now, on the side of the rug where the sun streamed in, a black cat with three white paws and one black one lounged, fixing its green eyes on him as if he was the intruder.

Its gaze seemed to say to him, 'what are you looking at?' And perhaps 'now you're here, you may as well bring my breakfast.'

Dante paused.

He'd never spent much time with animals. There was that one time in the Siberian tundra, but the cat in question had been so many times larger than this one, it hardly counted.

Then there was the elderly neighbour when Dante was a kid. She'd lived next door to Dante and his mother in the crime ridden council estate they'd called home.

The old lady had fed all the neighbourhood strays. When she'd died, the ambulance team had come to take her body away. The cats had all sat in silent witness, perched on concrete walls and balustrades. Dante approved of that. It seemed appropriate cat behaviour.

This cat, however, seemed to think it had a right to be here.

Dante frowned. The estate agent had never mentioned a cat.

"Shoo," he said experimentally.

The cat blinked at him. Its scorn radiated from six feet away. It had a point. 'Shoo' was hardly a war cry to rally behind.

"Go on," he said, "get out of here."

Dante advanced into the sitting room and opened the main sash window, and then the three windows that made up the bay window, as if the cat was a bird that would fly in panic towards the nearest light source.

The cat did not move. It did not look like it had any intention of ever moving.

There was always the option of physical removal. Dante took two steps towards the cat and looked down at it doubtfully.

In the secret cupboard he'd installed on moving in, he had kevlar body armour and combat gloves. Removing the cat could result in scratches, but full body armour might be overkill. The cat might laugh at him. Silently.

"It's time for you to go. I mean it," he said, advancing closer, and winced.

He had never, ever, said 'I mean it' to anyone he'd been in a confrontation with, whether they held the gun or he did. It was an automatic tell that the person doubted their authority. In conflict situations, he took such threats as an invitation to attack.

The cat took his words as an invitation to roll on its back, stretching full length on the fluffy wool rug. It showed a white belly, the hair longer and finer than its back.

Dante knew this for a fact because he found himself crouched over the cat, cautiously running calloused fingers over its fluffy belly fur. A rumble started up, like a small contented lawnmower.

The cat was purring.

Dante wasn't sure how long he spent stroking the cat. He must have sat down cross legged on the carpet, because that's where he was now, with the cat curled comfortably in his lap.

Sun warmed his shoulders, and the purring soothed his morning restlessness. There was a word for this, he thought. Contentment. Dante was pretty sure that was the right word.

Eventually, the pool of sunlight shifted away, leaving Dante in the shade. The cat yawned and stretched again, revealing needle white teeth. It sank its claws into Dante's jeans just enough for him to feel their points.

With a lithe movement, the cat was out of his lap and padding for the door.

"Hey, wait," said Dante, suddenly aware that he'd lost all control of the situation.

But the cat was already through into the corridor, tail curled in a question Dante didn't know how to answer.

Dante followed the cat into the kitchen just in time to see it disappear into the pantry. Inside, it twined in and out of the boxes on the floor.

These boxes were full of plates, pots, cups, cutlery - all the things Dante knew belonged in a kitchen.

With three quick strides, Dante crossed to the laundry and opened the door to the backyard again.

"Look, enough's enough," he said. "There's the outdoors. Your home. Off you go."

The cat poked a curious head out from the pantry. It saw Dante and the open door. It said 'mrrr?'

Dante crossed his arms over his chest and glared. It irked him to be in a standoff with a four legged creature one tenth his size.

But if he simply picked the cat up and dropped it out in the yard, he would lose the moral high ground.

"Go on." Dante waved his hands at the cat. "Off you go."

The cat responded by winding around his legs.

Dante leaned down to stroke its back. It promptly arched its back, its purr starting up like an internal two-stroke motor.

"I don't have to let you stay," he informed the cat. "If I do, it's one hundred percent my decision. And you're only here on a provisional basis. If you bring in fleas, or have other cats around to visit, you're out."

The cat blinked its vivid green eyes up at him, its tail waving nonchalantly in the air.

"Right," said Dante. "My decision. Which I've just decided to make."

And then, because Dante always followed through on his decisions, he went down to the dairy to get milk.

Back in the kitchen, he poured milk into a bowl extricated from the boxes at the bottom of the pantry.

He set it down in one corner of the kitchen. The cat began to lick delicately at the milk, then got down to business. Somehow, it managed to both drink and purr like a miniature Royal Enfield.

Dante watched, feeling a certain pride in his handiwork, balanced by a faint sense of embarrassment. Was he a cat person now? What did that even mean?

If it all got too much, he could always put tranquillisers in the cat's milk and take it to the next town. But that was a dilemma he could deal with another day.

He sorted the small stack of mail he'd collected from the postbox. Mail — another novelty. People were sending things to his house.

It was puzzling, and not altogether welcome. There were bills, an invitation to join the community choir and another to join the folk dance society. And at the bottom of the pile was a plain white envelope with 'Dante Reid' handwritten on the front of it.

Dante slipped a surgically sharp knife from his wrist sheath and opened the envelope, slicing cleanly along one edge. He peered inside, alert to the dangers of poison powders, acid, micro-explosives, and cheery gift card tunes.

The envelope appeared to contain none of these threats, so he slid the letter out onto the table with the knife point. It was a simple white card, folded in two. Inside was typed this message:

As I said before, I would consider it a personal favour for you to accompany me to the Jubilee night celebrations. In return, I can ensure your stay in Te Kohe is free from malicious rumours and nosy neighbours.

- *Ted*

The threat was clear — refuse, and Ted would prime the town gossips with dark speculations about Dante and his past.

Dante sheathed his knife. On the one hand, he didn't like to give in to anyone. On the other hand, the one thing harder to fight than a remote activated incendiary device was a rumour. It looked like he was going to the Te Kohe Jubilee.

5

In which many things are set in motion

Ted slid out of his stretched Hummer and strutted up the path to the Pepper Tree Hotel, a glamourous hired model on each arm. Behind him, Dante glided like a dangerous shadow.

It was twilight, and the building glowed, decked out like an aged dowager in hundreds of fairy lights. It was the night of the 120th Te Kohe Jubilee, and the entire town had turned out for the celebration.

Ted cast a proprietary eye over the main street of Te Kohe before he mounted the stairs. It was his town. For now, anyway.

He waved at the maitre d' and smirked at the models as they peeled off to flank the entrance and greet the other guests as they arrived. A few years ago, he would have let the hands cupping the models' waists drift lower, but times had changed. He wasn't about to risk an 'indecent conduct' lawsuit. Not when he had so many irons in the fire.

"A drink, sir?" A waiter offered him a flute of champagne.

Ted emptied the glass, the sparkling wine heading down his throat with a pleasant fizz. For Ted Andrews, everything was going according to plan.

This summer was going to be the big one. The one he'd been working towards for years. This Jubilee, he'd managed to pull in some big investors from Auckland and further afield. If they took the bait, Te Kohe would stop being a sleepy village, home to generations of local families and their ageing villas. Mansions with helicopter pads and gated communities would spring up, and hopefully high-density housing just off main street, after the century old villas had been bulldozed.

Of course, by the time the developers had finished with Te Kohe, they would have ruined what attracted them in the first place. But by then, Ted would have taken his fat stack of cash and left for greener pastures. Sydney, maybe. Or Dubai. Somewhere where the drugs and hookers were plentiful, and the casinos never closed.

"Almost all the guests have arrived, sir," said the head waiter, greeting him at the entry to the dining room. "Dinner will be served at 8pm sharp."

"That's just swell, Jackson," said Ted, pleased he'd probably gotten the man's name right. He grinned, scoping out the dining hall.

It was a glamorous scene. Whoever said money didn't buy happiness clearly didn't have as much money as Ted. Sixty guests at four large tables. Silver cutlery glinting in the light from the crystal chandeliers. Everyone in evening wear, with serving staff flitting around discreetly filling glasses and plying the assembled throng with fresh plates of hors d'oeuvres.

His special investor guests were placed at the main table where Ted would also be seated. They looked relaxed and happy, already well into their twelve hundred dollar bottles of pinot noir.

"Not bad for a kid from the wrong side of the tracks," he murmured as he crossed to stand at the head of the main table.

Dante sat on the chair next to Ted's, silent and watchful. Ted stifled a frisson of unease. He'd known Dante would agree to guard him this evening. Part of him felt proud to have found the lever that could move a man like Dante. But Ted's hindbrain knew Dante was dangerous, and wasn't going to be soothed by thoughts of cleverness.

The other occupants of the main table were mostly known to Ted — investors and their plus ones, as well as a few people seated here for political reasons.

The head waiter started to tap on a wine glass, and Ted plastered on a broad smile as the sound cut through the conversation, quieting the room.

"Ahem," said Ted.

Everyone turned to face him - local business owners, district council members, his own special guests, and the various hangers-on an event like this always attracted.

The locals, he knew, were here to drink as much of his wine and eat as much of his food as they could, hoping it would help them stomach the high rent he charged them. His smile widened. He didn't think it would.

The investors, well. They were all seasoned professionals, and wouldn't make any decisions without consulting their team of lawyers, accountants, quantity surveyors and soothsayers. But tonight would be a good start in the wooing game.

It was time for his speech.

"Greetings, all. It's just wonderful to see you all again. You're all looking so fine, it's like you haven't aged a day." Polite laughter sprinkled around the tables. Ted smirked. "Every year, I ask myself, is it worth footing the bill for all this? Just so as you can all drink my best wine and stuff your faces with the finest cuisine this side of the Bombays?"

An uneasy silence fell. "And then there's the fireworks. Eighty thousand dollars, going up in smoke. What's it all for?" The silence was, if anything, heavier.

Ted spread his arms and gave them what he liked to think of as his 'roguish' smile. "But then I say to myself, Ted, you only live once! And what's a bit of dosh between friends? For you lot, I'd do it every year until I die. Eat, drink, and be merry, for tomorrow the tax man cometh." The laughter that greeted this was louder than necessary, uncomfortable laughter that sought to smooth over the social tension.

Ted raised his glass. "Here's to us: may our misdeeds never catch up with us, and may we always give the devil his due."

"To us!" Drunken laughter and the clinking of glasses filled the hall as Ted sat down, beaming.

"That was quite a speech," said Janice, a sharp-featured lady sitting across from Ted.

"Which bit did you like best?" Ted speared a piece of venison steak from the perfectly arranged confection in the centre of his large white plate.

"The bit where you said it's all worth it for us. Why even pretend you actually give a damn?"

Ted bared his teeth in a smile. "Janice. Might I say, you're looking fine. All those," he gestured at her neckline, "glittery things. And is that a Versace dress? Who died and left you all their worldly goods?"

"Oh, this old thing?" Janice gave a tinkly laugh. "You know what they say, save a penny here and there, and pretty soon you'll have pounds a plenty."

Noah, a wealthy investor from Wellington, had been watching their exchange with interest, like someone at a tennis match. Now he chimed in. "Janice, I'm Noah. Tell me, how do you know our charming host?"

Janice simpered. Noah was expensively good-looking, with dark Mediterranean features.

"Ted and I go back a long way. I'm the assistant to our town lawyer, and we always handle his local affairs."

She managed to pack a tonne of innuendo into the last two words, and Ted shuddered internally. Janice was so far from his type, she might as well be on another planet. "Janice and her boss have helped with a few legal matters over the years. Small fry deals."

"And yet you're here at the main table," said Noah, his smile gleaming white. "And your boss is?"

"Over there at table three," said Janice, looking smug. "Ted owes me—"

"Noah," said Ted. "See anything you liked on the town tour today?"

"I'll let you know if I want to invest," said Noah. "I like what you've done with the place, though."

Janice snorted not so quietly into her wineglass. "Ted doesn't actually own this town."

"Just the bits that are worth anything," said Ted.

"Amazing how most of Te Kohe seems to be in your pocket," said Noah. "How did that happen?"

"Leverage," said Ted, his smile sphinxlike. He raised his glass.

"What would you say?" said Noah, turning to the lady on his left. "Is or is not leverage the eighth wonder of the world?"

Ted followed his gaze to Noah's companion. She was around sixty, an elegant lady with an understated style. A true classic. He knew he'd seen her before, but was having difficulty placing her.

"I would go with plausible deniability as the eighth wonder." She spoke with a pleasantly mellow American accent. New York, perhaps, but upper crust. "Hello, Ted, I'm Eleanor. Eleanor Graham. We met at last year's Jubilee. By the flower arranging area."

"Ah. Yes." Ted remembered. Every year, the local yokels put together a display of flower arranging, baking, and other homegrown crafts in a large marquee on the waterfront. He usually never saw it, but last year he'd been avoiding Teresa, his soon-to-be ex-wife. He'd ended up lost in the rows of flower bouquets, looking for his latest mistress. He had found her throwing up over an irate lady's magnolias. Eleanor had diffused the situation before his mistress and the magnolia lady came to blows. Ted had been quite disappointed.

"I rather liked your toast," Eleanor said. She had an enchanting smile. It was almost enough to make Ted reconsider his policy of only dating women thirty years younger than him. Almost. "When did you give the devil his due?"

"Last Thursday," said Ted.

"Intriguing," said Noah. "Care to elaborate?"

"No," said Ted.

Eleanor's gaze flicked between Janice and Ted. "I prefer to be on good terms with the devil myself. And I am looking forward to your fireworks display. Anything special planned?"

"Oh, it'll be special," said Ted. "Like I said, eighty thousand dollars buys you quite the show."

"Ted likes to splash his money around," said Janice. Her smile was all teeth. "Keeps the local population in check."

"Bread and circuses, m'dear," said Ted. God, he wished Janice would choke on the scallop ceviche and expire on the dining room floor. Preferably quietly, under the table.

"How do the locals feel about Te Kohe being developed?" said Noah.

"The council's with me," said Ted. "And the local businesses. Full community support."

"So much support you felt the need for your own security detail tonight?" said Eleanor. Her gaze shifted to Dante, seated silently next to Ted.

"Allow me to introduce Dante Reid," said Ted. "Recently moved here from abroad. And no one's unhappy with my investment plans. It's just that there's been someone hanging around my estate and leaving threatening notes on my car. I don't think it's anything serious. Just being a bit cautious, that's all."

"Someone with a grudge?" Noah swirled a mouthful of pinot noir in his mouth before swallowing. "That's hard to believe for you, Ted."

"I think your mystery enemy is trying to stop the development," said Janice. "By any means possible." She smiled demurely and sampled her filet mignon.

An uneasy silence followed this pronouncement. Then Noah said: "How would you stop this development, Dante? If you were the mystery enemy?"

Dante fixed Noah with a flat look. "I just learned that plausible deniability is the eighth wonder of the world."

There was a moment of silence, and then Eleanor favoured Dante with a radiant smile. "I look forward to getting to know you better, Dante. Welcome to Te Kohe."

———

The dinner progressed towards dessert and Dante watched the diners become mellow with alcohol and full bellies. He checked his watch. Just an hour to go, and he could be done with Ted, his cronies, and people in general. *Enjoy the small things. Don't kill—*

"Seriously, Ted," said Noah, pushing back in his chair, "a few years ago in the last building crash, we thought you were a goner. Washed out to sea like Henderson and De Voors. How did you stage your comeback?"

"That's for me to know," said Ted, baring his teeth.

"And us to find out?" finished Noah.

"I don't think so." Ted leaned back in his chair. He was still in his dinner jacket and a fine beading of sweat covered his forehead.

"I guess with your upbringing, it's easy to cut expenses to get through a downturn," mused Noah.

"What do you mean by that?" A slow flush crept across Ted's face.

If Dante had been guarding Noah instead of Ted, this would have put him on full alert. Noah, taking a long swig of his wine, didn't appear to have noticed.

"I've looked into your background," said Noah. "Solo mum, state house, welfare kid... I hope the government's getting some tax off you to pay for all those handouts when you were little."

Ted was quiet, and Dante saw something ugly stirring behind his eyes. Instead of lashing out though, he gave a twisted smile that reminded Dante of a skull he'd exhumed in Salar de Uyuni while on the trail of human traffickers.

"I'll tell you how I made my fortune during a market crash, Noah. But you'll have to win it off me."

"Oh yeah?" said Noah. "And how's that work?"

"You beat me at my own game." Ted's eyes gleamed. "Your fancy watch if you lose."

"And if I win?" Noah slouched back, expensively disinterested.

Ted shrugged. "Whatever you like."

Noah flicked his fingers. "Anything?"

"Within reason," said Ted.

"But this is a Patek Philippe Nautilus," said Noah, twisting the gold watch around his wrist. "It's priceless."

"You could ask for my Hummer," said Ted.

"You're confident of victory," observed Eleanor, a slight smile on her lips. "That's suspicious in itself."

Noah put his head on one side to study Ted.

It was probable, thought Dante, that a sober Noah would have told Ted where to stick his wager. But this Noah was more than a few glasses into his pinot noir. It was one of several reasons Dante never drank.

"Just admit you're scared to lose," said Ted. "No hard feelings."

"You wash the dishes down in the hotel kitchen tonight, and we have a wager," said Noah.

Ted looked momentarily uncertain, eyes flicking left and right as if seeking a way out. But Dante saw his hand, hidden under the table, clench tight with fury.

"Oh, come *on*," said Janice, her face flushed, her voice too loud. "Get on with your party trick, Ted. The fireworks are starting soon."

Dante wondered briefly if Janice and Ted were in on the scam together. He doubted it, though. Their mutual loathing seemed too real to be an act.

"I'll wager whatever you did to escape bankruptcy would put you in jail if anyone knew about it," said Noah with a sardonic smile.

Ted shrugged. "Do we have a bet or not?"

Noah looked around the table. Everyone's eyes were on him. Dante saw the trap was set. Noah would look like a fool if he ducked out now.

"Fine," said Noah.

"Excellent." Ted beckoned a waiter over. "Three espresso cups, please. And something small and round - like a marble."

Dante saw Eleanor relax back in her seat slightly. She had guessed what Ted was about to do. He wondered how a respectable looking lady in her sixties had come by this knowledge.

"It's called the Shell Game," said Ted, as a black-clad waiter handed him the three cups and a polished round stone, probably taken from the hotel mantelpiece display. "It was played in ancient Egypt and Rome. It's still played, anywhere tourists want to lose a little — and maybe win a little."

The conversations around the table ceased as the other diners stopped to watch the show.

"The rules are simple," said Ted, tipping the cups up so that Noah, Janice and Eleanor could see they were empty. He placed them upside down on the tablecloth, covering the round stone with the middle cup. "All you have to do is guess where the stone is, and you win, my friend. Follow the cup, follow the ball, round and round she goes." As he spoke, the cups circled in a complicated dance designed to confuse anyone trying to follow the cup with the stone in it.

Dante recognised the patter of an experienced hustler and wondered where and when Ted had acquired his skills. Eleanor's face had a small, appreciative smile as she watched Ted shuffle the cups.

"How's your luck, holding?" said Ted. "You guess right, I'll wash dishes tonight." He grinned. "Guess wrong, and your watch is mine for a song."

Noah didn't answer. His attention was fixed on following the ball with the stone under it through changes in direction, circles, and crossovers.

"You ready?" said Ted.

Noah pointed at one of the cups, and Ted's face fell.

"You have a good eye," he muttered and lifted the cup. The small blue stone winked up at them. A low murmur of amusement arose around the table. Everyone liked to see Ted lose.

"Not so bad, eh," said Noah.

"I was going slow on purpose," said Ted gruffly. "That was just a practice."

"Whatever, old man," said Noah.

"First to win three games," said Ted. "And I'll wash dishes for a week."

"You're on," said Noah, the gleam of alcohol-fueled conquest in his eyes. "Go."

This time Ted moved the cups faster, the white porcelain flashing under the chandelier's light as he spun and swirled the cups over the tablecloth. Eyes narrowed, Noah followed the cup with the stone in it.

"That one," he said, pointing at the middle one. And there was the stone.

"Three's the charm." Ted's smile was that of a crocodile spotting a young faun on the way to its watering hole.

Dante had seen the Shell Game played many times, in many forms, on streets in many crowded tourist traps. The most memorable time had ended in a knife fight, and he'd melted back into the crowd to avoid the inevitable arrival of the local gang boss.

The point of the game was that Noah didn't stand a chance, and he never had. Anyone who knew how the game was played knew that the dealer won whenever he wanted to.

This point was proved as Noah lost the next two games.

Now they were tied at two games each. Whoever won the next game would triumph. Noah leaned forward as Ted shuffled the cups. His eyes followed the cup on its route, pushed here and there by Ted's surprisingly nimble hands.

"Follow the ball, follow the cup, follow it fast, follow it slow, if luck is with you, win you will," said Ted. He was watching Noah now, smile gloating.

The cups stopped.

"Make your guess," said Ted.

Noah's eyes were fixed on the cup on the right - the cup where the stone had originally been placed. He moved to point to it, then hesitated.

Dante knew Noah had guessed correctly the last two times. But the stone hadn't been there.

Noah bit his lip, then pointed at the cup in the centre.

With a smirk, Ted flipped it up. Empty.

"Show me the other cups," growled Noah. "I want to see."

"Sure, no problem." Ted flipped the one on the left. Empty. Then, with a showman's pass, he slipped the right hand cup back, and Dante saw the stone flick under it from its resting place in Ted's palm, where it had been since the start of the game.

Ted lifted the cup and there was the stone.

"Dammit! I knew that's where it was!" said Noah. He glared at Ted.

"Fair's fair," said Ted. "You played, you won, and then..." he leered, "you lost."

"This watch was a gift," said Noah. "It has sentimental value."

"I assure you," said Ted, "I'll look after it."

"I'll pay you the watch's monetary value," said Noah. "My father left it to me in his will."

"Then you shouldn't have wagered it," said Ted. His eyes were cold, and Dante tensed, on alert for the possibility of violence.

There was a taut silence. With a glower, Noah flicked open the watch strap and tossed it onto the table cloth. Like a greedy five year old, Ted snatched it up, gloating.

Noah sat back, arms crossed. "You really are a piece of work, Ted Andrews."

Ted grinned, sliding the watch into his coat pocket. "I'm going to make you millions. Surely you don't begrudge me this small win?"

"Some more pinot noir please," said Noah, turning to Eleanor.

She obliged, pouring with an easy grace.

A waiter glided up to Ted and whispered in his ear.

"Alright!" Ted bounced to his feet. He raised his voice. "Ladies and gentlemen, it's time for the fireworks."

Guests began standing up, gathering their possessions and getting ready to follow the maitre 'd up the staircase to the balcony.

Dante scanned the crowd. At this stage, he hadn't decided if he was pleased that no attempt had been made on Ted's life.

The elegant lady in her sixties — Eleanor — gave Dante a sympathetic smile as he followed Ted out of the dining room. It was time to watch the show.

6

In which the plot thickens

Eleanor checked the card with her assigned seat number. Around her, the other guests, pleasantly full of food and alcohol, spilled out onto the balcony of the Pepper Tree Hotel to watch the fireworks display.

Eleanor sank gracefully into her seat. The wine she'd drunk gave a pleasant glow to the surroundings, and she smiled in anticipation, looking at her surroundings.

The balcony was at the back of the building, facing the harbour. It was flanked by two wings that reached out towards the sea, creating the courtyard where a hundred year old pepper tree raised gnarled branches to the sky.

Ted's staff had set up two rows of tiered seating on the balcony. Eleanor glanced sideways at the other guests. Her seat was in the front row, and Ted was stationed a few seats down from her next to Noah.

Dante stood by the door, a solid shadow silhouetted against the interior lights, until Ted beckoned him over. A brief exchange, and Dante disappeared back into the hotel on an errand.

Seated at the end of the row top, Janice looked pleased. Her fingers wrapped around her pearl necklace, and Eleanor wondered how an attorney's assistant could afford such finery. A recent inheritance, perhaps? The relationship between Janice and Ted intrigued her. They clearly loathed each other. Why had Ted invited her at all, let alone seated her at the table with the best wine?

One hundred metres offshore a barge floated, packed to the gunnels with high-grade explosives ready to shoot fiery colours across the sky in a display of wondrous wealth and waste.

Eleanor leaned back in her seat and smiled. She had loved fireworks ever since her first Fourth of July celebration. Now, fifty eight years later, she was still enamoured with them. To her mind, they perfectly embodied the ephemeral nature of life.

We're all here and then gone in a flash, she thought, leaving no trace of our existence, fireflies vanishing with the dawn.

A waiter with a silver tray came around for one last drink refill, and then the porch lights switched off.

The crowd stirred with excitement. The show was about to begin.

The first rocket burst into the sky with an explosion of gold and crimson, spreading out into the sky like a phoenix flower. A cheer came up from the locals crowded down on the waterfront walkway.

Ted had been right - eighty thousand dollars did buy quite the show.

Great blossoms of fire spread across the sky, accompanied by oohs and ahs from the crowd.

Eleanor sipped her martini, then nearly spilled it as someone jostled past behind her, heading for the exit. It was Ted, holding an empty glass. It seemed he couldn't go ten minutes without liquid entertainment, she thought, then forgot about him as a shower of violet sparkles crackled across the blackness above.

The fireworks built to a crescendo, filling the sky with fiery fountains blooming in the darkness, bursting into fractals across the night sky.

Finally, with a triumphant thunderclap, the last salvo of rockets soared across the heavens and silence fell.

The audience stirred, making sure it was over before they began a round of applause.

Then came a 'bang' loud enough to make Eleanor jump, and someone behind her yelled in pain.

"Arghh! Shit!" It was Ted's voice. "I've been shot!"

The guests reacted like a flock of startled pigeons. Half of them rushed towards Ted, while the other half crowded the door back into the hotel, frantic to get off the balcony.

Eleanor set her drink down and took stock. Ted was ducked down in his chair, his hand clapped to his upper arm. A woman was screaming, and two others were fighting to get past her and back into the hotel.

Jackson, the owner of the local pistol club, was pointing towards the other wing of the hotel where you could just see, in the uplighting from the garden, that a window was broken. Was that the shooter's position?

Dante appeared on the balcony, moving fast. He lifted Ted out of his seat as if he weighed nothing, then vanished with him into the hotel.

In the mad scramble, Eleanor saw one thing out of place. A lady sat, head bowed, unmoving as the guests jostled past her.

A rush of cold swept through Eleanor, banishing the glow of the martini. She slipped between the seats and made her way to where the lady sat.

It was Janice.

There was a small dark hole in the side of her head, in the smooth soft circle of her temple. Eleanor put two fingers to Janice's neck to feel for a pulse, but she already knew what she would find.

Janice was dead.

Eleanor looked back towards the dark wing of the hotel where the shooter might still be, then ducked into the stream of people hustling through the door into the relative safety of the hotel. Where she had least expected it, amidst the beauty of the fiery display, a public murder had taken place.

7

In which Eleanor provides assistance to the police

Inside the hotel, people were shouting, half in shock, half in excitement.

It seemed no one else had noticed that Janice's murder.

Eleanor went in search of Ted. Dante would be with him, and he would have ideas about finding the shooter.

How unusual, she thought distantly, for something like this to happen in Te Kohe. It was much more the kind of thing to occur in her old world of high art, New York billionaires, and highly flexible morals.

And who had been the target: Ted, Janice, or someone else entirely?

Down in the kitchen, a shaky Ted was being examined by Dr. Galway, a small man with a grey goatee and round glasses.

Eleanor eyed the shallow gash. It seemed Ted had been lucky tonight. Or, if the intended target was Janice, rather unlucky.

Ted looked pale and suddenly sober. His shirt was off, and blood leaked from a wound on his upper arm.

"Steady on there, Ted," said Dr Galway. "It's not that deep, just a graze. I don't think it'll even need stitches, just a good dressing. You're a lucky guy."

"Yeah." Ted clasped his hands together to stop them shaking, and Eleanor felt a momentary stab of sympathy.

"Where's Dante?" she asked Charlie, who was standing in the crowd of white uniformed kitchen staff.

"He said he was going after the shooter," said Charlie. He also looked pale.

"Has someone called the police?" said Eleanor.

"I did," said a tall Polynesian man wearing a chef's hat. "Rosie is on her way."

"Just Rosie?" asked Eleanor. She recognised the tall man as Sione, the sous chef.

"Yar. Hemi's off chasing those guys who prank the police station every Jubilee. This year they're planning to steal all the lightbulbs," said Sione with a grin.

"So Hemi is chasing Zak and his mates?" asked Charlie.

"Oh yeah," said Sione.

Charlie looked at Eleanor. "They'll have gone bush. Hemi won't be back for a while."

"Well, someone will have to find him fast, because there's a dead woman on the balcony," said Eleanor. Gasps of shock echoed around the crowd of staff. Eleanor scanned the throng, searching for reactions that looked unnatural - either overstated or understated. Unfortunately, they all looked genuine.

Ted flinched. "That could have been me. It was probably meant to be me."

"Dante is looking for the perpetrator," said Eleanor crisply. "I suggest you stay here until he is back."

Ted's gaze sharpened. "You're pretty calm for someone who just found a dead body."

Eleanor raised an eyebrow. "I'm simply trying to help manage a difficult situation. Having hysterics would not be useful."

"Just curious," said Ted with a tight smile. "Seems like you're a bit too used to this sort of thing."

"Exactly what are you trying to imply, Ted?" said Eleanor.

"You seem a bit too... prepared under the circumstances," said Ted. "Everyone else is panicking or drinking, and you're taking charge, almost like you knew this was going to happen."

Eleanor made her face sympathetic. "You've had a near miss, Ted. That takes people all different ways." She addressed Dr Galway. "I think Ted may be going into shock. Elevated cortisol, adrenaline... pressure can make people paranoid."

"Now see here," said Ted, leaning forward. "I know what's what. And I think you're way too comfortable with people being shot dead."

The kitchen staff were watching this exchange like a crowd at a tennis match. Eleanor did a quick calculation. Insinuation was a powerful tool, and Ted wielded it well. But she also had cards to play.

"It's..." she blinked rapidly, as if forcing back tears. "It's just too awful. But someone's got to do something. I was a nurse for a while, back in the States. I just want to help."

She saw the moment the crowd turned against Ted. He knew it too and slumped back, glowering at her. Unfortunately, this brought him in contact with the alcohol swab in Doctor Galway's hand, and Ted winced as the solvent touched his wound.

Never show your hand, thought Eleanor. She smiled bravely at Ted. "I'll tell Rosie you're making a speedy recovery."

In the corridor outside the kitchen, Eleanor stood for a moment, considering. Was Ted the kind of person to sling accusations around when he felt threatened? Probably.

Eleanor hummed softly to herself as she walked back towards the dining room. Upstairs was a dead woman, downstairs a wounded man, and somewhere in the town of Te Kohe, a murderer. This evening was getting interesting indeed.

Up in the dining hall, confusion reigned.

Constable Rosemary Kimble was in the middle of the room, unconvincing in her severe black police uniform. It was her freckles, Eleanor supposed. They lent her an air of youthful innocence that made it impossible to see her as an authority figure.

The young policewoman was currently attempting to get the guests to gather and give their details to her. Unfortunately, the guests, in a state of high excitement, were much more interested in reacting to the dramatic events of the evening.

Mrs Williams was having hysterics in one corner, with a small crowd gathered around her to watch. The Jamesons were attempting to leave the hotel — his face grim, hers tear stained. Mr Aberman was sure the shooting had been a prank and was trying to go back up to the balcony so he could find the hidden cameras. And Buz Edy was telling anyone who'd listen that he'd been shot at once in Palmerston North, and the best thing to do was keep calm and keep drinking.

Eleanor sighed. It was time someone took charge.

She climbed on a chair and gave a piercing whistle. Everyone turned to stare.

"Your attention, please." Eleanor smiled down at the throng. "I am assisting Constable Kimble in her duties this evening until Sergeant Hemi arrives. You will all please line up along the far wall, and Rosie will take down your names and contact details. You will then proceed to the foyer, where refreshments will be served, and further questions may be asked of you. Everyone who was on the balcony please go to the front of the line. Thank you."

She watched in satisfaction as the guests lined up and Rosie gave her a relieved smile.

That was one thing sorted. Next would be arranging the refreshments, so the guests stayed in the foyer. But first, she wanted to take another look around the balcony. It was possible there was vital evidence still there.

Eleanor met Dante on the stairs leading up to the balcony.

"Dante," said Eleanor. "What have you been up to?"

"I was looking for the shooter," said Dante.

"And?"

"There's a small pantry with a window that looks towards the balcony," said Dante. "One of the window panes is broken. Whatever broke it blew the shards of glass outwards."

"A bullet?"

Dante shrugged. "The shooter could have broken the glass before taking the shot. No one would have heard during the fireworks."

They stepped onto the balcony, now lit up in a blaze of outdoor lights.

Janice was still slumped in place. The two of them navigated the tiered seating to stand over to the body.

Eleanor took several photos of the scene on her phone. Dante sighted from Janice's head to the broken pantry window in the wing of the hotel.

"Could a bullet aimed at Janice have grazed Ted?" asked Eleanor.

"Perhaps," said Dante. "Although you'd want forensics to check the angle the bullet entered the target's head."

"It could have been a bullet aimed at Ted that missed and killed Janice," Eleanor mused. She stepped back and photographed Janice.

As she put her phone away, the full force of what had happened struck her. In an instant, this woman had gone from a lively, if not particularly likeable human being, to an empty shell.

It was a somber moment, but in the privacy of her thoughts, Eleanor had to admit Janice's murder intrigued her. Who in Te Kohe would commit a murder? And in such a public manner?

"Could the bullet have been fired from somewhere else?" she asked Dante.

He stepped back and surveyed the scene. They both appeared to remember exactly where Ted had been seated.

"It would have to be close by," said Dante. "For it to have grazed Ted's arm and hit Janice."

They both looked towards the hotel facade.

"All the windows on that side of the building are fixed pane," said Dante. "The shooter couldn't have used any other window without breaking the glass."

"What did Ted tell you at the start of the fireworks show?" asked Eleanor.

"He wanted me to go check on his Hummer," said Dante. "He said someone had been hanging around the garage, and he was worried they'd pick this moment to vandalise the car."

"Did you go check on the car?"

"Yes. There was no one there."

Eleanor pictured the garage — one of just a few private car parks supplied to senior hotel staff. It was roofed over and trellised all around, and located in an unlit part of the back of the hotel.

She sighed. Someone going to check on Ted's gaudy Hummer could easily have passed unnoticed by anyone in the busy crowds of the Jubilee.

"Did anyone see you in the garage?" she said.

"No," said Dante.

"Did you shoot at Janice? Or Ted?"

"No."

It was said simply, with utter conviction. Eleanor found herself, if not convinced, then satisfied for now.

"This might put you in a difficult position."

Dante was silent. Eleanor had no idea what was going through his mind.

"I would like to remain here in Te Kohe," he said at last. "Charlie Wilson has been teaching me how to garden."

"Gardening can be therapeutic," said Eleanor.

"I would rather not be involved in a murder investigation," said Dante. "This is a small town, full of people who have known each other for years. Rumours can be damaging."

"It is entirely that kind of place," said Eleanor. "But it's best not to borrow trouble from tomorrow."

Dante looked at her in puzzlement.

"I mean, take each day as it comes."

"I always do that," he said.

They both stood for a moment in silent contemplation. The last glow of alcohol and adrenaline drained away and a wave of sadness swept over Eleanor, surprising in its intensity.

The balcony blurred as unshed tears welled up in Eleanor's eyes. She blinked them away and pushed her emotions down into a well-sealed compartment where they could be unpacked later.

"I didn't know Janice well," she said. "She seemed an unhappy person, who preferred displays of wealth to real friendships. However, she stayed married to her husband Derek for twenty six years. I imagine her loss will affect him profoundly."

Dante nodded slowly. "We can all learn from each other. I hope she has found peace now. And is in a better place."

He said the sentences carefully, as if reading from an inner handbook labelled 'demonstrating empathy and showing respect for the dead.'

Eleanor squared her shoulders. Hopefully, someone would locate Hemi in the thickly forested hills behind Te Kohe where cellphone signals were nonexistent. Until then, she could help Rosie bring order to the chaos.

"I'll find a staff member to lock the doors to the balcony." Eleanor took one last look at Janice's body and turned away to reenter the hotel. The night was far from over.

8

In which Dante expresses his doubts, and Eleanor's curiosity is piqued

Eleanor strode back into the foyer and took stock. Rosie did not appear to have things under control. It was true, all the guests were there, and Rosie was scribbling frantically in her notebook. However, she had an air of desperation that Eleanor attributed to the fact that her boss, Hemi, had not appeared to take charge.

Eleanor beckoned one of the serving staff over.

"Has anyone found Hemi yet?"

"Yes…" the waiter was middle-aged, with a sharp face and quantities of thick black hair that framed his face like a wolverine. "He called to say he's on his way. But he's not in the most professional state right now."

"Call him back to say there's a dead woman up on the balcony of the Pepper Tree Hotel," said Eleanor. "She's been shot through the head." At the man's shocked expression, she made a shooing gesture with her hands. "Well, go on! See to it."

The man hurried away, casting a doubtful glance over his shoulder.

Eleanor joined Rosie as she took a statement from Mr Whittaker, town council member, and one of the guests up on the balcony.

"Let me check I've got this right," said Rose. "You were up on the balcony, four seats down from Ted Andrews. The fireworks ended, then you heard a bang that could have been a gunshot, and then Ted yelled that he'd been shot."

"Yes, that's it," said Mr Whittaker. "Except that could you put in a bit about me being a pillar of the community?"

"That isn't relevant," said Eleanor. "The police are only interested in the objective facts of the evening - what you saw, what you heard."

"Well, then I reckon one of the hotel staff did it," said Mr Whittaker. "They're always going on about how they work long hours for not enough pay. Hear them at the pub all the time. One of them must have finally snapped, decided to take matters into his own hands. Or hers," he added generously.

"That is a theory, not a fact," said Eleanor. "Rosie, can I have a word?"

Rosie followed Eleanor a short distance from the queue of people, white-knuckled fingers gripping her notebook like a shield. "Is Hemi going to be here soon?"

"He's on his way," said Eleanor. "I've gotten the staff to lock the door to the balcony. Ah, here comes Hemi at last."

Officer Hemi was a big man. He was the same height as Dante, and his shoulders were as broad. But where Dante's impressive torso tapered down to a slim waist, Hemi was shaped like a tree trunk, solid muscle all the way.

Hemi was trying not to look like a man who had spent the last two hours scrambling through thick back country bush. In this, he was only partially successful. His irritated glance took in the hall full of inebriated guests, the worried face of Rosie and the righteous Mr Whittaker. Eventually, it settled on Eleanor.

"You organised this menagerie?" he asked.

"Oh, Rosie did most of it," she said. "I was just assisting."

"Much obliged," said Hemi. "But it's police business. Not yours." He straightened, wiped his brow, and then addressed the room, his voice growing to parade ground stature. "Right, you lot. Thank you for your cooperation. Have you all given Rosie your contact details?" There was a murmured chorus of assent. "Then you're all free to make your way home. Please be aware you may be required to come back over the next few days for further interviews. Good night."

His voice held the finality of closing time, and it was clear that he expected all the guests to leave.

Eleanor was unsurprised to see they did no such thing.

Here, they had an open bar, someone playing jazz on a grand piano, and all their mates to gossip about the most exciting event in years. Why would anyone go anywhere? And who knew what exciting thing might happen next?

Hemi growled something at the maître d' and stumped upstairs to look at the body, Rosie a nervous shadow flitting behind him.

Her work complete for now, Eleanor snagged an espresso martini from a passing waiter and prowled to one side of the room. Dante didn't want to get involved in this affair, and that was a sensible attitude to take. So how much did she want to be involved?

The espresso martini and her natural curiosity said she'd like to know a little more. Against her better judgement, Eleanor left the dining hall and headed in the direction of the kitchens.

The scene in the kitchens hadn't changed much. Ted was bandaged up now, and the kitchen staff were still standing around, watching.

Ted looked up as Eleanor entered, and scowled.

"There's the useless bodyguard," snapped Ted. "You're not getting paid for tonight I can tell you that right now."

Eleanor started. Dante was standing just behind her. For a big man, he moved silently as a shadow.

"There will be payment. With an additional fee for becoming entangled in a murder investigation." Dante gave Ted a dead-eyed stare.

"So, did you catch the bastard who tried to shoot me?" said Ted.

"No," said Dante.

"What makes you so sure you were the intended target?" asked Eleanor.

"Don't be daft, woman," growled Ted. "I'm an important man. Who would go to the trouble of offing Janice?"

"It might have been a personal matter," said Eleanor.

"Whatever it was," said Ted, "they missed. Will the police do anything? I doubt it."

"I think you'll find they will," said Eleanor. "This is a big event for a small town."

"I suppose," Ted sounded sullen.

"Do you want me to guard you tonight?" Dante sounded remarkably reluctant.

"No need of that," Ted shot back. "I'll be on my estate, with full security: lights, burglar alarms, deadbolts, and a panic room. A sight better than you could do."

"Do you still have that French Bulldog?" asked Eleanor. "Patrick, was that his name?"

Ted scowled. "You think you're so clever." Then he ordered one of the staff to fetch his driver and limped out of the kitchen.

Dante and Eleanor stood on the porch of the Pepper Tree Hotel and watched Ted's driver bundle him into a stretched Hummer.

"What a night," said Eleanor.

"Yes," said Dante.

"Even though I don't like him, I can't help feeling sorry for Ted," said Eleanor. "He's had quite a shock." And yet, her inner sense whispered. Something is off.

There was a long moment where Dante failed to say anything. Eleanor supposed small talk was not his strength.

"Good night, Dante," she said. "I'm sure I'll see you again soon."

9

In which Dante learns the subtle art of pruning and Charlie receives unsolicited advice

Dante awoke to early morning light and warm rumbling. There was something warm and furry nestled against his neck.

He froze, assessing the threat. His sidearm was within easy reach on the bedside table, but the warm rumbling thing was on that side of the bed. He might dislodge it when he made a grab for his gun.

Then the warm furry rumbling thing butted its head up under his chin, and Dante felt the tickle of its whiskers. He realised what it was.

The cat had insisted on coming into his bedroom last night. All efforts to evict it had failed, as the cat retaliated by meowing outside his bedroom door and scooping its white socked paws under the door as if it were trying to catch fish.

Dante couldn't sleep with such interruptions. At midnight, he had folded and allowed the cat inside, wherein it hopped onto the foot of his bed with a self satisfied air.

Now, instead of waking up to his usual danger assessment, Dante awoke to surprise, and then a gradual unwinding. The cat's purring vibrated against the side of his neck and his muscles relaxed.

"You're lucky I didn't attack first and find out what you were later," he muttered.

The cat, utterly unimpressed, purred louder. Its tail passed across Dante's face, and he brushed it aside.

Dante checked his watch: seven in the morning. Charlie would be here soon to do the garden. Dante wanted to see what he did, just in case something happened to Charlie.

From his many assignments abroad, Dante had learned that danger lurked even in small towns like Te Kohe. Granted, often the danger had been him, but the point still held true. And after Jubilee night, he was reassessing the safety of this town.

At precisely seven thirty, Charlie knocked on his front door. The young man's curly hair was neatly brushed, his side parted fringe emerging from under a broad brimmed cricket hat. Dante supposed that someone with skin like Charlie's would need to keep out of the strong New Zealand sun.

"Hi Mr Dante," said Charlie. "I'll just fetch a few tools from the toolshed and then I'll meet you out back."

"How are you going to get into it?" asked Dante.

"There's a key hidden on the door lintel," said Charlie. "Erm, I would have told you about it if you hadn't given me the job." Charlie hesitated. "About last night. What happened at the fireworks — it isn't normal. Not in Te Kohe. Not in New Zealand, really. I hope it hasn't upset you too much."

Dante sorted various responses to find the right one. His therapist's coaching suggested that saying he wasn't at all upset would not be the best reply. "It's ok," he said. Then after a pause as he reran his therapist's advice in his head, he added: "Thank you."

"Right. Er... I'll get started."

Dante retreated to his bedroom to ponder the question of footwear. He had combat boots with flexible soles for silent movement and, well, combat. But he didn't want to wear them gardening. He liked to keep his gear in purpose specific silos.

In the end, Dante joined Charlie in the back garden wearing his leather sneakers. They were too well made to be covered with soil, but they were still his best option. Charlie seemed harmless enough. He doubted combat would be called for while trimming the garden.

Charlie was halfway up the ladder with the pruning shears when Dante emerged from the back door, looking dangerous in his form fitting dark clothes. Actually, Dante always looked dangerous. Charlie wasn't sure he wanted to let Dante near this tree with an edged weapon.

"Hey!" Charlie waved to him, and Dante came to stand at the foot of the ladder, arms crossed. "I'm trimming the branches that grow in towards each other," Charlie explained. "This will give the tree a better shape and healthier foliage."

"What kind of tree is it?"

"It's a Kōwhai. You just missed it flowering when you moved here. They have beautiful yellow blossoms, and the tuis and kererū go crazy for them. A tree full of tuis is quite a sight."

"What are tuis and kererū?"

"Native birds. Tuis are black with a white ruff of feathers at their throat. They have the most beautiful and varied song. Kererū are our native wood pigeons. Their plumage is iridescent turquoise and cream. They're great fliers, but clumsy when they've landed. I've seen one drunk on pūriri berries almost fall out of its tree."

Dante regarded the tree doubtfully. "Early spring, you say? That's when it'll flower?"

"Yes. Even better after I give it a haircut."

Charlie snipped away, and Dante gathered the fallen foliage into the bag. The sun rose higher, and sweat trickled from under Charlie's hat to run down his face.

"Son, you look fit to kill."

In the shade of the lilac bush, an old man stood looking up at Charlie, craggy face softened by the shadows, arms crossed in an unconscious imitation of Dante.

Charlie's shoulders tightened. Now was not the time for a lecture, but if he knew Pete Morrow, that was exactly what he was going to get.

"I heard about last night."

"Yeah." Charlie leaned towards the fence to cut a protruding branch. His godfather Pete Morrow had been the only police officer in Te Kohe for thirty years before he retired and Hemi took over. "How much have you heard?"

"Enough to know you're probably one of the suspects. Tell me, how bad is it?"

"It's bad," said Charlie in an undertone.

"What was that?" asked Dante.

"Just talking to myself," called back Charlie.

Dante frowned. "Is that a gardening thing?"

"Er, yes?" Charlie started to attack the small branches and twigs under the spreading canopy of the kōwhai.

"So, did you do it?" asked Pete.

"No," muttered Charlie.

"I won't tell anyone if you did." Pete's grin was transparent, the lilac leaves visible behind his spectral figure.

Charlie gave a noncommittal grunt.

A not-so-innocent smile played around Pete's mouth. "After what went down between Ted and your old man, I bet you wish you had tried to kill Ted."

Charlie made an involuntary noise of protest.

"C'mon son. Don't tell me you hadn't considered it. Ted's got heavy history with your family. In any case, it's time for you to man up and face reality."

"Reality." Charlie snipped a particularly stubborn branch with a vicious cut. He was tired of inhabiting a reality different from every other living person. "I'm not a murderer. Hemi will believe me," he whispered, loudly enough for Pete, but hopefully not Dante, to hear.

"What are you talking about?" asked Dante. He had gathered all the branches into the garden waste bag already, moving with a speed and precision that surprised Charlie.

"Just... talking out loud," said Charlie. He wished Pete wouldn't harass him when there were people around. "Hey, would you mind getting me the Philips screwdriver to tighten these shears? It's in the garage."

"Sure," said Dante.

"Look," hissed Charlie, eyeing Dante's retreating back, "I didn't murder anyone. I'm innocent."

"You have that much faith in the justice system? Pity." Pete sighed. "Believe me, Charlie boy, you're not going to find any friends on the force. Hemi's a good man, but he'll do his job. And you've got the full bingo card: means, motive, and opportunity."

Charlie's blade scythed through another branch. "I still didn't do it." But he couldn't prove it.

"You're being naïve." Pete rubbed his stubble.

"So, what do you want me to do?"

"Charlie, you're a grown man. It's not what I want that counts. You're the one who's got to step up and make a decision."

Charlie snipped the last branch and let it fall. He took his gloves off, flexing his fingers. "I know."

"About that..." Pete paused, and Charlie could just about hear the wheels turning in his mind. "You need an ally. Someone smart, who knows how things work, and can figure out how to get you off the hook."

"Sure," said Charlie, wishing Pete would leave him in peace.

"It's just as well I found you," said Pete sagely, "because I know exactly who you need to talk to."

"Who's that?"

"Mrs Graham."

"Why?"

"She knows a lot more about this stuff than you do."

"What do you mean?"

"She has an interesting past."

"How do you know?" Charlie snipped the last branch.

"An old copper has a sense for these things."

"Why would she help?"

Pete shrugged. "She likes hopeless causes."

Charlie wiped sweat out of his eyes, smearing sap across his forehead in the process. "I suppose."

"I was just down at the station, boyo. Hemi is getting ready to call you up for an interview. He's aware you went off the grid at the time of the murder. And there's a hotshot homicide detective come down from Auckland too. He looks to be a sharp one."

A chill unrelated to ghosts shivered up Charlie's spine. "Right."

"Can you please stop talking to yourself?" Dante had reappeared, holding the Philips screwdriver like it was a knife. "It's distracting."

"Sorry," said Charlie. He glared down at Pete, who grinned.

"Easiest time to lecture to you, son," said Pete. "But, since you think you know what's best, I'll leave you to your gardening. Just one final word of warning…"

"What?" growled Charlie.

"Your new employer here? He's no ray of sunshine. There's serious stuff hanging around this guy. You take care, Charlie boy." The old ghost turned and disappeared, like he'd just walked through an invisible door to another dimension.

Charlie breathed a sigh of relief. It was exhausting, trying to act normal when he was anything but. He finished trimming the kōwhai in peace and descended the ladder.

Dante took the shears from him and examined the blades. "I can make this sharper. A lot sharper." He inspected the kōwhai.

Charlie had the feeling Dante was carefully cataloguing exactly what Charlie had done, comparing a mental before and after picture of the pruning job. Then his employer lifted the full gardening bag without seeming to notice that it weighed rather a lot.

"Some of that will make good kindling," said Charlie. "I can stack it in the shed, ready for winter."

"Winter." Dante looked like he'd never considered the fact of seasons changing.

"For the fireplace," prompted Charlie. "Mrs Davison has a modern one installed in the living room and the main bedroom. Old houses are hard to heat, but those two burners will keep you toasty all winter if you use them. I can chainsaw you some firewood, too."

"Right," said Dante. "There's a chainsaw in the shed?"

"It's about twenty years old, and there's no safety guard, but it works just fine."

"I will sharpen it as well," said Dante.

"I'll go on and weed the garden beds on the South side," said Charlie. "And then I'll compost the vegetable beds ready for late summer planting. There's still time to plant basil, tomatoes, zucchini, runner beans, rocket, and even corn if we're quick about it."

"Ok." Dante looked at Charlie like he'd just spoken in a foreign language. "Vegetables. Right."

"Mrs Davison has a legendary veggie patch. The soil's been worked over and composted for decades. And she saved all the seeds from the best producing veggies. Her heritage tomatoes are the envy of the village." Charlie wasn't sure why he was trying so hard to sell Dante on vege gardening. Deep down, Charlie believed everyone should have a vegetable garden. It would make the world a better place.

"Ok," said Dante. He tucked the shears under his arm, ready to hone them to a state of lethal sharpness, and that seemed to be the end of their conversation.

10

In which Eleanor considers a request

In Te Kohe, the Returned and Services Association — or the RSA for short — was handily combined with the croquet lawn, bowling club and pétanque court. Thus, people could exercise all their rivalries in one location, then retire to celebrate or lick their wounds over a pint of lager.

On Monday mornings, the main club room was given over to the flower arranging club. That meant tables of flowers, green foam, razor sharp implements, and the elderly women who wielded them.

Eleanor snipped at the spray of tiny white flowers blooming around a daylily. She was sitting at the table with her two best Te Kohe friends: Grace and Billy.

Grace was large, round, and comfortable, with thick black hair curling in a bob around her face and horn-rimmed glasses. Billy was small and blonde, with pixie-like features and a haircut that missed out on being a mullet only by virtue of her long trailing fringe.

Since they'd first met, Grace, Billy and Eleanor had helped each other through several trials and tribulations, including the great sponge cake debacle, the masquerade ball mystery, and the case of the missing groom.

By the successful conclusion of the first escapade, they were fast friends. Eleanor felt fortunate indeed that two such intelligent and resourceful women had decided to make Te Kohe their base of operations.

"Have they come up with a chief suspect yet?" said Billy, binding two aspidistra flowers together with wire.

"Hemi's been doing a lot of running around, but no dice yet," said Grace. Hemi was her nephew, and she made sure he kept her well informed.

"Do all the hotel staff have alibis?" asked Eleanor.

Grace hmmmd, and plucked a dahlia from the pile on the table. "Hemi's still working on that one."

Eleanor supposed there were limits on how much information Grace could extract from her nephew. Especially if there was a new police officer brought in to oversee the case. It could make a man raise his professional conduct standards, even in a laid-back town like Te Kohe.

Around them, tables hummed with less informed, but just as enthusiastic gossip about the events of Jubilee night. Eleanor caught snatches of conversation like 'to think it could be someone we all know,' and 'said it was a precision shot. Right to the temple.'

Truly, this is a gossip rich environment, she thought. If only there was a way to arrange all this rampant speculation into a pleasing bouquet to present to the authorities. She smiled to herself.

"Someone to see you, Eleanor," said Billy.

Eleanor glanced up. Outside the seventies glass sliding door that did duty as the main entrance stood Charlie, looking awkward.

With a bright smile, she waved him in. He hesitated, then stepped inside. There was a hush in the conversation as the many ladies of the flower arranging society took note of this new arrival.

"Charlie," she said. "You know Grace and Billy."

"Hi Charlie," said Grace with a comfortable smile.

"Do you want to talk in private?" asked Billy.

For a moment, Charlie looked like he was going to say yes, then he slumped down in the chair beside Eleanor.

"It probably doesn't matter," he said. "Everyone in town will know soon enough."

Eleanor lowered her voice. "Know what?"

"I don't have an alibi for the time of the murder," said Charlie. "When the fireworks started, I got sent to the store room. And when I got back, Ted was being patched up in the kitchen. No one saw me when the actual murder was taking place."

Billy tsked. "A lack of an alibi isn't definitive proof."

"Are you positive no one saw you?" asked Eleanor.

Charlie nodded. "And I don't want to ask anyone to lie for me."

There was a sombre silence.

Then Billy leaned forward and fixed Charlie with her bright green eyes. "Did you do it?"

"What kind of question is that?" huffed Grace.

Billy shrugged. "Just the one everyone's thinking, but too polite to ask."

"I didn't kill Janice," said Charlie. "Or shoot at Ted. Though he's not my favourite person."

"I don't think Ted's anyone's favourite person," said Eleanor. "Though I'd downplay that part when the police interview you. They do so love to find a motive. What's yours, by the way?"

Charlie flushed. "Ted's... not a nice man."

"We all know that," said Billy. "We want specifics. Why do you dislike Ted?"

"He's... I guess he's alright," said Charlie.

"Why did you go to the store room?" asked Grace.

"Sous chef Sione wanted port. It was going to be served to the guests straight after the fireworks."

"And he asked you to go just as the fireworks were ending?" asked Eleanor.

"Well, yes. The kitchen was crowded. We didn't want to have the bottles just sitting there, taking up space."

"Hmmm," said Eleanor.

"Have the police taken a witness statement from you yet?" asked Billy.

"'My presence has been requested,'" Charlie quoted hollowly.

"By the visiting police inspector?" said Eleanor.

"How did you know?" asked Charlie.

Billy and Grace exchanged a look.

"We like to keep informed," said Billy.

"I think he's a bit scary," said Charlie. "I saw him at the hotel yesterday, directing the forensics team. So serious."

"I think he'll do this investigation properly," said Eleanor. "I would tell him the truth about what you were doing on Jubilee night, and nothing more. Don't volunteer any information."

"What if he asks me a whole lot of questions?" said Charlie.

"Just answer them," said Grace, while at the same time, Eleanor said:

"Questions you don't want to answer?"

"Yes," said Charlie.

"You know the saying 'the innocent have nothing to fear?'" said Eleanor. "Load of rubbish. What are the rules regarding lawyers in this country?"

"Lawyering up makes you look guilty as," said Billy.

"What are you afraid he'll ask?" said Eleanor.

"I dunno," said Charlie. "Why I don't like Ted?"

"Suppose for a moment you did do it," said Eleanor. "Why do it now? If you had a massive axe to grind with Ted, why wait until the most crowded night of the year to try and off him?"

"Ted's about to make a fortune," said Grace. "Everyone knows that. As soon as he manages to sell all the land he owns to developers."

"Do you own a gun, Charlie?" said Eleanor.

"No."

"Do you know how to shoot a gun?" said Billy.

"Of course," said Charlie. "My cousin Ralph's taken me hunting every summer since my dad died."

Eleanor sighed. "Maybe you should lawyer up. You're eligible for legal aid, right?"

"You're all assuming Ted was the target," said Billy. "Supposing it was Janice. Do you have any motive for killing her, Charlie?"

"I wish you wouldn't keep saying that," said Charlie. "I don't want to kill anyone."

"Just answer the question," snapped Billy. When they all looked at her, she shrugged. "I'm being the bad cop here. It's good practice for Charlie."

"I don't have anything against Janice," said Charlie. "I've only ever talked to her a couple of times."

"Well, that's good news at last," said Eleanor. "Hard to find a motive when you hardly know the person."

"Although she did spread a lot of nasty rumours about my dad after he died."

Eleanor sighed.

"What are you most afraid you'll be asked?" said Billy.

"I don't want to say," said Charlie.

"Is it relevant to the murder?" said Eleanor.

"Yes. Not really. Maybe," said Charlie.

Grace sat back, puffing her cheeks out in a sigh. "You're not helping matters, Charlie."

"I know," said Charlie apologetically.

"You know you can tell us anything," said Eleanor. "We're on your side."

"That's right," said Billy. "Friends don't ask questions. They just help bury the body, and never speak of it again."

"Not helping," said Grace.

Charlie shrugged. He looked miserable. "Look, can you just tell me what to say if I get asked a question I don't want to answer?"

"You just say, 'I don't know,'" said Eleanor. "Or, 'I'm not sure.' Or 'I'm not comfortable answering that.'"

"What if they keep me in there for hours and hours until I'm sleep deprived and can't think straight, and they good cop, bad cop me till I break down and confess to everything they tell me to?"

Eleanor reached out and gave Charlie's hand a squeeze. "I'm sure it won't come to that, dear. We're in New Zealand after all. They'll probably give you a lamington cake every half hour. In fact, one of us could come with you as a support person if you like."

"Could you do that?" said Charlie, his face bright with hope.

For a moment, Eleanor considered saying, 'only if you tell me the thing you're keeping back.' But that wasn't fair. Charlie was under a lot of stress. And she was fairly certain she'd get him to tell her sooner or later anyway.

"I'd be happy to," she said.

11

In which Dante compares the art of making cheesecake with managing a murder investigation

To his not very great surprise, two mornings after the Jubilee night, Dante opened the door to admit Mrs Eleanor Graham.

"What can I do for you, Mrs Graham?" he asked.

"Please, call me Eleanor," she said, presenting her hand. He shook it reluctantly.

"I've brought New York cheesecake," she said. "Shall we go through to your sitting room to discuss matters?"

For a moment, Dante considered blocking the doorway, refusing her entry, and then leaving town in the dead of night, never to return. He could fly out of New Zealand using one of his alternate identities. No one would ever know.

Then he sighed and waved her inside. "Please."

In his sitting room, Eleanor arranged herself gracefully on a wingback chair. Dante set down two cups of tea on the coffee table and sat opposite her, bracing himself for whatever she was going to ask.

"Have you heard the latest news of the investigation?" said Eleanor.

"No," said Dante. He'd banned himself from reading newspapers as part of his strict retirement regime and hadn't talked to anyone about the events at the town jubilee.

"As far as I can determine from talking to the Jubilee celebration guests," said Eleanor. "Only two people present don't have an alibi for the time of the murder."

Dante frowned. "I said didn't want to get involved."

"I think that ship may have sailed." Eleanor leaned forward. "The two people are you and Charlie Wilson. And I'm sure Charlie didn't do it."

Based on Dante's time with Charlie, he agreed for the most part. Though you never knew, when someone was sufficiently motivated, what they might do. "That leaves me as the prime murder suspect. Do you think it's wise to interview a potential murderer alone in their house?"

Eleanor smiled, quite at ease. "I don't think you did it either."

"Why's that?"

She raised one eyebrow. "If you'd wanted Ted dead, you wouldn't have missed. And if you were to murder someone, you'd do it with rather more subtlety."

"And how do you know that?"

"I don't know anything and I can't prove anything," said Eleanor. "However, in my time on this earth, I've met many people from many walks of life. I've met people like you before, Dante Reid. Enough to form rather accurate assumptions."

Dante didn't argue. He'd never seen the point of arguing, especially when the person was right. "Why are you here, then?"

"Because I want to clear Charlie's name."

"If I help you clear Charlie's name, that leaves me as the prime suspect."

"True. But I want to clear Charlie by finding the real killer. Which we've agreed isn't you."

"Why would I help you? Why would I help Charlie?"

"He's your gardener."

Dante considered. He had quite enjoyed gardening with Charlie. Even the damn corpse plant was starting to grow on him. Figuratively, not literally, because it hadn't shown any signs of life yet. He wondered if it would need extra attention when it sprouted. Would he be able to consult Charlie in jail?

"I don't think him being my gardener is sufficient reason."

"Clearing this up quickly will help you stay here in Te Kohe in relative peace and quiet. But there's another reason." Eleanor fixed Dante with her piercing green eyes. "I'm telling you this as someone who might become your friend. When you retire from a life such as yours, it's difficult to form new bonds. Having seen the worst sides of human nature, it's easy to follow one's natural instinct to cut oneself off from all human interaction. From attachments. From people who might come to depend on you."

"I don't like... people much," said Dante.

"Understandable, given your experience of them thus far." Eleanor picked up her teacup and sipped her tea demurely. "Let me tell you something I learned the hard way."

Dante focused. He preferred to learn from other people's mistakes, rather than his own, as in his business, mistakes could often be fatal.

"It's about settling down. If you don't fill your new life with things - hobbies, connections, people - you leave a void. And what comes to fill it? Your personal demons. Unless," she held up one finger, "you keep yourself occupied. By clearing an innocent man's name, for example."

Eleanor unfolded a parcel wrapped in grease-proof paper and laid it on the coffee table, revealing neat squares of creamy cheesecake.

"I imagine a man like you might have a few demons hanging around. Cheesecake?" She nudged the paper with its slices of cake towards him.

Dante took a square of cheesecake and bit into it. It was delicious, the smooth creaminess of the topping contrasting perfectly with the light and crunchy base.

"You have experience with demons?"

"Oh, yes," said Eleanor.

"So you want me to help Charlie get off a murder charge because you think that'll silence my demons?"

"No, I want you to help because you have a rare and useful skill set. And because Charlie's one of my favourite people. And because he's innocent. And because when we find the murderer, you'll be free of suspicion, too."

Dante noted the order of those last three sentences.

"And it'll be fun, Dante. I guarantee it."

Dante could feel his mouth begin to shape the words 'thank you, but no,' when Eleanor looked straight at him.

"And I'll owe you a favour."

"What kind of favour?"

"I'll help you when you need it most. You'll find," she said, sipping her tea, "that I too have quite a formidable set of skills."

Dante watched Eleanor open his garden gate and disappear behind the hedge.

He already regretted his decision. He could see a dozen ways the mission to clear Charlie's name could go wrong. The most egregious scenarios ended with him falling off the wagon and having to change his AA wristband to the other hand and start his tally of days without bodies all over again.

With a deep sigh, he went back into the sitting room. The cat was stretched out in a pool of sunshine, and the remainder of the cheesecake was on the coffee table. That was something, at least. He put a piece in his mouth, where it promptly crumbled and melted on his tongue.

Someone who baked cheesecake to such perfection did have a formidable set of skills, he thought. It was possible they would conduct a murder investigation properly, too.

Whether it could be done without arousing the ire of the police and assorted townspeople was another matter. On that, only time would tell.

12

In which Eleanor encounters the long arm of the law

The morning three days after what would become known as 'Jubilee Murder Day,' dawned warm and golden. It put Eleanor in mind of her mother's apple cake, a hallowed dish that never failed to raise her spirits.

By the time she'd had her morning coffee and dressed to meet the day, there was a buzz in the air. The murder was still big news in town, and the whole village was waking up to a world where exciting things happened.

The fact that this particular exciting thing had turned out poorly for Janice didn't seem to bother people much. Apart from Janice's husband, Derek, and her niece, Angelina, no one seemed terribly upset.

Since the special policeman from Auckland had arrived to do his special police work, everyone had become an expert in the criminal mind.

Charlie was looking more and more like suspect number one, and Eleanor was determined to have a good look at the rest of the crime scene. It should be doable, now that the police had completed their due diligence, and the hotel was once again open for business.

Eleanor was sure that something about this particular crime did not add up. She was equally certain that she couldn't trust the police to do things properly.

Sometimes it's best to go see for yourself, she thought. You never knew. She might find something that would get Charlie off the hook.

Calling at the Pepper Tree Hotel early in the morning was easy. Delia, Charlie's mum, was a friend, and as such, was quite happy to let her in via the kitchen entrance.

On her way into town, Eleanor slipped a note into Dante's letterbox, telling him where she could be found.

The people she met on the walk into town waved cheerily at her. Everyone had an air of extra alertness, as if the whole town had caught the bug of 'amateur sleuth.' Eleanor had no doubt that, at this very minute, the Frog and Gumboot cafe was a veritable hotbed of theories and surmises, and more suspects than a game of Cluedo.

Eventually, people would lose interest, or it would turn nasty when an arrest was made, and someone they knew was accused of the crime. But for now, the entire affair lay in the area of morbidly fascinating, and as such was fair game for all the village armchair detectives.

The Pepper Tree Hotel hove into sight, looking slightly less majestic than it had on Jubilee night. Now, it looked a trifle forlorn, missing the glow of the myriad fairy lights and the excited crowd of guests.

The service door to the kitchens was ajar, so Eleanor slipped through.

Inside, the kitchen was controlled chaos — the breakfast prep was nearly done, but no one knew yet how hectic the morning was going to be.

Charlie's mum, Delia, looked up with a smile as Eleanor gave her a friendly wave.

She pushed the last tray of croissants into the oven, closed it with a bang and wiped her hands on her apron.

"I'm glad you're here," she said without preamble. "A new policeman's turned up. Our guys and him spent all yesterday going over this place. Later today they want to question us staff. What should I say?"

"Just tell them the truth."

"The truth is that if Ted was the target, I could have shot him myself."

"Maybe don't tell them that," said Eleanor. "Are the police still around?"

Delia shook her head. "Not till this afternoon, I think. Also, I wanted to say, I'm worried about Charlie."

Eleanor glanced at the door to the main hotel. "Is Ted here today?"

"Maybe. He was lurking yesterday. I wouldn't be surprised if he was bothering the police, trying to tell them how to do their jobs. Anyway, about Charlie."

Eleanor sighed. "Yes?"

"He's gone all quiet - not like him at all. You know, when he was a kid, everyone used to tease him about being weird, talking to people who weren't there. He grew out of it, but when bad things happen, he backslides. So I'm worried."

"I'll check in on him later," promised Eleanor. She eyed the door to the hotel again. "Where is he?"

"Probably out on the harbour. Or in the bush. He likes to get away when he's worried like this."

This ranked among the least useful directions she'd been given to find anyone, thought Eleanor. She said goodbye to Delia, and had a warm, freshly baked croissant wrapped in a napkin pressed into her hand.

A murmur of conversation issued from the hotel restaurant, where guests and locals were having their breakfast. From the sounds of it, it was more packed than usual. Notoriety will do that for you, thought Eleanor.

She slipped upstairs, checking around for any stray police investigators. She had a choice of revisiting the balcony, or taking a look at the store room where Dante said the bullet might have been fired from.

Eleanor had already photographed the balcony on the night of the murder. But the store room was new territory and might yield interesting information.

She sauntered down the corridor, heading away from the guest areas of the hotel and into the service rooms.

Eleanor passed three doors, comparing her mental map of the hotel to the windows she'd seen from the balcony. She tried the handle of the fourth door and was surprised to find it opened easily.

The pantry was a wood panelled room with one window on the back wall. Floor to ceiling shelves lined the walls, packed with condiments, bottles of wine, vinegar and pickles.

Hastily removed vestiges of crime scene tape indicated that the police had already been through here and finished their work.

Standing on tiptoes, Eleanor could look out the window and across to the balcony. It was certainly possible that someone with a gun had shot Janice from here. Someone taller than her, though that wasn't unusual.

She didn't know how difficult a shot it was, though she was sure Dante would know.

Eleanor turned around the room, looking for anything that might suggest... something.

A few minutes later, she sighed in frustration. It was hardly likely the killer had left a calling card. Though she did know one professional back in the New York days who'd used to do just that. It paid to advertise, she supposed.

Look for the thing that's out of place, she thought.

Eleanor scanned the stacks of provisions one last time, and quite unexpectedly, found what she was looking for.

At the end of one shelf, three bottles were not as dusty as their companions. Eleanor carefully shifted them aside and peered into the dimly lit wall at the back of the shelf.

A small circle of putty had been hurriedly applied to the timber, close to the corner of the room. Eleanor flicked a small pen knife from her handbag and dug into the putty. She scraped it back, and behind it was a dark, hard object.

She slid her knife further into the wood and levered against the object. With a small metallic sound, it fell out onto the shelf.

Eleanor shone her cellphone light onto the object. It was a bullet, small, grey, and deadly.

"Interesting." Eleanor tapped it with her knife. What was it doing here, and why had someone tried to hide it?

"I'm sure you have a legitimate reason to be here. Otherwise, you're acting rather suspiciously."

Eleanor didn't jump. That would not have done. Instead, she turned around easily, her face arranged into a mask of innocent surprise.

"Surely a civilian is allowed to enter a hotel pantry early in the morning and find interesting items buried in the woodwork? What could possibly be suspicious about that? I'm Eleanor Graham, by the way," she said. "And you are?"

"Police Inspector Avery," said the man dryly. "At your service."

The policeman was pushing sixty, his dark hair now liberally peppered with grey, which contrasted nicely with his tanned skin. He was also, Eleanor had to admit, quite good-looking, in a formal, straight-laced way.

He extended a hand, and Eleanor shook it.

"Perhaps," the inspector said, nonchalantly putting a hand in the pocket of his navy jacket, "you can explain what you're doing here, at one of our crime scenes?"

"Perhaps I could," said Eleanor.

The police inspector raised one dark eyebrow.

"As you're probably already aware," said Eleanor, "since Jubilee night, this town has been afflicted with an epidemic of amateur detectives."

"That has come to my attention, yes," said Inspector Avery.

"You're probably wondering if I'm one of them."

"The thought had crossed my mind."

"Well, you're quite correct." Eleanor gave him one of her more vapid smiles. "Guilty as charged. Only, I'm not so much an amateur sleuth as an...interested bystander. This whole situation struck me as so unlikely I've been wanting to satisfy my curiosity. Which I now have."

"I see." Avery's face gave nothing away. "Were you a witness to the events of the Jubilee night?"

"I was up on the balcony," said Eleanor. "Though I haven't been called in to do a witness statement yet."

"We will have to rectify that," said Avery. "I take it the local police have your contact details?"

"Of course," said Eleanor. "Would you like a croissant?"

"That could be seen as an attempt to bribe a police officer."

"It's a delicious croissant. Delia is an excellent pastry chef. I'm sure she would be quite happy to give me another if you took this one."

"No thank you."

"I was wondering if the boys in blue have any suspects yet." Eleanor didn't quite bat her eyes, but it was a close thing.

"That would be police business."

"Oh, come on," she cajoled. "What am I going to tell everyone at the Frog and Gumboot if you don't spill just a few beans?"

Inspector Avery was unmoved. He was a full head taller than her, and looked down at her from this height with a deadpan expression.

"I mean, modern policing is all about community outreach," said Eleanor. "So as a member of the community, I'd love to know just a little of what's going on."

Inspector Avery was studying her intently. "Have we met before?"

Eleanor returned his gaze with an airy smile. "I don't think so."

"You look familiar."

"My photo was in the local paper recently. An article on the Te Kohe Flower Arranging Society."

He smiled faintly. "I must have missed it."

"I expect you're far too busy with police work." Eleanor simpered. "It must be quite thrilling, chasing murderers around the country."

"Quite so."

Eleanor wondered if she was laying on her airhead society lady act a bit thick. Police officers were used to people trying to deceive them, after all. It was a good act, though. One she'd used many times in the past.

"And you're unable to share any information on the case with the public? Is that your last word on the matter?"

"I could book you. It would fall under obstructing police enquiries and tampering with evidence."

"How thrilling," trilled Eleanor. "Would you handcuff me? Read me my rights? Sit me in one of those interrogation rooms with the one-way mirror?"

Inspector Avery pinched the bridge of his nose. Now he looked tired, and mildly repulsed. "Please, get out of here now. If I find you near this crime scene again, there will be consequences."

"Aren't you interested in what I found? That would be assisting the police with their enquiries."

Avery gave the shelf a dismissive glance. "Looks like a 9mm bullet has been embedded in the wall, and then covered up with matching wood putty."

"Hardly of interest, then?"

"Mrs Graham, I won't ask you again to leave."

"Of course, of course. So sorry to obstruct you." Eleanor fluttered her hands in apology. She retreated to the hotel lobby, a little disappointed her airhead act had worked so well.

Still, she told herself, it was better the police inspector regarded her with contempt. Easier all round to be underestimated.

Eleanor bit into her croissant as she exited the Pepper Tree and descended to the street. The warm white pastry and melting butter embraced her senses.

Nothing like a croissant, she thought. First thing in the morning, freshly baked, and made by someone who truly understands about the flaky lightness balancing the inner core of mushy dough. Delia is a treasure, she thought. I hope we can do right by her and her son.

13

In which Dante establishes a moral baseline

Dante read the message Eleanor had left him on her way into town. She hadn't messaged Dante on his phone. Dante detested phones. He'd seen so many people come undone (sometimes terminally) because they failed to protect their phone from being hacked, being tracked, or simply because it distracted them at a crucial moment.

In retirement, he refused to own one.

Instead, as instructed, Eleanor had left a small card in his letterbox. In flowing copperplate script it said: 'meet me at the Frog and Gumboot today, 9:30 am.'

Dante had spent the first two hours of the day doing his workout routine, while the cat watched with wry amusement. He hit his heavy punching bag and did chin-ups, press-ups, and situps until his muscles ached. It was good. It stopped him thinking about the near future and the prospect of having to meet people. And talk to them. With no option of violence as a way out if things got awkward.

Finally, it was time to go and meet Eleanor. There were two cafes in the town of Te Kohe. The first cafe only survived because it was next to the petrol station and truckers taking the coastal road went there to fill up on coffee and cream buns.

The second cafe was the Frog and Gumboot. This was where all the locals and the occasional tourist went. It sat next to the Foursquare in the centre of town, a wonderfully golden, warm and comfortable place to be.

When the Frog was first built in the 1920s, it had been a dressmaker's workshop. Now, the large fabric cutting benches had been converted to cafe tables, and great yards of coloured cloth hung down from the heavy timber roof trusses.

Dante entered and found Eleanor seated at a small table in the corner. The table had a view of the entire cafe, and backed onto bare walls, rather than a window. Dante appreciated this.

The noise of people eating and talking almost drowned out the loud blare of the coffee machine steaming milk and the grinder milling the freshly roasted beans. The air smelt of delicious things being baked with lots of honey and butter.

A waitress set an elegant bone china kettle in the centre of the table, then placed two cups and two saucers next to it. Eleanor smiled in thanks.

"I come here so often, they know I always take Assam tea in the morning. Though of course if you prefer coffee, I can see to that too."

Dante used to drink his coffee black and extra dark, Turkish style. He used to strain the dregs through his teeth to filter out the coarse grounds. Perhaps, now he was retired, it was time to enjoy the finer things of life.

"Tea is fine." He waited while Eleanor poured tea into china cups so thin that the light shone through them. A wisp of steam wafted up, and Dante caught the scent of malt and the faintest hint of caramel.

"We're here to make a plan of attack," said Eleanor. She brought a small leather journal out of her handbag and detached a fountain pen from its spine. "I have a few ideas on how to proceed."

Dante was sure she did.

"Before we begin, though, do you have any initial thoughts?"

Dante considered.

"I would rather not have to kill anyone," he said.

"Duly noted." Eleanor made a small footnote in her book.

Dante felt he ought to elaborate.

"It's just that — on most missions, when I get the directive that there's not meant to be any lethal intervention... those missions generally end up having the highest body count."

Eleanor shut her notebook with a snap. "Dante, I am not one of your unimaginative, dry, and bureaucratic ex-bosses. If we're not making progress, we will simply get creative. I promise I will not ask you to kill anyone."

"Ok." Dante took a sip of his tea. It tasted clean and aromatic. He rather liked it.

"Our objective is to clear Charlie and you of suspicion of murder. Preferably by finding the real killer. To do that—"

"Excuse me."

It was a waitress. She had jet black hair, an oval face, and wide green eyes that matched the emerald silk dress she wore.

Eleanor smiled. "Dante, this is Crystal. Crystal, Dante."

"Hi." Crystal beamed. "I know you've got your tea, Mrs Graham, but perhaps you'd be wanting something to eat?"

"What a lovely idea. I would like a slice of carrot cake. It's particularly good at this cafe," she said as an aside to Dante.

Dante blinked. The waitress, Crystal, was looking expectantly at him, her pen poised above her notebook.

"I, uh," he glanced across at Eleanor. "I'd like something to eat." Eleanor nodded encouragingly.

"Would you like savoury or sweet?" said Crystal.

"Uh... sweet?"

"In that case, might I recommend the red velvet cake? It's this week's special." Crystal smiled at him.

"Yeah, great. Ok."

Eleanor watched the girl bounce away to the kitchen. "Crystal's lovely. She might try to slip you her number when she delivers the cake."

Dante blinked in confusion. "Why? Is she an operative?"

"No, Dante. She's flirting with you." Eleanor smiled wryly. "I don't usually have pretty young ladies come over to offer me extra cake."

Dante considered this piece of intelligence. "I'm not ready to date yet."

"I don't suppose you are. Don't leave things too long, though. You never know when time might run out." For a moment, Eleanor looked sad, then she shook her head, and the expression vanished. "I found something quite interesting in the hotel pantry. A bullet embedded in the wall. Someone had taken pains to hide it. I would very much like to know if it was fired by the same gun that killed Janice."

"Eleanor!" An elderly gentleman in a checked Swanndri jacket and corduroy pants shouted from across the cafe. He strode towards them, brushing past patrons with abandon.

Dante focused, assessing the new arrival as a possible threat.

The man reached their table, huffing slightly like a land-bound walrus. "Good to see you, m'dear! How's tricks?"

"Bernard." Eleanor bestowed a dazzling smile on him. "How lovely. This is Dante." She waved a hand in Dante's direction and gave no further explanation for his presence.

"Pleased to meet you, I'm sure," said Bernard. "Mind if I join you? Just for a few minutes. My coffee's to go and I've got to get back to the boat. Bilge pump's gone, and she's listing to one side, poor thing."

"Of course." Eleanor swirled the teapot and poured both her and Dante another cup. "Please, take a seat."

With a certain amount of huffing, Bernard sat. He combed his moustaches with one finger, his bright brown eyes peering out from his tanned and wrinkled face.

"What a business, eh? Can hardly believe it."

"You mean the Jubilee night?" said Eleanor. Her journal had disappeared out of sight the moment Bernard appeared.

"Of course, of course. What else? There hasn't been a murder here for what... twenty five years? Unless, of course, it was an accident. Doesn't look like an accident though. Who do you think did it?"

Bernard could combine several thoughts in one long stream of commentary. Dante hoped Eleanor was keeping track of it all.

"Bernard, it's hardly fair to hypothesise ahead of the facts," said Eleanor.

"Ha! Don't you quote Sherlock Holmes at me, m'lady. I'm sure everyone in town's got their theories. It's looking bad for Charlie boy though, isn't it? I mean, I heard he had an opportunity, and he's surely got a motive. Charlie's a good lad, but maybe Janice just went too far. All that resentment, building up, then bursting out all at once."

"What do you mean?"

"Well, you know. Back in the day, Janice spread all those rumours when Charlie's dad died. That he was drunk when he had the boat accident, and that he owed Ted a whole lot of money from gambling debts. It was a bad enough time for poor Charlie and his mum. Janice made it much, much worse. Maybe seeing her that night in all her finery, while his mum Delia laboured away in the kitchen... well, perhaps the boy just snapped."

Eleanor shook her head. "Charlie isn't the type to snap like that. He's a nice, calm person."

"You never know," said Bernard, darkly. "What do you think?" he asked Dante.

Dante paused in raising the teacup to his lips. He put it down carefully. There was a drawn out silence while he considered his reply.

"If an amateur was going to kill someone," he said, "they wouldn't do it when the target was surrounded by people."

"That's a good point," said Eleanor. "Perhaps someone with more experience, then? Bernard, who else do you think had a grudge against Janice? Or Ted?"

"Ted now..." Bernard combed his moustache again, thinking. He snapped his fingers. "The Hellhound boss — Thrasher Jake. They've been enemies since school, you know. Ted's development plans are going to mess with the gang headquarters. Jake's not happy about it."

"Well, that's a possibility," said Eleanor. "Thank you, Bernard."

The barista called out: "Bernard. Bernard! COFFEE!"

"I heard you Val!" Bernard yelled back. "Just because I'm old, they think I'm deaf. See you round, Eleanor. Nice to meet you, Dante." He wrapped on the table top and lumbered off to collect his coffee.

Eleanor raised an eyebrow at Dante. "That is something odd about this murder. Why kill someone in the middle of the most crowded night of the year? Sure, fireworks would mask the gunshot noise, but the murder happened after they finished. Do you think that was a mistake?"

"Depends who did it," said Dante. "I wouldn't have done it that way."

"Our first item, then," said Eleanor. "I'd like you to review the scene of the crime. I'd thought the police were finished with it, and they should be properly gone soon. Delia will let you in early tomorrow morning if you're free. What is it, Dante?"

Dante wondered how she knew he was thinking about something. Then he thought about how to phrase his question. Perhaps there was no good way to say it. "What if we find out that Charlie did it?"

"Ah." Eleanor put down her tea cup. Her green eyes met his, and he saw she'd been waiting for this objection. "This is assuming that Ted was the target, not Janice."

"Yes."

"Do you think someone like Charlie could shoot at Ted in cold blood?"

Dante stared into the distance. "I've learned that people are capable of anything."

Eleanor steepled her fingers. "If Charlie tried to kill Ted, I'm sure he had a good reason."

"Ted's still alive, though. Janice isn't."

"Charlie is a fine young man. Everyone makes mistakes, Dante. Intent matters."

Dante shook his head. His hand wrapped around the fragile china teacup, and he wondered how much pressure it would take to shatter it.

"Besides," said Eleanor, "how many people have you killed?"

"That's different," said Dante.

Eleanor took another sip of her tea. "I don't think we'll find that Charlie did it. I'm a pretty good judge of character, and Charlie can't lie to save himself. He had no idea what was going on that night."

"But if he did do it?"

Eleanor tapped a staccato rhythm on the table. "People who work for institutions are always looking for absolutes. Thinking there's an unassailable moral high ground, a *manual* that lets you know what is right and what is wrong. Life is not like that. The people giving you your assignments were deep in shades of grey. You must have realised that before you left."

"Rules are there to keep people safe."

"No, rules are there to control people and trick them into thinking they're safe. They're there to give people an easy out, so they don't have to think and decide for themselves."

"Eleanor." Dante waited until she met his eyes. "I need to know that if we find Charlie guilty, you'll let this go. I can't be part of freeing someone who's guilty. Or framing someone who is innocent."

"Oh, very well." Eleanor looked sharply away. "I agree. And I would never frame an innocent. I have my own moral code, even if it's not as right-angled as yours. We'll find that Charlie didn't do it, though. Since he has no alibi for the time of the crime, proving it will be the difficult part."

Dante slowly unclasped the bone china mug.

Eleanor followed his gaze down to his hand and smiled.

"Porcelain is fragile - a slight tap with a hammer would shatter that cup. But like that - with pressure coming at it from all around? It's so strong you could squeeze as hard as you like and it'll make not a jot of difference. Now, shall we make our list of action items?"

Dante nodded. An agreement had been reached. And he'd discovered that he liked Assam tea.

14

In which we find out what Dante does every Thursday morning

It was Thursday, 9:00 am New Zealand time. That made it Wednesday 3:00 pm in New York, noon Pacific Time, and other times at various unknown locations around the globe where Dante's fellow AA members were situated.

Dante sat in front of a plain wall with no distinguishing characteristics and logged in using multiple encryptions, scramblers, and VPNs that bounced his signal around the world.

He clicked to join the meeting, entering in the long string of letters and numbers he'd memorised from a note passed to him by a hooded stranger he'd encountered in a crowd watching an underground bare-knuckle fight in Caracas.

One by one, the other members of his AA group tuned in, their rectangular screens appearing on the meeting panel.

"Welcome to the three hundred and twenty-fifth meeting of the non-denominational AA," said John, their meeting leader. John had an ageless face, somewhere between thirty and sixty, with chiselled cheekbones and an ascetic's calm eyes.

"As always, it's a pleasure to see you all."

"Hi John," the members chorused.

Dante slowly relaxed. Everyone was there. Which meant, presumably, that no one had fallen off the wagon. That was good.

John glanced down, where Dante supposed he had the meeting agenda.

"A special congratulation is in order for Aubrey, who has completed one year homicide free."

"Congratulations Aubrey," came the refrain.

They used only first names, and no one talked in any detail about their life. However, Dante assumed that the names given were in fact their real ones. It was Assassins Anonymous, and anonymity was important. But if you couldn't be upfront with your fellow ex-assassins, when were you ever going to go straight?

Dante gripped his Colt Peacemaker's handle as he listened to the minutes from last week's meeting. He found the solid weight of it calming as he studied the faces staring back at him from his screen.

Some of his fellow AA members had likely been government employed, like himself. Others, he suspected, had been freelance killers-for-hire. Dante didn't judge. He doubted the people he'd killed felt any different, knowing they'd been targeted by a hostile arm of the secret service rather than a private individual. Dead was dead.

There was a pause in the conversation, and Dante became aware that everyone's eyes were on him.

"My name is Dante," he said, "and I am an assassin."

"Hello, Dante," they chanted.

"It is now one hundred and four days since my last kill," he said.

A general rumble along the lines of 'well done' and 'keep it up' went around the group. John gave him a tiny nod of approval.

Unlike the other AA, there were just five steps to the Assassins Anonymous creed.

1. Admit that killing people is wrong
2. Make a list of all persons you've terminated, and become willing to make amends
3. Stop killing people
4. Continue to not kill anyone, even if you really, really want to, or have a pressing reason to do so.
5. Having had your ethical awakening, carry this message to other assassins, and support them in their journey towards redemption.

Dante had the feeling that John (possibly his real name) was the real deal when it came to lethal force. Something in his eyes, that wide awake but deathly still quality, made him glad, deep in the tiny corner of his soul that still cared about mortality, that he hadn't gone up against John back when he was still active.

Although if work had brought him into conflict with John, it would have been memorable. Dante was sure of that.

"I'd like to welcome a new member," said John. "Jasmine has been sponsored into this group by Caleb. Welcome Jasmine."

A chorus of welcomes filtered around the group.

Jasmine raised a shy hand in a wave.

"Hi everyone," she said. "I'm thrilled to have found this group, and I'm ready to put the past behind me."

Jasmine was a bottle blonde. She had wide blue eyes with long eyelashes and a cheeky smile. Dante imagined that smile, distracting as it was, had been responsible for more than a few fatalities.

"Caleb, if you want any support in your role as sponsor, let me know," said John. "We want Jasmine to have a strong start in her new life."

"Thanks," said Caleb. "Appreciate it."

Caleb was a classic working stiff, burnt out, sad-eyed, probably with an alcohol or other strong substance habit on the side to help cope with his PTSD. Dante thought it likely Caleb also attended the other type of AA meeting. He wondered if the man ever got the two meetings confused and made the wrong introduction. He hoped not.

"Hey, John," said Frankie. "I gotta question for ya."

"Go ahead," said John, folding his hands. His dark eyes half lidded as he prepared to listen.

"Well, it's more of a situation," said Frankie. "But yeah, I guess it's a question too." Frankie was classic New York: dark features, slicked back hair, leather jacket. Every part of him said 'mob hitman trying to kick the habit.' Dante wondered if Frankie had fallen off the wagon this week and had to bury a body in the woods upstate.

"Fire away," said John. "Or rather, go ahead, please."

"So we're at parent-teacher meetings," said Frankie, "and this asshole at the next table is doing stuff on his phone, y'know? And it's noisy. It's like those dumb videos kids are into these days. And I give him a look, y'know? Like I'm trying to tell him to shut the hell up, or he's gonna end up dead. But he doesn't get it. And I thought, it would be so easy to follow him home after my kid's teacher is finished telling me why he needs to spend more time on his math homework. And then I would let that asshole know he needs to show some respect. Not kill him, just rough him up a bit. Give him something to think about. But I'm like, no, that could easily get out of hand, and then I'll be left with no choice. I'll have to whack the guy just to shut him up."

"So what did you do, Frankie?" asked John.

Frankie grimaced. "I called my sponsor, Aubrey. He talked me down. And then the guy drove off in his shiny Lambo. He had no class, you know what I mean? What kind of grown man watches dumb kid's videos in a parent teacher meeting? What example does that set? Maybe I should have—"

"Frankie," broke in John, "you did the right thing. What do we say?"

"Killing people won't solve the problem," they all intoned.

"But sometimes you gotta send a message," said Frankie. "All right, all right," he held his hands up. "I'm gonna sit tight. No problem. I'm one hundred and sixty three days, no fatalities. I won't break the chain."

"Well done," said John crisply. "Moving along — Dante, how has your week been?"

Dante thought about his week. "I didn't kill anyone."

"Good, that's good," said John. "Any pressures? Has it been hard to stay cool? Or was it a regular week?"

Dante thought about Janice's body on the Pepper Tree Hotel balcony. He thought about Charlie's worried face. He thought about Ted's smug smile and whether a body would fit in the corpse plant pot in his greenhouse.

"A little harder than usual," he said at last.

"Anything we can help you with?" said John.

Dante gathered his thoughts. "There's a situation developing. I might find it hard to keep to the code." He could feel it in his bones, that urge towards action that would lead to someone lying on the ground with the light dying in their eyes. "I might need to kill to save a life."

"The code is not negotiable, Dante," said John. "No reason is sufficient to justify murder."

"Isn't it all too late for that?" said Dante. "For us?"

"No," said John, simply. "That's why we're here."

"Hey, just a thought," said Frankie, "does keeping to the code include arranging for someone else to do the deed? Because I know a guy…"

"What do you think?" said John.

Frankie ruminated on this for fifteen long seconds. "Ok, ok," he said. "I get it. No arranging jobs either. Because killing people is wrong. Sheesh, tough crowd."

John steepled his fingers. "Even if we think our past is too deep in shadow for the light to come through, we must carry on. In the fullness of time, there is a way forward for everyone."

"It's just that some people don't know how to read between the lines, y'know?" said Frankie. "You have to hit them right between the eyes just to get the message through."

"Frankie…" said John, a tiny warning note in his voice, and Dante wondered why Frankie wasn't already ducking for cover.

"And it's not like I'm being unreasonable here," said Frankie. "I mean, a guy can only take so much crap from people who don't show no respect."

"Frankie," said John, "Dante has the floor now."

"Ok, ok," said Frankie. "I'm just sayin'."

"What do you advise if things get heated?" asked Dante.

"Keep to the code." John's dark eyes met Dante's. "And feel free to reach out if you require additional guidance. My satphone line is open 24/7. Now, who else has something they want to discuss? Someone other than Frankie." John's voice never deviated from his usual calm tone, but Frankie shut up and stayed that way for the rest of the session.

Fifteen minutes later, the meeting concluded with John leading them in the AA invocation.

"May Life grant me the serenity

To accept that not all things are solved by violence,

That sometimes the right thing to do is walk away.

Allow me to tolerate this world with all its flaws,

And never seek to improve it,

By removing from it,

Those whom I deem unworthy of life.

May I possess the wisdom to know,

That burying the bodies

In a place they'll never be found,

And leaving no witnesses,

Is not the same as living a life of peace."

The members chanted to the end, Jasmine finishing a little behind everyone else. Then, one by one, the members blinked out and Dante's screen went black as John ended the meeting.

He stared into space for a full minute, then flipped his laptop closed and stowed it away in a lead lined drawer.

He had a murder to solve.

15

In which Dante encounters croissants and bullet holes

Dante knocked on the service door of the Pepper Tree Hotel. Moments later, it was answered by a slender lady with high cheekbones, curly auburn hair, and rosy cheeks. It was easy to see that she was Charlie's mother.

Her face looked like it was meant for smiling, but it was currently creased with tension.

"Dante?" she said, her voice low.

"Mrs Wilson," said Dante.

"Please, call me Delia," the lady said with a small smile. It made her look years younger and dimpled her rosy cheeks. She motioned Dante inside.

"Eleanor said you were going to look for more clues," said Delia.

By the state of the kitchen, Delia had already been at work for some time. Dante supposed this was normal for a pastry chef.

In his line of work, regular hours weren't part of the job description. Sometimes a job started at nine in the morning, sometimes at midnight. Sometimes Dante would work straight for thirty six hours, and sometimes he'd be flown halfway across the world for a job that lasted half a day. He wondered if Delia liked her consistent schedule, or whether she'd prefer the type of job that had no routine at all.

He didn't think Delia would be cut out for work like his. Although you never knew. He'd certainly been surprised in the past by others in his profession who didn't appear to fit the mould.

Dante followed Delia through the kitchen, full of the aroma of baking, and into the service corridor.

"Eleanor said you'd want to see the pantry, and then the ground outside the pantry window," Delia said in that same low voice.

Dante supposed she thought she was being secretive. He didn't tell her that covert operations didn't work like that. Half the time, people who thought they were being stealthy were as transparent as glass. The real key to keeping things secret was when nobody knew you even existed. It was rather too late for that here.

"Thank you," he said, and followed her down a long corridor and up a flight of stairs.

Delia flicked on the light to the pantry, illuminating panelled wooden walls, and shelves lined with jars and bottles of preserves.

Dante's eye immediately went to the corner where Eleanor had described finding the bullet. He shifted the jars and examined the hole. He thought about the angle of the bullet's entry into the wall. It looked like the gun had been held close to the wall when it was fired.

Then he looked at the pantry window. Someone had taped clear plastic over the broken pane as a stopgap before the glazier arrived to repair it.

The window glass was old and brittle. It would have been simple for the shooter to break a pane with one tap of the butt of their gun. With fireworks exploding across the sky, no one would have heard.

It struck him as sloppy work. If he'd had to shoot from the pantry window, the procedure was to scribe a small circle in the glass and remove the piece with a suction cup. Letting broken glass fall could have attracted attention, even with the fireworks. He wouldn't have risked it.

Few people were as professional as Dante, though. And he doubted many could be found in Te Kohe.

There was a clear sight line to the balcony. In his mind's eye, he replayed the Jubilee Night fireworks display. His memory placed Janice in her chair at the end of the row of seating. It would be an easy shot from here with the right firearm.

He recalled where Ted had been seated. Could a bullet aimed at Janice's head have grazed Ted's arm? At a casual glance, the angles worked, but Dante was never casual when it came to murder. It was close, but Janice was just a bit out of line for Dante to be one hundred percent convinced.

Dante gazed up at the sky, pale with the dawn, and thought. If he had been tasked with terminating Janice, he wouldn't have picked this situation.

The only reason to assassinate her in such a public place would be so that many people observed the event. Many witnesses present, who could provide convincing alibis for everyone on the balcony at the time. And people absent, like himself and Charlie, would be automatically suspect. It was a good setup.

Dante glanced at the bullet hole in the wall one last time, then left, flicking off the light switch.

It was time to find a way up onto the hotel roof. The angles from the shot hadn't been quite right, and Dante wanted to see how the shot looked like from the roof of the West Wing. Maybe the shooter had been careless enough to let a bullet casing slide down into the gutter.

He found a way up a few minutes later - standing on the balcony railing and boosting himself up onto the sloping green corrugated iron roof. His rubber soled combat boots gripped the steep slope of the roof as he made his way over to the West Wing.

Dante sat, surveying the spot where a sniper might have shot Janice. There was no sign of bullet casings in the gutter, or any other trace another human had been here. Below him was the pantry window. It had a small hood over it - a miniature roof to stop driving rain.

And in the middle of the green corrugated iron roofing of the window hood was a black and smoky mark — a small circle of soot. Dante couldn't imagine why this was there, but he took a photo of it, using a compact high-grade camera that did not go online and contained no tracking capability whatsoever.

He took a few more establishing photos, then made his way back into the hotel and down to the kitchen to thank Delia.

The smell of fresh baking was even stronger now. Perhaps Delia would need someone to check that the first batch of pastries was acceptable.

"Hi, Dante." Delia favoured him with a smile as she straightened from peering in the oven door. "The almond croissants are nearly ready. Would you like one? They'll be out in two minutes."

"Thanks."

"Good to see you're hard at work, Delia. Not slacking off and yacking with non-hotel guests." Ted Andrews stepped into the kitchen and leaned against the wall just inside the door, a smirk on his face.

Delia turned back to the oven, ignoring Ted. She opened the door and a blast of heat rushed into the room. Dante leaned on one of the stainless steel benches and levelled a cool stare at Ted.

"You're not meant to have anyone in here who isn't an employee," said Ted. "Food hygiene rules."

"He hasn't touched anything," said Delia.

Dante quickly pushed off from the kitchen bench.

"I don't need to tell you, Delia, you're on thin ice here," said Ted. "Your own son is a suspect in a murder. And now you're inviting members of the public into my hotel kitchen, while you're supposed to be working. If you're lucky, I'll let you off with a written warning. I could start formal proceedings to have you fired right now."

Delia bit her lip as she dragged a tray of hot almond croissants out of the oven. Dante doubted whether he was going to get to taste a croissant. He wondered if leaving now would help the situation, or make things worse.

"Your own son," said Ted, an unpleasant smile on his face. "His dad would be so disappointed if he were still with us today."

Delia dumped the tray of pastries on the oven bench with a crash and spun around, her face reddening in anger.

"Don't you say one word against Charlie," she said, her voice low and tight.

"Or what?" said Ted, his smile widening. "You'll do something you'll regret? I'm sure it'll cause me no end of trouble to find a new pastry chef. Oh wait," he snapped his fingers as if a thought had just occurred to him. "I'm guessing you'll need to move soon, anyway. You'll be looking for employment in Wellington. To be close to your son when he's in Rimutaka prison."

Delia took a step towards Ted, her hands clenched into fists.

Dante smoothly stepped in front of her, his bulk effectively blocking her path.

"Ted," he said, gazing calmly at the hotelier. "If you don't leave immediately, I will break into your house at night while you're sleeping. After knocking you around a bit, I'll tie you up and attach a twenty eight kilogram kettlebell to your feet. Your infinity pool is twelve feet deep at one end. I'll throw you in and flip a coin. Heads, I'll pull you out, and tails, I'll walk away. Even odds."

The room went quiet.

"You wouldn't dare threaten me," hissed Ted.

"It wasn't a threat," said Dante.

"I have state of the art security systems," said Ted.

"I've seen them." It was likely Ted now regretted giving Dante a tour of his mansion before they went to the Jubilee celebrations.

"I have a bodyguard."

"I've seen him too."

"You'll never get away with it," said Ted.

Dante just looked at him, and whatever Ted saw in his eyes made him uncross his arms and step back a pace.

"Please," broke in Delia. She had retreated to the oven, and her hands were clasped in her apron. "Please, everyone, just stop it. I need..." she trailed off, her eyes darting around the room. "I need a good atmosphere in my kitchen. Or the pastries won't turn out well."

Dante could understand this. He liked a peaceful atmosphere too, when he was planning his missions.

Ted had regained his usual bluster. "If I see you in here again," he said. "I'll..."

Dante turned his most dead-eyed gaze on Ted, and the man shrank away.

"Delia, you can keep your job," Ted muttered at last. He shot Dante a poisonous look, then exited the kitchen, his footsteps speeding up as he disappeared down the corridor.

"Thanks for that," said Delia. Her cheeks were flushed, and she looked both worried and grateful.

"No problem." Dante hoped this altercation hadn't affected the pastries too much.

"Here." Delia took a serviette and wrapped it around an almond croissant. She handed it to Dante with a smile that wavered a bit around the edges.

"Eleanor said she intends to get Charlie off the hook," said Dante.

"Oh, that's good." Delia's smile became stronger, and it was amazing how different she looked.

The corners of Dante's mouth turned up without conscious effort. He thought this might be what his therapist called 'interacting in a sympathetic way.' He liked it.

"Do you mind leaving by the courtyard door?" said Delia. "And please don't let Ted see you with the croissant."

"I don't think he'll fire you," said Dante.

Delia's smile turned crooked around the edges. Now she looked impish. "No, I don't think he will. You certainly know how to make a good threat."

Dante considered telling her that he'd already come up with three different ways to murder Ted this week and get away with it, then decided not to. Besides, he did want to keep to the code.

"Thank you for the croissant," he said, and ducked out the door.

16

In which Ted takes action

In his mansion, on the peak of the highest hill above Te Kohe, Ted lay on a white leather sofa, chosen as much for its price tag as its elegance.

At his feet, on a special heated rug to insulate him from the polished concrete floor, Ted's French Bulldog Patrick dreamed, his toothless mouth slightly open, his gnarled paws kicking faintly as he chased an illusory postman.

Keeping Patrick alive for the last few years had cost almost as much as Ted's latest Hummer. He'd tried his best, but Patrick would soon be going to the great Shangri-La in the sky, where posties visited twice a day, cats were slow and clawless, and there were no baths after rolling in something divinely foul.

With a sigh, Ted leaned down and scratched Patrick between the ears. The threadbare, arthritic dog growled in satisfaction, either at the ear scratch, or catching his imaginary prey.

Ted tried not to get sentimental. The timing was probably for the best, as Patrick didn't like change. He wouldn't cope well with the heat and humidity of Dubai. Although Patrick mostly slept these days, the tiny voice of his conscience reminded him. He probably wouldn't even notice he'd changed countries.

Anyhow, this wasn't the time to debate whether to call the vet for Patrick's last visit. Ted had other fish to fry.

He heaved himself off the couch and pushed open the three storey sliding doors that led from his lounge to the courtyard. A neat box hedge surrounded the paved area, and a few steps descended to an infinity pool that stretched out to merge with the blue Pacific ocean.

It was a marvel, this mansion, and Ted knew he deserved it. The monthly mortgage payments were more than what he used to earn in a year, back when he was a young man with big dreams and an axe to grind with the whole world.

But he'd shown them. All of them. He'd wrenched his dream from a world that didn't want to give it to him. And if a few people had been trampled in his climb to the top, well. That was how the world worked. Not his fault.

But now...

He ran over the events of the last few days. That woman. Eleanor Graham. He was sure finding Dante in the hotel kitchen earlier today had been her doing. She was a meddler, a woman with no morals, a manipulator extraordinaire.

She was here to take away Ted's happily ever after. He had a cast-iron sense for these things, and he knew she was trouble.

Dante was a threat, but she was the mastermind. Without her, Dante would go away, either pursued by the police, or deciding to stay out of things that weren't his concern. Eleanor was the ringleader, so she was going to have to be handled.

Ted pulled out a slim cell phone of the sort that could not be bought off the shelf, and cost more than an average family vehicle. He scanned through his contacts until one leapt out at him.

With a satisfied smile, he dialled the number.

"Crowley, old pal!" Ted crooned. He was fairly sure Crowley was not the man's real name, but it certainly fit his persona. "Yes, I have a little situation here. I'm looking for a bit of extra help. Muscle, yes, but I want brains too. You have just the person? Excellent! Yes, always a pleasure. I'll be seeing him soon? Capital!"

Ted grimaced as he pocketed his phone. For some reason, talking to Crowley always made him put on a posh English accent. It was something in the other man's smooth voice - like he was in the middle of playing polo. Ted knew he would never be highbrow, but Crowley made him want to try.

He crouched down and scratched Patrick's belly, right on the spot that made the dog's stiff back legs kick in appreciation.

"Never fight fair if you can avoid it, old fella. That's how you win, every time."

Ted certainly intended to win this game. It was the only way to get what was his.

17

In which Charlie is embarrassed

Charlie sat in the back seat of the Buick as Dante navigated the new subdivision on the edge of Te Kohe. The houses were all variations of beige, with faux plaster walls and grey tiled roofs.

Following Eleanor's directions, Dante pulled up outside a tea coloured house and cut the Buick's motor. Charlie gazed at it without enthusiasm. He was not looking forward to this meeting.

Charlie wasn't even sure why Eleanor had asked him to come. However, since this was mainly for his benefit, and Dante's, he supposed, the right thing to do was climb into the Buick and ride along. Which is what he'd done.

"What are we going to say to him?" asked Charlie. "I hardly know him."

"The truth," said Eleanor. "Or rather, a version of it. Let me do the talking."

The three of them got out of the car and walked up to the gate through a rocky, low maintenance garden composed mainly of flaxes, alpine grass, and yuccas.

Eleanor knocked on the door. It was three on a Friday afternoon, but the house had the peculiar silence that suggested no one was awake.

They waited. Silence. Eleanor knocked again.

At last, they heard stirrings within the building. Footsteps approached, and then Janice's husband Derek opened the door.

He was in his forties, but he looked older, with a redness to his eyes that hinted at barely suppressed grief and poor quality sleep. He was dressed in a faded beige dressing gown and blue and white striped pyjamas. The neck of a rum bottle poked out of one dressing gown pocket.

"Who are you, and what do you want?" he asked.

"I'm Eleanor Graham," said Eleanor, putting out a hand. "An old friend of Janice's."

Derek shook it blearily. He peered at Charlie and Dante. "And these are?"

"Dante Reid, and Charlie Wilson."

"And what do you want?" he asked. "The funeral is on Sunday. If you've come to offer condolences, that'll be the best time for it." Derek's hand still grasped the doorknob, and Charlie could tell he wanted to slam the door and go back to what he was doing - either snoozing, drinking, or watching daytime television. Maybe all three.

"We're here because all of us have been affected by your wife's murder," said Eleanor.

"How have those two been affected?" said Derek. "Don't tell me they're old friends of Janice."

"Charlie and Dante are the chief suspects," said Eleanor calmly.

At this bald statement, Charlie wanted to disappear into the earth of the spiky garden. The look Derek levelled at him confirmed this sentiment.

"And this would make me want to talk to you because?" Derek's voice took on an acid note.

"I believe they're both innocent," said Eleanor.

Charlie, blushing furiously, did not think he looked innocent at all. While Dante, standing at an angle so he could keep an eye on the street and Derek at the same time, looked as far from innocent as a silent, hulking, impassive crewcut man could look.

Derek crossed his arms. "So you're a sleuth, as well as a friend of Janice?"

"Oh, you know as well as I do that Janice didn't have friends," said Eleanor. "She had allies, and she had enemies, and she had people that she had a use for."

Derek leaned against the doorframe. A ghastly grin stretched across his face. "And which one are you?"

"In this case? I'm an ally."

"My wife's dead. She doesn't have allies any more."

"I'm an ally who wants to find her killer."

"What could you possibly hope to find here on a Friday afternoon? Gods," groaned Derek. "I'm meant to start work again next week." He scratched at his four day old stubble.

"I'm interested in the killer's motive," said Eleanor. "You're an observant man, Derek. It must have occurred to you that Janice seemed to afford a lot of luxuries on a lawyer's assistant wage."

At this, Derek made to shut the door, but Dante's hand was suddenly there. He leaned nonchalantly against the door near the hinges, where the leverage was least, but the door didn't budge an inch.

"My wife had a rich aunt," said Derek tightly.

"With such small and seemingly unimportant lies is marital peace maintained," said Eleanor.

"Look," said Derek. "She's dead, ok? Did you come here to insult her? Or me? Have some decency, for god's sake!" His voice broke on the last word.

"Do we have to do this?" said Charlie in an undertone.

Eleanor ignored him. "Derek," she said, and this time her voice was gentle. "I didn't come here to insult anyone. I want what you want — to know the truth about who killed Janice. The police think Charlie did it because Janice spread rumours about his father when he died."

"I remember that." Derek stared at Charlie as if finally recognising him, then looked quickly away.

"I think whoever killed Janice did it because she knew something dangerous. A secret that was worth killing for."

Derek rubbed his eyes. Charlie couldn't tell if it was to wipe away unshed tears, or because he was tired and hungover. Again, it could be both. "My wife was always too clever for her own good," he muttered. "Look, you can come inside. But I don't know anything, ok?"

"Thank you," said Eleanor, and stepped past him into the wide, carpeted corridor.

The house was what someone's idea of a posh house looked like, if they hadn't actually been in many posh houses, and relied instead on glossy magazines.

The couches were white leather, and Charlie was sure that in a desk drawer resided the furniture shop labels and prices. The carpet was cream, as were the drapes. It was a colour scheme dreamed up by someone who never planned to have children, dogs, cats or possibly food.

The stylishness of the living room was compromised by the fact that Derek had clearly been following a strict regime of daytime drinking and no house cleaning. Beer bottles sat on every available flat surface, losing ground only to larger bottles of spirits and the occasional wine glass.

"Take a seat." Derek waved a hand vaguely at the designer furniture. He slumped down on a couch, which still bore the impression of a man lying horizontally.

Charlie brushed cigarette ash off one white leather cushion and sat next to Eleanor, while Dante stood near the door.

Derek looked at them with tired dislike. "I also want to find out who killed my wife. That's what the police are supposed to be doing."

"Of course," said Eleanor. "We're just concerned that they're looking in the obvious places, rather than the right places. When did Janice start receiving extra income?"

Derek wiped a hand across his eyes. "It's hard to keep secrets in a marriage. Sometimes harmony comes from not finding out things you don't want to know..." he gazed into the distance, seeing something other than bland designer furnishings. "The first time I knew about it was when she bought a car — a BMW. We had a huge argument about it. I told her we couldn't afford the payments. She said she'd bought it cash. I wanted to know where she'd been hiding the cash. And she told me about her rich aunt in Dubai."

"And how long ago was this?" asked Eleanor.

"The All Blacks had just won the Rugby Sevens in Adelaide," said Derek. "So...about nine or ten years. About the time that Adrian Wilson..." his voice trailed off, and he suddenly seemed to find the floor interesting.

"And since then? Have there been other cash injections?"

As if acting on autopilot, Derek's hand pulled the bottle of rum from his dressing gown pocket. He sat forward, holding it in front of him like a totem. "I don't know. Probably."

"You work as an accountant. Average wage, maybe 80 to 100k," said Eleanor, mercilessly. "This house is, what, 1.8 mill? Then there's the Porsche Janice drove, your own Tesla, the Versace suits, the pearls, the twice yearly vacations to Bora Bora and Santorini, the—"

"Ok!" barked Derek. He unscrewed the rum bottle top and took an aggressive swig. "Ok," he said in a calmer tone. "So my wife was doing something dodgy, alright? Something that paid her a bunch of money. And I, moral coward that I am, never wanted to find out what it was. Satisfied?" He glared through red-rimmed eyes.

"It's not about you," said Eleanor softly, "or Janice. This is about Charlie being locked away for twenty years for something he didn't do."

A long silence permeated the house. In the distance, a lawnmower droned.

Derek slumped back on the couch. His head rocked back, and he closed his eyes. "I don't know anything that can help you. I'm sorry. I didn't ask Janice when she was alive, and now it's too late."

"It's never too late," said Eleanor.

"Ha!" Derek's bark of laughter lacked any humour. "Unless you can speak with the dead, I think it is."

Charlie tried not to meet anyone's eyes.

"I believe that secrets are always revealed in their own time," said Eleanor calmly. "I'm not asking you to do anything that would hurt your memories of your wife. All I'm asking you to do is call me if you remember something that could lead us to her murderer."

With that, she laid a simple white business card in the centre of the table, and stood.

"That's it?" said Derek. "You're going to just leave?"

"Unless you have something else to share with us," said Eleanor.

Charlie looked up from studying the carpet to meet Derek's blurry gaze.

"So you're Charlie Wilson," he said. "How time flies."

Charlie thought he should make a reply to this. Something pithy, like: 'and things still don't change.' Or, 'and justice waits in vain.' But it felt like kicking a man who was already on the ground.

"I'm Charlie Wilson," he said.

Derek heaved a deep sigh. "You know how to play your cards, don't you, Eleanor. Fine. I remember something."

Eleanor simply waited.

"There was this one time when we went to a party, and Janice woke in the middle of the night. She was still drunk, but it was clear there was something on her mind. She said that if anything were to happen to her, she had insurance - something that would take the murderer down. I asked what the hell she was talking about. She said 'I know what I'm doing. It's a dangerous game, but I'm smarter than he is. And if anything goes wrong, I've got what I need, so he doesn't get a happily ever after.' She mentioned something getting sent to Adrian's boy." Derek flicked his eyes to Charlie and then looked away.

"Did she say who 'he' was?" asked Eleanor.

Derek scowled. "No. She was asleep next minute. Denied everything in the morning. Refused to speak of it ever again." His gaze drifted out the window to the pocket of lawn and the tastefully grey concrete landscaping. "Fool woman. She was always trying to get one up on everyone. And now she's dead." He closed his eyes, and Charlie felt a throb of sympathy both for Derek's grief, and his no doubt horrible hangover.

"Do you want me to make you a Bloody Mary?" asked Eleanor. "It's the best hair of the dog I know of."

"No. Thank you." Derek opened his eyes. "That's all I've got for you. Really."

"Thank you," said Eleanor. "We'll go now, but if you need anything, please call."

Derek waved one hand in farewell, his eyes closed again as he lay back on the couch.

Eleanor led them out of the silent, well heeled house.

Outside, Charlie took a deep breath of the fresh morning air. He hadn't sensed Janice's ghost anywhere inside the house, something he'd been dreading. Fresh ghosts were needy, sucking the energy right out of you in their desperation to be heard.

"Well, that went better than expected," said Eleanor briskly.

"What do you think Janice had as insurance?" said Dante.

Eleanor made a face. "Hard to say. Could be incriminating evidence of the forged will, could be dodgy paperwork from the lawyer's office Ted didn't want exposed."

Charlie thought about Janice's life, cut off by the man she'd blackmailed for years. He tried to calculate the value of the house, the expensive furniture, the Porsche. He wondered if it had been worth it to Janice. He hoped her ghost had moved on.

"It's unlikely Derek knows more," said Eleanor, "although I've been wrong in the past. Not often, but it does happen. If we're lucky, Charlie, you have an interesting package headed your way. In the meantime, I have a job for the two of you." With this, she marched back to the Buick, Charlie and Dante trailing behind.

18

In which clues are uncovered and new acquaintances made

Dante drove his Buick down the main town road. In the passenger seat, Charlie had his arm hanging out the window. The young man's shirtsleeves were rolled up past his elbow, revealing a strong tan line that Dante suspected came from being a fair-skinned gardener.

"Did Eleanor tell you what we're looking for?" asked Charlie.

"No. She just said to look for anything unusual. She said we'll know it when we see it."

"I don't know what that means. Do you?"

Dante shrugged his large shoulders. In his experience, the future came at you in its own time. Sometimes it came all at once. It didn't pay to try to get ahead of it.

The Te Kohe dump was located fifteen minutes' drive outside of town. The day was hot and windless, and the road shimmered as Dante followed it around the coast. A hundred metres below, the deep blue Pacific ocean crashed against black rocks. Dante hummed quietly to himself as the road cut inland, winding between low foothills forested in mānuka and kānuka.

The dump was advertised by a sign that would not have looked out of place in a post-apocalyptic world. Letters made out of rusted metal, machinery and assorted debris made up the words 'Te Kohe Scrapyard.'

It was clear the curator of the dump was an artisan.

Dante coasted into the car park and cut the engine. He pocketed the keys and emerged from the car. He left the driver's window cracked open, but he knew that by the time they returned, the black vinyl steering wheel would be hot enough to cook on.

"Eleanor said to let you do the talking," he told Charlie. "Do you know the man who runs this place?"

"Ian Cunningham? Sure." Charlie smiled easily. For an unknown reason, he'd eschewed his usual heavy duty gardening gear and dressed nicely for this trip - faun chinos and a dress shirt.

Dante wondered if perhaps being under suspicion of murder inspired a man to dress smart. For his part, he had his usual black jeans, grey long sleeved sweatshirt, and a black leather jacket. That way, his sidearm stayed hidden, and he was somewhat protected from whatever rusty metal they'd encounter.

"Have you had your tetanus shots?" he asked Charlie. Dante's grandad had been a stickler for tetanus prevention. Any cuts or grazes had to be doused in a stinging chemical that, years later, Dante thought might have been bleach. So far, he had stayed tetanus-free.

"I think so," said Charlie. He waved a greeting as a small, bandy-legged man in blue overalls beetled his way out of a shipping container. Over the door, the words 'office' were again sculpted from mismatched rusty iron.

"Charlie!" The little man grinned, revealing a smile that contained perhaps six teeth in total. "My boy! Good to see you. Welcome to the dump," he addressed Dante, gesturing towards the scrapyard like a butler granting access to a stately home.

"Ian! Great to see you too," said Charlie. "This is my friend Dante."

"Always good to see a new face," said Ian. "What brings you here?"

"We want to go through the trash from the Pepper Tree Hotel. We're trying to find the truth of happened on Jubilee night," said Charlie.

Dante stared. What had Eleanor been thinking, getting Charlie to do the talking? Most of Dante's missions had not involved talking. They had been silent, deadly, and above all covert. He was sure that coming right out and saying what they were after, and why, was not a good idea.

"Hmmmm." Ian tugged at his earlobe. "Pepper Tree Hotel, eh? The trash from their skip came through just yesterday. Let's see." He stood for a moment in silent thought, then nodded to himself. "I know where we put it. Back East corner. I'll show you the way."

The trio picked their way between small hillocks of trash to a concrete platform overlooking a flat expanse of wasteland.

Seagulls circled overhead, their hoarse cries giving Dante a sense of exposure.

Ian gestured to the slope of the rubbish pile that dropped away from their perch.

"That's where all the Pepper Tree hotel junk goes. I chuck it there, have a quick look in case there's anything interesting, then shift it over to join the rest of the stuff." He gave them a gummy grin. "It's been an exciting couple of days. That's why I'm a bit slow off the mark. Luckily for you, I haven't bulldozed the latest pile yet."

"Go on," said Dante to Charlie.

Charlie looked down at his chinos and sighed. "These are my only smart pants."

"Better than wearing prison orange," said Dante.

Charlie grimaced. "Thanks for reminding me." He hopped off the concrete platform and forged his way into the pile of trash, stumbling and swaying as it shifted underneath him.

"When I first got this job, I nearly died on one of them trash piles," said Ian. "Sometimes big gaps open up, large enough to swallow a man. I didn't see one until it was too late. Took me four hours to wriggle my way out."

Dante watched Charlie pick his way across the pile. He hoped he wouldn't have to go in and haul him out. Although, unlike Charlie, he was not wearing his best pants. Dante didn't have best pants. His wardrobe was full of identical black jeans, white t-shirts and grey sweatshirts. He just didn't like getting dirty. The trash pile smelt bad from here, and he was sure it was even worse up close.

"Do you have any idea what we're looking for?" called Charlie.

Dante shook his head, and Charlie returned his examination of the rubbish pile.

A shadow fell across his back, and Dante looked over his shoulder, and then up.

A man had come up behind him so quietly that Dante, who was usually hyper-aware of these things, hadn't noticed him.

The man was huge, a veritable mountain of muscle. He seemed to have picked his features straight from the 'villainous' section of the catalogue, with an overhanging brow, scarred cheeks, a nefarious goatee, and a gold earring in one notched ear.

He smiled, revealing a further flash of gold in his front tooth.

"I am Viktor," he said. "From Belarus."

"Ok," said Dante.

"You do not introduce yourself," said Viktor, "but I know who you are. You are Dante Reid, the man who let Ted Andrews get shot."

Dante was not entirely sure this was a good moniker to follow him around his prospective hometown. On the one hand, Ted Andrews probably deserved to be shot. That was a mark in favour. On the other, Dante had not been the one doing the shooting, which was a definite mark against.

"You after anything particular?" asked Ian, scratching his stubbly jaw. "There's a few cars you could carry away if you want them."

Viktor grinned. "Ha. You make good joke. One in each hand, yes?"

"That was my thinking."

Viktor surveyed the slope of trash as Charlie foraged industriously through it, getting his smart clothes torn and stained.

"That's the boy, yes? The one they say did it."

Dante did not dignify this statement with a reply.

"He does not look the type."

"Charlie's a good lad," said Ian. "He's a good shot too, but none of us think he did it."

Viktor considered this. "Crime is not up to a vote," he said at last.

"It is if you're being tried by a jury," said Ian.

"Mr Dante," called Charlie. "I think I found something." Grinning, he held up a strange assembly of metal. "This has got to be it."

Dante looked at Viktor.

"I think you had better go now," he said.

Viktor smiled with another flash of gold. "Are you going to try and make me?"

"You arrived in this town," said Dante. "Right after a murder occurred. Why?"

"I am employee."

"Did your employer send you to spy on us?" said Dante.

"Maybe I just like to see a nice scrapyard," said Viktor.

"Thank you," said Ian.

"Charlie, stay right there," said Dante. He squared up to Viktor. "Unless you want to leave in an ambulance, you're going to go. Right now."

Viktor looked down at Dante. "Last time someone threatened me like this," he said reflectively, "he had to start a new job."

"Why's that?" said Ian.

"He was a prize fighter," said Viktor. "Hard to do that with two broken arms and a broken jaw."

"I wasn't planning to fight you," said Dante. "I'm just asking you, politely, to leave." His eyes didn't waver from Viktor's. In the distance, a seagull cried.

"I don't think I want to." Viktor crossed his arms.

Dante shifted so that his back was slightly to Ian. He deliberately unzipped his jacket. The butt of Colt Peacemaker shone dully in the sun, visible only to Viktor.

Viktor grinned. "I see you brought your friend with you." His hand strayed towards his belt. "Maybe I brought friends too."

One hundred and six days, no bodies, thought Dante.

He could see the path that lay ahead, clear as day. Viktor dead. And then he'd have to kill Ian too, and stage things to look like they'd killed each other. Charlie wouldn't like that.

Keep to the code, he thought. But every one of his senses was poised on a razor's edge, a hair trigger away from lethal action.

"Dante?" called Charlie. "Can I come up now?"

"If you don't leave, now," said Dante. "I will regret my actions."

Viktor's smile faded. "You," he said, "are full of the zlo - the darkness. Many times have I faced men like you. And I am still here."

Dante didn't reply. His focus was on Viktor's right hand, and the micro-expressions in the muscles around his eyes that would telegraph when Viktor went to draw his gun.

"Dobra." Viktor's right hand relaxed to hang by his side, and his massive shoulders settled into a more casual stance. "Is free country. I come to see this fine scrapheap, and now, I have." He looked around the scene one more time, then he turned and strode away.

Dante watched him go, counting his heartbeats as his pulse returned to normal.

"Phew," said Ian. "I wasn't looking forward to you two having a fight. It would have made quite a mess." He looked around his scrapyard with a proprietorial air.

"Like I said, I wouldn't have fought him," said Dante.

"Really?"

"No point trying to fight someone bigger and stronger than you."

Ian considered this wisdom. "I reckon you're a smart man, Dante. And I reckon that with a philosophy like that, you don't get into many fights."

With a cheery smile, Charlie staggered up the mountain of trash, carrying his find like a bizarre appendage.

"What do you think this is?" He handed the contraption to Dante, who took it gingerly.

It was smeared with a substance that could have been aioli. Dante hoped it was aioli.

It consisted of two steel struts welded together with smaller steel struts, so they stayed a fixed distance from each other. There was a wire cage at the one end, and a string attached to the cage that ran back to the other end of the device. The string threaded through a series of small holes drilled in the horizontal struts.

Dante turned it over. An idea was forming in his mind. He studied the cage at the one end of the device. He pictured it with a simple addition and sighed. It was dispiriting to find his worst beliefs about human nature confirmed. And to find out that, on the balance of things, Eleanor was probably right about Charlie being innocent and the forces of darkness arrayed against him.

"I think," he said, "that Eleanor will want to see this." He gestured with the contraption towards Ian. "Is there any charge to take this with us?"

Ian sucked at his remaining teeth. "That'll be a tenner," he said.

"How about I give you a hundred," said Dante, "and you forget we were ever here."

Ian considered this. "Alright. It'll help our lad Charlie, right?"

Dante peeled two fifties out of his wallet and handed them over.

"Thanks, Ian," said Charlie with a sunny smile. "I owe you one."

"Well, I know where to find you when I want to collect," said Ian. "Good luck with whatever it is you two are up to. Happy to not know anything more about it."

19

In which Charlie tells the truth, and Eleanor doesn't

On exiting the Te Kohe dump, an unwelcome sight greeted them. All four tyres of the Buick had been slashed.

Dante regarded his car for a full minute. Then he told Charlie to stash the item they'd found in the trunk.

"Do you have a phone?" he asked Charlie.

"There's no reception here," said Charlie. "But Ian's bound to have a landline. He's old school."

"Sure, no problemo," said Ian, once Charlie had explained their predicament. "Mi casa es tu casa, amigos." He ushered them inside his cramped office and waved a gallant hand towards the landline, half buried by drifts of paperwork and takeaway cartons on his slowly disintegrating desk. With a vague salute, Ian left to do unnamed junkyard business.

Charlie brought up Eleanor's phone number from his out-of-signal phone and relayed it to Dante, who punched it into the grimy landline buttons. The phone cord was so curled and tangled that Dante had to anchor it in place to stand to his full height.

The phone rang a few times, and then Eleanor's voice, polite as ever, came down the receiver.

"Hello Dante."

"How did you know it was me?"

"I can think of no other reason someone would phone me from the dump."

"Can you arrange to have four P215 tyres delivered to the tip? Mine have been slashed."

"Do you know who did it?"

"Yes."

There was a brief silence on the other side of the line. Then: "I'll be there in half an hour."

Dante strode back to his injured Buick. He wondered what he should be feeling right now. Angry, perhaps? Upset?

Instead, all he could summon was a detached feeling that this was a stupid thing for Viktor to have done. What would slashing his tyres accomplish? Surely it made little difference for them to be stuck here for another hour or so.

Charlie and he sat on the Buick's hood and watched the seagulls circle while they waited for Eleanor to arrive.

Dante supposed he was meant to do some talking in this type of situation. Either that, or smoke a cigarette. He did neither. He simply folded his leather jacket neatly on the hood and let the sun beat down on his back while the birds wheeled overhead.

Charlie opened his mouth at a couple of points during their wait, then shut it again, and joined Dante in watching the birds.

Eventually, a car motor broke the silence.

"That's not a Jaguar Mark II," said Dante.

Charlie looked impressed. "What is it, then?"

"It's a Holden Commodore."

"Our local police chief, Hemi, drives a Holden," said Charlie. His brow creased. "Eleanor said her car was being serviced today. Maybe Hemi gave her a lift."

Dante mused on what species of policeman would bother driving out to look at a car with slashed tyres. Where he came from, police only bothered with drug busts, knifings, and dead people. He wondered if Hemi had brought them fresh tyres.

Hemi's police car came around the corner, travelling at a respectably slow and serious pace. It parked next to Dante's Buick Riviera, and Eleanor emerged from the passenger side of the car. From the driver's side rose a man Dante didn't know. This man had a patrician profile and intelligent brown eyes that didn't miss much.

Eleanor gave them both a sunny smile. Her eyes were wide, her movements extravagant.

"Dante *darling*, how awful! I just simply cannot believe anyone would do such a horrible thing. I never know what to do in these situations, but Inspector Avery was kind enough to give me a lift. Isn't he a sweetheart? I'm so glad you're both all right. The tyres are in the trunk."

Dante blinked. He hadn't known Eleanor could put on an act like this. From Charlie's puzzled expression, neither had he.

"Inspector Marcus Avery, homicide," said Avery, sticking out his hand in a businesslike manner.

Dante shook it carefully. "Dante Reid."

"And Charlie Wilson." The inspector's gaze lingered on Charlie's torn clothes. "We will be interviewing both of you later this week in relation to the murder."

Charlie bobbed his head and looked uncomfortable.

Dante was glad they'd stowed their find in the boot of the car. With Eleanor putting on a show like this, it was possible she wouldn't want the inspector to see it.

Dante moved to the trunk of the police car and popped it open. He lifted out the four tyres and stacked them carefully by his car.

"Thank you for the tyres," Dante told Avery. He turned back to his car.

"Just one minute," said Avery. "What were you two doing here?"

"More importantly," said Eleanor, hands fluttering, "who was the villain who slashed your tyres?" She turned anxious eyes on Avery. "Can you see any clues?"

"Hmmmm." Avery bent his gaze on the Buick's ruined tyres. "I would say the perpetrator was a tall man, maybe six four, heavily built, with a black goatee and a scarred face."

Eleanor gasped. "Amazing! You can tell all that just by looking at the scene of the crime?"

Avery gave her a wintery smile. "A man of that description was seen loitering around Dante's house earlier today." He looked Dante up and down. "And I doubt many other people in this village would be keen to make an enemy of you."

"You know a lot about this village," said Dante. It came out sounding like an accusation.

Avery gave a gallic shrug. "Sergeant Henare has been bringing me up to speed." He stalked around the car, examining it from all angles. "And I still want to know what you two found at the dump."

"We didn't find anything," said Dante.

"I wasn't asking you," said Avery. "I was asking Charlie."

Charlie's face went red. He looked desperately to Eleanor, then Dante. "Ummm..."

"Failure to answer would be obstructing the police," said Avery.

"In actual fact," said Dante, "all someone who is not under arrest has to supply is their name and address."

"Arrests can be arranged," said Avery, his lips thinning.

"Can't you see the poor boy's in shock," exclaimed Eleanor. "All this horrible business with Janice, and then the car tyres being slashed! Are any of us safe, with murderers and vandals at large?"

"What did you find in the dump, Charlie?" Avery's voice had taken on a dreadful patience, like he would go on asking this all day.

"Er..." Charlie had turned a hue similar to that of a beetroot. Dante gave him perhaps twenty seconds until he broke.

"I can see someone with grease-stained hands has recently opened the trunk of this car," said Avery, looking pointedly at Charlie's blackened fingers. "What will I find when I open the boot?"

"Nothing," said Dante. "It's my car, and the boot stays closed."

"Oh, dear!" Eleanor looked distraught. "Surely the good inspector can see there's nothing of interest here? The only question is where the tyre slasher has gone! And will he strike again?"

"Open the trunk, Charlie," said Avery calmly.

Charlie gave Eleanor a hopeless look.

"I won't ask again," said Avery. He took a small notebook out of his pocket, and, pen poised, shot Charlie a loaded stare.

"Maybe we should show him," said Charlie in a stage whisper.

Dante folded his arms over his chest. His pecs strained against his shirt.

"The trunk, Charlie," said Avery.

"Oh, you're just impossible!" said Eleanor. She huffed and flapped a hand. "Go on Charlie. You may as well open the boot. He's bound to carry on asking until you do."

His face a mask of worry, Charlie moved to obey. The click of the trunk opening sounded loud in the quiet.

"Interesting," said Avery. He loomed over the open trunk. From his pocket, he flicked a gunmetal grey phone and snapped a few photos.

Then he sent a slow, disapproving look, from Charlie, to Dante, to Eleanor, who was hovering close enough to peer into the trunk over his shoulder.

"Thank you for helping the police with their enquiries. I assume this item came from the Pepper Tree Hotel dumpster?"

Dante gave a small growling noise, deep in his throat.

"Well, this has been a most interesting visit," said Avery. "Good luck changing your tyres." He wrapped once on the Buick's hood, then dropped smartly into Hemi's car and drove away.

Dust swirled in the hot wind stirred up by the police car departing.

"I'm sorry," said Charlie. "I just couldn't not show him." He sighed. "It's a hereditary thing. My uncle was a police officer, and I grew up calling him sir."

"Yes?" Eleanor came back from whatever headspace she kept the society lady airhead. "On the contrary, that went better than expected." She smiled at Charlie's mystified expression. "Inspector Avery wouldn't have believed us if we'd just shown the item to him. It would've triggered all his suspicions. This way, he's started thinking along the right lines all by himself."

Charlie's mouth formed an 'o' of surprise. "That's... rather clever," he said at last.

"Yes, well, we have quite a task to prove your innocence," said Eleanor. "I'm beginning to think that someone is certainly up to something. And this tyre slasher — what was his name?"

"Viktor," said Dante.

"He's from Russia, I think," said Charlie.

"Belarus," said Dante.

"Well," said Eleanor briskly, "we will keep an eye out for him as well. This summer is becoming quite intriguing." She smiled in a way that made Dante think that she liked this kind of summer more than the usual Te Kohe summers.

"I'll go see if Ian has any lemonade," she said. "While you change the tyres."

Half an hour later, Charlie and Eleanor sipped lemonade and watched Dante check the newly re-tired Buick for other traps, like car bombs, severed brake cables, fuel leaks, and incendiary devices.

That done, they headed back to town.

"So this device," said Charlie. "What's it for?" He was sitting in the back on a towel to keep the seats clean, and he was on his third lemonade.

"I'm not sure," said Eleanor. "Dante?"

"It might hold a gun," said Dante. He was enjoying the roar of the Jag. He wondered if he should have fought Viktor. He wondered who Viktor's employer was.

"Someone threw it in the Pepper Tree skip bin in the last week," said Eleanor. "Meaning it was on site during Jubilee night."

"Could someone have used it to fire at Janice?" asked Charlie.

"Maybe," said Eleanor. "Murdering her in such a public way created a lot of people with rock solid alibis, but…"

"But what?" asked Charlie.

"I think we shouldn't discount the people on the balcony," said Eleanor. "The crime feels staged, and that usually means misdirection."

"Why did you put on an act?" asked Charlie. "I could tell Inspector Avery didn't like it much."

Eleanor looked irked. "It was how I got out of a mess when I first met the inspector. Keeping this act up is only going to get more awkward, but I haven't yet decided when to drop it."

"He'll flip out when you do," said Charlie as they slid into place outside Eleanor's house.

"It'll be interesting to find out," said Eleanor.

20

In which Dante acquires a bell

There were few unforgivable things in Dante's moral code, but the things that were, did not change. The intentional murder of children was unforgivable. As was killing for pleasure, and the torture of innocents.

In far flung corners of the earth, far from the law, there had been times when Dante had used lethal force to punish those breaking his code.

He was not sure whether it was fair to apply this code to the cat.

After all, in nature, it was considered normal for a cat to climb a tree to eat baby birds. Perhaps nature, in all its ruthless beauty, had its own innocence that excused such things. Unlike humans, who should know better.

As a precaution against needing to enforce his moral judgements on animals, on returning from the dump and dropping Eleanor and Charlie home, Dante decided to purchase a cat collar with a bell on it.

He left the Buick with their mysterious item in the trunk and walked into town. A faded decal on the front window with a kitten and a puppy advertised the Te Kohe pet shop. A bell rang a cheerful 'ding' as Dante entered the crowded store.

The Te Kohe pet shop doubled as a veterinary clinic, farm supply and fishing & hunting store. This meant that aquariums and pet food were shelved next to spear guns and skinning knives.

Dante found the juxtaposition familiar. The morally grey area of uncomfortable truths most people avoided thinking about was where he'd spent most of his working life.

"Can I help you?" The lady behind the counter wore green scrubs, and a facemask pulled down around her neck. She was mid thirties, with black curly hair pulled into a thick plait that wound around her head in an elaborate coil.

"Do you sell bells?" asked Dante. Then, in case she thought he was an itinerant Morris dancer, he clarified: "for cats."

"For sure," she said, waving a friendly hand at the shelves to her right. "There'll be something there with the cat collars."

Dante conducted a brief search of the shelves and extracted a small red collar with a silver bell. He calculated it would fit the cat's neck when tightened to the third belt hole.

He placed the collar on the counter, where it rang faintly.

"You're the new guy," said the woman, smiling. "In Mrs Davison's old house."

"I am," said Dante. "Did Mrs Davison have a cat?"

She shook her head. "Has one adopted you?"

Dante relaxed. Maybe having cats move in was normal once you had a house. "Do I need to feed it?" The thought hadn't occurred to him before. Now it seemed vital.

She shrugged. "Depends if you want it to stay."

"I think it's already decided," said Dante.

She smiled as if he'd made a joke. "Well, we have plenty of cat food. I'm Andrea, by the way. I'm the local vet. And shop owner. Though Agnes usually runs the shop during the week."

"Hello," said Dante. "I'm Dante."

Gravely, he shook her offered hand.

"That's an interesting necklace," said Andrea. "Were you a soldier?"

Dante froze, then looked down. His shirt was open a button lower than usual. He must have been distracted by the cat attacking his shoelaces as he got dressed this morning. Andrea had caught a glimpse of the one item of jewellery Dante owned.

It was a small piece of shrapnel strung on a leather cord that would easily break if someone caught hold of it in a fight. Dante knew what a hazard ties and necklaces could be in close combat, and made sure that his could never be turned into a garotte.

"I was an accountant," he said, carefully buttoning up his shirt and tucking the necklace out of sight.

"I feel like there's a story behind it," said Andrea, with another warm smile.

"What should I feed the cat?" said Dante. His therapist had told him to change the subject if he didn't want to answer questions. 'Simply staring someone down can be seen as hostile, Dante.'

Andrea's smile slipped a little. "You'll find all our cat food options over there," she said, pointing at the far wall. "Next to the duck decoys."

"Thank you," said Dante, and Andrea's smile regained its warmth.

He picked out a random assortment of tins with pictures of fish on them.

"Do you want a bag?" asked Andrea. "Here." She held out a paper bag with two string handles. It had a pink heart on it. "It's my early Valentine gift bag. From my sister," she explained with an embarrassed laugh. "Since I haven't had a Valentine card in three years, she said she'd send me something."

Dante felt there was a secret code being communicated here. He just couldn't tell what it was. Valentines... meant dates. Romance. Marriage. He cast his mind back to an assignment where the target had kidnapped girls from an orphanage and smuggled them into Somalia to be married off as child brides. That probably wouldn't help in this situation.

"Er, would you like flowers for Valentine's day?" he asked.

Andrea looked, if anything, more embarrassed. "No! I mean sorry, that's kind of you, but I wasn't trying to imply..." She shrugged helplessly. "I'm sorry. I'm bad at this."

"At what?" asked Dante.

"Flirting."

So that was what they were doing. Dante felt relieved to put a label on it. "That's alright," he said. "I've never tried it either."

"That's not what I meant..." Andrea sighed. "Can we just pretend this conversation never happened?"

"Ok." Dante never forgot events, but he was excellent at pretending things never happened. Since their conversation was going so well, he decided to test out an idea he'd had. "Have you seen a big guy recently? About this tall," he showed Viktor's height with his hand, "and a black goatee. He's not from around here."

Andrea stared at him with a slightly mystified expression he was beginning to associate with talking to people outside of work. "Er, yes, I have. He was hanging around the Bin Inn. I was just opening up the shop, and I saw him through the window."

"The Bin Inn?"

"It's next to Ted's Automotive." Andrea frowned. "Or maybe he was waiting for Ted's Automotive to open. I'm not sure."

"Oh." Dante was surprised that asking for information got such a ready reply. He stacked the tins into the pink Valentine's bag and put the collar with the bell on top. Then he counted out several green New Zealand twenty dollar bills. "Thank you for your help."

"Sure, no worries."

"I enjoyed our conversation," he assured her. "Which never happened."

She gave a startled laugh, and an unusual warm glow grew in the vicinity of Dante's chest. He didn't think he'd ever made someone laugh before.

He gave a brief nod and headed out of the vet clinic / pet shop / hunting and fishing store before he said something else to wreck the good impression he may have made.

21

In which Dante learns the price of family secrets

On the return journey to his house, the bell jangled faintly as the Valentine's bag bounced against Dante's leg.

Turning onto the side road where his house was situated, Dante considered the problem of his and Charlie's lack of alibis for the time of Janice's murder. He thought back to his AA meeting, and the mantra 'killing people doesn't solve the problem.'

The first time Dante had heard that, he'd found it hard to believe. In his line of work, killing people always solved something. The few times it didn't, it was because someone higher up the chain of command needed to be dispatched.

Since he started AA, Dante had kept a list in his head of things that couldn't be solved by killing people. There were a surprising number of items on it, and now, here was another item to add to the list. Clearing suspicion from Charlie and himself would probably not be aided by offing Ted.

He swung open his front gate, stepped into the garden, and stilled. Something was wrong. Dante sniffed the air.

There was a faint aroma of dill and fried potato. It seemed someone had recently been here, and consumed a herb pastry. Draniki, perhaps, thought Dante, who had spent time in East Europe.

His pistol slipped into his hand, seemingly of its own accord, as he continued his walk up the garden path. His heartbeat doubled, beating out a rapid rhythm that he nevertheless found calming. His field of focus widened, taking in the front garden, his porch, the greenhouse, and the small single car garage where the Buick was stabled.

Viktor will not confront you on your own turf, he thought. His instincts told him the man had already departed, but the hairs on the back of his neck worked as antennae, searching the air for subtle signs of movement.

Dante drifted to his front door. The latch showed no signs of tampering. He was ninety eight percent sure the lock he had installed could only be picked by the top one percent of burglars in hotspots like London and Macau. It was, therefore, unlikely the thief had gained access to his house. Also, the military grade alarm system he'd installed had not gone off.

He turned, set his shoulders to the solid oak door, and scanned the garden. There was a broken pane of glass in the greenhouse door. Dante had thought it odd for a greenhouse to have a lock on the door until Charlie had explained how much some of the plants inside were worth.

Clearly, the intruder had found it necessary to gain access to his greenhouse.

A quick scan of the greenhouse interior revealed no one hiding in the dense tropical shrubbery. The large planter where the corpse plant resided had not been disturbed. Dante was glad. If it had been damaged, he might have had to take steps.

Leaving the greenhouse, he ghosted over to the garage door. It had been kicked in with a heavy blow, the blue painted timbers splintered with the impact. Dante halted just outside the door and listened.

The air was deathly quiet. Even the cicadas seemed to have paused their insectile hum. In one oblique movement, Dante whirled inside the garage and crouched low, scanning the interior.

It was cool and dark, his car a resting shadow in the dim light. He dropped to look under the Buick. There were no boots, shoes, or feet of any kind to suggest an intruder waiting in ambush on the other side of the car.

A circuit of the Buick revealed that the boot had been forced. It looked like someone had simply shoved a screwdriver into the lock and turned. Dante ran a finger over the ravaged lock. It was a classic car. Breaking in would not be a challenge for any half-decent criminal.

Popping the now defenceless boot revealed what he predicted: the item they'd found at the dump was gone.

Dante retreated to his house and checked the alarm records. No one had tried to enter here. Next, he reviewed the security camera footage of the garage. Someone the size and shape of Viktor kicked down the door. The intruder wore a red and green balaclava with a pattern Dante recognised from the Belarusian flag.

He sighed. Clearly, Viktor did not believe in stealth.

Dante made himself a cup of herbal tea. He had never owned a house before, and he wasn't sure how he should feel about a break-in. He knew that homeowners joined neighbourhood watch groups to prevent just this sort of thing.

Perhaps it was time to get better acquainted with the neighbours. Who knew? They might even have a neighbourhood watch he could join. Maybe being a member would give him a licence to inflict grievous bodily harm on intruders. He thought it unlikely, but you never knew.

Dante wondered whether homeowners would feel better or worse, knowing an ex-assassin wanted to join their ranks. Eighty year old Mrs. Haddock across the road had a steely glint in her eye and he thought she'd probably like the idea. She seemed the type of lady to sleep with a sawn-off shotgun under her bed.

Five minutes later, Dante was in Mrs Haddock's rose-coloured drawing room, sipping a cup of tea. Dead ancestors and living descendants looked down on him from every available space, glaring out from black and white photos, or smiling from heart framed pictures.

Mrs Haddock returned from the kitchen with a small plate in which she'd neatly arranged twelve shortbread biscuits.

"I hope you like shortbread," she said brightly. "This is an old family recipe. My mother passed it on to me, and it came from her mother, all the way from the Orkneys. My daughter-in-law has been trying to pry it out of me for twenty five years, but she'll never succeed." Mrs Haddock smiled in satisfaction. "I shall take it to my grave."

Dante cautiously dipped the biscuit in his tea, withdrawing it before it could break off. The shortbread crumbled delicately in his mouth. It tasted faintly of rosewater and an indefinable flavour he suspected he would never discover.

"Now, Mr Dante," said Mrs Haddock. "Was there a reason for your visit? I'm always happy to have a neighbour around for tea, but I reckon you're not a man for socialising."

"Did you see anyone break into my garage earlier this morning?" said Dante, grateful that he didn't have to do any small talk.

"Oh." Mrs Haddock sat back, folding her hands in her lap. They were wrinkled and spotted with age, but Dante saw she had callouses. They looked like strong hands. "I didn't see anything. I was out the back this morning, seeing to a new bed of asparagus. Do you know you need to cultivate the soil down to a depth of three feet if you want to see any decent growth?"

Dante admitted that he did not.

"Have you told the police? Hemi will want to know. We hardly ever have any break-ins here. The last time it happened, Hemi just went over to the thief's place and got her to give the items back."

"I think I'll sort it out myself," said Dante. The last thing he wanted was a police officer poking around his house and asking questions.

Mrs Haddock looked him up and down. "I suppose you could, at that," she agreed.

Dante swallowed down more tea and took another biscuit. He was only half way through his cup and knew he couldn't leave before he finished it. That meant small talk had to happen. He sorted through things his therapist had told him were normal topics of conversation, hoping one would present itself as an obvious choice.

"How's the weather going?" he said.

Mrs Haddock blinked at him for a moment, then put her teacup down with a smile. "It's alright, Dante. You don't have to make polite conversation. Let's talk about this murder."

Dante's shoulders relaxed in relief.

"You know, I think Ted had something to do with it," said Mrs Haddock. "He was always trouble, even as a child. I taught him at Te Kohe Elementary, back in the eighties. We never talked outside of school, of course, but in the staff room, we'd all voted him most likely to end up in jail. Then he surprised us all by making a lot of money, but that's beside the point. He was a bad 'un when he was little, and he hasn't reformed. He's just got sneakier."

Dante decided Mrs Haddock was a shrewd judge of character. She'd known Ted for years, and might have inside information. He thought about the kinds of questions Eleanor would ask her.

"If Ted was going to commit a murder, how do you think he'd do it?"

"Ted has interesting character quirks." Mrs Haddock paused in her oration to sip her tea. Her sharp brown eyes measured Dante over the rim of her teacup. "But you probably don't want to hear about all this ancient history from an old lady. You're probably wanting to read twitter, or do candy crush, or whatever it is you young people are into these days."

Dante forbore to tell her that the longest he'd owned a cell phone was 36 hours. Burner phones tended to burn a hole in his pocket, and he couldn't wait to get rid of them.

"I am interested," he said.

Mrs Haddock made a slight sucking noise between her tongue and lips. "Well, we could do a tit for tat. Quid pro quo."

Dante slowly put down his teacup. "What kind of information are you interested in?"

"I like to know a bit about my neighbours," said Mrs Haddock. "Just to make sure they're not murderers or hitmen or anything." She gave a deprecating laugh.

"Yes," said Dante. He picked up his tea again and sipped it. He took another shortbread.

"So, tell me about yourself," said Mrs Haddock. "What is it you do?"

Dante ate his shortbread in two bites. "If I was a murderer or a hitman, what would you do?"

"It would depend if you were retired or not." Mrs Haddock eyed him like a chess grandmaster, lining up her next move.

"I'm retired," said Dante.

Mrs Haddock tapped her fingers on her teacup. "And what did you do before retirement?"

"I worked for the government. In England."

"MI6? James Bond? 007?"

"I had a desk job in Kent. There was a lot of paperwork."

"If you say so," said Mrs Haddock. "You know I am superb at keeping secrets."

"I can see that. What would it take for you to reveal your shortbread recipe?"

She shook her head. "My mother would have to rise from her grave, god rest her soul, and command me to share it."

Dante was impressed. He'd never seen a ghost, but he supposed they were possible. He tried not to assume he knew how the world worked. False assumptions frequently proved deadly.

"You could put the shortbread recipe in a hidden place," he said. As a child, Dante had seen Indiana Jones and the Temple of Doom, and been impressed by the giant rock rolling down the passage to crush Indie. "You could plant clues people have to solve and hidden traps they have to navigate in order to get to it. I could help you set up the traps."

"That's a kind offer, dear," said Mrs Haddock. "Which brings us back around to the question of Ted's character, and how he would commit a murder. You used to do a desk job in Kent, you say?"

Dante nodded.

"Then I'm afraid I can't help you."

It was like running into a brick wall. Mrs Haddock was as polite as ever. But her eyes held nothing more for Dante.

Dante was still for a long moment. Then he said: "would you take this to the grave, along with your shortbread recipe?"

"You have my word."

"I used to be a wetwork specialist for MI6."

Mrs Haddock appeared to have no problem with this piece of jargon, leading Dante to believe she watched a certain species of tv, and perhaps read a particular class of book.

"I am retired though," he offered. "And planning to stay that way."

"Well, that's nice," said Mrs Haddock. "Have another shortbread, dear. Have two, and let me tell you about Ted."

22

In which Dante and Eleanor encounter consequences

"So you met Mrs Haddock," said Eleanor. "I'm glad. You'll want to stay on her good side."

They were walking through the farmer's market, which made an appearance every Friday evening.

Eleanor had already bought bunches of fresh greens, which Dante could not identify or begin to imagine how to cook.

Normally, he subsisted on protein powders, energy bars, and vitamin shakes made to precise formulas - a combination of nutrients that would give him the required sustenance for each day while taking the minimum of time and effort to consume.

In various locations around the globe, Dante had studied cooking shows hosted by assorted celebrity chefs. It all seemed quite intimidating, though he did approve of their knife handling skills. He'd always put off the actual preparation of real food for a later date.

"Did Mrs Haddock see Viktor break into your place?" asked Eleanor.

Dante appreciated that Eleanor had already guessed the culprit.

"She didn't. I have Viktor on camera, but he was wearing a balaclava. Also, I'm fairly sure he's working for Ted."

"That's good to know," said Eleanor. "Getting him arrested would be a nuisance for Ted, but not worth all that much. We need to get real evidence if we're going to clear Charlie and you."

They stopped in front of a stall crowded with bottles of homemade relish, chutney, jam, and jars of bright yellow substance. Dante picked up the container and read the label: 'lemon curd.'

"That spread's delicious on toast," said Eleanor. "Hello Arjun," she beamed at the storekeeper. "These look wonderful, as ever."

"Thank you," said Arjun. "Have you tried our lemon curd? It goes on toast extremely well."

Dante realised Arjun was addressing him. He put the jar down. "I don't own any bread."

"We'll get some at Keller's stall," said Eleanor, and gave Arjun a selection of coins.

Dante looked nonplussed as Eleanor handed him the jar of lemon curd. "You'll need to toast the bread, then put a thin smear of butter on it. Once the butter's melted, apply the lemon curd. It's quite sweet, so use to taste."

"Thank you," said Dante. He was fairly sure he'd seen a toaster somewhere in his kitchen.

They walked on, past stands of plants ready for an enterprising villager's vege garden, tables stacked high with knitted sweaters, placemats made from 60s blankets, and a stall that seemed to consist entirely of glass bongs.

Dante wondered if Eleanor knew how to cook. He was fairly sure she did - she seemed that sort of person. Perhaps he could come around one evening and see how it was done.

"Did Mrs Haddock have any other information for you?"

Dante refocused. "Yes. She had a theory about Ted, and how he'd commit a murder."

Eleanor smiled faintly. "That sounds like our catnip."

Dante had no idea what that meant, so he continued. "She said he was always a lone wolf. His partnership with Adrian was unusual, and he only did it because there was no other way he'd get a bank loan with his criminal record."

"How did he get that?"

"Minor stuff. Petty theft. Drug possession."

"And her theory?"

"She thought that if Ted were to commit murder, there's no way he'd have an accomplice. She said he was pathologically unable to trust anyone, because he was such an untrustworthy character." Dante repeated Mrs Haddock's words verbatim, like a good operative would.

He himself was also disinclined to trust people. But he was coming to realise that perhaps this was because the people he'd mixed with over the last twenty years were, for the most part, violent, dangerous, and highly untrustworthy. This may have influenced his judgement.

"Mrs Haddock also said that he held grudges and liked to get back at people in nastily inventive ways."

"For example?"

"There was a guy who used to bully him at school. Years later, after Ted became rich, he purchased the building the bully had his mechanic workshop in. He raised the rent until the man was forced to close his business. Then he turned the building into 'Ted's Automotive.' That same guy has to walk past it every day on his way to working at the Bin Inn."

"So Ted likes to flaunt his victories. That's a useful trait in an opponent," said Eleanor. "It also fits with how poor Janice died. Why else do it in such a public way? Though I suppose there's also the utility of creating yourself a cast-iron alibi, and framing someone else. Ted does like to be clever."

"Whoever shot her was a good marksman," said Dante. "It was dark, and Janice was shot with considerable accuracy for a handgun at that distance."

"I have no idea whether Ted is a good shot or not," said Eleanor thoughtfully. "He did leave his seat at the start of the show, but he came back before the end. I saw him leave but didn't see exactly when he returned - I was enjoying the fireworks too much. If I'd known I was about to witness a murder, I would've paid more attention."

They stopped in front of a stall loaded with loaves of bread, buns, and assorted baked goods. It smelled delicious, although, Dante told himself, not as good as Delia's baking.

"Eleanor, so good to see you!" A lady with a brightly spotted head wrap smiled sunnily at Eleanor. Her smile dropped when she saw Dante.

"Hello Angela," said Eleanor. "Lovely evening, isn't it?"

"Quite." Angela turned away, as if trying to avoid looking at Dante.

"We're here after your wonderful sourdough," said Eleanor.

"I don't know if I can," said Angela slowly.

"You have loaves right there," said Eleanor. Her smile was still in place, but the friendliness had retreated.

"I'm sorry." Angela swallowed, her jaw tense. Her eyes flicked sideways to Dante. "You're always welcome to buy bread when you're in good company, Eleanor. But we need to make sure this town is a safe place, for good, honest folk."

"Honest folk," murmured Eleanor. She was still a long moment. Behind her green eyes, Dante could see rapid calculations, various responses playing out in the theatre of her mind. "Rumours have been circulating, I see."

"Facts." Angela folded her arms over her apron covered chest and scowled.

"I don't need bread," said Dante. It seemed to him that real food was perhaps more trouble than it was worth.

"Angela," said Eleanor. "You've known me for some time, yes?"

"Yes..."

"Could you perhaps give my friend the benefit of the doubt?"

Angela's arms tightened. "The police know he didn't have an alibi. And he's ex-CIA, or FBI or something. They'd know how to do away with anyone."

"Dante is English," said Eleanor calmly. "Also, it's hardly fair to convict someone on a rumour, no matter who you know in the police force. Let the police, or a judge and jury, decide who's guilty and who's innocent. No need to jump in ahead of proven facts."

"I can choose who to sell my bread to," said Angela. She looked directly at Dante for the first time. "Janice was a good — well, I'd known her for a long time. She was a good — well, she had a husband who cared for her. Te Kohe is a nice town. We don't need people coming from outside, causing trouble."

"That's an interesting viewpoint," said Eleanor.

Angela huffed.

"It's ok," said Dante. "Perhaps I will learn to bake bread myself." He gave Angela a friendly smile.

For some reason, Angela took a step backwards, her hands coming up in a defensive gesture.

"Goodbye, Angela," said Eleanor. "Have a lovely rest of your day."

Dante considered smiling at her again, then decided not to.

"Dante," said Eleanor as they walked away, "have you ever studied the art of social interactions?"

"Yes," said Dante. "I have been taking an intensive study course for the last three months, ever since I handed in my notice at my previous place of work."

They walked past a stall selling wooden bowls and breadboards, and another filled with brightly coloured paintings of boats and beaches.

"I'm afraid Ted is trying to make this town slightly disagreeable to you," said Eleanor. "Spreading rumours is a petty move, but it might be effective in hampering our investigations."

"Should we stop associating in public?" asked Dante.

"No," said Eleanor. "There is something you should be aware of, though. You and Charlie are the two best suspects the police have right now, and everyone would much rather it was you than someone they've known all their lives. Especially someone like Charlie."

Dante nodded. He almost wished it had been him. It would make solving the mystery a lot simpler. Of course, if it had been him, he would've made it look like an accident. Unless there was a reason to make it obviously murder.

"It wasn't me," he said, just in case that needed clarification.

"I know, dear," said Eleanor with a smile.

23

In which Dante learns of the relative virtues of the local gang

"Do you want me to go in there and reconnoitre before you ask the questions?" Dante looked dubiously at the large industrial shed where the Bonebreaker Gang had their headquarters. "I can if you want me to, only they might not like it. People tend to get upset when I turn up unexpectedly."

Eleanor tsked. "Of course not, dear, though I do appreciate the offer. What I'd like you to do is to wait while I go inside and talk to them. If I'm not out in ten minutes, then you should probably come in and check on things."

"If you're sure…" Dante did not quite like to see Eleanor go in there by herself. "Why don't I come with you now?"

"Because they'll find you threatening, and will attempt a show of dominance. And then you probably will end up having a fight, and someone could get hurt."

"Ok." Dante checked his watch. "Ten minutes."

He watched the slender form of Mrs Graham make her way up the cracked pavement to the black painted door of the Bonebreaker Gang's headquarters. She opened the door and disappeared inside.

Dante leaned back in the leather chair of his Buick. He checked the side mirror and rear view mirror for people trying to sneak up on him, then concluded that, unlike every other gang headquarters he'd surveilled, the Bonebreakers didn't seem worried about people in cars loitering on their doorstep.

It was slightly unsettling.

Jake 'Thrasher' Thompson was engrossed in the morning paperwork, spread all over the table, still littered with last night's beers and ashtrays. It was a summary of all the members' dues and who owed what from their last road trip.

It was exhausting work, and he perked up when a slim white woman walked in the door. She was wearing a pale grey linen pantsuit and could have stepped from the pages of a magazine for glamorous people over sixty.

She nodded cordially at Big Jim Kingi and crossed to where Jake was sitting. He hastily pocketed his reading glasses and shoved the paperwork into a pile, obscuring another sheet of paper that tallied that month's sales of marijuana. (Labelled 'gardening services' in Jake's heavy scrawl.)

"Hello Jacob," she said pleasantly, seating herself opposite him. "I'm Eleanor Graham."

Jake scowled. "I know who you are. I know everyone in this town."

"That's nice," said Eleanor. "Then you'll know my friend Charlie Wilson."

"Charlie? Sure. His old man and my old man were friends. And now the boy's in a place where his friends are running for the hills."

"I am not one of those friends." Eleanor folded her hands in front of her on the table. "Let's get the ball rolling, Jacob. I would like to help Charlie clear his name. But to do that, I need to know who else might have shot Janice and Ted. You know everyone. Do you have any information that might help?"

"I heard," said Jake, "that in the future, wars will be fought with information rather than weapons."

"Wars have always been fought with information," said Eleanor.

"Maybe so." Out of the corner of his eye, Jake saw the other gang members drifting closer, drawn by the prospect of live entertainment. "That being said, information is valuable. Priceless, for some. Like young Charlie, for instance. Information is not something to be given away for free."

Eleanor tapped her fingers delicately on the cracked melamine of the table.

"Value..." she said. "I could pay you, I suppose, but I don't think you're a man to be bought."

"That's right." Jake's jaw jutted. "I don't give secrets to outsiders. Not now, not ever. "

"Can we come to an alternate arrangement? I think Charlie's been framed, and the right information might give us a shot at clearing his name."

"Can't help you, sorry," said Jake. "Ain't my problem, and no upper-class white bitch is going to make it my problem."

Eleanor smiled. It was a sweet smile, and Jake felt like he may have underestimated her. "How about a wager? Charlie could do with a lucky break."

He leaned back in his chair. "I have been known to play the odds from time to time. Cars. Horses. Boxing."

"Poker?" Eleanor indicated the card table in the corner.

"Maybe." Jake flexed his biceps. They were rather large, the result of working out with heavy weights every day and training in the boxing gym he owned with his brother. "What do I get when you lose? Far as I can see, you've got nothing I want. You're well past your prime, lady."

The men behind him chuckled appreciatively at this. Eleanor nodded thoughtfully.

"I would pay with information. Like... who was responsible for the noise complaint calls at your cousin's fortieth last weekend? Or why your main buyer in Gisborne has switched to another source."

Jake's face darkened. "You know that? How?"

Eleanor gave a small shrug. "People tell me things. I suppose I have one of those faces."

"One of those faces." The interruption of his weed sales to the East Coast was bothering Jake. He considered he might have to force the information out of Eleanor, no matter what. Which he wouldn't like doing. Eleanor didn't look like she'd be easily intimidated by purely verbal threats. As a rule, he only beat up people who deserved it — people who were trying to steal from him, for instance, or who belonged to rival gangs. Not elderly ladies in linen suits.

"So, Jacob, do we have a deal? Texas hold'em, first to ten, winner gets three questions answered."

"No." Jake had done enough wagers to know never to let your opponent choose the terms. "We'll play snooker." He grinned. "And when I win, I get my questions answered and a thousand bucks from you for wasting my time."

"Why Jacob, you drive a hard bargain," said Eleanor. She didn't look in the least flustered. "I accept." She checked her watch. "Perhaps before we begin, you could send someone outside to invite my associate in. Otherwise, he might do something rash."

Jake jerked his head towards Terry 'Slugger' Collins. "See to it." He studied Eleanor, sitting across from him so composed. "This had better be worth it. Or I'll make sure you never do business in this town again."

"You can do that?" said Eleanor. "I'm impressed."

Jake tried not to think what his mother would say if she found out he was trying to intimidate a woman the same age as her. Just as well the old girl was still in jail.

"I can do all that, and more," he said. "Let's play."

———

Exactly nine minutes and fifty-five seconds after Eleanor entered the building, a burly man in a leather jacket and oil-stained jeans slouched outside and approached Dante's car. The man held up both hands and waved the right one slightly in greeting.

Dante wound down the window and the man leaned in to talk. His grin revealed a silver-capped tooth winking out from salt and pepper stubble.

"The lady says to come on in. There's a snooker game, see, and she wants moral support." He managed to invest that last sentence with enough ooze to oil Dante's Buick and the adjacent Bedford truck.

Dante slid his revolver back into the gap between the driver's seat and the gearbox.

The man in leathers was already halfway back up the path to the building. He turned back and growled, "Tick tock, mofo."

Dante uncoiled from the car and checked the street one more time before following the man. There was still no one watching, and this bothered him.

He loosened his shoulders, ready for action as he stalked up the path and into the building.

Inside, the lights were dim. The space smelled of tobacco, weed, and engine grease. Somewhere deeper in the building, a bass thudded in a dull rhythmic beat. There were a dozen men engaged in various activities - lounging around the sofas, leaning against the bar, and doing nameless mechanical tasks around a motorbike that lay in one corner of the room in a state of semi-dismemberment.

In the centre of the room, a skylight shone slanting golden light onto a snooker table, giving it the entirely inappropriate air of a Renaissance painting.

Eleanor stood facing a giant of a man with an honest to god eye patch and a jagged scar that ran from his hairline down the length of his face to his jaw. Four large men stood in a semi-circle behind the man. They were facing Eleanor with their arms crossed and muscles bulging.

Eleanor smiled in greeting as Dante crossed to stand next to her.

"Dante, this is Thrasher Jake, the leader of the Te Kohe chapter of the Bonebreaker Gang. He's agreed to help us with our enquiries, provided I beat him at a game of snooker."

"That's right." Thrasher Jake was giving him a look Dante recognised. It was a fighter's assessment. Dante endeavoured to look peaceable, and Jake's eyebrows drew together in a frown.

"Lads," said Jake, "set the table."

One man placed balls on the table while another hurried forward to hand Thrasher Jake a custom-made snooker cue, glossy black and lethal looking. Jake twirled it between his fingers, looking smug.

"I was Waikato County champion six times running," he said.

"Goodness me," said Eleanor. "I'll have my work cut out for me on this one."

"Lady," said Jake, "you might as well fork over the thousand bucks now and spare yourself a thrashing."

There was appreciative laughter at his self-referential joke.

Eleanor examined the pool cues. She weighed up a pale wood one, then a darker one. Eventually, she settled on a medium-weight cue of battered brown wood. She sighted along the length of it and took the blue chalk a tattooed man passed her.

"Thank you, darlin'. Now, it's been a while since I played, and I usually play pool. Could someone remind me of the rules?"

There was a small crowd now, all hairy, muscled and tattooed men with stubble, leather jackets, and scarred faces. They broke into a gabble of instructions, and Eleanor listened, head tilted slightly to one side.

"So I sink the red balls, alternating with coloured ones, then the coloured ones in a special order." She shook her head. "Dear me, seems rather complicated."

"You can always quit now," said Jake. "Spare yourself the embarrassment."

"Oh no. I'm always keen to learn."

Dante thought she might be putting on the helpless old lady act a little thick, but the Bonebreaker Gang seemed to buy it.

They tossed a coin, and Jake won the break.

Dante could tell from the first shot that Jake knew what he was doing. He sank four balls in quick succession and set up the fifth one perfectly. A chorus of low voices showed the gang's approval.

Eleanor made polite comments as Jake sank seven more balls. He played with aggressive speed, and the crowd murmured in appreciation.

Finally, Jake missed, the red ball bouncing off the edge of the pocket to spin into the middle of the table.

Eleanor stepped up to the table and took stock of where the balls lay. Dante had the sense she was calculating the odds, taking into account not just the snooker game, but Jake and his assembled men as well.

It reminded him of seeing a soprano take the stage, years ago, when he was on an assignment in Vienna.

He'd tracked his target to the Vienna State Opera House and been momentarily distracted by this lady's virtuoso performance. It had seemed she was singing only to him. His target had also been distracted, and that error had proved fatal for the Estonian drug runner.

With a small gesture almost like a stage bow, Eleanor started to play.

The room grew quieter and quieter as she cleaned up. She sank all the red balls, alternating them with high-scoring coloured balls. She left the white ball perfectly positioned with each shot, set up for the next score.

Dante watched Jake carefully out of the corner of his eye. If the big man turned out to be a sore loser, Dante would need to react with extreme prejudice.

If things turned nasty, Dante calculated the odds of them escaping with only minimal injuries at 10%. With minor flesh wounds, he put it at an attainable 35%. With someone dead (not him or Eleanor), escape would be a more comfortable 75%.

Eleanor sank two of the coloured balls before she made a mistake —

sending a ball skimming along the felt barrier to bounce gently off the end of the table, rather than into the pocket.

There was an expectant pause as Jake smacked the end of his cue into his palm and lined up the next shot to sink the brown.

Dante's eyes flicked to the scoreboard. It was still a close game. If Jake sank the final three balls, he would win. However, the next ball — blue — was tucked away in a difficult position - up against the far side of the table, and partially shielded by the pink ball.

Jake tried several positions, measuring distances. The tension grew as he sighted the angles, sitting half on the table for one possible shot.

Eleanor smiled encouragingly. "It's never good to second guess yourself, dear. Play to your strengths."

Thrasher Jake shot her a surly look. "This is advice from someone who doesn't play snooker?"

"Quite so."

Jake chose his angle and lined up the shot, glaring along his cue with one ferocious eye.

The white ball shot down the table, bounced off the end, missed the pink ball, and struck the blue, sending it rolling towards the pocket. There was a collective sigh that turned into a groan as the ball hit the cushion, ricocheting away from the pocket.

Eleanor didn't hesitate. She stepped smoothly up and in less time than it took to describe what was happening, 'click clack' - she had sunk the blue and pink balls.

That left only the black, shining in the sunlight. Eleanor paced to the far end of the table, leaned over her cue, and struck the white ball. It hit the black, which rolled down the length of the table, and into the corner pocket, leaving the white ball spinning gently in the middle of the table.

There was an expectant silence.

Jake swung his pool cue and smacked it into his palm. Thwack. Thwack. A muscle jumped in his jaw.

He looked across the table at Eleanor and Dante standing beside her.

Dante's sense went on high alert. If there is going to be violence, he thought, it will be now.

"You think you can just swan in here and win a game like this? And now I'll answer your questions?"

Eleanor looked directly at him.

"Yes," she said simply.

The silence stretched taut as Dante's nerves. It was all he could do to keep still. Striking first would even things somewhat, he thought. He could take out two of them with Eleanor's pool cue before the fight properly began.

Then Jake's eyes crinkled at the edges and a huge, wickedly ugly grin spread across his face.

"You are a piece of work, lady."

"Thank you," said Eleanor. "It takes one to know one."

Chuckling, Jake handed his pool cue to one of the assembled crowd. "Alright. You won fair and square. So you and I are going to go over to the bar there. We'll get a drink, and you can ask your questions. And you'll get my honest answers."

Eleanor smiled. "Thank you, dear. That sounds wonderful."

———

Dante started the car and drove Eleanor away from the Bonebreaker's headquarters.

"Well, that was interesting," she said at last.

"What did you ask Thrasher Jake?"

"I asked him who might have a grudge against Janice. He couldn't think of anyone with a beef big enough to kill for, although she wasn't much liked. But half a dozen people have it in for Ted, including Thrasher Jake himself."

"What was Jake's grudge?"

"Ted's development is going to put townhouses all around the Hellhound club, and Jake's not happy about it. Another one is that Ted charges all his tenants top dollar. It's angered a lot of people. Jake also mentioned that mechanic Ted put out of business — the one Mrs Haddock told you about. And then there was what happened to Delia."

"Charlie's mum?"

"Yes. Charlie's dad, Adrian, used to be in business with Ted. They were equal owners of the Pepper Tree Hotel, with Delia, Adrian's wife, working in the kitchens. Then Adrian died in a boating accident. Everyone thought Delia would get half the hotel, but she didn't. Ted got the entire hotel, and Delia got nothing."

"Adrian's lawyer was Janice's boss?"

"Yes."

"Hmmm."

"In a town like this, there's going to be dozens of intriguing connections."

"Doesn't look good for Charlie," said Dante. "Since he has no alibi for the time of the murder."

Eleanor sighed. "It does not." She tapped her fingers on the car window sill. "I'm rather glad Jake went for the snooker option. I'm rubbish at poker. I could have cheated, I suppose, but I prefer not to cheat whenever possible."

"How did you know he'd want to play snooker rather than cards?"

"I suggested it to him. Subliminally, of course. It's an old grifter trick. I put several verbal and non-verbal cues into our conversation, and his subconscious picked them up and ran with it. Poor dear, he thought it was his idea."

Dante digested this. He wondered if Eleanor had done anything like this to him.

"Of course not," said Eleanor, appearing to read his mind, which was equally disconcerting. "That trick only works for a minute or two, so I only use it on marks. You and I are in a mutually beneficial partnership."

"That's good to know," said Dante. "Where to next?"

"You have your police interview soon, don't you? Perhaps you could drop me home first. I have gardening and thinking to do."

Dante nodded and turned right at the bookshop. They drove towards Eleanor's house.

24

In which Dante regrets helping the police with their enquiries

Dante shifted in his seat, feeling how he would grip the chair if he needed to use it as a weapon.

"No comment," he said.

Across the table from him, Inspector Avery and Hemi were two dissatisfied police officers. Dante could tell that Hemi, at least, was used to far more cooperative witnesses. People brought into the Te Kohe police station were either innocent, and eager to help the police with their enquiries, or guilty, and trying hard not to show it.

Dante was neither.

"Key witnesses said you left the balcony just before fireworks began, and reappeared just after Ted was shot," said Avery. "Where did you go?"

This was the third variation on the same question in about five minutes.

"What I said before," said Dante. He didn't see any reason to waste words.

Right now, Charlie was doing garden things in the greenhouse, and he'd wanted to see what they were. Charlie had also been making excited noises about the corpse plant maybe springing into life. Dante hadn't noticed anything different in the large dirt-filled pot, but perhaps Charlie had a special gardening sense, in the same way that Dante had a sense for exactly how hard to hit someone so they fell down and didn't get up again.

"You said that you went to check on Ted's Hummer when he asked you to," said Avery, looking down at his phone where he'd been taking notes. "Did you see anyone during this time?"

"Yes," said Dante.

"Who?"

"I don't know their names."

"If you could give us a bit more detail," said Hemi, trying hard to be friendly in the face of Dante's blank stares. "We're trying hard to sort this out, mate, and the more information you can give us, the sooner we can clear you of suspicion."

There had been a lot of people on the street outside the Pepper Tree Hotel, but Dante had moved to the garage in the shadow of the wisteria covered pergola. He doubted anyone had seen him.

"You do realise," said Avery, "that everyone else in the hotel has an alibi for when Janice was murdered."

Dante knew this was not true. Both he and Charlie were unaccounted for. But he kept quiet. It was generally the best policy when talking to police.

Besides, the Te Kohe interview room was a veritable palace compared to the places he'd been interrogated. And neither Avery nor Hemi looked likely to bring out batteries with jumper leads, waterboarding equipment, or any of the less sophisticated enquiry techniques Dante had encountered during his time working abroad.

"You haven't eaten your biscuit yet, mate," said Hemi. "Something on your mind?"

Dante took his biscuit (a cameo cream, quite good fare for a police station) and deliberately dipped it in his PG Tips tea. The tea cup was of the dark smoked glass variety, popular in the eighties, seemingly indestructible. He waited until the exact moment before it would become soggy enough to break. Then he lifted it out and ate the entire biscuit in one bite.

A small silence followed.

"We want to be sure we're not missing anything," said Avery. "Go over the night's events again, starting from when you arrived at the Pepper Tree Hotel."

Avery had opted for the 'wear them down with endless repetitions' style of questioning. Dante could repeat his story ad nauseum, he knew. Apart from anything, it was the unvarnished truth. In his world, that gave it an air of novelty.

However, it was a lovely summer's day outside, and Dante didn't want to be here.

"How about I spare us all the time," he said, "and tell you both what you want to hear?"

Both police officers perked up.

"And that would be?" asked Avery.

"I didn't kill Janice. My story is true, and if you ask enough witnesses, you'll find someone to corroborate it. Janice's killer used a handgun with 9mm bullets fired with considerable accuracy. That's the mark of a professional. The pantry window was broken, yes, and the glass scattered outwards. However, if you use a laser measurer from the pantry window, and sit someone where Ted was, and someone else where Janice was, you'll see the angles don't quite check out. Which means the crime you are looking at is different from the one you think you're seeing. Now, are we done here?"

Avery remained where he was, regarding Dante with professional interest.

"Yesterday, I went to the hotel and checked the angles with a laser beam. You are correct in your assessment. How did you know?"

And that was why it never paid to volunteer information to the police.

Dante sighed. "The angles didn't look right."

"How did you check?" asked Avery.

"They didn't look right."

Avery leaned back. "It was only slightly off. Did you just eyeball it?"

"I guessed?"

"And you said your occupation was…" Avery made a show of checking his phone, "an accountant. In Kent."

"Yes."

Avery exchanged a significant glance with Hemi. "We'd like you to remain available over the next few days. We will likely have further questions for you once we finish going over the rest of the witness accounts."

In other words, Avery would like to arrest Dante as soon as he had adequate proof.

"Sure." If Dante decided to vacate Te Kohe, he could be on the other side of the world before anyone had time to put out a BOLO. "I'd like another biscuit, please."

"Here, mate." Hemi pushed the packet of cameo creams towards him, and Dante took one.

"Make sure you stay in town," said Avery. His gaze appeared to be measuring Dante for a set of prison overalls.

Dante left the interview room without another word.

When he stepped outside, the bright sun was blinding after the relative dimness of the Te Kohe police station.

Dante stretched his shoulders. Perhaps high intensity gardening might relieve the tension that had been building up over the last forty five minutes.

He'd never had dealings with the police like this before. At home, there'd always been someone further up the chain of command to make these kinds of problems go away. And when he worked in other countries, police were to be avoided at all costs, as no one would help him if he became entangled with local law enforcement.

Dealing with the police like a regular citizen was new. Dante didn't think he liked it. And between himself and Charlie, he already knew who looked the more likely suspect.

25

In which various theories are expounded, and an agreement reached

They were gathered in Dante's sitting room, where Dante had been sure he'd never actually have guests.

Eleanor sat on a wingback leather armchair, while Charlie sat cross-legged on the rug with the cat stretched out in his lap. A brief frisson of emotion flared in Dante. Was it jealousy? He told himself he didn't want the cat in the first place — it had just invited itself into his home. And it was looking increasingly like he wouldn't be in Te Kohe much longer, anyway.

Neither of these thoughts helped much.

"Please, sit down, Dante," said Eleanor. "Let's begin."

Dante didn't feel like sitting. He wanted to do something strenuous. A rooftop chase through the slums of São Paulo, or a bare knuckle boxing match in Latvia.

"She's a gorgeous creature," said Charlie. "Ouch!"

The cat had just caught his fingers with its sharp claws. Dante felt gratified. He pushed off from the mantlepiece of the sitting room hearth and sat on the couch.

"I was going to do a summary of where we've got to so far," said Eleanor, "and then we can decide what to do next."

Dante wasn't fooled by this statement. He was ninety four percent sure Eleanor had already decided what she was going to do next. She was merely keeping himself and Charlie informed.

"How soon do police start making arrests in a case like this?" asked Charlie. He stuck his finger in his mouth and sucked on it. "Your cat's got sharp claws."

"I'm sure Grace will let me know if that is imminent," said Eleanor. "Let's start by putting down everything we know, then we can look at what we don't know, and what we can do to find those things out." Eleanor took a sip of her tea, then returned the cup to its saucer on the coffee table.

"There's the device we found at the dump," said Charlie. "What do you think it was for?"

"It's to fire a gun," said Dante. "It would fit a Glock, a Sig Sauer or a Beretta fairly well."

"Do you think it would help shoot more accurately?" asked Eleanor. "Do you think it was used to fire at Janice?"

"Maybe," said Dante. "It's an odd design. I'm not sure."

"There was that bullet buried in the wall in the pantry," said Eleanor. "Someone had tried to conceal the hole it made. Did you find anything else when you visited the hotel, Dante?"

"There was a burn mark on the roof over the pantry window," said Dante. "Something left a circle of soot there. I only saw it because I went up on the hotel roof."

"Interesting..." Eleanor tapped fingers on her teacup. "A bullet buried in the wall inside the pantry, soot on the window hood... it all adds up to something. Locating the murder weapon would be handy, but it could be anywhere. Best place to put it would be the bottom of the ocean, I suppose."

"If I were going to shoot someone on the balcony," said Dante. "I'd position myself on the roof, and use a sniper rifle, something like a Remington 700 or a Barrett M82. I wouldn't be inside the hotel - too likely to run into someone. This is just theorising, of course," he added at Charlie's frown.

"So the details of the crime suggest either an amateur, or, I think more likely, an angle that we've missed," said Eleanor. "On the subject of motive, the Hellhounds thought you might have a grudge against Ted, Charlie. Because he inherited your dad's share of the hotel."

"You went to see the Hellhounds?" said Charlie, eyes wide.

"Thrasher Jake's a lovely man, once you get to know him," said Eleanor. "Motive is important, though. It seems more and more likely that Ted murdered Janice because she was blackmailing him. It also looks like Ted intended to frame Dante, and you got caught up in it when Sione sent you off to fetch wine at just the wrong moment. Unless you were a backup fall guy. Or maybe Dante was." She trailed off, looking thoughtful.

"Mum always said she couldn't believe dad would leave his share of the hotel to Ted," said Charlie. "She wanted to contest it, but lawyers cost too much. And she didn't want to lose her job at the hotel — then we would have lost our house."

"There's a line of people with a motive to get rid of Ted," said Eleanor. "Thrasher Jake admitted he has one, as well as all the people who don't want the development to go ahead, and all the people who owe Ted money. If Ted was the target, we have a lot of suspects to discount. However, if Janice was the target, things become much simpler."

"Janice's husband said she was getting paid each month," said Dante. "If she was blackmailing Ted, what was the angle? Money laundering? Drugs? It's usually drugs."

"It would be good to know exactly when the blackmail started," said Eleanor. "Janice was a lawyer's assistant. Presumably, she had insight into Ted's business. Perhaps one of Ted's property acquisitions was illegal."

"He owns a lot of Te Kohe," said Charlie.

"How much you own is only half the puzzle," said Eleanor. "The other half is how much you owe. I could find that out — I know someone who could delve into Ted's financial dealings. I have the feeling Ted's an all sizzle, no steak guy."

"Derek thought the blackmail payments had been going on for years," said Dante. "Why kill Janice now?"

"Ted's about to make a lot of money," said Eleanor. "Suppose Janice demanded a cut of the new development profits?"

"Ted wouldn't like that," said Charlie.

"I also suspect that Ted may not be able to just sit back and wait for the development to happen," said Eleanor. "I think he's running out of time, which makes him dangerous. I want to find out more about his finances. Which means I'lll be taking a trip to Auckland in the near future."

"In the Viking Age," said Dante, "if someone was judged guilty of a serious crime, they had two choices - pay the wergeld fine, or be outlawed. If they were outlawed, anyone was allowed to kill them and there would be no repercussions."

There was a small silence while everyone digested this statement.

"I don't think modern New Zealand law works like that," said Eleanor. "They don't even have the death penalty."

"Could that Russian guy — Viktor — have done it?" said Charlie. "If he's working for Ted."

"He's from Belarus," said Dante.

"That's a possibility," said Eleanor. "I shall try to find out when he arrived in Te Kohe."

Dante found himself pacing the floor. "I'm not going to prison. Especially for something I didn't do."

"Of course not, dear," said Eleanor.

"How do you know the police are going to listen to us?" said Dante.

"I'm sure I can arrange things so that they do," said Eleanor.

"If I don't see real progress in clearing my name soon," said Dante, "I'm out."

"Out?" said Charlie. The cat in his lap stretched full length now, bearing its white furred belly to the sun.

"I'll go. Away. Somewhere." Dante thought about the many other places he could disappear to — places he'd visited in between assignments and liked the look of. Antigua, in the West Indies. Nicaragua. Tanzania. However, none of them had a cat with three white socks, and an as yet unseen corpse plant.

"How could you leave the country if the police want you to stay?" asked Charlie. "I thought they had a thing to stop that?"

Dante's face didn't change, but he thought about the secret panel he'd installed in the bathroom cupboard, and the several passports stored there with entirely different names below his photograph. "I need to know that you have things well in hand," he told Eleanor.

"That is a fair request," said Eleanor. "Can I ask you for perhaps five day's grace? Until we get a break in this case?"

Dante wondered whether this was a good idea. His instinct told him that the tide was soon going to turn against either himself or Charlie. His instinct had kept him alive through many situations. He wasn't going to stop trusting it now. But a strange feeling of inertia was tugging at him. Perhaps this was the result of owning a garden?

"Five days," he said.

"Thank you, Dante," said Eleanor. "What we need to do is find the proof Janice stored away as her blackmail security against Ted. There must be some way to find out what it is. And if my trip to Auckland is successful, I might be able to trace the payments from Ted to Janice."

"What should I do?" asked Charlie. "My police interview is coming up soon." He stroked the cat's belly, and it seized his hand with both front paws, claws temporarily retracted.

"I want you to take time to think back on the Jubilee evening. Try to remember any unusual details that stand out. And we should talk to Sione, the sous chef who asked you to go and get the port. I think the timing of that was suspiciously perfect."

"Sione's alright," said Charlie, flushing slightly. "I'm sure he's not... a murderer."

Dante felt Charlie needed an education in what people would or wouldn't do when sufficiently motivated. He wasn't sure he was the best person to give it to him.

"He doesn't need to be a murderer to help with setting you up," said Eleanor. "He might have been bought off, threatened, or someone may have simply instructed him, and he did it because he's a good employee."

Charlie gently freed his hand from the cat's paws. "I don't think I'll ever get the hang of thinking like this."

"Luckily," said Eleanor, "with us helping you, you won't have to." She took out her slim cellphone and tapped in a message. "I'll arrange to go to Auckland in the next few days. Dante, thank you for sticking around to help us sort this mess out."

"Ok," said Dante. The cat chose that moment to roll out of Charlie's lap and do a magnificent full body stretch. It sauntered over to Dante and rubbed against his calf, purring. Dante leaned down and scratched it between the ears. The purring increased in volume.

In an ideal world, Dante could stay and see this through. That didn't mean he would, though. On any mission, getting in at the right time was important. But ten times more important was knowing when to get out. And Dante didn't believe in ideal worlds.

26

In which Charlie is unwise

Charlie turned over a shovelful of soil. This late in the summer, the earth in the small church graveyard was dry and crumbled as he pitched it out of the trench.

He told himself that this job was important - urgent, even. It wasn't. There was no point planting this time of year. But it was a good way to take his mind off his upcoming police interview.

"Ready for the big day?"

Pete Morrow appeared, sliding out of thin air in the way of ghosts.

"I guess." Charlie leaned on his spade, turning to face him.

"What does this remind me of?" Pete tapped his fingers on his knee as he thought. "You're like that guy in the play — what was his name? Had to avenge a murder, couldn't summon up the stones to do it? Did a lot of talking."

"Hamlet. He got to it eventually."

"Yeah. Saw it in '05 with the late Mrs Davison. Local theatre group. She likes the theatre. Got a lot more culture than me."

"You two still going out?" Charlie hadn't seen them together for a while.

"Oh yes. There's even less to argue about when you're dead," said Pete. "Though she's not entirely happy with how you're looking after her corpse plant."

"I'm sure she isn't," sighed Charlie. Mrs Davison had been an exacting employer.

"There was a good graveyard scene in Hamlet," said Pete. "Alas, poor Yorik."

"I knew him well, Horatio." Charlie supposed there were plenty of skulls around to re-enact the scene. He even had a shovel to play gravedigger.

A brief chill raised the hairs on the back of his neck, and Charlie glanced behind himself. Just beyond the borders of the graveyard, a figure stalked the pavement.

Pete grimaced. "Looks like our chieftain's up and about."

It was chief Hōne Te Whetū, sole surviving ghost of a battle between two tribes that had taken place a hundred and fifty years ago. When Charlie was a kid, he'd been terrified of the chief's shade, a fact that had caused no end of problems when his mother had tried to take him to church. The walk to the chapel went right by the ghostly warrior's post, where he stood, covered in spectral blood, hands still clutching a splintered taiaha.

"Has he ever spoken to you?"

"Yeah, course," said Pete. "We have regular weekly catch ups."

"Really?"

Pete snorted. "'Course not. A ghost that old is already half in the next-next world."

"Why does he hang around here?"

"His bones are buried under the pavement. Everyone else from that battle, too. Guess he objected to not getting the proper sendoff and decided to stick around."

It always puzzled Charlie why some people became ghosts, while others slipped away into the afterlife without a backward glance. If it was stubbornness of will, he supposed Pete was a good candidate. But he'd known other headstrong folk who'd vanished into eternity without a trace.

Asking the ghosts didn't help. They often didn't know. He'd offered to try to find the key to getting Pete to move on, but the old copper told him (nicely) to mind his own goddamn business.

"Here's my advice: just answer the questions, play it straight," said Pete. "On the evidence they have, they'll have to work hard to convict you. And you've got a good face for this sort of thing. Juries will be sympathetic."

"Thanks," said Charlie, feeling worse than ever. The thought of being hauled in front of a court with press photographers, hostile prosecution lawyers, and implacable judges made his stomach churn.

"You know what they say," said Pete.

"What doesn't kill you makes you stronger?"

"It'll be alright in the end, lad. And if it's not alright, it's not yet the end."

As the ghost of his godfather faded, Charlie reflected that this was not altogether reassuring advice. After all, Pete had reached the end, and, judging by the fact that he was still here, not everything was alright.

Charlie tried to stop fidgeting. The easiest way to do this was to sit on his hands, but this wouldn't give the best impression. He blew out a slow breath. He needed to stay calm, cool, collected — like Eleanor, who unfortunately wasn't allowed to be here. The police had been quite definite about that. Instead, sitting next to him in the police interview room was Leonard Finch, the Wilson family lawyer.

Leonard was a short, dark-haired man with a vague air, as if he was trying to remember whether he'd left the gas on at home. His presence did nothing to bolster Charlie's confidence. They were both seated at a table, and across from them sat Sergeant Hemi Henare and Inspector Marcus Avery.

Avery had introduced himself in a friendly way, but Charlie saw how keenly his eyes studied Charlie, and his nervousness crossed over into nausea.

He tried to remind himself he hadn't done anything, but that didn't help. Something about being in a police station made him feel guilty. He could believe people confessed to anything if kept in a station for sufficient length of time.

Hemi pressed a button on the desk and a small red light began to shine.

"I haven't seen one of those since last century," murmured Inspector Avery, and Hemi frowned at him.

"It was cutting edge in its day." Hemi cleared his throat. "The date is the 15th of January, time is eight thirty am. Present in the room are myself, Sergeant Hemi Henare, Inspector Marcus Avery, Leonard Finch, attorney, and Charlie Wilson, the interviewee. Charlie, please state your date of birth for the record."

"Um, hi," said Charlie. "I'm Charlie." Hemi made a small motion with his hand as if to say 'go on.' For a moment, Charlie couldn't remember his birthday, then it came to him. "I was born in 2003, September twelfth."

"Cheers, mate," said Hemi. "We're ready to begin. Charlie, I want you to know that you are not under arrest. You have the right not to answer any question you're asked, though that might prejudice your case later if you end up in court. Please note that anything you say will be recorded and may be used later in a court of law."

Charlie resisted the urge to say, 'wow, it's just like in a cop show.' But it was. He just wished he wasn't the person on the hot seat in this show.

"Charlie," said Inspector Avery, "do you understand the charges that could be levelled against you?"

And just like that, Charlie understood that Avery was going to be the bad cop.

"It's a murder investigation, right?" he said. "You're trying to find out who killed Janice Enderby." He paused. It seemed important that he say this right. "It wasn't me."

Leonard gave him a small smile of encouragement and a thumbs up under the table.

"Charlie, at this stage, we're just trying to get a timeline of events," said Inspector Avery. He had a cultured, calming voice, like a radio presenter from the fifties. "Can you please walk us through your movements on the night of the Jubilee?"

"Uh, ok," said Charlie. "So, I got there at about three o'clock in the afternoon."

"Got where?" said Avery.

"The Pepper Tree Hotel. I was working in the kitchen, and it was going to be a big night. My mum, Delia, works there full time, and I sometimes go help out as a kitchen hand when they're busy. Jubilee night is the busiest of the year, so they called in a bunch of extra staff."

Avery sat back and interlaced his fingers as he listened. Charlie wished he could read something on the man's face. Hemi was fairly easy to read - his face was big and expressive, and emotions moved across it in waves. Currently, Hemi was being grave, mainly because this was the first murder in Te Kohe in over ninety years.

The last murder had been in the thirties, when a farmer called Johanus had shot his neighbour, then shot himself. Johanus still lurked around the cemetery, but he vanished whenever Charlie tried to talk to him and see if he could help move him along.

Charlie faltered in his account. He'd gotten distracted, and both policemen were staring at him. It didn't help that the ghost of One-eyed Percy, local thief and troublemaker, deceased 1908, was leering at him from the doorway.

"You were saying that you were working in the kitchen," prompted Hemi. "Starting at three pm."

"Right," said Charlie. "We were busy doing prep until seven, when guests started to arrive. Then Sione, he's the sous chef, sent me to Foursquare to get more eggs. It was about to close and nothing else would be open until tomorrow. Unless I went to Glenhaven where the Pak'n Save is."

"What time did you get back?" asked Avery.

"About a quarter past," said Charlie. "I had to walk, because there was no way I could drive with town being so busy."

One-eyed Percy hid behind Avery's head and then popped out, like he was playing peek-a-boo. Charlie closed his eyes and tried to concentrate. His cheeks went red and he felt the same frustration as when he was a kid, and 'acting normal in public' had been impossible.

"I think Ted arrived around eight," said Charlie.

"How did you know that?" asked Avery, his eyes sharp.

"Mum sent me to get champagne and start serving it to guests. Ted was there. Everyone was about to start dinner and there was going to be a speech and a toast," said Charlie. "So I served wine until the dinner ended and the guests went up to the balcony to watch the fireworks."

One-eyed Percy stood between Avery and Hemi and mimed being hung with the noose around his neck, his head tilted sideways and his face in a grotesque grimace.

Charlie focused on the table. This was the important bit, he knew.

"Once the guests were up on the balcony, Sione, the sous chef, sent me to get the port and the special port glasses. They're in the pantry on the East wing of the hotel, away from the main food storage because they don't get used much. It took me a while to find the port glasses, because someone had put them on the top shelf, behind the Christmas decorations. When I came back, the fireworks were over."

Dead silence greeted this statement.

"The East Wing?" said Avery.

"It's on the opposite side of the hotel from where we think the shot was fired," said Hemi.

"Did you see anyone when you went to get the port?" asked Avery.

Charlie tried to control the adrenaline coursing through his veins. He knew his statement looked bad. He'd known all along it would. He'd just somehow managed to keep his hopes up until now, to retain his faith in the justice system and the belief that the innocent had nothing to fear. That hope was crumbling now, like pastry cut too soon after coming out of the oven.

"No," he said, as One-eyed Percy jerked around behind the two policemen in a macabre simulation of the hemp fandango. "I didn't see anyone."

Avery sat back in his chair and exchanged a weighty look with Hemi. "So no one can confirm your location at the time of the murder."

"No," said Charlie.

"Could you have gone to the West Wing without anyone seeing you?" asked Avery.

Charlie stared straight ahead, feeling the walls closing in around him. He wanted to run out of the room and keep running, all the way until he found somewhere safe, far away from all people and all ghosts.

"Charlie?" said Avery. "Remember that failing to answer a question could prejudice people against you if this goes to court."

"Ahem." Leonard cleared his throat, the sound loud in the silence. He sat forward and laced his fingers together. "You've asked my client a lot of questions, and he's given you a lot of detail about the other night. Unfortunately, no one saw him go to fetch the port. But lack of evidence doesn't mean he's guilty. You're supposed to presume innocence until proven guilty."

There was a brief silence as Charlie's spirits sank further. Hemi and Avery exchanged another glance.

"Do you remember exactly what time you returned to the kitchen with the port?" asked Avery.

"No." Charlie clenched his hands under the table. "But Ted was just coming down to the kitchen with Doctor Galway. Everyone had stopped work to watch him get stitched up."

"What happened next?" asked Hemi.

"Ted got stitched up, and then Eleanor sent all the staff up to the dining hall so Rosie could get their details."

Avery gave him a sharp look. "Going above and beyond the call of duty must be a habit for her," he murmured, as if to himself.

"And?" said Hemi. Charlie could hear his foot tapping under the table.

"And I gave Rosie my name, address, and phone number, though she already knows where I live." Charlie blushed. That had come out all wrong. "And then I helped the staff clean up everything. I got home around three am."

Avery leaned forward. "Charlie, I won't lie to you — this looks bad. So far, you're the only person who we know was there on the night that doesn't have an alibi for when Janice was shot with a Glock 22."

Charlie frowned at the last statement, then tried to clear his expression when Avery's eyes sharpened. "What I said is what happened. I went to the East Wing to get two bottles of port and the port glasses. When I came back, Ted was down in the kitchen." And Janice's dead body was up on the balcony. The thought circled in his head like a dog on a chain.

"We are coming to a crossroads," said Avery. "At this juncture, you can come clean and tell us anything else you know. Your willingness to cooperate with the police will help you if this ever comes to trial."

"That's right," said Hemi. "We know you're a good lad, Charlie. If there's anything you aren't saying because you're protecting someone, now's the time to come clean."

Charlie stared. Did they know something? Were they trying to trap him into a confession?

"Hey, wait a minute," said Leonard. "My client has provided you with all the information he can. Let's not get ahead of ourselves and jump to any conclusions."

"We're not trying to—" said Hemi, while at the same time Avery spoke.

"You saw someone on the stairs, Charlie, just as you were coming back to the kitchen. The stairs to the West Wing."

Charlie blinked. One-eyed Percy made a 'woooo,' noise from under the table. Charlie wanted to kick him, but his foot would go right through the ghost. Knowing his luck, he'd probably end up kicking Inspector Avery.

"You never mentioned seeing anyone to me," said Leonard in a whisper that was clearly audible to everyone present.

Charlie wanted to hide his face in his hands. Why couldn't he have a hotshot lawyer like in those courtroom dramas?

"If you don't answer the question," said Avery, his voice deep and serious, "we will record you as refusing to answer."

"I didn't see anyone else," said Charlie, but his ears were burning. He knew his face would be going pink, and he cursed his skin for being such a giveaway.

"Charlie," said Avery, and paused. The small room fell absolutely silent. "I don't believe you."

Charlie opened his mouth, but he couldn't think of anything to say.

"Now see here," said Leonard. "This is subjecting my client to undue pressure. I don't think it's fair."

"I am investigating a murder," said Avery. "I have the right to demand answers to my questions."

"Steady on," said Leonard. "There's no basis to even suggest what you're suggesting. My client is innocent."

"Right now, he's our primary suspect." Avery shot an irritated glance at Leonard. "And your obstruction is not appreciated."

"I object to that," said Leonard. "I'm well within my rights to stick up for my client."

"Guys, please maintain calm," said Hemi.

And Avery said over the top of him, "We can do this now, or in front of a stand of hostile jurors."

"I object," said Leonard. "You're just fishing for information."

Avery leaned back and pinned Leonard with a basilisk stare. "One of the hotel staff heard Charlie talking to someone on the West Wing stairs."

"That's... just hearsay," said Leonard, but his fingers beat a nervous tattoo on the tabletop. "Also, Charlie hardly knew Janice. There's no motive for murder. Right, Charlie?"

Charlie felt like he ought to back Leonard up, but at the same time, he didn't want to join the losing side of the argument. Even if the losing side was his side.

Avery raised one eyebrow. "I've been fortunate to have Sergeant Henare on this case, who has a rich and detailed knowledge of this community and its history."

"I've been the Wilson family lawyer for thirty years," said Leonard. "And like I said, there's no motive."

Charlie had hoped this segue would give him time to think, but he couldn't come up with anything. He wished that Pete was in the room with him, instead of One-eyed Percy.

"Charlie knew Ted," said Avery. "It's quite possible Ted was the target all along, but the bullet missed him and killed Janice. It turns out Charlie and his family have quite the history with Ted."

"Now see here," said Leonard. He paused with that 'did I leave the gas on,' look on his face for a moment, then found inspiration. "Pretty much everyone in this town has beef with Ted. He's that kind of guy."

"How did your father die, Charlie?" said Avery.

"I object to this line of questioning," said Leonard. "Could we stick to the present day, please?"

"I'm just a newcomer here," said Avery, "but I heard your dad was out fishing, drunk, after running the business he and Ted owned nearly into the ground."

"That's not true," the words came out through Charlie's tightly clenched teeth, and his face was suddenly red, not with embarrassment, but with anger.

"I heard they never found him, that maybe it was a suicide, from shame," continued Avery.

"Hey now..." said Hemi. "That's hardly—"

"I heard he'd made such a mess of things, Ted had to buy the whole operation back from his grieving widow, and pay out of his own pocket to save the business," said Avery.

Leonard cleared his throat. "Charlie, you don't have to—"

"And that he was so irresponsible, he left his wife and child with nothing. Nothing at all to help her raise her only son. I heard he was a total waste of space—"

"That's not true!" Charlie yelled. It felt like all the air had been sucked out of the room. "Ted stole everything we had. He's a lying, thieving, murderous bastard and he deserves to—!"

He stopped short of finishing his last sentence because Leonard kicked him under the table. Hard.

There followed a few heartbeats of silence, and Charlie realised he was half standing, fists crashed down on the table. He was hot, like a fire that had been smouldering inside him for longer than he could remember had suddenly sprung into flame.

"Charlie, are you accusing Ted of murdering your father?" said Avery. He leaned forward, eyes intense.

Charlie collapsed back into his seat, breathing hard.

'Ooooo,' jeered One-eyed Percy, smirking out from behind Avery. 'You messed up big time, Charlie boy.'

"With all due respect, this has gone too far." Leonard drew himself up, his face serious and worried, like a dignified rabbit. "Hemi, we've known each other a long time. What's the meaning of pressuring my client like this? It's not keeping to the spirit of how we do things here."

Avery's face was implacable. "I still have questions for you, Charlie."

"I think," said Charlie shakily, "that I'd prefer not to answer them at this time, officer." He gripped the table's edge to stop his hands from trembling. He couldn't tell if it was anger or despair that made his legs feel like water.

This was the point, he knew, that suspects in cop shows were supposed to say 'I'd like to have my phonecall please,' and their maverick genius lawyer would swoop in and fix everything. But his lawyer sat beside him, looking like a man who'd not only left the gas on but also forgotten to turn off the kitchen tap.

Hemi gave a gusty sigh. "We just want to get the record straight, mate."

"Failure to answer our questions won't look good on your file," said Avery.

Just for once, thought Charlie, I'd like to be able to cast a hex. People like me are supposed to be able to do that. I'd hex Avery for being a proper bastard.

"Can I go now?" he said.

"I'd like to pass a motion—" began Leonard, but Avery cut him off.

"Charlie Wilson, you are to remain here in the station," said Avery. "You are being detained for the suspected murder of Janice Enderby, and the attempted murder of Ted Andrews."

"I'd like to make a phonecall please," said Charlie.

27

In which many birds come home to roost

Eleanor sat on the marble bench and reviewed the situation. After listening to Charlie's shaky voice on the phone half an hour earlier, she'd contacted Inspector Avery. A brief conversation, and Eleanor had arranged to meet him at the small Te Kohe church graveyard.

The graveyard had several points in its favour. It was quiet (as the grave) and quite beautiful, with ancient oak trees and moss covered tombstones. And it served to remind her that, in the end, no matter what triumphs and disasters your life contains, we all end up in the same place. Death had been Eleanor's constant companion throughout her eventful life, and she appreciated the reminder of a peaceful graveyard when she was about to have a difficult conversation.

Eleanor looked up as police inspector Avery approached. He was dressed in a tailored light grey suit with a blue button-down shirt and patent leather shoes. Despite the fact he was in the enemy camp, she did appreciate a man who knew how to wear a suit.

"An appropriate place for a meeting," said Avery. "Considering the reason I'm here in Te Kohe."

Eleanor smiled. "Thank you for coming to meet me." For this meeting, she had decided to drop the airhead act. She looked forward to seeing Avery's reaction.

His eyes narrowed. "It seems you have undergone a personality transformation."

"Well, there are times to be overlooked and ignored, and times when one wishes to be taken seriously." Eleanor sat back on the bench, the marble cool against her back.

"It makes me wonder what else you've been hiding," said Avery. He sat next to her, his suit pants riding up to reveal matching grey socks.

"I'm always honest when murder is involved," said Eleanor.

"I'll take that under advisement," said Avery. "You said you had information of vital importance to the case, and you wanted to cut a deal."

Eleanor laced her hands around one knee. She was wearing an immaculate beige linen skirt and jacket, with a light cotton shirt underneath — what she thought of as her work uniform. She knew she had an excellent good poker face, but she suspected the inspector could read more of her than she liked.

"You know, this cemetery dates back to the earliest settler days," said Eleanor. "There are inhabitants from English and Scottish pioneers, as well as the first Maori converts to Christianity."

"I'm sure crimes were committed even back then," said the inspector drily, "but I doubt any of the people buried here had anything to do with Janice Enderby's murder."

"I imagine police back then had to take the law into their own hands a lot more."

"Is that what you're doing? Because that's a dangerous game, Eleanor Graham. I would advise against it."

Eleanor smiled faintly. "All the best things in life are inadvisable."

"Much as I enjoy a quiet cemetery on a Tuesday morning," said Inspector Avery, "I have rather a lot on my plate right now. If you have information, please spill it. If not, I will be leaving." He made to rise.

"Fine." Eleanor rolled her eyes. "You're no fun at all. All work and no play makes inspectors excessively dull."

"But efficient."

It was hard to say, but perhaps Inspector Avery looked just a tiny bit amused.

"I would like to have Charlie released from your custody."

"That is police business. Certainly not something the general public has any sway over."

Eleanor looked sidelong at him. It was like he was quoting from the police manual with every second sentence. Surely no one could be that straightlaced. It might be an act as polished as her own.

"I know that Charlie is innocent," she said.

"That would be because you can provide him with an alibi for the time of the murder?"

"No, it's based on my knowledge of human nature."

"I mean no offence, but your knowledge, accurate though it may be, will not be admissible as evidence in a court of law."

"If I were able to provide evidence that isn't admissible, would you be able to consider that as you build your case?"

Inspector Avery looked pensive. "The problem with modern policing is that you can't give evidence provided by a concerned citizen the same weight as, for instance, evidence gathered from an uncontaminated crime scene by your forensic consultant. Every year, the internal affairs department has to deal with a policeman who just knew who the guilty party was, and tampered, just a little, to make the evidence fit what they thought was the crime. It's called police corruption, and I don't condone it."

Condone, thought Eleanor. Who uses words like that in polite conversation?

"I would never ask anyone to bend the law." Somehow, Eleanor managed to say this with a straight face. "It's simply that I've uncovered information that would lead to an alternative picture of the crime. And, if you were open to consulting with me, I might be able to get the murderer, in an entirely admissible way, to reveal their identity."

Inspector Avery's eyebrows drew together. "I think what you're proposing is known as entrapment."

"Not at all," said Eleanor. "It's the difference between giving someone enough rope to hang themselves, and actually setting the noose up for them."

"From where I stand, that's a distinction without a difference."

"Do you have enough evidence to convict Charlie?"

Inspector Avery made a show of checking his watch - an expensive Swiss affair that probably showed the time in three countries and ran on clockwork.

"I believe you promised me information?"

"Release Charlie, and you'll have it."

"You know," said Avery, "as a young police officer, I made it my business to master memorising faces. It's a skill that's served me well over the years."

"It's a useful skill in many professions." A frisson of unease crept down Eleanor's neck.

"I remember a case, about, oh, eight years ago now. An art theft in Auckland involving a high profile painting on loan from the Guggenheim in New York. That is to say, it appeared at first to be a theft, and the police were called in."

"Imagine that," said Eleanor. Her face was smooth as ever, but a sinking feeling in the pit of her stomach sent her a signal she couldn't act on: get out, get out now.

"Our police department ran around like headless chickens for 24 hours, trying to locate the missing painting. It had the makings of an international incident. I think the prime minister was about to get involved. And then the painting turned up, unharmed, in the museum basement. It seems a mistake had been made with a packing crate label and the moving company. How that happened with such a high profile painting remained a mystery, even after the dust had settled."

"Life is full of such little mysteries. It keeps things interesting."

"As the officer in charge, I spent quite some time reviewing the suspect list," said Inspector Avery. "And I remember a well dressed lady making an appearance both the day before and after the disappearance and reappearance of the painting. A lady about five foot four, bottle blonde—"

"Excuse me," said Eleanor.

"Fast approaching sixty years of age—"

"That's hardly fair."

"And dressed in a tailored suit, jade earrings, and patent leather shoes. Not at all who you'd expect to be involved in a serious crime."

"I should think not."

"I recall she drank espresso martinis at the exhibition opening. She was one of the VIP guests and admired the Cezanne as well as the other post impressionists on display."

Eleanor remembered that episode. She'd been freshly arrived in New Zealand, and it'd been great fun. One last blast, for old time's sake. She rapidly replayed the event in her memory and yes, in the aftermath, she remembered a photograph that accompanied an article in the Herald. The recovered painting took centre stage, flanked by the museum curator and a man who, though in plain clothes, was obviously a police officer. He was a slightly younger version of the man now sitting next to her.

She considered that the whole affair must have been tremendously embarrassing, professionally, for the officer in charge.

It's true what they say, she thought. Live long enough, and all your birds come home to roost. No morally questionable deed goes unpunished.

"What else do you recall about this interesting occasion?" she said lightly.

"It struck me at the time how unlikely it was that a Cezanne would disappear, and then reappear. The authenticators were satisfied, though. They said the original had been returned. The genuine article."

"And what do you think?" said Eleanor.

"The case was never resolved to my satisfaction. And it was a definite black mark on my career."

Your distinguished career, thought Eleanor.

"And so," she said, feeling her way, "if you received information that cleared up the Cezanne case to your satisfaction, you might also consider receiving information that would lead to the resolution of this current case?"

"Got it in one." Inspector Avery's smile had a sharp edge to it that, while disconcerting in its current application, Eleanor couldn't help preferring to his previous puritanical demeanour.

"And the information about the Cezanne case would lead to the recovery of the original painting?"

"It would lead to the apprehension of the mastermind behind the theft."

"Mastermind is such a gendered term, don't you think?"

Inspector Avery's smile grew even more sharklike.

"You know I'm retired," said Eleanor, slightly wistful. She'd been enjoying her retirement immensely.

"I'm not."

She eyed him judiciously. "You're close to it, though. Does a case from eight years ago mean that much to you?"

"I ended up being shifted out of art crimes into homicide." His lip curled. "Hence my presence in this case."

Birds coming home to roost indeed.

Eleanor contemplated the various angles of the situation.

"Are you going to send Charlie to jail?"

"That's on a need to know basis. Also," said Inspector Avery, folding his arms, "I will be keeping to the letter and the spirit of the law in this case. However, I will be open to examining any evidence you may come up with. If you can bring it to my attention in a lawful way, that would be even better."

"How long do we have?"

"Not long at all." Avery's face grew serious. "This is high profile — a shooting in such a public place draws a lot of media attention. There's all kinds of pressure on me from higher up. As soon as we get to the 'beyond all reasonable doubt' phase, one of your boys is going to jail."

"A timeframe, please?" Eleanor worked well under pressure. Although, retirement and, she had to admit, being over sixty, had made the last few days tiring.

"I can give you a week," said Avery. "Then, unless we have compelling evidence otherwise, I'm going to have to arrest Charlie as our most likely suspect, and the case will go to court."

"Seven days..." Eleanor shook off the tiredness settling into her shoulders and fluttered her eyelashes at Avery. "So my society lady act didn't fool you?"

"Oh, it did at first," said Avery. "I found it excessively annoying. But it was... too perfect. And on reflection, you seemed strangely familiar. After forty years of policing, you learn to pay attention when your subconscious raises a red flag, even a small one."

Eleanor sighed to herself. As Honest Abe (or possibly Bob Marley) had once said, you can fool some people sometimes, but you can't fool all the people all the time. Such was life.

Her gaze traced the tombstones' mossy, faded lettering, lit golden in the slanting sunlight. Charlie was young, his whole life ahead of him. While she had lived a long life, brimful with excitement, glamour, and boatloads of fun. She would prefer to end her days in similar style, but doing the right thing rarely came without a hefty price tag.

She fixed Avery with her most direct and honest gaze — the one she had used on art collectors and museum authenticators around the world.

"On Charlie's acquittal, you will get all the information you require." After all, there was many a slip between cup and lip. Eleanor was an optimist, and life had taught her never to give up on chickens before they're hatched.

Then, with a mischievous grin, she spat on her palm and held it out to the inspector.

The expressions that crossed his face were priceless. Shock, outrage, then an answering sly amusement.

With an elegant gesture, he took her hand and raised it to his lips, brushing the backs of her fingers. Then he wiped his hand on his trousers.

"Eleanor," he said, standing. She was sure that if he'd been wearing a fedora, he would have doffed it. "It's been a pleasure."

"Not entirely," said Eleanor, "but it's not over yet."

She didn't watch Avery depart. Having made her deal, the less time spent in police company, the better. Instead, she watched as the sun sparkled on the spiderwebs, and the cool air of the graveyard gave way to the summer heat.

28

In which Charlie escapes police custody

Charlie followed Rosie down the corridor and out into the police station foyer. He was not having a great day.

They hadn't put him in the holding cell, and he appreciated that. Instead, he'd been seated in the briefing room with strict instructions not to leave. He wanted to ask if that included bathroom breaks, but didn't, in case the answer was yes. Charlie felt the loss of autonomy keenly. It was like being back in school, but with an extra helping of guilt and anxiety.

His unhelpful imagination was supplying him with images of how much worse prison would be when Rosie appeared with a scrabble set.

"It'll help pass the time," she said.

Charlie's first word (for 14 points) was 'warrant.'

At half past ten, Hemi poked his head around the door.

"Someone here to see you."

At reception, Eleanor's small delegation looked, well, small, against the bulk of Hemi in full dress uniform, and Avery in his tailored suit.

"We've come to pick you up, Charlie," said Eleanor. She smiled cordially at the officers arrayed before her.

Standing next to Eleanor, Charlie's mum was practically vibrating with worry and outrage.

"Er, I may have already filed the paperwork," said Hemi. He also was eyeing Avery with speculation. "We're letting the lad go?"

"On the condition that he doesn't leave town," said Avery.

"I still need to photograph him and take fingerprints," said Hemi. "I've read him his rights, but there's more paperwork to complete before he walks out of here."

"My son is leaving with us right now." Delia's brows drew down in a fierce frown. "Or there will never be another pastry gift box delivered to this station. Ever."

They were all arguing over him like he wasn't there. Charlie wondered if he should say something.

But at the same time, Pete had appeared behind Avery, and was making urgent signals at him.

Charlie sighed. The dead had all the time in the world, so they assumed everyone else did, too. He made a 'not now,' gesture, and Pete rolled his eyes. He mouthed something at Charlie, but Charlie couldn't make out the words.

"It's just a bit of paperwork," Hemi was saying. "If I don't, I'll have Senior Sergeant Melvin on my case later. No one wants that."

"Charlie's coming with us, now," said Eleanor. "He hasn't been arrested, so you don't need mugshots and fingerprints."

"It won't take long," said Rosie. "We've just bought a new camera."

"I might just go to the interview room," said Charlie. "Since you all seem set to decide without me."

"Technically, he is under arrest," said Hemi. "Sorry! The new I3 forms came out, and I may have ticked the wrong box. I might need reading glasses..." His voice dropped to a mutter under the combined glare of Avery, Eleanor, and Delia.

"If Charlie's under arrest, then we can let him go on bail," said Rosie.

Everyone stopped glaring to look at her.

"That would work," said Eleanor grudgingly.

"How fortunate this meets with your approval," said Avery under his breath.

Eleanor folded her arms. "What's the bail set at?"

"Since you're involved, quite a lot," said Avery.

Eleanor reached into her handbag and examined the contents of her purse. "Would two thousand do?"

"Whoa, steady on," said Hemi. "That's way too much. What do you reckon, Rosie? A dollar?"

"And some almond croissants," said Rosie firmly.

"Done," said Eleanor, and held out a shiny one dollar coin.

Hemi took it with a broad grin.

"Unbelievable," said Avery.

"Eh, big city cop," said Hemi. "This is how we do things around here."

"Fine," said Avery. "Charlie, we're going to—" he stopped and looked around. "Where's he gone?"

———

Charlie followed Pete down the corridor into the interview room, where he could have a conversation without looking like a crazy person.

"What's up?" he asked.

"I thought you'd want to know," said Pete. "A few of the other spooks reckon they've seen Janice."

"Oh..." Charlie tried not to feel a surge of hope in his chest.

"She's not properly connected to this world," said Pete. "You know how it is with murdered souls. She's flitting here and there, fading in and out like a radio with bad static."

"If I can find her, she might be able to tell me where she hid the proof to blackmail Ted," said Charlie.

"Reports put her anywhere from the lighthouse down to the main crossroads," said Pete. "And she's only appearing for a few seconds at a time."

"She might stabilise though? With help?"

"I'm allowed to speak ill of the dead, being one myself," said Pete. "That skeevy woman was nothing but trouble in life. She's the same in death."

"Finding her might get me off the hook. And she deserves justice," said Charlie.

Avery appeared in the doorway, closely followed by Rosie, Hemi, Eleanor, and Delia.

Charlie froze. He couldn't think of a single thing to say.

"Needed a moment alone?" said Hemi, looking sympathetic.

"Yeah," said Charlie. "Thanks."

Pete chuckled. "You need to work on your 'not talking to dead people' act."

"We'll get you processed and out of here as soon as possible," said Hemi.

"Sure," sighed Charlie. He hoped he'd be able to locate Janice's ghost soon. He hoped even more she'd lead him to something that would get him permanently out of police custody.

Ten minutes later, Charlie left the station, straight into his mum's rib crushing hug. They both got into the Jaguar Mark II, and Eleanor drove off.

She pulled up outside the Pepper Tree Hotel and his mum got out, dabbing at her eyes. Charlie felt awful. It would be his fault if his mum lost her job.

Eleanor didn't say another word until Delia had disappeared inside the hotel. Then she turned to face Charlie. Even though he was half a head taller than her, Charlie wanted to back away from her level gaze.

"Charlie," she said, "we need to talk."

29

In which Charlie has ice cream

Charlie leaned back in the passenger seat, feeling like his skin was too hot and too tight around his chest.

"We're going to get ice cream," said Eleanor firmly. She put her sunhat on, wrapped a silk scarf around her neck, and slipped on large Jackie O sunglasses.

Charlie wound down the window, glad to feel the cool breeze on his face as they headed out of town.

There was just one place people in Te Kohe meant when they said 'We're going to get ice cream.' It was Land's End Creamery, a tiny ice cream shack on the furthest bend of the ocean road between Te Kohe and the next town. It sat on the seaward side of the road, with a window where you got served ice cream, and a long bench facing out to sea where you ate the ice cream.

Charlie had eaten ice cream out there on summer days so hot the ocean glittered like a mirage, and the air barely moved, like it was too hot to be bothered stirring. He'd eaten ice cream in autumn storms, when the sea was purple and grey with rainstorms and the thick transparent plastic sheets rolled down to shield customers from the wind flapped in the gale like the shack was about to take flight.

In winter, Land's End Creamery closed, and the owner, Rajesh Patel, went to visit his relatives in Fiji. Charlie liked to think there was an ice cream mecca on the island, where Rajesh sought the wisdom of the ice cream sages, and returned with new recipes to serve across his battered rimu countertop.

He'd never asked, partly because he didn't want to lose the illusion, and partly because Rajesh might say it's true.

In any case, Land's End Creamery served an uncommonly good Taro ice cream, an exceptional Meyer Lemon Sorbet, and a divinely inspired Manuka honey Hokey Pokey.

Eleanor's car rounded the final corner, and there it was, perched on the side of the steep drop down to the Pacific ocean. There were already a few cars in the unsealed car park. It was a sunny day after all, and Charlie was not surprised people had headed out for a leisurely ice cream. A low rock wall surrounded the car park, with a small strip of grass serving as a place for customers to sit when the bar leaner was full.

Eleanor parked up and strode to the ice cream shack, handbag slung across one shoulder. She was still angry, Charlie realised, though he wasn't sure who she was angry at - Inspector Avery, or himself. Maybe both. Maybe she was still deciding which one she was more angry at, and then the sparks would fly. The problem with that hypothesis, Charlie realised, was that Inspector Avery was no longer present, and he was.

"Good afternoon," Eleanor smiled at Rajesh. "I'd like a manuka honey hokey pokey, please. In a cup. Charlie, what would you like?"

Rajesh was perhaps thirty, with a deep gravitas that gave the ice cream shack a hallowed air. He nodded and scooped two rich, creamy curls of ice cream shot through with golden honey and barley sugar into a paper cup.

"I'll have the same," said Charlie. "Thanks." He'd never told Rajesh that his father sometimes haunted the back of the shack, his maroon turban brushing the low roof beams and his long beard glowing silver. He thought Rajesh might already have a sense of this.

Eleanor and Charlie retired to the wooden bench on the lawn by the carpark. It faced out to sea, timbers weathered silver by the bright New Zealand sun.

Charlie was glad to have his ice cream. Difficult conversations were easier with ice cream.

"So, Charlie," said Eleanor. "Tell me what happened in your interview."

Eleanor listened without interrupting to Charlie's account of the police interview and its aftermath.

"I'm sorry, Charlie," said Eleanor when he'd finished. "I should have prepared you better for the interview. I didn't expect Leonard to be so useless. Or Avery to go after you quite so hard." Her eyes narrowed, and Charlie thought Avery might be coming out on top as the person Eleanor was most annoyed with.

Charlie took a mouthful of ice cream, the rich manuka honey balanced perfectly against the full cream of the vanilla. "I guess he was just doing his job."

"Not to put too fine a point on it — you screwed up royally in there," said Eleanor. "Avery thinks he's got his man. Is he wrong, Charlie?"

"What? No! I mean yes! He is wrong. I didn't kill Janice. Or try to kill Ted."

"But you have a powerful motive to kill Ted, at least. Juries love that. Why are you certain Ted murdered your dad?"

Her tone was casual, but Charlie saw her fingers tense slightly around the ice cream spoon. This was important.

When he was a kid, Charlie and his friends used to jump off the bridge that went over the narrowest part of the harbour. Standing on the bridge guardrails, the water always looked a long way down. With friends yelling dares and taunts, backing away was never an option. There was only one way to get out of the situation - jump. But there was always a moment just after you leapt when you realised there was no going back. Before: uncertainty. After: the feeling of no return and the rushing wind as you fell.

Charlie felt the uncertainty now. There was no going back once he'd told her.

"You won't believe me," he said.

"I might," said Eleanor.

"Most people don't."

"I'm not most people."

Now was the moment of no return. Charlie braced himself for the way this conversation usually went - polite disbelief, condescension, and then a subtle distancing. He could almost hear people internally crossing Charlie off the list of people you'd want to be friends with.

"I know my dad was murdered because I saw him on the night of the Jubilee."

Eleanor took a long, thoughtful spoon of ice cream. "This is the point when most people say: 'Oh, that's interesting,' and back away slowly, am I right?"

"Yeah." Charlie took a big spoonful of ice cream.

"I don't believe you, Charlie. No wait," she held a hand up. "I don't believe you because it's hard to believe something you've never seen.

But, I believe *you*. Does that make sense? I believe you, Charlie Wilson, because you're the most truthful person I've met."

"Oh." This was new territory.

"Is this the first time you've seen a ghost?"

"No. I, er, see them quite a lot. Since I was little."

"And they talk to you?"

"Yes."

Eleanor contemplated the horizon. "Well, it does explain some of the things you've done in the past."

"It does?"

"Yes. Is that why you visit the hospice every so often? My friend Grace mentioned it but was reluctant to give out any details."

Charlie gave an uncomfortable shrug. "Sometimes, old folks pass on, but they don't move on. Grace calls me in to sort it out."

"How does she know to call you in?"

"The cats. They have two of them - adopted from the animal shelter. They get antsy when there's restless ghosts around. The patients and staff notice it eventually, but the cats are an early warning system."

"Hmmm. I never picked Grace for a believer, but maybe that's what happens if you spend enough time tending the dying. Is this why you sometimes look over my shoulder when you're at my house? Do I have ghosts?"

Charlie gave an uncomfortable shrug. "There's just Old Mrs Grincham. I can try to move her on if you want. It's tricky, because she only fully shows on moonlit nights. That's why I haven't managed it yet. But if you give me free range of the place next full moon…"

"I may just do that, dear. I don't particularly want unauthorised guests in my house. So, what time did you see your dad?"

Charlie felt a sense of disorientation. The conversation kept twisting in directions he didn't expect. "You believe me?"

"I don't disbelieve you." The reflection of Eleanor's sunglasses made her eyes unreadable. "Did your father speak to you?"

Charlie huffed a laugh with no humour. "Like the ghost of Hamlet's dad?"

"Exactly like that."

Charlie took a spoonful of ice cream and sighed. It was hard to be morose while eating Land's End ice cream. "He didn't speak. I don't know what that means. Usually it's only recently passed ghosts that are hard to hear."

"How did he seem?"

"I didn't get an unhappy feeling. That's strange, isn't it? Considering he'd been murdered."

Eleanor looked sharply at Charlie. "And how did you know that?"

Charlie looked away. "I came down the stairs from the East Wing carrying the port glasses. I was about to go into the kitchen when I saw him on the stairs to the West Wing. We were looking at each other for a long moment. I said 'hi dad,' and 'can you talk to me?' and I don't know what else. He didn't say anything. Then he turned to go, and I saw the back of his head was all bashed in." Charlie closed his eyes, a deep weariness seeping into him. "Ghosts don't always show how they died. They usually retain a memory of how they were when they were alive. But he wanted me to see."

Eleanor gave his shoulder a squeeze of sympathy. "I'm sorry."

"It's ok," said Charlie. "I mean, it sucks. Big time. The thing is, the only person I can think of who'd gain by dad's death is Ted. My dad thought Ted was his friend. He trusted him. It's all I've been able to think about since the Jubilee night. That, and why my dad showed up now, after all these years."

"He probably wants to help you, dear."

"But why now?"

"Well, you certainly need help. And you're turning twenty one soon, correct?"

"In April."

"That's an age when you come into your majority. Sometimes legacies and so on are released then. It's possible Ted knows about something due to you on your twenty first that could incriminate him. It might explain why he made an effort to frame you for the murder, even though he has Dante as a backup fall guy."

"If there's something coming my way, and Ted knows about it, surely he'd have already destroyed it?"

"Perhaps. But maybe it's going to be delivered by someone Ted doesn't know about." Eleanor swirled her spoon in a circle to gather up the last of the ice cream.

"I also just heard Janice's ghost has been seen," said Charlie.

"That could be helpful."

"But she hasn't anchored herself yet. Meaning she'll be hard to find and talk to."

"Well, then that's another person to be on the lookout for," said Eleanor. "Is there any chance your father could tell you who killed him, and how to prove it?"

"I...don't know."

"Can you contact the dead? Is there a phantom phone number index, a departed directory, or anything like that?"

"Mrs Graham, are you making fun of me?"

"Not at all," she said briskly. "I'm just trying to sort out the next practical steps. Now I know you have this ability, I want to add it to our skill set."

"I can contact the dead," said Charlie slowly, "but it's not an exact science. Thursday evening at the RSA is usually the best time to do it. But as for contacting my father, well... This is the first time he's shown up in ten years. I've no idea how to get in touch again."

"Your father didn't do anything else to communicate?"

"He just... looked at me. And he looked the same as he had when I was a kid. And I realised... someday I'm going to be older than him. I keep changing, but he's stayed the same..." The sharp line of the sea's horizon went blurry and Charlie blinked rapidly to clear the tears.

"I'm sorry, Charlie." Eleanor patted him on the shoulder.

"Seeing him wasn't as much of a comfort as I thought it would be," said Charlie shakily. "I wished for it so often when I was little, and then when I got bigger, I thought it was a good thing: it meant he'd moved on. But now, I don't know what to think."

The ice cream was melting fast in the summer heat. Charlie ran his spoon around the edge of the cup and scooped up the semi-liquid cream. "Do you believe me that I didn't do it?"

"Charlie." Eleanor gave him a look that was both warm and pitying. "I find it easier to believe you can see ghosts than to believe you're a cold-blooded killer."

Charlie found he was smiling a genuine smile of relief. "So you'll carry on trying to prove my innocence?"

"You've already been arrested as the most likely suspect. It'll be an uphill struggle from here."

"I really, really, don't want to go to jail."

"You really, really messed up in your interview," said Eleanor. "But there's no point trying to change the past."

They sat together in silence while Charlie finished the last of his ice cream and Eleanor pretended not to notice him sniff and wipe his eyes with the back of his sleeve. The paper ice cream cups went into the recycling bin, and Eleanor waved goodbye to Rajesh. The ocean blue perfectly matched the sky in the side mirror of the jaguar as they drove back into town.

Charlie had no idea what they were going to do next. But for the first time in his life, he had an ally who believed something about him that most people deemed impossible. It felt good.

30

In which Eleanor is threatened

That afternoon, Eleanor was on her porch, sipping a gin and tonic in the fading gold of the late afternoon, when her phone rang.

It was an unknown number. Normally, she would ignore such intrusions, but her subconscious gave her a nudge, and she answered the call.

"Mrs Eleanor Graham?" came a familiar voice.

"Ah, Ted," said Eleanor brightly. "How lovely to hear from you."

"I made it clear back in the hotel that there would be consequences to sticking your nose where it doesn't belong," said Ted.

"The thing about communication," said Eleanor, "is that it's rarely as clear as we'd like it to be."

"I heard the police were ready to make an arrest before you got involved," said Ted. "Interfering in police business, asking questions all around town. You think you're so clever."

Eleanor didn't bother answering this one. She knew she was clever. Also, letting other people speak their mind was usually the best option.

"Eleanor Graham. You think you're so secure here in this town, with your heritage villa, and your little flower arranging group, and your gardening, and your new friends," Ted went on. His voice dripped sarcasm and malice. "Well, I have news for you."

"I would love to hear your news," said Eleanor. Her heirloom roses were blooming, spreading their sweet, soft scent into the warm summer air. Bees and bumblebees were gathering the last pollen of the day, their sleepy humming a low and comforting drone.

"I've done my homework on you, dearie," said Ted, and Eleanor made a face. Everyone she knew who used the word 'dearie,' had been an unspeakable villain. "Let's see… I own the hall where your little flower arranging circle meets every week, and the lease is up for renewal next month. I'll either double the rent, or simply boot you all out and lease it to someone else."

Eleanor took another sip of her G&T. Ted could be vicious, she knew, and he had fingers in a lot of pies, but this was small fry. She'd been expecting more.

"Oh, don't worry, I'm just getting started," said Ted, as if he'd read her thoughts. "You know how I'm about to develop main street? I've been working closely with the town council members. They'll basically do whatever I say. Very amenable. And you know what I think?"

"I'm sure you're about to tell me," said Eleanor. She did appreciate it when villains revealed their evil plans.

"I think the new access road would be better if it went on a slightly different route. It could go, for instance, right over an old but not particularly valuable row of houses. One to seventeen Fort St."

Eleanor's home was number one Fort St. She looked out over the golden English country garden, seeing it replaced with tarmac and painted road markings. And Ted was planning to do the same to her neighbours too? Just to satisfy a grudge. It was truly villainous.

"You are a piece of work, Ted Andrews," she said.

"Thank you," said Ted. "Now that you know I mean business, let me extend an olive branch. The town council meeting is at the end of the week. That's when I'll push through this road change. And you better believe it will go through. But if you stop poking around into Janice's murder, the road stays where it is."

Right. So she had a deadline. Eleanor always worked well under pressure.

"Well? Do we have a deal?"

Eleanor rolled her eyes. People like Ted wanted you to know they were more powerful and that they had you in checkmate. "I'll think about it."

"What do you mean, think about it?" Ted's voice turned rough with anger. "I'm going to demolish your house, you stupid bitch!"

"Please don't do that," said Eleanor hurriedly. She put fear into her voice, knowing that was the reaction Ted was after. "I'm just trying to help out a friend. You know how it is. This puts me in a difficult situation."

"Not my problem, sweetheart," said Ted. "You either back off now, or pay the price."

"Just wait," Eleanor flapped her hands in the air. She found acting helped put emotion into her voice on the phone. "Let me think."

"You've had your warning," said Ted. "You'll find I don't mess around, I don't compromise, and I always get what's mine."

The phone clicked off, leaving Eleanor in the ruptured peace of her scent-filled garden.

"I suppose I should consider myself warned." Eleanor's eye traced a spray of roses curling out from the pergola towards the small white bird bath in the centre of the front garden.

Ted had not, in her estimation, made an idle threat. She was sure he did have the political clout to move the road, over the protests of her and the other houses in this street. *But he can't do that if he's in jail*, she thought.

Eleanor had enjoyed her settled life in Te Kohe. And she had a duty of care - to protect her garden, her neighbours' gardens, and Charlie. On the balance of things, she thought, it was worth fighting for.

31

In which Dante learns the virtues of an appeal to justice

Te Kohe had one lawyer's office: Finch and Bailey, which resided in a squat seventies building next to the bank.

"What's the plan?" said Dante, following Eleanor up the narrow stairs to the law office door.

"I'm sure you'll know exactly what to do as the occasion arises," said Eleanor. "Just be prepared to back my play."

The waiting room was painted a uniform beige, with a curved reception desk that probably dated back to the nineties. Air conditioning circulated tepid air and a few aged magazines spread on the small coffee table completed the picture of a workplace where aspirations went to die.

Dante took an immediate dislike to the place. It reminded him of the dreary offices where he'd met handlers and received assignments.

Eleanor strode across the waiting room, ignoring the desk where

Janice would normally have sat. She opened the door with a small brass plaque on it saying 'Leonard Finch, Attorney.'

Inside, a small man with an untidy mop of black hair looked up from behind his desk. He blinked at them like a shortsighted turtle, his vague expression quickly turning to surprise as he took in his uninvited visitors.

Eleanor smiled calmly and seated herself in one of the two client chairs facing the lawyer. She motioned for Dante to do the same. Dante sat, pulling his chair sideways so he could keep an eye on the entry door behind them.

"Hello Leonard," said Eleanor. "I'm Eleanor Graham."

"Hi, Eleanor." Leonard laced his fingers together on the desk and looked at them with raised eyebrows. He probably thought this made him look dangerously perceptive, but in reality, he just looked bewildered.

"I was not impressed with your part in Charlie's police interview," said Eleanor.

"Well now," said Leonard. "Well now. I, um…"

"Yes?"

"Well, you can't just come in here and say things like that. The lad was clearly upset. He went off the rails. He should have let me do the talking."

Eleanor gave a flash of a smile. "That's one thing we can agree on. But we're here to ask you a few questions about a different matter."

Leonard's gaze shifted to Dante. "Are you wanting a lawyer for something?"

"No," said Dante.

"I'm quite happy to pay your hourly fee while you answer a few questions," said Eleanor.

"What's this all about?" A note of wariness entered Leonard's voice.

"You've been the Wilson family lawyer for a long time," said Eleanor.

Leonard sat back, frowning. "Are you with the police?"

"We're working in parallel with the police," said Eleanor.

"I don't think I can answer any of your questions," said Leonard. "It's client confidentiality, you know? I can't just talk about my clients' business."

"If you want, I can get Charlie to join us," said Eleanor. "But you might not want him to hear what you have to say."

"Excuse me?"

"To begin with," said Eleanor, "I'd like to know about Janice and her relationship with Ted."

Leonard shuffled the papers on his desk, his hands unsteady. "If you're with the police, or in parallel, or whatever, you ought to have documentation."

"Documentation? Certainly." Eleanor reached into her handbag and held out a small booklet. "My police consultancy licence. Feel free to examine it closely."

"Ok, ok." Leonard didn't even look at it, which Dante thought was a mistake. He wondered what, exactly, Eleanor had found to show him. A kitchen appliance instruction manual, perhaps?

"Ask away," said Leonard. "But I'll be calling Hemi to follow up on this."

"That is a sensible step to take," said Eleanor. "Would you please tell me, in your own words, about Adrian Wilson's death, and the aftermath?" She had adopted a professional tone, authoritative and calm.

"I don't see how that has anything to do with Janice's death," said Leonard.

"We want to clarify the possible motive for Janice's murder," said Eleanor. "I'd like to know your views on how Charlie's father died, and what, if any, role Ted or Janice may have had to play in it."

"Oh, I see." Leonard relaxed fractionally, but he still looked unhappy. "Charlie's a good lad. I don't want to make things worse for him."

"Things are not looking good for Charlie," said Eleanor. "But I agree, he is a good kid. We'd like to help him if we can."

"Oh." Leonard's face brightened. "In that case, let's see… it was a long time ago. Almost ten years now. Charlie was just a boy, about nine or ten. Adrian's boat was found offshore, drifting with the tide. He'd gone out fishing earlier that day, but he hadn't made it home, so his wife, Delia, raised the alarm. The Coast Guard searched the area, along with almost every other boat in town. His body was never found."

"Ted was Adrian's business partner, correct?" said Eleanor

"Yes, they owned the Pepper Tree Hotel together."

Dante could see Leonard was getting restless. He wondered if the man had any appointments today. Any potential witnesses…

"How is it that Delia didn't inherit her husband's share in the business?"

"Well, when we came to read the will, it turned out Adrian had left it all to Ted. Delia was quite surprised. Shocked, even."

"You were there?" asked Eleanor.

"As the family lawyer, I read the will," said Leonard. "It was not a happy affair."

"And Janice was your assistant as well?"

Dante could tell Eleanor was building a case of some sort, but he wasn't sure where she was driving.

Leonard looked down at the papers piled in front of him, like they might contain the answers he sought. "Janice has been with me for nearly twenty years."

"Why do you think Adrian left his business shares to Ted?" asked Eleanor.

"I don't know. It struck me as odd, though."

"Could you hazard a guess?" said Eleanor.

"People do odd things sometimes?" said Leonard.

"Did Adrian and Delia get along? Were they happy in their marriage?"

"I thought they were. But you never know, right? I mean, I thought my wife was happy, and then she upped and—"

"Yes, quite." Eleanor tapped her fingers on the table. "Did you witness the original will?"

"What do you mean - the original will?" Leonard's eyes darted away.

"Adrian leaving his share of the hotel to Ted was an alteration, was it not?" said Eleanor.

"Well, yes." Leonard steepled his fingers. Again, this gesture didn't have the intended effect. "Why do you ask?"

Dante could see the tension gathered in the lawyer's shoulders, his neck, and his clasped hands. He prepared himself to act if Leonard became obstructive.

"Did you witness the alteration to the will?" said Eleanor.

"Of course I did," said Leonard. "I witnessed all Adrian's business documents."

"Did you, though?" said Eleanor.

"Well, I would have had to. You can't just go changing a will without proper witnessing," Leonard's fingers clasped together, tight as a clamshell.

"You don't remember, do you? Just before, you said: 'when we came to read the will,' like it was a surprise to you as well." Eleanor's face was perfectly polite, her voice as precise as a sprung steel trap. "This was about the time of your divorce, and there, up on that shelf, is an Alcoholics Anonymous coin for nine years sober."

There was a long silence as Leonard continued to stare at Eleanor.

"If the signature on the altered will was forged, I will know it," said Eleanor. "Could you, as Adrian's attorney, say with complete confidence that you witnessed him revising his will? Would you be willing to swear that under oath?"

Leonard drew himself up to deny everything, then paused. Eleanor was looking at him not with accusation, but with sympathy.

He slumped and spread his hands on the table. Leonard stared at them like they might contain redemption. "If I admitted anything, I'd be disbarred. I might even go to jail."

"I believe in justice," said Eleanor. "I also believe in second chances. Otherwise, I would be a terrible hypocrite. My main concern is Charlie. I want to discover who killed Janice, so Charlie doesn't go down for this."

"Are you with the police?"

"Of course not," she waved dismissively. "How could I get anything done, working with all those rules? Leonard, please tell me what happened to Adrian's will."

Leonard's shoulders hunched. "I don't want to be disbarred."

"I won't let that happen," said Eleanor.

"But if you revealed the will was fake, I'd be guilty of gross negligence."

"I can do that without incriminating you," said Eleanor. "I can think of at least three ways off the top of my head."

"Legal ways?"

"What do you think?"

"You could do that?" Leonard leaned back in his chair. Now he looked almost cheerful. "It'd be good to see Ted go down. He's such a bastard. I mean, cheating a grieving widow out of her inheritance. Who even does that?"

"Well, it appears Ted does," said Eleanor. "Was there enough time in between Adrian's death and the reading of the will to substitute a fake?"

"I think so." Leonard looked vague again. "It was all a bit patchy back then."

"What about Janice?" said Eleanor. "Did she do anything unusual? Out of character?"

Leonard hesitated. "It seems strange talking of her in the past tense, but yeah… she did seem pleased with herself around that time. And she bought a new car. A flash one. Way better than her last car. Better than mine."

"That's certainly suggestive," said Eleanor. "Are there any other details from that time that could be helpful to our investigation?"

"Not especially," said Leonard. "I'm sorry."

"Very well. Thank you for your time. Dante?"

Leonard jumped to find Dante standing behind him.

"I'm happy to help you with anything else," he said as Eleanor and Dante headed for the door. "As long as it's legal."

"I will keep that in mind." Eleanor favoured him with a wry smile.

Outside in the street, Eleanor walked with a spring in her step towards Dante's Buick.

"I'm glad I didn't have to break any of his fingers to get information," said Dante.

"I know, dear," said Eleanor. "Talking things through is usually better in the long term."

"Did you find what you were looking for?"

"I think so," said Eleanor. "Janice helped Ted steal the hotel from Delia, then she blackmailed him. It's highly likely the package she planned to send to Charlie will be proof of the forged will."

Dante thought about this. "That still doesn't help Charlie get off a murder charge."

"Not yet," said Eleanor. "But Shakespeare said it best: 'what a tangled web we weave, when first we practise to deceive.' We simply unpick the net of lies, piece by piece, until we arrive at the truth."

"What do we do next?" said Dante, opening the Buick door for Eleanor.

"I need to talk to Sione, the sous chef of the Pepper Tree Hotel. It will require a fair bit of tact, though."

"I can break fingers in a tactful way," said Dante.

"I appreciate that," said Eleanor. "But hopefully, that won't be necessary. Can you please take me to Kowhai Drive?"

32

In which Eleanor is finally grateful for the lessons learned in Sunday School

Eleanor walked down the street to her intended destination, and was intrigued to see a Toyota Hilux parked on the curb in front of the house she wanted to visit. She was relieved to see the inspector was still sitting inside the vehicle, doing something business-like on his phone.

Either that, or he's playing candy crush, she thought. You never can tell.

He got out smartly from his car when he saw her turn up the small concrete pathway to number 23 Kowhai Drive.

"What are you doing here?" he said, blocking her way.

"Going to talk to Sione," she said. "Obviously."

"I think not," he said.

"I got here first," said Eleanor with a slight smile.

"I have jurisdiction," said Avery.

"That only works on other police officers," said Eleanor.

"Our deal doesn't include you getting in the way of my investigation," said Avery.

"Funny. I also didn't think you'd try to manipulate an innocent witness into a confession."

"It worked, though," said Avery, a trifle smugly. "Now we have a cold case to look into that might have a bearing on this case."

"Yes, yes, you're very clever. After your last interview, I'm certainly not allowing you to talk to Sione on your own."

"I don't see how you have a choice in the matter."

"I'm dropping in to see a dear friend's second cousin. There's no law against that," said Eleanor. "You can tag along if you like. I doubt you'll be welcome, though."

"I think Sione and I will get along just fine," said Avery. He checked his watch. "You can accompany me to the interview, as long as you don't interfere with my questions."

"I wouldn't dream of it," said Eleanor. Her smile was not meant to fill the inspector with confidence.

"Don't push me on this," said Avery, his voice low and dangerous.

Eleanor rather liked this aspect of him. "I'll be as well behaved as a churchgoing girl scout," she assured him. It sounded like a good promise, providing you didn't know the cons Eleanor had pulled as a churchgoing girl scout.

Sione's house was a modest seventies brick and tile house. It sat in what had been a flash new subdivision, back in the seventies when everyone was sure Te Kohe was set to boom.

Now, the neighbourhood had settled into a blue collar suburban doze, with comfortably flaking paint and well tended gardens.

Eleanor climbed the concrete steps to Sione's front door, keeping one step behind the Inspector. She was still peeved at how he'd treated Charlie. Although, she had to admit, it had served a purpose.

She had not yet made up her mind whether to believe Charlie saw ghosts, or to chalk him down as delusional. She had, however, resolved to keep an open mind about it. Eleanor had a great capacity for keeping an open mind, and it had gotten her out of (and into) some interesting situations.

For instance, the 1970s party and subsequent road trip with a reporter called Hunter, and his many hallucinogenic substances, would definitely not have happened if she'd kept strictly to the script. Never mind that the script had been to pose as a hotel maid in order to relieve an oil baron's mistress of her blood diamonds.

Eleanor brought her mind back to the present as Avery knocked on the sun faded white door. The jaded yellow glass with its circle pattern was as seventies as bell bottoms and discotheque.

Avery waited twenty seconds, then knocked again.

"It's Wednesday," said Eleanor. "Sione would have been working until late last night."

Heavy footsteps came towards them, and through the yellow glass, a dark shape approached.

"Hey." Sione opened the door and gazed down at them from his six foot four height. He wore basketball shorts and a Breakers singlet. His large feet were jammed into battered plastic sandals. "What's up?"

"Mr Sione Faleafa." Avery held up a card in a smart leather sheath. "I'm Inspector Avery, homicide division of the Auckland police. I'm here to question you about the Jubilee night."

Eleanor was reminded of Doctor Who and the psychic paper. She wondered if she should have forged herself credentials for this occasion.

But Sione just nodded and said, "Ok," as if police inspectors and members of the public knocked on his door to ask about murders every day.

The house smelt of carpet cleaner and crispy fried bacon. Sione kicked a small red truck out of the way as he lumbered down the dark corridor. At the back, the space opened out into a large living room, with a huge flatscreen TV, and a galley style kitchen.

"You want to sit on the couches, or at the table?" said Sione with an expansive wave that encompassed the large corner couch and a seventies Melteca dining room table.

"The couch is fine," said Avery, which Eleanor thought was a mistake.

There was a fine line between setting your interviewee at their ease and having them too relaxed. The leather couches looked comfortable enough to swallow them both whole.

"So," said Sione, throwing himself onto a couch and flicking back his impressively afro fringe, "what do you want to know?"

Avery took out his phone and an electronic stylus. "Is it ok if I record this meeting?"

"Sure, sure."

"For the record, this is just a routine interview. You're not accused of anything, you're not under arrest. However, you have the right to a lawyer, and anything you say may be recorded and used in court against you."

"If I'm not accused of anything, why would I need a lawyer?" asked Sione

To Eleanor's mind, this was a fair question.

"It's standard procedure," said Avery. "I have to tell you that."

"O-kay…" Sione looked unconvinced. "Is she with the police?"

"Eleanor Graham is here as a private consultant," said Avery smoothly. "Now, can you walk me through what happened that night?" said Avery.

"I already talked to Hemi and Rosie about all this," said Sione.

"Yes, but since this is a murder investigation," said Avery, "we want to be sure everything is as accurate as possible. It's possible you'll remember something more."

Sione flicked his eyes towards his wristwatch. "The missus and the kids are going to be home in half an hour. Can we get this wrapped up before then?"

"We'll try," said Avery. "You were the sous chef on the night of the Jubilee, correct?"

"Yeah," said Sione.

Eleanor's gaze flicked to his hands for telltale signs of nervousness, and found them. Sione's large hands were clasped around his knees. The right hand index finger beat a rapid rhythm. She smiled inwardly. Sione have the nervousness natural for anyone being questioned by the police. Just as likely, he had something to hide.

"And what time did you start work on the night of the Jubilee celebrations?"

"About three in the afternoon," said Sione. "Lots of prep to do."

"And dinner started at?"

"Eight. But there were plenty of hors d'oeuvres to get out first."

"And Charlie Wilson was working in the kitchen the whole time?"

"Yeah." Sione leaned back and crossed his well-muscled arms over his chest. "He'd been in since around three too."

"Now, when the fireworks started, at 10:30, what were you doing?"

"I was getting the canapes ready. Lots of little profiteroles, truffles, petit fours, and tiramisu. Also cheese platters."

"When did you tell Charlie to go and get the port and port glasses?"

Sione's arms tightened around his chest. "About 10:30. He needed to have them back by the time the fireworks ended. And getting the port glasses down from the top shelf can be tricky, so I sent him with plenty of time to spare."

"And when did he get back to the kitchen?"

"I don't know, man," said Sione. His thick black eyebrows drew together. "I was hella busy. You know how it is in a kitchen. There were a million things to get done, and it all had to happen yesterday."

"When was the first time you noticed Charlie was back?" Avery's stylus was poised above his phone, ready to note it down.

Eleanor tamped down her inner frustration. This line of enquiry was not going to get the answers she needed.

"I dunno," said Sione. "Maybe when Ted was down here, getting stitched up by the doc? I wasn't paying attention."

"Oh, but you were," said Eleanor.

Avery shot her a black look, which she ignored.

"I said I wasn't paying attention." Sione glowered at Eleanor. "Why is she here again?"

"I was there when Ted was getting stitched up," said Eleanor. "You were the person who knew where Hemi was, where Rosie was, and where to find the doctor."

"So? When someone gets shot, you start to notice things," said Sione. "I was in the kitchen busy the whole night. Everyone knows it."

"You wouldn't have known Janice was shot then," said Eleanor. "You were in the kitchen the whole time, remember? You would have only known when I told everyone there."

Silence filled the living room, punctuated by Sione's plastic sandal clad foot tapping on the carpet "I don't know what you're trying to say, lady," he said at last. "You trying to trick me or something?"

"We're just establishing each person's whereabouts at the time of the murder," said Avery, glaring at Eleanor.

"What I'd like to know," said Eleanor, "is who told you to send Charlie for port as soon as the fireworks started."

"He just happened to be free at the time," said Sione.

"I don't think so," said Eleanor. "Someone gave you specific instructions to send Charlie to a place far from everyone, so that he wouldn't have an alibi for the time of the murder. I want to know who that person was."

"Do I have to talk to her?" Sione said to Avery. "I don't want to answer questions when people are just making stuff up."

"This is a witness interview," Avery told Eleanor. "You don't lead the conversation and introduce conspiracy theories. If you can't keep to simple questions, I'm going to ask you to leave."

Eleanor's eyes rested on the wall opposite the TV. The faded paisley wallpaper was hardly visible under the photos of family - grandparents, uncles, aunts, nephews and cousins. There was a small dresser pushed up to the wall, and on it sat a figurine of Jesus, palms raised, next to a golden cross, and a small electric candle.

A long ago Sunday School lesson filtered into Eleanor's memory — having to write the Ten Commandments in a shaky hand in her exercise book. The memory mixed with the time she'd spent a peaceful eight days masquerading as a nun in order to evade pursuit.

"There's an innocent man's freedom on the line here," she said softly. "Don't you think Delia's worried about her son?"

Sione looked away, his gaze resting on the wall of photos.

"You don't need to answer that question," said Avery. "However, I find I'm now curious. Why did you decide to send Charlie to get the port?"

"I dunno," said Sione. "He was free at the time."

"On the busiest night of the year?" said Eleanor.

"Yeah," said Sione, jutting out his chin. "He'd just finished a job, and was looking for something else to do."

"Are you a churchgoer?" asked Eleanor.

"Of course," said Sione. "Our church is just up the road."

"So you must have gone to Sunday school when you were a child?"

Avery frowned, seeing the wall of photos and the small religious shrine.

"Yeah, why?"

"You're with the Tongan church," said Eleanor. "And I'm sure Pastor Kautai taught the Ten Commandments. There's one in particular I'm hoping you remember: 'Thou shalt not bear false witness against thy neighbour.'"

Sione blinked rapidly and uncrossed his arms, reverting to his original knee-gripping posture. He was silent for a long time. Eleanor shot a quick glance at Avery, hoping he wouldn't break the tension and give Sione an easy out. Experienced interviewer that he was, Avery simply waited.

"Look, if I tell you something, do I have to go on the record?" said Sione. "Can you do, like, witness protection or something? I don't want this to be known outside this room."

"You can do that, can't you?" said Eleanor to Avery.

"It depends on the nature of what you want to tell us," said Avery. "If it's something along the lines of, say, conspiring in a murder, then no, I can't promise any immunity."

Sione let out a long breath. "It's not that. I — our kid was sick this one time. She needed special medicine, and it wasn't subsidised. And so I might have taken a couple of bottles of the hotel wine. And sold them on Trademe to pay for the medicine."

"Let me guess," said Eleanor. "Ted found out. And instead of firing you, you ended up owing him a favour."

Sione nodded, face miserable.

"What did Ted ask you to do?" said Avery.

"It's like she said. Ted came and told me: if you do this one thing, all sins are forgiven. Send Charlie to get the port when the fireworks start. And if you breathe a word about it, I'll ruin you. Get you fired, get you a criminal record, make sure your cousin doesn't get a working visa, and he'll send someone to bust my kneecaps."

"Thorough," murmured Eleanor under her breath. More loudly, she said: "I can see why you'd want to keep this in strict confidence."

"If you don't promise to keep my name out of this," said Sione, "I'll deny everything. I'll say you used police brutality to force me into making it up."

Eleanor looked between herself, Avery, and the six foot four man opposite them. "If you say so," she said. "You're forgetting that if Ted's locked up for murder, he won't be able to do any of the things he threatened."

"We can keep this knowledge confidential," said Avery. "Though we may have to take it down in a formal deposition if the case comes to court. In which case, as Eleanor points out, Ted won't be able to fulfil any of his threats."

Sione blew out a breath. "Ok, I can do that. Sort of like taking the fifth amendment?"

"More like a sealed testimony," said Avery.

"It's been on my conscience," said Sione. "And I know if I told my pastor, or my wife, or," he grimaced, "my mum, they'd make me go tell you guys. So I'm glad I didn't have to. You came to me."

"We did indeed," said Eleanor, smiling slightly. *The good lord works in mysterious ways*, she thought.

Outside in the front yard came the sound of doors slamming. Sione's family had arrived.

"This talk stays just between us, ok?" said Sione. "I can't lose my job. And I don't want Ted Andrews as an enemy."

"You have my word this will remain restricted information," said Avery. "I'll only ask you to come forward if we are confident we can prosecute Ted. Deal?"

"Deal," said Sione. He relaxed back with a huge sigh, then levered himself off the couch. "Hey, you guys take care, eh?"

On her way out, Eleanor exchanged a brief greeting with Sione's wife, Malia. On the pavement outside the house, she and Avery faced each other.

"Your car isn't here," he said.

"Top marks, you're amazingly observant."

"You walked here?"

"Your powers of deduction astound me."

"Would you like a lift home?"

"Have you been to the Koru Ridge Estate vineyard?" said Eleanor.

"No, I've been busy conducting a murder investigation."

"It's worth a visit. They do an excellent salmon fillet. And a stellar pinot noir."

Avery stuck his hands in his trouser pockets and regarded her thoughtfully. "Are you trying to get me DUI'd?"

"Such suspicion!" Eleanor fluttered her hands, the society lady making a brief cameo appearance. "As you pointed out, I require a lift, you have a car, and it's lunch time. One glass of wine would keep you well below the legal limit. Or I can drive us home." Her smile skipped coquettish and went straight to wicked.

"Absolutely not," said Avery.

"Besides," said Eleanor, "If I'm to spend the remainder of my life behind bars, I need to enjoy every chance for luxury I can get."

"Don't be dramatic. Art forgery would be 2-4 years, max," said Avery.

"Orange just isn't my colour, mon cher."

"If you let your hair revert to its natural silver, it would be." Avery jerked his head towards the Toyota Hilux parked on the curb. "Let's go."

33

In which Dante goes bowling

In times past, Te Kohe had been an important town. The safe harbour attracted shipping, and the long river that wound inland had been used to transport goods and people. A railroad with a steam train had made its way out to the coastal town, and various people had made their living serving the travellers and merchants whose goods passed through the port.

Nowadays, the train station was all but abandoned. Old sheds stood silent with their great steel steeds - the steam engines of times past - sleeping inside.

In the eighties, however, the largest shed had been turned by an enterprising young man called Roy Webb into a ten pin bowling alley. In defiance of all good business sense, the bowling arena still functioned. Wednesday night was the main event, though some people headed in there on a Saturday afternoon, hungover and wishing the lights weren't quite so bright.

Eleanor, Dante and Charlie met there at five o'clock sharp, Wednesday evening. The bowling alley only got busy around seven, so it was easy to get a lane down one end.

Dante looked dubiously at the bowling shoes the bespectacled and pimpled youth held out to him. The soles were hard and smooth and would be no good in a combat situation. He took them anyway and followed Eleanor and Charlie over to their table to put them on.

"Why are we meeting here, Eleanor?" Charlie was saying.

"Because I love bowling," said Eleanor. "And Dante's never done it before."

"Oh. I see." Charlie's ears went pink. "It's a lot of fun," he told Dante. "I'm sure you'll enjoy it."

Dante examined the lane - smooth hardwood with a gutter on either side. At the end of the lane, the bowling pins stood arrayed like little soldiers guarding a pit. If Dante was guarding a position, he wouldn't stand in front of it. He'd take the high ground, sitting up on a building with a high velocity rifle to shoot anyone trying to enter.

"So you're meant to hit the pins with the ball?" asked Dante.

"Yes, dear," said Eleanor. "You put your thumb and two fingers in the holes here," she showed him, "and roll the ball down the lane. You want to hit the gap between the middle pin and the one just to the right of it."

"Ok," said Dante. He looked at the array of balls.

"You'll probably want one of the heavier balls available," said Eleanor. "I'll demonstrate the technique." She took two steps forward, releasing the ball onto the lane in a graceful motion, her weight transferring onto one leg. The ball rolled down the lane and struck the pins, scattering them. When the pins had finished falling, two were left standing.

"Nice one," said Charlie. He did a few stretches, then selected a ball.

A few other lanes were occupied now. Dante recognised a few Te Kohe residents: Dr Galway, Mr Whittaker, and the lady who'd refused to sell him bread at the market.

"Ten pin bowling is one of the main attractions around here on a Wednesday," said Eleanor. "Fairly soon, there won't be a single lane free." She went on to explain the rules and the scoring system.

In his mind, Dante simplified it down to 'knock over all the pins. Every time.'

They were just about to begin when Eleanor looked up towards the shoe hire booth. Her face tensed momentarily, before arranging itself into the expression Dante thought of as 'breezy and unfazed by anything.' In other words, classic Eleanor.

Inspector Avery was being handed a pair of bowling shoes by the teenager behind the counter. He turned and seemed to pick out their trio with unerring ease. He was dressed in smart casual attire - khaki dress pants, a dark blue button-down shirt, and a battered leather jacket that looked like he'd confiscated it from Steve McQueen in the 1960s.

"Inspector Avery," said Eleanor. "Care to join us for a game?"

"Thanks." Avery sat down and started putting on his shoes.

"To what do we owe the honour of your company?" said Eleanor.

"Hemi said there's only one thing going on here on a Wednesday night," said Avery. "Even policemen take breaks occasionally." He thanked an attendant as she gave him a lager in a plastic cup, presumably to avoid broken glass on the pale wood floor.

"I see... A pure coincidence you happen to be here," said Eleanor, raising an eyebrow. "Charlie, how about you start? Show us how it's done."

Charlie went for the shot, but his aim was off, perhaps distracted by

Avery's presence. The ball went off course and ended up in the gutter, rolling harmlessly past the carefully arrayed pins.

"You get two shots to try and knock the pins down," Eleanor explained. "Dante's never bowled before," she told Avery.

Dante thought two shots was more than fair. Usually, he only got one.

Charlie's second shot went better, and he knocked over eight pins.

Eleanor was next, and she took two shots to knock down all the balls.

"All right." Avery stood and selected a bowling ball. Dante could tell by the way he handled himself that he'd done this many times before. His shot rolled cleanly down the lane to take out all the pins in one go.

"Good shot. That's called a strike," Eleanor said to Dante.

Charlie had ordered chips and seemed distracted by something in the far corner of the bowling hall. Between that and his obvious discomfort with Avery being there, Dante doubted he'd be bowling well this evening.

For his part, Avery seemed unconcerned with whether he was a welcome addition to their party. He dispatched the next set of skittles in two shots with aplomb. Eleanor watched him with narrowed eyes, and Dante could see she had started working on a strategy.

"How's the case going?" she asked just as Charlie went to bowl, and the lad slipped onto one knee, the ball going wide and straight into the gutter.

"Oh, fine," said Avery. "Just chasing down a few stray leads. How are your investigations proceeding?" He dispatched another ten skittles with a fluid throw of the bowling ball, and Dante took note of his footwork.

"Very well thank you," said Eleanor, giving him a razor sharp smile. "I expect we'll be able to reveal the real culprit any day now."

"Just as well, since you are on a deadline. Care to share what you've uncovered?"

"Not especially," said Eleanor. "That reminds me, I'm going to be away for the next couple of days."

"Because?" Avery's dark eyes narrowed in surmise.

"A friend in the city might be able to help me gather intel on a certain businessman's shady dealings. I think we'll find a fairly strong motive for murder there."

"If you're using illegal means to get information, it won't be admissible in court," said Avery. "And I still want to know what you've found out so far."

"How about a wager," said Eleanor. "If you beat me in a game, I'll tell you everything we've found out so far."

"Interesting," said Avery. "What happens if I lose?"

"You answer one question about the case."

"Ah, but I want to know what you want to know," said Avery. "What question do you want answered?"

"I have so many questions." Eleanor smiled. "How about this — if you beat Charlie in the best of three frames, I'll answer all your questions. Or you answer one of mine. No information forthcoming until then. Deal?"

Avery flicked a glance at Charlie, who stood with his mouth open in surprise. One of his shoelaces had come undone and was trailing on the ground.

"Deal," said Avery.

"Ermmm," said Charlie, and fumbled the bowling ball, nearly dropping it on his foot.

"Charlie, dear, come this way," said Eleanor with a brilliant smile. "Just a minute," she said over her shoulder as she swept Charlie ten paces away for a quick talk.

Dante eyed Avery. He was certainly a good bowler, much better than Charlie, and he wondered what Eleanor was up to. He found Avery was studying him just as carefully.

"Your first time bowling?" said the inspector.

"Never had the opportunity before," said Dante.

"Accounting in Kent was too hectic for bowling?" said Avery.

Dante gave him a thin smile. "Hectic. Yes."

"Ok, let's play," said Eleanor, returning with Charlie in tow. "Who would like to go first?"

"I'll go," said Charlie. He looked determined, his shoulders set square and eyes focused.

"Be my guest," said Avery.

Just as Charlie was stepping up to begin his throw, Avery said, "I must say, though, we're fairly close to having this case solved."

Charlie shot a pained glance at Eleanor and retraced his steps. He took a deep breath and prepared to bowl again.

Avery took a meaningful look at his watch.

"Ignore him, Charlie," said Eleanor with a smile. "He's just trying to put you off your game."

"Yes, and it's working," muttered Charlie. He rolled his shoulders, trying to regain a semblance of poise.

"I have a lot of questions for you to answer," murmured Avery. "So let's get this over with."

Charlie took in a deep breath and fixed his gaze on the pins at the end of the lane. He started his runup. Avery opened his mouth to say something else, but Dante pinned him with one of his most dead-eyed looks, and Avery shut his mouth again.

The ball landed true in the middle of the lane and rolled towards the pins. It struck slightly to the right of what Eleanor had called the sweet spot, and knocked down seven pins, leaving a small trio standing on the far left of the lane.

"Well done," said Eleanor.

Charlie managed to hit the three skittles with his second shot, the last one balancing on one edge before finally toppling over.

"Phew." Charlie didn't try to disguise his relief.

It was lucky he was a gardener, not a poker player, thought Dante.

"Perhaps I should make comments as you get ready to bowl," Eleanor said to Avery with an innocent air.

"I'd expect nothing less," said Avery. He selected a ball and swung it a couple of times to test the weight.

He was just measuring his runup when Eleanor murmured: "I don't suppose police officers still carry those Smith & Wesson handcuffs? I remember them from a certain young NYC officer I knew in the eighties. That was quite a summer."

Avery's ball bounced on the lane as it landed, then veered off wildly into the gutter, rolling uselessly past the ranked pins.

Charlie grinned and blushed at the same time. "Gee," he said in a perfectly audible whisper.

"Did I say that out loud?" said Eleanor. "Dear me."

Avery gave her a quelling look that only made her smile deepen. He managed to knock down eight pins with his next shot, but Dante could tell he was rattled.

The secret, Dante knew, was never to allow anyone or anything to rattle you. But if you did get rattled, the next thing was never to continue to be rattled. Because then you ended up spiralling and screwing the whole mission. And people ended up dead. People who might be you.

Dante walked back that last thought. It was unlikely a botched bowling game would end in death. Although you never knew.

Charlie's next shot was a strike.

"Bravo," said Eleanor. Dante wondered briefly what she'd told Charlie to put him back on his game.

In Dante's estimation, Avery looked to be the class of man who wouldn't spiral. This was proved out by his next shot, which knocked down all the pins but one, which he cleared with his next shot.

"Since Charlie scored a strike," Eleanor explained to Dante, "He gets to combine the scores from his next two bowls. It's quite useful."

Charlie lined up his next shot. Dante studied the set of the young man's shoulders and how his feet met the floor. He reckoned Charlie would nail this shot. Unless he got distracted.

"I did hear unusual rumours about Charlie," said Avery, as if speaking just to Eleanor. "Something about talking to people no one else could see?"

Charlie took a deep breath. His gaze flicked over to the far corner of the bowling hall. As far as Dante could see, there was nothing of interest there. His shot went wide, only knocking over three skittles on the far left corner.

"Pity," said Avery. "You were set to win, there."

Charlie's next shot knocked over all but two of the pins.

"You did just fine, dear," said Eleanor. "I would have thought an officer of the law would play fair," she said to Avery.

"That's where you're wrong," said Avery. "Policemen cheat and take advantage any chance they get."

"Finally, something I can relate to," said Eleanor.

"But only in the pursuit of justice," said Avery.

"Eleanor doesn't take advantage of people," said Charlie. He looked indignant, and Dante was reminded of how young he was. He probably hadn't been much outside Te Kohe, let alone New Zealand.

"Only in the pursuit of what's right, dear," said Eleanor. "Let's see what the Inspector can pull out of the hat. Though I'd have thought," she continued, "that your lumbago would be giving you more trouble, in a seaside environment like this."

"Thanks for reminding me," said Avery. "It's fine, thanks."

"Your left knee looks a tad stiff though," said Eleanor. "Something about a bullet wound in the 90s?"

"You did your homework," said Avery.

"Know thine enemy," said Eleanor with a smile.

Avery's shot knocked over all but one pin, but Dante could see how he'd favoured his left knee just a fraction, making the shot miss the sweet spot. He'd never appreciated before how the power of suggestion could be used as a weapon. Probably because, in his line of work, there was no time to suggest anything. Typically, his targets never knew he was there until it was too late.

"Last shot," said Eleanor. "You can either draw or lose. Bon chance."

Avery's jaw was set, and his next shot demolished the remaining skittle.

"Well, what to do?" said Eleanor. "We can't have a draw."

Under his air of nonchalance, Avery looked peeved. Dante supposed the officer had been confident of beating Charlie.

"How about you play me?" said Dante.

"You said you've never bowled before," said Avery. "Is that true?"

"Scout's honour." Dante had never been a scout, but he'd spent plenty of time hiding from various bullies in the concrete jungle council estate where he'd grown up. Perhaps, if they had a scout group in Te Kohe, he could join as a scout leader. He could teach the kids useful survival skills. Like how to kill someone before they knew you were there.

"Hmph." Avery eyed the size of Dante's shoulders and the biceps that stretched his sweater. "I didn't know accountants had to lift heavy objects."

"Surely you're not backing down from a contest with someone who's never done this before?" said Eleanor. Her smile said exactly what her words didn't.

"Fine. Best of three shots," said Avery. "And I have the feeling I'm going to regret this," he said under his breath as he turned away.

"You understand the rules, dear?" Eleanor asked.

"Hit the pins with the ball," said Dante.

"That sums it up nicely," said Eleanor.

Dante swung the bowling ball, feeling the weight and smoothness of it. He measured the length of the lane in his mind, calibrating the size of the ball, the direction of the floor woodgrain and his estimated weight of the pins. Then he let loose.

There was a small silence.

"I've never seen anyone do that before," said Charlie. He was still staring at where the ball had struck the pins, scattering them like a mini explosion.

Avery looked like he wasn't sure whether to pull out his police badge and arrest Dante, or laugh out loud. "I think the owner of this place would prefer you not do that."

"Well done, that's definitely a strike," said Eleanor, serenely. "However, Avery's right. Roy will be upset if you carry on bowling like that. For one thing, the wooden floor might not survive. Perhaps try rolling the ball along the floor instead of firing it like a cannonball?"

Dante noticed the small piece of shrapnel he kept threaded on a cord around his neck had swung loose during his bowling efforts. He put carefully it back inside his sweater. He thought he would probably get to like bowling.

Avery gave a long suffering sigh. He limbered up his arms and shifted his weight. Dante could tell his knee was bothering him, and wondered who'd shot him all those years ago. Clearly, they hadn't been a good marksman.

Avery's bowl knocked down eight pins. The pins were reset by the machine.

Eleanor glanced over to the counter where the skinny youth was renting out shoes to the newly arrived bowlers. "Dante, dear, if you roll the ball from the start, it's less likely to make a hole half way down the lane. Roy will be so grateful."

"Okay." Dante loosed another shot. He made sure the ball contacted the lane at the beginning, but instead of rolling, it slid at speed, back spinning, to send all ten skittles flying. It stopped just before the edge of the pin pit and rolled back towards them, still spinning gently.

"I've never seen that before either," said Charlie, eyes wide. "Were you an athlete before? A fast bowler for England, maybe?"

"I've never played cricket." Dante didn't bother repeating his story about being an accountant. Neither Eleanor nor Avery believed it, and Charlie was so gullible he might one day ask Dante about double entry bookkeeping.

Avery grumbled something inaudible under his breath.

"You agreed to this," said Eleanor. She looked like she was enjoying herself.

"I didn't know I'd be playing against a one-man demolition machine," said Avery. Dante took this as a compliment. "Also, there's a bowling ball sitting in my lane."

"I can hit it out of the way with another bowling ball," offered Dante.

Avery gave another sigh. "Neither ball may survive the impact. I'll go get it myself."

By his third strike, Dante felt like he had the hang of ten pin bowling. He even got the ball to roll into the pin pit after the skittles, which made him happy.

"A deal's a deal," said Avery. A sudden smile crossed his face, making him look a lot younger, and a good deal more mischievous. "I have a story to tell my bowling buddies, at least." He sat down at the table and propped his chin on his hands. "What do you want to know about the investigation?"

Eleanor was abruptly serious. "In the ballistics report, did the bullet that killed Janice match the bullet I found in the wall of the Pepper Tree Hotel pantry?"

Avery nodded. "We're ninety nine percent certain it came from the same gun."

Eleanor's face didn't change, but Dante noticed a subtle relaxation in her shoulders. "What are your theories about the bullet in the wall?"

"You only get one question," said Avery.

"What I wonder," said Eleanor, "is if Ted didn't shoot Janice, who did? He must have had an accomplice. Viktor, perhaps?"

"Fine," said Avery. "You can have one freebie. Viktor seems a likely candidate, but it wasn't him. We have eye witness reports that put him at the Turkish baths in Rotorua on the night in question. He's clear."

"Oh well," said Eleanor. "Always good to narrow down the possibilities. Any more freebies for us?"

"I think I've given away too much already." Avery took a sip of his beer and grinned. "And now that I've had my ass handed to me by someone who's never bowled before, how about we get in some games before the owner throws us out for destroying the lane?"

Eleanor's smile was warm, and maybe even genuine. "In that case, I'll get the next round. What would you all like to drink?"

34

In which Charlie receives unwelcome guests

It was the middle of the night when Charlie woke up from a complicated dream. He had been trying to find a particular plant in his potting shed, but every time he thought he had located it, he discovered the plants had changed their position.

A slight sound had woken him. Charlie opened his eyes, then closed them again and listened. The house he and his mother lived in was small, a two bedroom bungalow out the back of Te Kohe, bordering the forest reserve. His mother had stayed the night at her cousin's after a late shift, and Charlie was alone in the house.

Something was scuffling around the front door.

No, thought Charlie. Some*one* is doing something to the front door lock. Someone is trying to get in.

Adrenaline rushed into his body and he sat up, throwing off the bedcovers. He pulled on a jumper and tiptoed down the corridor in his socks. Charlie's front door had an old fashioned lock, and from the quiet rattling of the door handle, someone had just picked it.

Heart thumping, Charlie took the short chain attached to the door and hooked it into its groove on the door frame. He jumped back when someone turned the handle and the door began to open.

With a sharp jangle, the door stopped short in its progress and the chain pulled taut. Someone outside hissed a curse. Charlie backed up, wondering desperately what he ought to do now.

Should he flee out the back door or his bedroom window? Call the police?

With a growl, whoever was outside slammed the door open. The chain stopped it, but the timber of the door frame cracked ominously.

That decided him. Charlie fled back down the corridor and into his room. He slid open the sash window and peered outside. There didn't appear to be anyone on this side of the house.

A louder crack came from the front entry, and then the sound of the door crashing into the wall. The intruder was inside. Cold with fright, Charlie grabbed his phone off his bedside table and slipped out the window. A moment later, his bedroom door smashed open, but Charlie was already swinging himself over the fence.

A muffled curse came from his bedroom as the intruder found his bed empty, then footsteps pounded along the fence line. There must have been two people.

Adrenaline swept through Charlie. If he'd tried to leave via the back door, he would have run straight into the second person.

Moonlight shone silver on the leaves as he scrambled up the small track that looped over the back of Te Kohe reserve towards the harbour. Behind him, someone shouted and two bright lights shone as the intruders entered the reserve.

Charlie sped up, his bare feet sure on the forest path. He'd been on this track a thousand times since he was a boy, and hardly needed the moonlight to find his way.

I just need to get off the trail, he thought, and let them go past me. Then I can call the police. Unless...

The lights were getting closer, along with thumping footsteps.

Charlie slipped off the track and ducked under a trailing liana vine to hide behind a puriri tree. His heart hadn't slowed from a gallop from the moment whoever it was had slammed his door open.

With a thud, his pursuers rounded the bend. They slowed down, lights flashing around the forest as they searched for Charlie.

"He must have come this way," said one voice, deep and growling.

"Doesn't matter," said the other. "By the time the police show up, his house will be well on the way."

"Eh," said the first voice. "Him getting out wasn't quite the plan, but I guess it'll do."

Charlie's heart dropped like a stone. Had they planned to set his house on fire? With him tied up inside? He shivered, the cool night air mirroring the chill in his heart.

"Let's get the hell out of here then," said the second voice. "I reckon our boy's well away."

The footsteps disappeared back down the track, but Charlie stayed frozen in place for long minutes after. Then, with shaking hands, he dialled the emergency services.

―――

Dante was instantly awake when his watch sounded a small buzzing alarm. His hand found the Ruger on his bedside table, the grip fitting comfortably into his palm. Only once he'd checked the safety and trained the gun on the door of the room did he look at his watch.

The small digital screen showed his front porch camera. Charlie stood there, looking scared, his arms wrapped tight around his chest, his feet bare below his striped pyjama pants. He kept looking back over his shoulder as he knocked on Dante's door.

Dante swung open the door and ushered Charlie inside, checking the front yard was clear of intruders before he swung the steel reinforced door shut.

"What happened?" said Dante as he led Charlie into the kitchen.

"Two guys showed up at my house," said Charlie. "I just talked to the police. They're on their way over. And the fire truck. My neighbours called them because the guys set my house on fire."

Dante checked his watch. "How long ago was this?"

"Maybe ten minutes?"

Dante frowned. "I'm sorry, Charlie, but your house might already be past saving."

Charlie's shoulders slumped. "Oh."

"Stay there," said Dante, and disappeared into the next room, carefully closing the door behind him. He put his thumb on a security pad, and a laser scanned his eyes. A moment later, hydraulics hissed and a section of the wood panelled wall slid open.

Inside, an alcove held a dozen firearms of different capabilities, as well as grenades, smoke bombs, ammunition, various edged weapons, and a small rocket launcher. Dante narrowed his eyes as he perused his options.

Eventually, he slung a Remington 700 across his back, hung a Kukri knife in its sheath on his belt, and slung a pair of night vision goggles around his neck.

He reappeared in the kitchen, and Charlie started.

"Uh, what are you doing?" he said.

"I'm going to have a look at your house," said Dante. "There were two people, you said?"

Charlie swallowed. "They followed me into the bush. I heard them say that me getting away wasn't the plan. I don't know if they planned to beat me up or..." he trailed off, looking paler than usual.

Heat spread across Dante's chest. It was an unusual sensation, and he concentrated on it, trying to figure out what it was. Heat, and a faster heart rate. Was he angry? Perhaps this was what happened when people tried to kill someone he knew.

"Dante?" said Charlie, his voice hesitant.

"Yes?"

"You're not going to kill anyone, are you?"

"Why do you ask?"

"You have a rifle over your back, and you're holding a pistol." Charlie's Adam's apple bobbed. "I don't think it's a good idea for you to go back there. I'm fine, really."

Dante loosened his grip on the pistol. "I'm fine too. I won't be long. I want you to stay here." He looked around the kitchen in perplexity. "I think there's something to eat. Maybe tea? Have some tea."

With that, Dante went into the front yard and checked the street outside. It seemed no one had followed Charlie here. Then Dante got into the Buick, placed the rifle on the passenger seat where he could easily reach it, and glided out of the garage.

Charlie stood in the kitchen, shifting his feet nervously. Dante's house was a gracious wooden villa, beautifully renovated, with golden wooden floors and high ceilings.

However, the furnishings were beyond minimalist. Cautiously, he opened the pantry, half expecting something deadly to spring at him.

All the shelves were bare except one shelf at eye height, which was loaded with protein powders, energy bars, and dehydrated food.

The cupboard above the kettle yielded one small box with an assortment of tea bags in it. It was like being in a hotel. Everything was spotless, hardly lived in. The kettle was empty, and didn't look like it had ever been used.

Charlie wanted to calm down and wait patiently, but his mind kept skipping back to the break in, and what the men following him had said. His phone buzzed, and he jumped.

The caller ID read 'Hemi' and Charlie thumbed his phone to accept the call.

"Hey, mate," said Hemi's voice. In the background, sirens sounded. "I'm at your place right now. Bit of a mess."

"Uh, what happened?"

"I was hoping you could tell me that," said Hemi. "There was a fire started in your kitchen, but the boys are putting that out now. The kitchen's ruined, and there's smoke damage throughout the house. The structure should be ok, though. We got there in time. You have insurance?"

Charlie sagged against the kitchen bench. His family home was alright. Mostly. "Yeah. We're with State."

"Should be alright then. Hey, it looks like your front door's been forced open. Where are you?"

"I'm at a friend's house," said Charlie. "I've messaged mum, but she probably won't read it her phone till tomorrow."

He wondered where Dante had gone. He hoped he hadn't found the guys who broke into his house. For a moment, something clinical and ruthless had looked out of Dante's eyes. Something that would not stop until whatever threatened it was utterly destroyed. Charlie didn't want anyone to get in the way of that.

"Well, sit tight until morning," said Hemi. "Then you can come into the station and make a statement. And we'll get a gang together, see about making your place livable until the insurance kicks in. Ok?"

"Thanks," said Charlie.

For the next half hour, Charlie prowled around the kitchen. He boiled the kettle and made tea. A glance inside the fridge revealed more bottled drinks with labels like 'max power' and 'boost,' so he drank the tea black. He briefly considered a trip outside to get lemon for the tea from the ancient tree in the back garden, but he was fairly sure he wouldn't be able to get back inside Dante's fortified villa. Also, he didn't like the idea of going outside right now. His hands still shook slightly.

The minutes ticked by, and Charlie was working up to trying a protein shake when Dante appeared in the kitchen doorway. For a tall, muscled guy, he moved as silently as a cat.

"I didn't find the men who broke in," he said. "They wore Timberland and Caterpillar boots and drove away on two Honda motorcycles."

"Did you see them?"

"No." Dante disappeared into the next room and returned without his rifle and belt knife. He looked at Charlie with a slight frown. "You need to stay somewhere, don't you?"

"Um... I can crash at my cousin's house," said Charlie. He wasn't sure where he ought to go. He didn't want his mum or his cousin to become a target for whoever was after him. Maybe he should drive down the coast and camp out on a beach for the rest of the night.

Dante was still frowning. "I have a couch," he said slowly. "And a blanket. You can stay here."

With that, he disappeared down the corridor. Charlie watched him go, feeling that if he refused now, he might hurt Dante's feelings. He also suspected that Dante had never had a friend stay at his place before. At this point, he wouldn't have been surprised to learn that Dante never slept, or maybe he slept standing up with one eye open.

Dante reappeared with a blanket over one arm.

Charlie followed him to a room half way down the corridor. Dante opened the door and Charlie saw he was right - Dante did have a couch.

It was an elegant cream affair and looked like it had never been used. It was also the only piece of furniture in the room.

Awkwardly, Dante handed Charlie the blanket.

"Is this ok?" Dante thought a bit more. "Do you want a weapon? I can provide several—"

"No, it's ok," said Charlie hurriedly. The less he knew about Dante's house and possessions, the less he might have to lie to the police about in the future. "This is, um, very nice. Thank you."

Dante's shoulders relaxed. "Oh. Good. Ok. Well. I'll see you in the morning."

And with that he was gone, leaving Charlie in the high ceilinged cream room, with one blanket, one couch, and a head full of worries.

Charlie switched off the light and lay on the couch. He stretched to full length, pulling the blanket up around his chin. He gazed up at the darkened ceiling, then at the wall where a shaft of moonlight pierced the gap in the curtains. It was a long time before he finally drifted off to sleep.

35

In which Dante discovers eggs benedict, and Charlie makes an unusual offer

Charlie awoke at dawn to the feeling that ghosts had gathered around him while he slept, staring down at him in silent vigil.

He saw the faint shimmering traces of them all around the room as he opened his eyes, like heat mirages fading as sunlight filled the room. He wondered who they'd been when they were alive, and how long they'd haunted this house.

It was an unsettling way to wake up.

In the kitchen, Dante was standing in front of the open pantry, staring at the one shelf with edible goods on it.

"Do you like protein shakes?" he asked as Charlie came in.

'I don't think I've ever tried them," said Charlie. "Do you have any coffee?"

Dante looked doubtfully at one large plastic screw top container with a gorilla and lightning bolts on the front product logo. "I think this one has caffeine in it."

"Maybe we could go out for breakfast," suggested Charlie. "And then I'd better head down to the police station."

"Do you want to have a look at your house?"

Charlie thought about it, then shook his head. "I'll do the police statement, then I'll head home. Let's have breakfast first, though."

The Frog and Gumboot was crowded, with Te Kohe residents occupying most of the tables and lined up along the bar leaner with coffees in hand.

Charlie and Dante waited in the queue that snaked along the bench of cabinet food and back towards the cafe entry.

"Heard about your house, Charlie. Crazy, huh? Glad you got out alright." A waitress bustled by with two coffees and two plates of eggs benedict balanced in her hands.

"Yeah, what did you do, Charlie? Leave the stove on? Fall asleep smoking in bed?" A man two places ahead of them in the queue smirked back at Charlie.

Dante gave the man a stare that made him mutter 'sorry' and face forward again.

"What would you like for breakfast?" said Charlie, mostly to avoid further comments from the assembled Frog and Gumboot patrons.

Dante studied the chalk covered menu boards suspended from the ceiling above the counter.

"Eggs?" he hazarded. "They have protein."

"The eggs benny they do here is legendary," said Charlie.

"Eggs benny?"

"What Sharona just carried past us."

Dante lapsed into silence, contemplating this as a possible breakfast. "They don't do protein shakes?"

"They do fruit smoothies. That one has protein in it." Charlie pointed at the smoothie section of the menu, where 'green booster' proclaimed its healthiness and delicious flavour.

"It has raw vegetables in it." Dante managed to convey that this was a step too far by about twenty miles.

"Well, the eggs benedict is always a good option," said Charlie.

At the counter, Dante ordered eggs benedict, with instructions that no vegetables were to be involved in the making of his dish. Charlie ordered the same, telling Greg that he could put any vegetables Dante didn't want onto his plate. And he ordered a triple shot long black.

They sat at a small table by the window that had become vacant just as they stepped away from the counter. Charlie twirled the steel stand with their order number in it as he stared out the window. He needed coffee before his brain would start processing the events of the previous night.

"Who do you think it was?" he said finally.

Dante didn't ask for clarification. He met Charlie's eyes and said, as if they'd already been discussing this topic for the last ten minutes: "The most likely candidate is Ted. Not him personally, but people he's hired. Both you and Eleanor are in his way. There's this package that might be on its way to you right now. And Eleanor's been hard at work to solve the murder in order to clear your name. So he has multiple reasons for wanting you intimidated or dead."

The way he ended that last sentence sent a chill running down Charlie's spine. It wasn't just that it could be true. It was the way Dante said it, as if he was discussing a routine event. Charlie wondered, not for the first time, what work Dante had done before he'd come to Te Kohe.

The eggs and coffee arrived, and Charlie dug in with gusto. It turned out that fleeing for your life in the middle of the night gave you quite the appetite. He was just polishing off the last of his breakfast and wondering if he could order more when his phone rang.

"It's Eleanor," he told Dante, and put the phone on speaker, laying it on the table between them.

"Hi Charlie," said Eleanor, "I heard what happened last night."

'How?' mouthed Charlie.

"Are you in the Frog and Gumboot?"

"Ah, yes," said Charlie. "Dante's here too. You're on speaker."

"Oh, good. Dante, I want you to keep a close eye on Charlie. Evidently we've annoyed the target of our investigation. They could just be trying to scare Charlie, but they might want him dead."

"Yes," said Dante.

"I'll be back as soon as I can. Finding the information I want has not been easy, but we're on the clock with this one."

"Do you want me to do your garden this afternoon?" asked Charlie.

"Only if you feel up to it, dear. One thing I would appreciate, though."

"What's that?"

"Could you go to the Te Kohe council meeting if I'm not back by then? I think Ted is planning something truly dreadful, and I'd like to know what it is."

"Sure, Mrs Graham. Will do."

"Thank you dear. And Dante?"

"Yes?"

"Can Charlie stay with you for a couple of days while we sort this out?"

Charlie and Dante exchanged a mutually uncertain glance.

"Yes," said Dante, at the same time as Charlie said, "it's no trouble. I can always stay at my cousin's."

"Out of the question," came Eleanor's voice. "You're in danger, Charlie. Anyone you stay with could also be a target."

"Won't staying at Dante's put him in danger?"

"I'm sure Dante can handle things," said Eleanor with such certainty that Charlie's next objection died in his throat. "So that's settled," she continued brightly. "I look forward to seeing you all soon."

―――

Outside the Frog and Gumboot, Dante retrieved his keys and slid into the Buick. "I'll drive you to the police station," he told Charlie.

"Thanks." Charlie, who had cheered up briefly over his breakfast, looked miserable again.

Dante supposed this was a natural effect of having someone try to burn down your house. He'd been involved in building damage in the past, sometimes by way of explosive devices. But he'd never been around to see the aftermath. All actions have consequences. When you stayed in one place, it was hard to escape this truth.

The Buick pulled away from the curb, heading towards the police station.

"Eleanor thinks I won't be able to go back and stay at my place until we find out who's after me," said Charlie.

"We could set a trap and ambush them at your house," said Dante. He stopped short of proposing a tripwire connected to a grenade, something he'd found effective in the past.

"I don't know if that's a great option," said Charlie. "For one thing, I doubt I'd be able to sleep at all."

"Then we'll find another way," said Dante.

"There is one thing I can do," said Charlie. "If we're properly, completely, stuck." He looked worried, like a kid about to use the credit card left by his parents only in case of emergencies.

Dante considered. "We are stuck." The next logical move would be to break into Ted's house and threaten to chop his hands off, but he wasn't sure that was a good move. Not yet, anyway.

Charlie stuck his hands in his pockets and drew in a deep breath, then blew it out again. His eyes were earnest as he told Dante, "I'm going to a thing this evening. If it works, I'll tell you all about it tomorrow."

"I'm coming with you," said Dante.

Charlie shook his head. "I'd rather you didn't."

Dante wondered if Charlie planned to break into Ted's house. "What are you going to do?" he asked.

"Oh, just talk to some people," said Charlie, then stopped as if he wished he hadn't said anything.

"Do I know them?" said Dante.

Now Charlie looked like he wanted to make his excuses and run away.

"I don't think so. They're just... people."

"Which people?"

"People who might know what happened on Jubilee Night. Or what happened to my dad."

Dante frowned. "If these people might help, why haven't you mentioned them before to Eleanor or myself? Who are they?"

Charlie stared at his shoes and made a mumbling noise.

"Either I go with you," said Dante, "or you're not going. Eleanor said to keep you safe."

"Fine!" said Charlie. "I'm just going to talk with ghosts, that's all." He had gone red in the face and was scowling.

Charlie was not good at scowling, thought Dante. Then he registered what Charlie had said. "Ghosts?"

"You heard me!"

Dante looked sidelong at Charlie. He appeared to be serious. "Ghosts," he said, testing the word out. "As in spooks? Dead people?"

"Yes." Charlie was looking huffy. "You can laugh now, if you want to."

"If it was meant to be a joke, it's not particularly funny," said Dante. "Do you mean you can talk to dead people?"

"Yes." Charlie's shoulders were hunched as if braced for ridicule.

"I've seen lots of dead people," said Dante. "But they all stopped talking after they died."

"Yes, well, some people come back after they die," said Charlie. "Some people, but not others. I don't know why. And I can see them, and talk to them."

"Are there any around now?"

Charlie scanned their surroundings with the vague look Dante had seen on his face before. He noted it down as 'Charlie's searching for dead people' look.

"There aren't. They don't often come out during the day. Especially in summer."

"Why?"

"I don't know. I've asked them, and they don't know either. I think it's because they get lazy, and don't like getting up early."

"Tonight is a full moon," said Dante. "Would they come out then?"

Charlie was looking at him strangely. "Do you mean you actually believe me?" he said in a small voice.

Dante shrugged. "I once met a man who could hear people's hearts beat, even through walls. I never figured out how he did it, but he could. He was good at his job." His job had been shooting people, often through walls, but Dante decided not to share that piece of information.

Charlie's shoulders slumped. "I didn't think you'd believe me."

Dante's lips curved upwards. Maybe this was what his therapist called a 'natural smile.' "Charlie, you're a terrible liar. If you believe you can see dead people, that's good enough for me."

"Oh."

"Are dead people good at helping to solve murders?"

"Not usually." Charlie still looked lost, as if he'd prepared a script for the next ten minutes of conversation, and things had gone wildly off track. "They're generally nosy, bossy, and want to tell you about how much better things were when they were alive. But I'll see if I can get something out of them tonight."

"Do you have to sacrifice a goat or anything?"

"Of course not," Charlie looked shocked.

"Oh. That's good." Dante had once surveilled a man for a whole day. He'd been across the street, looking through the man's window with binoculars. The man had spent seven hours watching The Omen, Rosemary's Baby, and The Exorcist I to III. Dante hoped talking to dead people wouldn't be anything like these movies. He liked goats, especially baby ones. They were cute.

"There's a place we can go talk to the spirits," said Charlie.

Dante wondered if it would include graveyards, pentagrams, and chanting.

"It's in Te Kohe," said Charlie, "at the RSA club. Fran, the manager, makes a special kawakawa gin."

"Ok," said Dante.

Charlie checked his watch. "If we go over to the RSA this evening, we'll probably catch them."

"Catch who?" asked Dante.

"The ghosts," said Charlie. "It's one of their favourite spots. They love to gossip. And if we sit in the garden under the Hoya vine, and drink kawakawa gin made from Fran's special plantation, they'll drop by for sure."

"Do we have to do all that?" said Dante.

"Well, I get bothered by ghosts all the time," said Charlie. "But they usually won't talk to me if there's anyone else there. Except at the RSA, under the flowering hoya vine, when we drink kawakawa gin. It's the rules."

"The rules?"

"That my grandmother told me. It's been like that ever since Te Kohe was founded in 1916 and the RSA was built."

"So I'll be able to see ghosts if we do it that way?"

"No. But you can ask any questions you have, and I'll relay the answers. Mostly, ghosts just want someone to listen to them. It gets a bit exhausting."

"Do ghosts tell the truth?"

"Maybe? It depends on how they were when they were alive. Also, you'll need to wear a hat inside the RSA. Fran says it's a sign of respect for the veterans."

Dante had inventoried his house when he bought it. Someone had left a fedora in the top of the linen cupboard, possibly by accident. It wasn't something he'd normally wear, but if it showed respect for veterans, then he would make an exception.

Charlie chewed on his lip for a moment, then said, "Also, there's quite a few ghosts hanging around this place. More than usual. I don't remember the house being this haunted when Mrs Davison lived here."

Dante reflected on this statement. "Can ghosts be attached to a person?"

"I don't know." Charlie looked unhappy. "It's probably nothing."

In Dante's experience, statements like this usually preceded a FUBAR of epic proportions. But he had no experience in the arena of hauntings. He didn't think even silver bullets would work on ghosts.

"I'll pick you up from the police station in an hour," he said. "Then we'll check out your house. Then we'll have lunch. And then we'll go to the RSA to question your ghosts." The last was a sentence he'd never thought he'd say.

As Dante pulled up in front of the police station to drop Charlie off, he reflected that his retirement to Te Kohe was turning out differently than he expected.

36

In which Charlie is evasive

Sitting in the Te Kohe police station interview room, Charlie fidgeted. He was becoming far too familiar with this place, and he hoped it wasn't a precursor to joining the ranks of the incarcerated.

"Sorry about the wait." Sergeant Hemi entered the room, followed by Avery. Tension coiled in Charelie's guts. Hemi was alright. Charlie had grown up with him being the policeman you went to if there was ever a problem. But seeing Avery in his perfectly tailored dark blue suit and immaculately side parted hair made him feel automatically guilty.

I haven't done anything, he thought. How guilty would I feel if I'd actually murdered Janice? He tried not to think about that, which had the effect of making him feel even worse.

"Sorry to hear about your house," said Hemi. "How are you holding up?"

"Ok, I guess," said Charlie.

"Garry's had a look at it," said Hemi. "He thinks it might be arson."

"Yeah," said Charlie, blowing out a shaky breath. "I thought it might be too."

"What made you think that?" said Hemi.

"Er, I just thought it might be," said Charlie. For some obscure reason, he didn't want to talk about the intruders. Perhaps it would make him look more guilty. He'd never had people trying to burn down his house before he was under investigation for murder.

Hemi jotted down notes on Charlie's statement into his phone. Glancing over at Avery, Charlie couldn't tell what the Inspector was thinking. He'd hardly said a word throughout the meeting, simply listening as Hemi's inquiry continued.

Finally, Hemi finished asking questions.

"Give me a minute, mate, and I'll be back with the paperwork." Hemi disappeared out of the room.

As soon as he'd gone, Avery leaned forward. "You need to be careful, Charlie. I'm investigating one murder. I don't want there to be a second."

Charlie swallowed. "I didn't murder anyone. And I'm not about to start."

Avery gave a tiny shake of his head. "You misunderstand me. You're in danger, Charlie. Don't think I didn't see the massive holes in your statement. I don't know what Eleanor told you to do, but your best option is to let us take you into protective custody. In here, I can make sure nothing happens to you. Out there, I can't."

"Oh." Charlie gathered his thoughts. "I, um…"

Hemi reappeared, holding a stack photocopied sheets in his hand. "Just a bit of paperwork. Your insurance company will want a copy of this."

"My insurance company," repeated Charlie. He wondered how long it would take for a claim to go through. He knew there were people in the Christchurch earthquake who had had to wait years for their insurance money to come through and their homes to be rebuilt. He hoped this wouldn't be the case.

"Don't worry, mate," said Hemi, clapping him on the shoulder. "We'll get this sorted out asap. The old place will be fixed up in no time."

"Thanks," said Charlie. He stared at Avery, perplexed, but the Inspector gave no sign that he was willing to carry on their previous conversation. Charlie gave up. He just wanted to get out of here.

"Sign here," indicated Hemi, "and there. And then you're free to go. Take a day off, eh? It's a shock to the system, something like this. You need to give yourself a break."

"Sure," muttered Charlie, and scrawled his signature on the page. He wanted to spend time in his garden. Then he remembered that his garden had been trampled on by firemen, and his house was probably still smoking faintly.

"Call us if you need anything, ok? Or if you think of anything that you forgot to put in your statement. Any details you can remember would help," said Hemi.

Charlie trooped out of the station door. Unexpectedly, Avery followed him. They stood, shoulder to shoulder, in the cool morning air.

"I get why you don't want to tell us everything," said Avery. "After all, you're part of an open murder investigation. That makes things adversarial. But we're still your best option if you need help. And," Avery's expression didn't alter, but Charlie heard sadness in his voice, "if you are in real trouble, Charlie... I don't want to see you end up dead."

"Uh, sure," said Charlie. Now he didn't know what to think.

"Let me know when you're ready to tell me what actually happened," said Avery.

For a moment, Charlie hesitated. But having already told Hemi a highly edited version of events, he didn't want to sit down in the police station and go over it all again. "Have a good morning, Inspector."

"Sure." Avery sounded tired, but he gave Charlie a faint smile as he left. "See you round."

37

In which Dante discusses the disposition of souls

After dropping Charlie off at the station, Dante returned home for his AA meeting. He logged into the secure connection, accessed via a satellite that, for all he knew, John owned personally.

Everyone was there, which was a good sign. The meeting proceeded smoothly, with even Frankie in a calmer frame of mind. Something about a new mistress upstate. Dante wondered how long that would last.

"Dante," said John. "I remember last week you said there was a situation developing. How have you been?"

"I have kept to the code," said Dante.

John's level gaze swept over him. "What's happening?"

Dante considered. How much did he want to share? He drew in a deep breath, then let it out slowly. "Do you believe in ghosts?"

John's brows drew together in the ghost of a frown. "I have never seen one. But I believe they exist. Why do you ask?"

"I've met someone who believes they can see ghosts. He thinks I might be haunted."

John's calm eyes regarded Dante. "At some stage, all those in our profession who are not entirely without conscience question how far the scales have tilted away from salvation. Even those who acted for a righteous cause, for king and country, come to realise that the blood we shed is still on our hands. If ghosts live in our shadow, they are only harbingers of what, perhaps, awaits us at the end of life."

Dante supposed an ex-assassin was not the best person to go to for reassurance. Still. "Have you ever heard of a way to get rid of ghosts?"

John sat back in his chair and laced his fingers together. He looked like a university professor about to give a lecture. A lethally dangerous professor. "In ancient India, it was thought that bathing in holy waters could banish ghosts. Other cultures believe a sacrifice can appease unquiet spirits if the sacrifice is of sufficient magnitude."

"I met a guy in New Orleans who said I was cursed, but he could fix it for fifty bucks," said Frankie, flexing his pectorals under his skin tight white vest. "Then again, he also told me I was a spiritually advanced soul living in harmony with the universe. I'd just killed three men and a rattlesnake, so maybe he wasn't as clued up as he thought he was."

"My grandma could see ghosts," offered Jasmine, her blue eyes widening with sincerity. "She had a touch of the sight. My mum said she passed it on to me, but I've never seen any ghosts. Gran did kill her third husband, so maybe she passed that on to me instead."

"What kind of sacrifice appeases ghosts?" asked Dante.

"The sacrifice would have to be deeply personal," said John. "Something with spiritual weight. Purely material goods would not be enough."

"I still don't know if I believe in ghosts," said Dante.

"I seen plenty of dead people," said Frankie. "No ghosts."

"That's what I thought," said Dante.

"One does not have to believe in a thing for it to be real," said John. "It may be more important to consider whether ghosts believe in you."

Dante squared his shoulders. "I can't kill ghosts."

Unexpectedly, John smiled, smoothing the austere lines of his face. "Knowing you, you're probably going to try anyway."

"That would be against the code."

"Maybe not. Ghosts are, by definition, already dead. Banishing one would move it on, perhaps giving it the closure needed to gain peace and continue its journey into the infinite."

Dante wondered if John had always been this poetic, or whether retiring from killing people had given his creative energies another outlet.

"So you're saying maybe I should try to kill these ghosts? Or move them on?"

"I think you should talk to your friend," said John. "The one who sees ghosts. If he's the real deal, he should be able to help you."

Dante's gaze grew distant as he thought about this. He wasn't sure Charlie would be able to help him. The young man had enough on his plate already. But maybe once they had resolved his current situation, he could give it a try.

"One word of warning," said John. "If ghosts are real, and they have attached themselves to you, they may not go gently. Vengeance is a powerful motivator, and it may be that these ghosts still seek revenge against you."

Dante stared a long moment at the black screen after he'd broken the secure link to the meeting. What kind of situation was he going into with Charlie and these alleged ghosts? In the past, he'd always planned meticulously before he acted. It was why he was still alive today.

Sun Tsu had said: *If you know the enemy and know yourself, you need not fear the result of a hundred battles.*

Now he was about to face an enemy he did not know. And it was possible he did not know himself as well as he had thought. His time at Te Kohe could be the beginning of a new chapter. Or perhaps it would turn out to be the last chapter in Dante's dangerously ordered life. Either way, he was determined to see it through.

38

In which Dante encounters a flowering hoya vine

Fran smiled as Dante and Charlie entered the Returned and Services Association. It was nine o'clock on a Thursday, and the regular crowd had shuffled in hours ago. A jukebox played hits from the golden years, and the patrons were washing down their burgers and chips with pints of beer.

Fran ran a slightly different RSA than some. There was no TV showing sports, no betting, and the dress code was smart casual with a hat, out of respect for those who had made the ultimate sacrifice for their country in the wars.

"One lager and one kawakawa gin please," said Charlie. "What would you like to drink, Dante?"

"Black tea. Milk, no sugar."

"Right, that," said Charlie. "And one large chips, please."

"Kawakawa gin, eh?" said Fran. "You want the usual table?"

"Thanks." Charlie gave her a sunny smile. He collected the lager and the gin and threaded his way through the tables of patrons to the courtyard out the back. A small table nestled in the corner under a lush green tropical creeper that had taken over one wall and looked like it was ready to make a spirited bid for the whole pergola above.

"That's a Hoya," said Charlie as he sat in the seat facing the wall.

"What is?"

"The creeper. It's a prime example of a Hoya Carnosa. It's going to flower soon, I think."

Dante studied the Hoya Carnosa, and then the rest of the courtyard dining area. Unlike RSA clubs back home, this was a mixed age group - families, young men and women, as well as pensioners. Dante supposed this was because only three places were open in Te Kohe after six: the pub, the hotel restaurant, and the RSA.

"It's good you're here," said Charlie. "Usually when I come here to speak to the dead I'm alone. I have to face the Hoya, otherwise it looks like I'm talking to myself. Nice hat, by the way."

Dante was wearing the dark grey fedora that came with his house. It made him look like a Chicago gangster, but Charlie didn't want to say that. He knew Dante was trying to blend in.

"So what happens now?" said Dante.

"We wait." Charlie took a sip of his beer. "By the time the chips show up, the first ghosts will arrive."

Dante didn't look concerned about a possible encounter from the other side. He nodded in thanks when a waiter placed a Royal Albert teapot, cup and saucer on his table, accompanied by a side plate with a slice of lemon on it.

"Will I be able to see them?" he asked.

"Have you seen ghosts before?" asked Charlie.

Dante thought about that, and Charlie wondered why that question would be hard to answer.

"No," he said at last.

"Then probably not," said Charlie. "I don't know exactly how it works, but so far, I'm the only person I've met who can talk with ghosts."

"What are you going to ask them?"

"If they know who killed Janice. And anything else about the murder."

"Were there ghosts at the Pepper Tree Hotel on the night of the Jubilee?"

Charlie shivered. A slight chill had crept down the back of his neck. That was something he hadn't mentioned to Dante. Ghosts liked gin, but they also liked the energy of the living.

It was tiring, talking to them, especially the needy ones. Usually, an order of chips was enough to fill the energy deficit. Sometimes an additional burger was necessary. But he would also like to have an early night, and a big glass of water with a panadol before bed. Too much ghost talking gave him a headache.

The edges of the bricks on the wall opposite him began to blur as a ghost took shape.

"Charlie?"

It was the elderly Scurringe, foremost expert on pre-1965 Te Kohe history. Charlie sighed. He'd hoped Scurringe was busy tonight.

"Hi, Mr Scurringe. How's things?"

"Passably good, me boy, passably good." Scurringe sat at the empty seat with the glass of gin in front of him and beamed at Charlie, his watery green eyes crinkling. He was wearing a horrible hairy brown hat, a large woollen scarf, a tweed suit, and ear muffs. The old man's chapped red cheeks and nose completed the effect of a Victorian arctic explorer.

Charlie guessed Scurringe had died on the coldest day of the year, but he'd never asked. It seemed insensitive.

"This is my friend Dante," said Charlie.

Dante nodded in greeting, but his gaze went straight through Scurringe.

"I heard about the Jubilee night," said Scurringe. He tapped the side of his nose meaningfully. It was something Charlie had only ever read about in old books, like those written by Dickens. "I 'spect that's why you're here. Want to know the word on the street. Well, you've come to the right place, you have. Why, this puts me in mind of the events of 1859, when Amelia Beureguard was murdered, murdered, I tell you, in sight of the chapel…"

And he was off. Charlie let the litany of historical events wash over him. It was probably too much, he thought, to get closer than 1985 in recency. Current day events were usually far beyond Scurringe. He had been dead a long time, and that seemed to give ghosts a certain lack of urgency.

The chips arrived mid-lecture, and Charlie gratefully dug in, dipping hot fried potato in spicy tomato sauce.

Dante looked dubiously at the small dish of vinegar the waitress had set out and gave his chip an experimental baptism.

"Proper malt vinegar," he said. "Good."

He said this just as Scurringe had built to the peak of his diatribe against what he called the 'immigrant scourge.' Charlie wasn't sure if this was meant to be Protestants, or Australians. Either way, Dante's comment stopped the old ghost in his tracks.

"You want to know what's going on?" he said. "Find Janice. That's all I'll say." His ghostly hand reached down to clasp the glass of gin. He lifted his hand, and a ghost gin was cupped in it. He toasted Charlie, then took a sip. "Ah," Scurringe gave a satisfied sigh. "Takes me back, that does. Summer of '54." And, like a photo fading in the sun, he shifted out of existence.

"Janice," said Charlie, and shivered. That was unlikely to be a pleasant encounter.

"Where's Janice?" asked Dante.

"I haven't seen her yet."

"Do all murdered people turn into ghosts?"

"It's a fairly high proportion."

Fran left the bar for a moment and made her way over. With a smile, she drew up an extra chair and sat in it, leaving the chair with the gin in front of it empty.

"How's tricks, Charlie?"

Once upon a time, Fran had been a champion sheep shearer, in an age when women didn't do that sort of thing. She still had a wrestler's arms, and rumour had it she'd beat Hemi in a no-holds-barred pea-knuckle match. The Te Kohe version of pea-knuckle thumb wrestling was vigorous, tending to violent. Those same rumours had put the casualty list at two tables, one bar stool, and a tray full of drinks. Charlie thought the stories might be true.

"The dead up to much this evening?" said Fran.

Charlie shook his head. "Not much so far." At Dante's slight frown, he said, "It's ok. Fran's one of the few people who knows. Her old man was desperate to get a message to her when I was a kid, so I passed it along."

Fran snorted. "He wanted me to know where in the boondocks he'd planted his secret Mach 4 Triple Zee pot plants. Like I was going to get into that. Cousin Merv was happy to know though." She bestowed a proprietorial smile on Charlie. "We've been friends ever since."

"We're trying to find out what happened to Janice," said Charlie.

"Her ghost hasn't shown up yet?"

Charlie shook his head. "No, and anyway, recently dead aren't always that helpful. They often don't remember how they died. I think it's a self-protection mechanism. To prevent trauma."

Fran sniffed. "I don't plan on coming back. Do you?" She turned to Dante.

Dante considered this. "No," he said at last.

There was a short silence. Dante reached out, took another chip, and dipped it in the malt vinegar.

"Well, alright then," said Fran. "Good luck tonight, Charlie. You want more chips?"

Charlie eyed the rapidly diminishing bowl. "Yes please."

With a wave, Fran shouldered her way back to the bar.

The hairs on the back of Charlie's neck rose.

"More ghosts?" said Dante.

"Yeah."

This time it was Mr and Mrs Patel, who'd run the greengrocers in Te Kohe for twenty five years. Mrs Patel had outlived Mr Patel by five years, but they reunited in death and seemed as content to haunt the grocery section of the new supermarket as they had been running their store.

"Charlie, how you've grown," beamed Mrs Patel. "Hasn't he, dear?"

Her husband gave Charlie the satisfied smile of a man secure in the knowledge that he would no longer have to unload cabbages at five in the morning.

The Patels knew nothing about Janice's murder. Neither did Anthea Adams, the past primary school headmistress, or Beena Murphy, the town bad girl who'd driven her mum's car off a cliff when she was nineteen.

However, they were all happy to gossip, tell Charlie what he ought to do, and offer unsolicited advice. It was coming up on ten o'clock by the time Charlie had a break from ghostly visitations.

He started on his second beer, then stopped as Reginald Harrington, local landed gentry, deceased 2012, a pillar of the community missed by many, faded into view.

"Did you ask them about Janice?" said Dante.

Reginald's hand froze on its way to lift the glass of gin.

"I mean no disrespect," said Reginald, "but I prefer not to comment on the recently dead's disposition when they are not here."

"Thank you, Mr Harrington, that's quite alright." Charlie cast a quelling look towards Dante. "I'm just wondering if you have any secret knowledge about the events of Jubilee night."

Dante's shoulders flexed slightly as he tensed. "Viktor's here," he said quietly.

"I don't think you can ask him to leave," said Charlie, equally quietly.

They both watched the mountainous form of Viktor cleave his way through the patrons of the RSA. There was only one empty table left in the courtyard - a small two person one quite near theirs.

"I could..." Dante didn't finish his sentence. He frowned and rubbed the back of his neck. "Did someone open the door to outside?"

Charlie started. Cold shivers ran from his head to his toes. Something strong was coming through. A new ghost. Or ghosts. With a quick sip of the ephemeral gin, Reginald Harrington put down his glass and vanished.

Charlie stared at the brick wall of the RSA club. A doorway was forming where there had been none before. It blew open, and now a corridor, dark and forbidding, took shape. Charlie's knuckles turned white where he gripped the edge of the table.

This was different from the affable Te Kohe ghostly scene. The feeling he had was of heaviness, dread, and anger. This was something new.

"Dante," he gasped, "do you think you may know some people who've died? People who perhaps aren't happy about being dead?"

Dante blinked at him. "Er..."

But it was now too late to say anything more because the corridor that shouldn't exist was filling up with ghosts. They gathered weight and substance, and Charlie's insides turned to ice as they sucked at his life force. He laboured to breathe, and his breath frosted as it hit the warm night air.

"Dante," Charlie whispered. "I think I might have gone a bit far..." With numb fingers, he tried to turn over the gin cup, but missed, toppling sideways in his chair.

Dante's eyes narrowed, and it seemed he'd caught a reflection in Charlie's eyes of the ghosts crowding thick at the entrance of the corridor. His hand strayed toward the underarm holster hidden under his jacket, but Charlie knew it would be no use.

The ghosts were getting ready to surge into the room, and Charlie was sure that if they did, the shock of it would stop his heart.

With a crash, a giant hand slammed down and smashed the gin glass onto the floor. Viktor loomed, glaring fiercely down into Charlie's frozen face.

"This gone on long enough," he rumbled. "Bad time to do this thing."

Dante was on his feet in an instant, every muscle in his body spring-loaded, ready to attack.

Viktor, however, was righting Charlie in his chair, giving him a shake to loosen up his locked limbs.

"Step away from Charlie." Dante's voice was low and dangerous. His hand crept under his jacket to where his gun nestled.

"Dante," Charlie wheezed. "It's ok. He's not here to fight."

"No." Viktor's face broke into a sly grin. "Too much good entertainment here, even without a fight. You," he pointed at Dante, "are not the right person to be near ghost boy when he does his spooky thing. Too much history. Too many how do they say," his grin widened, "skeletons in the closet. Too, too many."

"What is he talking about?" Dante asked Charlie.

"I just saved your friend," said Viktor. "Tell him." He stepped back and crossed his arms over his massive chest.

Charlie gulped in huge lungfuls of clean air. "I... there were too many ghosts coming," he said. "Angry ghosts. Rageful, lost souls. Viktor knocked over the gin in time. He broke the connection. He helped me." The last bit was said with wonder. How had Viktor known what was going on? Could he see ghosts too?

Viktor gave Charlie a clap on the back that nearly sent him into the bowl of chips. "You are a good boy, in way over your head. I like you. Him," he pointed at Dante, "I do not like. You should be more careful in your friends."

And with that, he marched to the RSA exit door, negotiating the crowd with remarkable agility.

They both watched him go, Charlie stunned, Dante contemplative.

Charlie let out a shaky breath. He stuffed half a dozen chips into his mouth and swallowed them just to feel warm inside. At last, after a hasty gulp of beer, he framed the question that was top of mind.

"Dante," said Charlie, "how many people have you killed?"

39

In which Dante is talkative. (For him.)

It was late, and Charlie sat on Dante's front porch, watching the bugs whirl crazily around the porch spotlight.

"I've never seen so many ghosts clustered around one person," said Charlie. He had his hands wrapped around a cup of tea Dante had made him. He was still cold, a seeping chill that seemed to come from inside him.

Dante took a long moment to reply. He gazed into the night, his features lit pale gold on one side, and hidden in shadow on the other. "I used to kill people."

Even though Charlie knew this must be the case, he still took a moment to take it in. Finally, his brain prodded him with the only question that mattered. "Why?"

Dante gave a slight shrug. "I worked for the government. MI6. The people I killed were all bad people."

"And... then you retired?"

"Yes."

Charlie took a sip of his tea, mind churning. It made sense — the dark glow that outlined Dante when the sun lit him just right, the sense of restless energy that gathered around him as the day faded. There were places, like hospitals and graveyards, that were more haunted than others. Dante was a haunted person.

"Did you kill Janice?" The question was out before Charlie could think better of it. He tensed, suddenly aware that if Dante had killed all those people, he was an exceedingly dangerous man.

"No. I haven't killed anyone for," Dante glanced at the leather band around his wrist, "one hundred and thirteen days."

Charlie had never thought of killing people as a bad habit, like smoking or daytime drinking. But maybe when you'd been doing it as a job for so long, that's what it became.

"You know, I could help you move those ghosts on," he said. "We could unhaunt you."

"Unhaunt me." Dante seemed intrigued by this. "How would you do that?"

"I have a few ideas." Charlie didn't want to say he'd be winging it. Well, he did have a few ideas, mainly from Grace, who loved to tell stories of the Tangata Whenua, and how the Maori dealt with violation of the tapu, or sacredness, of a place. Perhaps these principles could apply to people too?

Banishing the ghosts would improve Dante's life. Charlie was sure of it. And since Dante was helping him, it was only fair he did his best to help Dante with his ghost problem.

Dante eyed him. "Do you have magic powers?"

Charlie almost laughed out loud. But he didn't say 'no, everyone just thinks I'm a weirdo.' Or, 'it's hardly special to get bugged by dead people as well as living people.' The way Dante simply asked made him do a double take. Maybe I do have powers, he thought. Maybe I'm just not using them. "What do you think?"

"I thought people like you could do hexes," said Dante. "Cast the evil eye, or similar. It's what people were afraid of, back in the day. It's why so many people got burnt as witches."

"I've never tried to do a hex," said Charlie. "Mrs. Everly, who's been dead for thirty years, said all I have to do is wish super hard for the bad thing to happen. She's a bit mad, though. Even for a ghost."

"Sounds reasonable," said Dante. "Though it's not my area of expertise."

Charlie drank more tea, savouring the lemon flavour. He could practically hear the voice of Pete in his head, goading him to ask about the thing he'd been avoiding. "I've been thinking...." Charlie trailed off. "Well, it's about how we can stop Ted. I think he killed my dad. Ten years ago, when I was a kid."

"Ok," said Dante. "What do you want to do about it?"

Unlike everyone else, who didn't take Charlie seriously, Dante seemed to be thinking over why Charlie hadn't yet taken revenge against Ted.

"I was just ten, ok?" said Charlie.

"Ok."

"Anyway, I thought maybe if we could find evidence to show that Ted killed my dad, we could get him locked away," said Charlie.

"How did your father die?" said Dante.

"He disappeared off his fishing boat on a Sunday afternoon, on a mild sunny day, no bad weather, no evidence of foul play." Charlie closed his eyes, pushing away the painful memories. The grief, the shock, his mother's tears, the search with all the villagers out in their boats, his feeling of utter helplessness. People looking at him and whispering, then turning away. "His body was never found."

"I'm quite good at finding bodies," said Dante.

"Even bodies lost at sea?" asked Charlie.

"What about your ghost thing?" said Dante. "Can you use that to get us close to where his body might be?"

"Maybe..." said Charlie. "Ghosts often hang around where their physical remains are. I thought my father's ghost had moved on, but I saw him on the night of Janice's murder. It's possible he might help us." Again, the guilt over why he hadn't done this sooner hung over him.

"Whoever killed him probably took your father's body somewhere away from his boat," said Dante. "Did Ted have a boat back then?"

"A big fishing launch. I can't remember if he was out on the water that day. He might have been."

"We can start looking where your father's boat was found, then expand the search outwards from there."

Charlie liked how Dante talked about his father, like he was still a person. Not, as was more likely, a scattering of bones across the ocean floor, picked over by crayfish and sea urchins.

"I guess we could try," he said. "His boat was found drifting off the Hen and Chicken islands. But lots of locals, and the coast guard looked for ages, and never found him."

"What matters," said Dante, "is where Ted's boat was on that day. That's where we should look."

A shiver run up Charlie's spine. "Justine was a junior coast guard then. She's the chief now. She might remember."

"Ok," said Dante. "You or Eleanor can go talk to her. And then we'll hire a boat."

Guilt surged in Charlie again. "I don't know how to scuba dive." He'd developed a formidable fear of the sea since his father had disappeared.

"I can freedive," said Dante. "Down to about 55 metres."

"Freedive?" said Charlie, his eyes widening. "When you just hold your breath and go?'

"I don't like relying on tanks," said Dante.

"The coastal shelf around the islands is all around thirty metres. It only drops off several kilometres out to sea," said Charlie.

"That might work," said Dante.

"I suppose," said Charlie, "that we'll be looking close to shore - somewhere shielded from sight by an island." He shivered. The prospect of finding his father's final resting place filled him with both longing and dread.

"Ok," said Dante. "That's what we'll do when Eleanor gets back."

40

In which Eleanor calls in a favour

Eleanor hadn't been to Auckland for almost eight months. She liked the city, for all that it wasn't as flash as Sydney, or as fast-paced as Hong Kong, or as historic as London, or as exciting as New York.

Auckland was a combination city-overgrown town. It was only in the last decade or so that it had started to come into its own, with waterfront bars springing up, 24 hour nightlife in the central business district, and a thriving art scene.

She checked into her luxury hotel suite and looked out over the harbour. Winning the America's Cup in the 90s had done a lot for the central Auckland waterfront. Dockyards and fishing boats had given way to cafes, restaurants and highrise apartments. A few rusty fishing vessels, remnants of the old days, still retained the right to dock just below her hotel building.

Eleanor enjoyed this stubborn resistance to the gentrification of the port. It was part of why she liked New Zealand. Even the richest developers couldn't overturn a docking lease awarded eighty years ago to an enterprising fisherman.

Sunset turned the water pink, and the lights of Devonport across the bay were starting to glimmer golden in the twilight.

Later tonight, she would go and see the Auckland Symphony Orchestra and Choral group play 'La Traviata' in the Aotea Centre. Tomorrow morning, she would enjoy a leisurely brunch at the Viaduct before catching up on the latest art gallery exhibits. She might even pop over to Waiheke Island to see an old friend if she had time.

But right now, it was time to do what she came here for, and find out why Ted may have offed his business partner Adrian Wilson all those years ago. It was time to call in a favour.

The shop interior was dimly lit, with only the shelf lighting dialled up to make the merchandise glow. Eleanor strolled down the aisles, appreciating the artwork on display.

It wasn't the artwork she was used to, but the art of graphic novels. To her eye, it was just as creative and innovative as an avant garde artist trying to break into the gallery scene on the Lower East Side.

It was a wonder to her how this shop had survived all these years, located as it was in a backwater part of the world, far from the moneyed collectors. It was only when the shop's owner had run into trouble, and she'd lent her assistance to bail her out, that Eleanor realised the shop was a hobby — a front — for the real business.

"I didn't expect to see you again so soon," said a voice behind her.

"I'm like a bad penny, dear," said Eleanor, turning. "And how have you been keeping?"

The woman she faced had full lips, black eyeliner, an expensive purple and black hair dye job, and enough piercings to supply a small boatload of pirates.

"Good, thank you," the woman said, folding her arms. "Why are you here?"

Young people, thought Eleanor. No sense of style. No appreciation of the delicate dance of working out what the other person was up to without ever asking them directly.

"I'm here to call in a favour, Magenta," said Eleanor. "As we agreed."

"I'm hosting a Yugio game in an hour," said Magenta. "Do you think it'll take long?"

"I don't know," said Eleanor. "Maybe? You know I'm not up to date on all this techno stuff."

Magenta sighed. "Come this way." She strode down the aisle and through a door marked 'no entry.'

Eleanor followed her into an office overflowing with what she could only describe as 'tech.' Half built drones, complicated electronic gadgets, and piles of computer components crowded every horizontal surface. One wall was devoted to an enormous screen, with two more screens on either side of it for good measure.

Magenta flopped down in an ergonomic chair and spun around to face Eleanor. "If I do this for you, will it cancel out my debt? That'll be it?"

Eleanor paused and weighed this up. On the one hand, Magenta had useful skills. On the other, while she did not believe in the law, she did believe in fair play. "It will."

"Ok." Magenta cracked her knuckles and a wide smile curved her black lipstick. "Let's do this."

Half an hour later, Eleanor was staring over Magenta's shoulder at a screen full of code. It was all Greek to her, but she appreciated the art of hacking. It was like her skill set, but instead of opening people's minds, Magenta opened computer secure systems.

"This guy," said Magenta, tapping her long black-painted fingernails on a trackpad, "he's done some dodgy shit."

"Oh yes?"

"Like… there's money come in over the last few years, and I have no idea where it came from. Oh, it says it's from his Sackvale holdings, but that's a shell company owned by another shell company, and it hasn't done anything else since it was bought off the shelf. Also, the hotel makes way more than a small rural hotel should."

"Money laundering," mused Eleanor. "Seems like Ted's style."

"Then there's his crypto holdings," continued Magenta. "He bought at not a bad time, but he's been a bit reckless. He leveraged his money to the hilt in the crypto boom, then saw a fair chunk of change vanish in the crash."

Eleanor watched the windows open and close with dizzying speed as Magenta's fingers danced across the keyboard. She shut her eyes, momentarily queasy. Give me forged artwork or fake identities any day, she thought. So much simpler.

"So he needs to make money fast," said Eleanor.

"Heck yeah," said Magenta. "If he doesn't, his loan payments are due to go up in four, maybe five months tops. And then he's in real trouble."

"He couldn't just make money appear, like before?"

"Maybe," Magenta shrugged. "But the way this is looking, it would need to be fat stacks."

"Okay..." Eleanor felt a momentary longing for a Marlboro Red. She hadn't smoked in decades, but something about digging into illicit doings reminded her tastebuds of cigarette smoke and Hennessy.

"Is that it?" asked Magenta.

"Not quite. I need you to go back ten years and tell me what you can find. What were Ted's holdings, how leveraged was he, what debt did he have?"

Magenta leaned back in her chair. "To do that, I'm going to have to go to riskier places. Government records and suchlike."

"Which you can."

"Yeah, but... if anything goes wrong, and this leaves a trail, I could end up drawing heat."

"So be careful."

"Dammit, Eleanor! I'm not doing that stuff any more. I'm going straight. I've got responsibilities! I've got—" Magenta broke off, glaring at the screen.

"When you came to me for help," said Eleanor softly, "I helped you. Think about the consequences if I hadn't. Jail time would've been a mercy for you."

"Yeah, I know, but..." Magenta's eyebrows drew down in a scowl. "I'm not ungrateful, I just..."

"I don't need your gratitude. I just need you to find this information for me," said Eleanor. "And then we're quits."

"I'll never see you again?"

Eleanor smiled thinly. "Unless you screw up again and need someone to smooth things over with whoever's after your blood."

"You know that wasn't my fault!"

"In the world you strayed into, dear, no one cares whose fault it is. They just want the goods. And if the goods aren't as promised, well... They like to make an example."

"You're like, old enough to be my grandmother," huffed Magenta. "How do you even know people like that?"

Eleanor's smile deepened, though if Magenta had been watching her, she would have noticed a hint of sadness in her expression. "Live long enough, and you'll meet all kinds of people."

"It's just.. Is there anything else you want? Breaking into the IRD is going to look real bad on my resume."

"I'm afraid it's not up for negotiation," said Eleanor.

"Fine," said Magenta. "I've got my Yugio guys coming soon, and this will take a while. Come by tomorrow morning, and I'll give you everything I can find."

"Thank you dear," said Eleanor. "I have complete faith in you."

"Mum?" A toddler, eyes wide, poked her head around the door.

"Hi sweetie," said Magenta, a smile hastily plastered onto her face. "I'm coming soon. Two minutes."

Eleanor sighed internally. No wonder Magenta was going straight. Maybe she should just let it slide... but no. She steeled herself. If she didn't solve this murder, Charlie could be the one going to jail, and he didn't deserve that. Sometimes, doing the right thing felt like the wrong thing. And that was life.

"I'll come by tomorrow," she said.

41

In which Charlie ventures into new territory

On a Friday evening, the Te Kohe town hall was typically commandeered by the under-15s tap dance group, followed by the Spotted Skink Preservation Society.

But on this occasion, both those groups had been cancelled in typical high-handed fashion when Ted Andrews had announced an emergency town council meeting.

Charlie arrived early with Dante. Eleanor was still in Auckland, so Charlie was attending on her behalf. 'Ted's made convincing threats,' she'd said. 'Be a dear and see if he's ready to deliver on them, please?'

They stood at the back while Dante scoped the place out, and Charlie smiled and greeted people.

At eight o'clock, the hall began to fill up with members of the community. Snatches of conversation drifted into Charlie's ears as he strolled forward to sit with Dante near the front of the hall.

'And I heard Ted's bound to push it through this time, there's no one to stop him.' 'All those Aucklanders, ready to move in...' '...and our rates will go up, of course...' '...can't stop progress...' '...just as long as it doesn't go through my backyard...'

Gradually, the hall filled as the citizens of Te Kohe arrayed themselves on wooden benches facing the front of the hall.

There, a long table faced the assembled throng, with seats for six council members. The seats were currently empty. Presumably, the council members would make a grand entrance when the time was right.

There were also two podiums on each side of the table. One was for concerned members of the public to voice their complaints, and the other was for Ted, who had proposed to answer all questions. And then do exactly what he pleased, thought Charlie.

A small round lady at the front began to ring a bell, and the noise of many conversations dimmed to a murmur.

The council members strode in from the door at the back of the hall. Charlie knew the door connected to the kitchen, and he wondered what the council members had been talking about as they waited, crammed in between the tea bench and the row of hot plates.

With a certain amount of bustle and 'you sit there, oh no, you sit here,' the council members seated themselves.

Charlie had known them all since he was a child. The lineup hadn't changed much. There was Mr Whittaker, a tall, bespectacled man, with large ears and a beaky nose. Next to him sat Mabel Kirwin, a skinny lady with large round glasses and her hair in a messy grey bun. The third man was Timon Johns, round and red-faced, with a cheap synthetic suit half a size too large for him. The fourth was Ms Jacobs, a gruff lady with an honest to god mullet, and fifth was Damion Creighton, a man with a boxer's build and thick knuckled hands to match.

The sixth lady was stocky, in her thirties, with dark curly hair and a humorous tilt to her lips. Her olive skin shone under the cheap fluorescent lights and she looked twice as alive as anyone else in the room.

Charlie knew her from the Botanical Society - a Miss Andrea Kingi. She was also the local vet and pet shop owner.

Her eye caught his and a wry smile lifted one side of her mouth higher than the other, her hazel eyes crinkling up at the corners. Even though his stomach was full of nerves, Charlie found himself smiling back.

The bell-ringing lady stepped up to the podium, coughed into the microphone, and said: "Welcome to the January meeting of the Te Kohe town council. On the agenda tonight is the levy for the new rugby field drainage, the additional parking spaces outside the foursquare on main street, and a change to the roading for the development proposed by Ted Andrews."

Good-natured groans greeted the first item, boredom the second, and a tense silence the third.

Charlie tuned out as the councillors' voices droned on about drainage costs and whether removing an eighty year old pōhutukawa tree could be justified to provide the local Foursquare with two more parking places. (It turns out it wasn't. Charlie was glad of that.)

Then the third councillor passed the microphone down to the end of the table. Andrea took it and stood up, her face serious.

"We have reached the final issue on the agenda today," she said. "For those of you who don't know me, I'm Andrea Kingi, and we are here to find out what the community concerns are about the changes to the development plan proposed by Ted Andrews." She raised her voice above the sudden hubbub of noise from the audience. "We have not come to a decision yet. We will be voting on Thursday in a closed session - four days from now. This is your chance to let your elected council members know where you stand so that we can reach a democratic decision."

She sat down, and the crowd noise continued unabated.

One voice rose above the rest: "And we know Ted's paying you all off! It's illegal, what he's proposing. It'll put people on the street who've lived here for generations. Shame on you! Shame on you all. We will not be denied!"

The person yelling this impassioned appeal had risen to his feet - a short man with grey hair that stuck up in unruly tufts. He wore a tweed jacket with elbow patches and an expression of short-sighted outrage.

Councillor Damion Creighton took the microphone, his vast boxer's hands making it look small. "Now, Bennet, you'll have your say later. First, though, Ted Andrews is going to make his presentation. Then you can all line up to take the podium in an orderly fashion and let rip."

There was a small ripple of laughter at this.

"I'm just saying," huffed Bennet, "there's no democracy here. You're all bought and sold. That's all there is about it. Bunch of flunkeys." He glared around the room.

"Right," said Damion. "Let's kick this off. Please welcome Ted Andrews to the stage."

Rumblings and a chorus of 'boos' greeted this announcement.

"Load of bloody wimps," muttered Bennet.

Ted Andrews ducked out of the kitchen and walked to the podium, all smiles and self assurance. Behind him came the bulk of Viktor and an even larger man with facial tattoos and a black beanie covering his dreadlocked head.

The two heavies were carrying a large stand displaying glossy renderings of a modern town centre with broad avenues, glass and steel lowrise buildings, and obnoxiously happy families. The effect was incongruous, as if the two thugs had somehow gotten lost in a real estate convention. They put the display down behind Ted's podium and retired to stand at the back of the hall, looking menacing.

"Wonderful to see you all. Just wonderful. What a crowd." Ted bounced in place behind the podium, smiling like a toad who had just sighted a particularly juicy fly.

"Feck off and die, Ted!" growled Bennet. The people sitting next to Bennet laughed.

"Now, now," said Ted, "I understand you've all heard the worst about this development. But the fact is, Te Kohe has been stagnant for half a century. Population is shrinking, not growing. All our young 'uns are leaving, soon as they can, because there's no jobs here! And what I'm proposing is going to change all that. You'll once again be part of a thriving hub..."

Charlie listened with growing concern as Ted launched into a polished speech that hit all the right notes. There'd be an extra fund set up to renovate the retirement home, a new school gymnasium, and the main street shops would get a facelift. It all sounded rosy. People opposing the development were stuck in the mud, their 'not in my backyard' mentality depriving everyone else of the growth their town deserved.

Looking at the faces in the crowd, Charlie could see some of them nodding along. His heart sank.

"And lastly, there's something of a more personal nature I want to do," said Ted. "As you all know, my dear friend and business partner Adrian passed away ten years ago. I thought it would be fitting to erect a statue in the centre of the new development to memorialise him. A piece by a local artist. Adrian gave me the best start in life a man could want, and it's only right that I honour his memory now."

Ted's beady eyes scanned the crowd, looking for him, and Charlie turned away, nausea churning his stomach.

"Would you like me to kill him for you?" asked Dante. "Then you can banish his ghost."

"Thanks, it's alright," said Charlie. He straightened his spine and squared his shoulders. Funnily enough, Dante's offer did make him feel better.

"Any questions from the floor?" asked Councillor Damion, and half a dozen people sprang to their feet.

To no one's surprise, the first person to take the microphone was Bennet. The small man was practically vibrating with outrage.

"And what do you propose for the people whose homes you're going to bulldoze?" he asked Ted. "Who decides what 'fair compensation' is, you... you predator!"

"Bennet, we want to keep this civil," rumbled Damion.

"That's a fair question," mused Ted. "Everyone whose house falls within the proposed development road changes will get market rate cash for their house, and first dibs on the new apartments we're going to build along main street."

"Apartments!" blustered Bennet. "You're going to replace spacious, hundred year old villas with your cheap, crappy, shoebox apartments! You've got a bloody nerve."

"I'm replacing old, leaky, cold and damp villas with state of the art, all mod cons, apartments, each guaranteed a harbour view," said Ted smoothly. "And as you'll see, we've actually changed the proposed road route to accommodate a further thirty homes, in consultation with the community and the local iwi." At a nod from Ted, Viktor walked forward to pin a large map onto the display board with the new road highlighted.

Charlie winced. True to Ted's threat, the proposed road went right over Eleanor's house. Charlie thought of her garden with its stately roses and heirloom apple trees. Destroying it was a crime to add to the long list of Ted's crimes. But this one might actually be legal.

A heat started to build in his chest, then a burning behind his eyes. In the past, when Charlie had been this angry, he'd always turned his attention elsewhere before it grew too strong.

Now, however, he didn't have anything to distract him. And, he was realising, as the heat built and built, he was fantastically, incandescently, furious.

Ted had killed his father. He'd stolen from his mother. He'd murdered Janice, and tried to frame himself and Dante. And now, the bastard was trying to destroy his friend's house. With its precious, cherished, and irreplaceable garden.

As if in a dream, Charlie rose and walked down the aisle to stand in the line of people asking Ted questions.

Currently, occupying the podium was Xander Fields, owner of the local hardware shop, and one of Ted's tenants. It was clear Xander was a shill for Ted. The questions he lobbed at Ted were canned, setting him up for well polished answers.

"Of course, the refurbishment of High Street will be free of charge," Ted was saying. "It's my gesture of thanks to the community." He gave a huge off-the-shelf smile. "Thanks Xander. Who's next? My, my, it's Charlie Wilson. What an unexpected pleasure."

Charlie brushed past Xander and stood behind the podium. His hands were shaking, and he didn't know whether it was from fright or anger.

Speaking in public always terrified Charlie. But his fury at Ted hadn't abated when he took action. If anything, it was growing worse, the heat spreading down to his belly. He wondered distantly if he was about to have a stroke. He was too young for that, surely?

"So, Charlie, m'lad," said Ted. "What can I do you for today?"

Charlie took a breath and stopped. He'd come up here, propelled by outrage, and now he didn't have a single thought in his head.

"Sudden attack of nerves?" said Ted indulgently. "Happens to the best of us."

There was scattered laughter in the hall, and Charlie saw the slightly pained expressions of people who were seeing something embarrassing and hoped it wouldn't carry on for too much longer.

"Charlie," said Ted, a condescending tone entering his voice, "you know I have a lot of time for you. Your old man was one of my best friends as well as my business partner. But there's a lot of other people waiting to ask questions. Maybe we should talk after?"

Panicked, Charlie looked over the crowd, hoping for inspiration. Leaning back on his bench like a sinister shadow, Dante didn't inspire confidence. But a half-familiar shape right at the back of the hall gave him pause. A silhouette, hard to make out in the dim lights. But it was a shape so achingly familiar Charlie's heart surged in his chest.

The ghost of his father gave him a brief salute, and all at once, Charlie knew what he was going to do.

"I want you all to know about the Maori burial ground," he said.

"What Maori burial ground?" asked Ted. The friendly note had gone out of his voice.

"The one on the corner of Regent St and Bay Drive. Right where you want to dig up everything for the new road."

"There's no mention of that in any of the council documents," said Ted. "My lawyers have gone through everything."

"That may be so, but there is a significant burial site there," said Charlie.

"And how do you know this?" sneered Ted. "Spooky Charlie, still seeing things that aren't there?"

All the shame from his childhood came charging back, but Charlie faced it down. Now was not the time to let it own him.

"There are remains from the 1870s," he said. "From a battle between the Ngāti Hinepū and Ngāti Pātū. Chief Rangiheke is buried there, and digging up the ground would disturb his resting place."

"Where's your proof?" said Ted. "You can't just come in here, proclaiming this stuff. The iwi hasn't said anything about a burial ground."

"I just know," said Charlie.

"This is just another of your made-up fantasies," scoffed Ted. "Councillors, surely you're not going to take this seriously."

"Charlie," said Damion, "how do you know Maori remains are buried where Ted wants to put a new road?"

"He doesn't. He's just trying to block this thing from going through. Getting in my way, like—" Ted broke off in mid sentence and tried to look as if he hadn't.

"Like my dad?" said Charlie, and now he was getting mad again. "My dad, getting in your way, like he did just before he disappeared? Is that what you were going to say, Ted?"

"This has gone far enough," said Ted. "I've been tolerant because me and your family go way back, but I'm not going to let a little upstart like you spread wild rumours. And might I remind you all, this young man is a suspect in a murder trial. Charlie, step away from the mic now and let someone else have their say."

"Actually, Ted, we'd quite like to hear what Charlie has to say," said Andrea. Her smile was pleasant, but her voice didn't give an inch.

Charlie gathered his thoughts. He felt like he was swimming upstream against a strong current, but if he could just grab onto a root or tree branch, and get himself out of the water...

"All you have to do is dig down three feet and you'll find the bones," he said. "I can show you exactly where."

"I can't just go digging up someone's backyard because of your delusions," said Ted.

"You're planning to bulldoze the whole row of houses and gardens," said Charlie. "This will take all of fifteen minutes, and leave a hole about two feet square."

"We could ask an iwi representative to do the honours," said Andrea. "I'd like to see if Charlie's right."

"Oh, you would, would you?" snarled Ted. "The problem with you people is you can't stand anyone else succeeding. It sticks right in your craw. You're like those crabs in the barrel that pull down anyone who's trying to make it in this world. I don't have to listen to any of you. I've got everything I need to—."

"To push this through?" Charlie's head was finally clear, though the fires of anger still warmed his soul. "To what exactly are you referring? What leverage do you plan to use on the Te Kohe council?"

"You're mad, boy," spat Ted. "Always were, always will be. What I said was that the council's made their decision. You can't overturn it with some bullshit story."

"They haven't made their decision," said Charlie. "That's why we're here."

"Your dad was half mad too," said Ted, and with that, Charlie saw red.

Ted, mistaking his white face for fear instead of fury, smirked. "No one will listen to your tales. What are you going to do — hex me?"

And with that, the rage inside of Charlie took elemental form. With a joyful 'whoosh' the display stand behind Ted, with all its glossy development photos and colour coded maps, burst into flame.

"Holy shit!" "Fire!" "Help!" Shouts of shock and fright filled the air as people in the front row leapt back from the fire. Black smoke billowed as the photos curled in the blaze.

Ted's frightened gaze lit on Charlie, and Charlie knew that, no matter what he might do or say later, Ted was suddenly afraid of him.

"Stand clear!"

AJ Simpson, the local volunteer fireman, had seized an extinguisher from the kitchen. He tore off the safety tab and aimed a torrent of foam at the flames. With a hiss, the foaming CO_2 engulfed the display stand, letting loose even more acrid smoke.

"I don't feel so good," muttered Ted. His face was pale and sweaty as he leaned on the podium, swaying gently.

"Show is over, time to go home," said Viktor, stepping away from the wall where he'd been lounging. "I will call doctor."

"Yes, do that," said Ted.

Viktor shot Charlie a sardonic look as he and the other minder hustled Ted away.

With Ted gone, the meeting soon broke down in confusion.

Charlie stood behind the podium, watching the chaos of people arguing over what started the fire, and trying to get the smouldering remains outside before the sprinklers went off.

He was empty, spent. And he was also deeply, intensely, wonderfully satisfied.

Finally, he'd done the thing he'd always feared he could do. And it had worked.

"Did you do a hex?" asked Dante as they left the hall. Bennet had still been congratulating Charlie, though his enthusiasm dimmed slightly as Dante had loomed over his shoulder.

"I think so," said Charlie.

Dante nodded thoughtfully. "A hex would be a useful concealed weapon. Do you know what range you can cast hexes from?"

"Er, no," said Charlie. He'd never thought of a hex as a weapon with a set of specifications. But then again, he'd never tried to cast one before. It was an evening of firsts.

42

In which Dante encounters New Zealand fur seals

Dante eyed Bernard's boat — a grey aluminium craft with two strong motors and a small cabin. It was most definitely kitted out for fishing, with rod holders, nets, lures and sinkers neatly arrayed around the boat.

Eleanor had arrived back late last night, and promptly agreed to their plan. She'd organised a friend to take them out in his boat, and found likely places to look from Justine, who'd been in the Coast Guard when Adrian had disappeared.

Bernard grinned up at them as he pulled alongside the dock. He was wearing a red woollen hat, his large walrus moustaches damp with morning mist.

"Nice morning for it! Glad to finally get you out in my boat, Eleanor." He handed Eleanor down into the boat like the Queen. Charlie thumped in after. Dante lowered his freedive bag into the boat, then stepped aboard.

He scanned the dockyard as Bernard swung the tiller to take off from the pier. There was no movement, and no sign of anyone observing them. That proved nothing in Dante's world, though.

The motor chugged and then growled as they headed out of the harbour. Mist lay close around them, and the water was a deep emerald green.

The swell was slight, which Dante was glad of. He didn't know how deep he'd have to dive, and a calm surface would make preparations easier.

"Where are we headed?" said Bernard, voice raised above the noise of the engine.

"To start off, we want to anchor off the seaward side of Saddleback Island," said Eleanor.

"Right you are." Bernard turned the boat south into a thicker cloud of mist.

The island loomed out of the whiteness, a rocky bluff with a double peak that gave it its name. In the grey uncertain light it was ghostlike, the black rock and dense bush cover rendered ethereal by the mist.

Charlie scrambled to the bow of the boat and opened the anchor locker. At Bernard's command, he heaved the anchor overboard. The boat engine roared as Bernard threw it into reverse and the chain links rattled into the ocean as the boat backed into a small rocky bay.

"That'll do," said Bernard, and Charlie flipped the anchor lock into place. The boat engine cut to a low hum, and they drifted for a silent minute while Bernard checked the anchor was securely set.

Then he cut the engine entirely and the world was filled with quieter noises: the lapping of waves against the boat, the cry of a black-backed gull high above, and the suck, hiss of the ocean meeting the seaweed clad rocks of the island.

Charlie climbed back into the boat and gazed towards the island, his eyes going unfocused as the mist blew past.

Dante opened his dive bag and pulled out his wetsuit, snorkel, mask, weight belt, dive knife, and flippers. He wrapped his towel around his waist and methodically stripped off, folding his clothes back in the bag. He caught Eleanor giving him an admiring glance as he pulled off his sweater.

Dante knew he kept in good shape. He supposed no one had seen him topless in a long time. Something about the job discouraged intimate relationships. Anyway, he didn't think Eleanor was actually interested, just appreciative.

He pulled the wetsuit hood over his head and then spat on his mask, spreading the saliva evenly across the glass to prevent it fogging.

"Where do you think I should look?" he asked Charlie.

The young man was gazing into the mist. His face had lapsed into the vague, introspective face Dante had labelled as 'Charlie listens for ghosts.'

"I haven't seen anything yet," Charlie murmured. "I thought maybe he'd be here..."

Dante didn't need to ask who Charlie meant. He snapped the diving mask into place on his face, then pushed it up to rest on his forehead.

"I can start doing a sweep of the area," he said.

"When I talked to Justine, there was one detail that stood out," said Eleanor. "Adrian's boat had a large metal storage chest at the back of it. When his boat was found, the chest was missing. If he was murdered, and his body was dumped, that becomes quite suggestive."

"That's what you're looking for?" Bernard joined their tight circle, swaying slightly with the motion of the boat. "I remember Delia saying it was missing from the boat and wasn't that strange. Of course, no one listened to her."

Charlie stiffened. "I see something."

He pointed towards the island's shore, where a deep gash in the rock face cut down into the green waters.

"I think I saw him," Charlie whispered. "Can you take a look over there?"

"Ok," said Dante.

"Can I do anything to help?" asked Charlie. He was looking worried.

"It's fine," said Dante.

"It's at least twenty metres down to the seabed here," called Bernard. He was looking at his depth sounder. "It'll be similar over there. This island comes straight up out of the sea floor."

Dante sat on the small deck at the stern of the boat and pulled his flippers on. They were the long, flexible fins of a freediver, built for slow, graceful movement. He checked his mask was well sealed onto his face one last time, then slipped into the water.

It was summer in Te Kohe, but this far south, the waters of the Pacific were still cool. Dante peered into the depths, seeing nothing but emerald green with shafts of sunlight cutting through it like an oceanic cathedral.

Here there might be Kahawai, Hapuku, Moki, Kingfish. And there might also be Bronze Whalers, Makos, and even Great Whites, the empress of sharks. The salt waters only allowed for five metres of visibility. Like life, dangers could lurk here unseen until it was too late.

A dark shadow loomed up ahead. He was coming close to the island. Dante surfaced briefly to check he was headed for the vertical gash in the rock that Charlie had pointed to.

Another minute of finning, and he was close enough to the island to see black volcanic rock and the swirling brown tendrils of kelp clinging to them.

A rush of silver bubbles, and a brown shape sped past him. Surprised, Dante coughed into his snorkel. The shape doubled back, and now he knew it: a fur seal, dark eyes curious, spiralled past him, keeping well out of range.

Near the rockface, the water was misty with the myriad bubbles caused by the waving branches of kelp. The swell that had seemed slight when they were on the boat surged three feet up the rocks with every pulse. Dante finned backwards, careful not to get thrown against the rock wall.

There was the cleft in the rock, a dark crevasse leading down into the water.

Dante tread water for a few seconds, looking up at the dark island wreathed in mist. He removed the snorkel from his mouth and floated on his back, slowing his heart rate and relaxing every muscle. Then he took a deep breath, and dived.

A few kicks with his fins, and the pressure of the water closed in around him. He equalised his ears and pushed deeper. Now he was speeding down the rock face, past kelp forests, past starfish clinging to the rocks, past sea anemones and barnacles shining white against the obsidian rock.

Dante glanced over his shoulder. The surface of the water rippled silver, a long way above him. The seal had followed him down and danced in the ocean's eddies, an inquisitive onlooker.

This far down, the surge of the ocean around the island had stilled. Kelp waved gently in the dark jade waters, a ceaselessly rippling forest that obscured the crevasse.

Far below, Dante saw the sea floor, where black rock met silver sand. His lungs burned, but he was fairly sure he could make it to the bottom and back up again. A stray strand of kelp fluttered against the back of his neck, startling him.

His heart beat slowed as he carried on down. Now he had reached the point where he no longer needed to kick his flippers. He sank like an anchor, gliding into the depths, the tightening pressure on his lungs the best measure of how deep he'd gone.

At last, Dante reached the sand. He rested the points of his flippers delicately on the ocean floor and looked up. The surface was a long, long way away. The light was dimmer here. He checked his dive watch and saw that he was thirty metres down.

The seal flashed past, at home in this environment in a way he would never be. Down here, far from life and air, was peace. Down here where he couldn't breathe, his heart beating slower and slower, Dante had at last reached a place where he could rest.

Death is all around you, he thought. If Dante waited down here long enough, he would lack the strength to return to the surface. He would black out on the way up, and drift back down again, to float away with the tide. No one would ever come looking for him.

But he knew that wasn't true. It had always been true, up until a week ago. Now, he had friends, people who cared about him. It was a strange, not altogether unpleasant feeling.

So. Dante twined his fingers around the kelp and floated into the crevasse of rock. There was nothing there - just sand and crabs which scuttled into their hiding places as he approached.

The beginnings of the contractions in Dante's solar plexus meant he was running low on oxygen. He began the journey up, but this time, he swam inside the fissure of rock.

Kelp curled close around him, and he resisted the urge to wave his arms to clear his path. An octopus glimpsed him and took fright, vanishing into a crack in the rock, leaving an inky cloud behind it.

Halfway up, Dante found what he was looking for.

There, wedged deep inside the cleft in the rock, hidden by thick kelp, was a metal chest. Dante only saw it because of the glint of eyes catching the light. Deep in the fissure of rock, a moray eel hovered, mouth agape, predatory gaze sweeping over him.

Dante drifted closer, and as the kelp parted in the ocean current, he saw the edge of something that was not natural. A straight edge of metal, hidden in the seaweed.

He put out one hand to touch the chest, and the moray eel undulated, eyes fixed on him. Dante knew that moray eels would strike without warning when threatened. He could easily lose a finger or two if that happened. Gently, he tugged his dive knife out of its sheath, and the blade glinted.

The kelp swayed, and he caught a glimpse of the whole object - a rectangular grey chest, wedged tightly into the crevasse, half covered by barnacles.

His midriff shuddered as a contraction shook him. His lungs were running out of air. Dante glanced up. The surface was still a long way off.

Deliberately, he started kicking, his body sluggish with lack of oxygen. He had been too long, he knew. Gravity pulled against him as he fought his way upwards. Black spots began appearing in his vision, early warning signs of an impending blackout. A high whining filled his ears.

Dante resisted the urge to go faster, knowing this would only use up more precious oxygen. It would be a remarkably peaceful way to go, he supposed. Euphoria followed by a loss of consciousness. An unusually tranquil end for someone in his profession.

The last metres seemed to take forever. Finally, Dante's head broke the surface. The sun shone full in his face, burning through the mist. The island, which had been a grim shadow, now sparkled, every dew covered leaf on every bush lit bright by the sunbeams.

He gulped in a shuddering breath, then another one.

"Are you ok?" Charlie bellowed from the boat. The young man was leaning over the side. He looked like he had been ready to leap overboard, jeans and all.

Too breathless to speak, Dante held up one hand - thumbs up.

"I found it!" He called after a few more gasps of air.

A few paces from him, the seal popped up and peered at him. Then, unconcerned, it lay on its back, combing its whiskers with a flipper.

"Well done!" called Eleanor.

"We were worried!" yelled Charlie. "You were gone for ages!"

"I'm ok," said Dante.

The seal winked one large dark eye at him, then with a flash of sleek wet fur, it dived and disappeared.

"I'm ok," said Dante softly to himself. And this time, he believed it.

43

In which coincidences abound

Back on the boat, Charlie crossed his arms tight over his chest. Somewhere down there in the ocean waters was a chest that probably contained the body of his murdered father.

He thought back to when he was fifteen, and a particularly ambitious English teacher had put on a school production of Hamlet. It was fairly awful, with kids mangling the Shakesperian phrases and forgetting their lines.

Charlie had played one of the gravediggers and quite enjoyed it. But the one kid in the whole school who could act had played Hamlet. Charlie remembered when this kid - his name was Dean - had grabbed his sword and stabbed through the curtain where Pelonius was hiding, thinking he was dispatching his father's murderer.

When he thought of someone stuffing his father's body into a chest and heaving it overboard, Charlie could see the appeal of swift justice.

Eleanor's hand fell on his shoulder.

"Charlie," she said softly, "I won't ask if you're all right. Of course you aren't. Do you want a moment? Or can we radio the coast guard now?"

Charlie blew out a long breath. "Now is fine."

Dante pulled himself up onto the boat, streaming seawater. He pulled his mask off and shook his head, droplets scattering in the sunlight. There was still an imprint of the mask on his cheekbones and forehead.

"The chest is maybe eighteen metres down. In that cleft in the rocks. It's well hidden by seaweed. I could swim down and tie ropes around it if you have them," Dante told Bernard.

"The Coast Guard should have all that gear." Bernard huffed into his moustache. "I don't. And I'm not entirely sure I want to be caught up in all this."

"Oh, it'll be fine," said Eleanor. "Something to gossip about for the rest of the year, I suspect." She drew her slim phone out of her jacket and made a call. "Yes, this is Eleanor. We've found the chest that was missing from Adrian's boat. Quite well hidden off Saddleback Island. We're about to radio the Coast Guard for assistance. Of course they'll come out. Justine is a good friend. Yes, she'll give you a ride. Bye for now." She shut off the call.

"Who was that?" asked Charlie.

Eleanor smiled grimly. "Our dashing police inspector. A valuable witness to ensure we're not planting evidence. Bernard, please radio the Coast Guard. Justine's on duty this morning. Let her know we require non-urgent assistance just off Saddleback Island."

Bernard harrumphed into his moustache. "I hope you know what you're doing, Eleanor."

"Always." Eleanor smiled brightly. "Dante, dear, are you alright to swim down there again soon?"

"Sure." Dante wrapped himself in a towel and sat on the side of the boat. "You're certain it's the chest we're looking for?"

"Ninety nine percent," said Eleanor.

Charlie shivered. "I don't think I want to see it opened, if that's ok."

"Of course, dear," said Eleanor.

Charlie studied the island. The morning mists were vanishing fast now as the sun rose higher. What had he seen that directed his gaze to the fissure where the chest had been hidden? Not a ghost - not exactly. A smudge of darker shadow, accompanied by a presence. It had a warning feeling, cold and ominous.

"Maybe you should look in the chest first," said Charlie.

"If we do that, it won't be admissible as evidence," said Eleanor.

Bernard thumbed the radio and had a brief conversation with the coast guard. He switched off the comm link and sat in the captain's chair. "They're coming." He patted his coat pockets and drew out a bag of tobacco and cigarette papers.

They waited, the boat bobbing in the green ocean, the sun rising higher and the smell of homegrown tobacco drifting through the air.

Bernard's radio crackled into life.

"AKL 7583 Z, are you there?"

"Yes." Bernard blew out a cloud of smoke. "What's up, Justine?"

"We've had a distress call. A boat has gotten engine trouble off Roeback Island. There's a grandpa and two children on board, so we'll go there first. Be with you soon."

"Fine." Bernard cut the radio connection and took a deep drag of his cigarette. "So now what?"

"I suppose we'll just have to wait," said Eleanor. "How far is Roeback Island?"

"It's about thirty minutes south," said Bernard. "Nice place. Good fishing."

"I don't like coincidences," said Eleanor, drumming her fingers on the side of the boat.

"I hope they don't take too long," said Bernard. "My boat's due for a hull clean tomorrow, and I have to get her into the dry dock while the tide's high."

Charlie cast another glance over at the island and the jagged gash in the rock cutting down into the water. "I guess we'll just wait."

"Anyone like a spliff?" said Bernard.

"Bernard," said Eleanor reprovingly. "The Coast Guard are coming, and with them will be the esteemed officer of the law, Inspector Avery."

Bernard checked his watch. "So we have an hour before they get here. Just as well — I haven't brought enough for that lot too."

Eleanor smiled. "No thank you, Bernard. Another time, maybe."

Charlie watched the green waters ripple and shimmer with hypnotic grace. Unlike everyone else in Te Kohe, he'd never felt at home on the ocean. It frightened him — a place people could go out into and never come home. Charlie liked to feel the earth beneath his feet and be surrounded by the scent of things growing. A garden was the proper place for him, not this wild and untamed watery jungle.

Still, the pattern of the ocean swell was starting to work a magic on him, soothing him into a semi-conscious trance.

Bernard's radio crackled into life.

"AKL 7583 Z, it's Justine. We can't locate the boat that sent the distress call, so we're headed your way."

"Great," said Bernard. "See you soon."

Time passed. The sun dancing on the water flashed in Charlie's eyes, mesmerising him.

"What's that?" Dante's voice broke into his stupor. He was looking west, where a motor boat had dropped anchor about a hundred meters away.

"Just another fishing vessel," said Bernard. "Looks like one of Andy's charter boats. Probably diving for crays — they're excellent around here."

Dante didn't reply, but he watched the boat with concentration. "They're putting up a dive flag."

"There you go," said Bernard. "Nothing to worry about." He turned away from the wind to light his spliff and the sweet smell of marijuana wafted out across the water.

"Coincidences," said Eleanor. She exchanged a glance with Dante. "Dante, dear, do you think you could go down and check on the chest?"

Dante stood, shedding his towel. "Ok."

"Eleanor." Bernard's expansive hand wave trailed a plume of smoke. "You need to unwind. Chill out. Take it easy. You're so sharp you'll cut yourself."

"Bernard, dear," said Eleanor. "I'm starting to think we should have a go at retrieving it ourselves. You must have ropes on board we can use."

Bernard harrumphed into his moustachios. "They're called lines, not ropes. And you're all far too on edge."

"I'll take a look," said Charlie. He climbed over the side of the boat and began to shuffle towards the forward rope locker.

Glancing back, he saw Dante carefully put on his goggles and slip into the water, swimming swiftly toward the island.

"I'd quite like to know who chartered that boat," said Eleanor. She examined her phone. "Not enough coverage to call Andy's Charters."

Eleanor didn't say 'damn it,' but Charlie thought she wanted to. Anxiety built up inside him. He flipped open the forward hatch to reveal a bundle of ropes, all neatly coiled and ready for use. He picked five of the most likely and laid them out on the bow. Perhaps they could combine them to haul the chest up.

Dante had nearly reached the island. Charlie eyed the boat. It wasn't unusual for someone to charter a boat and dive here — especially in summer. Maybe Bernard was right? He'd become paranoid from hanging around Dante too much. And being accused of murder. And having the people trying to burn down his house with him inside. Charlie sighed. That didn't sound paranoid at all. Maybe he should be more paranoid.

There was a brief flash of fins as Dante dived, and then the ocean surface was empty once more.

Charlie checked his watch.

"How long do you think Dante can hold his breath?" he asked Eleanor.

"Probably somewhere between 4-8 minutes?" she said. "The world record is nearly 12 minutes."

"I wish I knew what's going on down there," muttered Charlie. He checked his watch again. Thirty seconds. How had thirty seconds taken so long?

The minutes ticked by.

"He's been down there four minutes," said Charlie. Unease caused a leaden weight in his stomach. What if the divers from that boat are here to steal the chest?

Charlie scanned the ocean. Anything could be happening down there, he realised. His imagination peopled the invisible underwater world with great white sharks and divers fighting one another like a 1960s Bond movie.

"There's our coast guard," said Bernard, and Charlie caught the roar of twin outboard motors, coming closer.

"Six minutes," muttered Charlie. He wondered who Dante's next of kin were. He had an awful feeling that the answer to that was 'nobody.'

At the seven minute mark, Eleanor pointed. "There."

A small dark shape had surfaced fifty meters away.

"That's your guy," said Bernard.

"Why isn't he swimming this way?" said Charlie.

The shape appeared to be barely moving. Or maybe that was just the motion of the water.

"Shallow water blackout," said Bernard. "Happens all the time. Free-divers get to the surface low on oxygen and pass out."

"Here," Eleanor thrust a long red plastic float into Charlie's hands.

Charlie stared at her.

"Well, go on," she said. "Swim out to him. Make sure he's ok." When Charlie made no move, Eleanor gave him a measuring look. "Unless there's a reason you can't. In which case, I'll go." She bent down to start untying her shoes.

"No, no," said Charlie. "I'll go." He peeled off his sweater and pants, shivering in the cool sea air. On the edge of the boat, the float clutched in one hand, he hesitated. The ocean was an opaque emerald green. All his childhood terror of the sea returned with a vengeance, freezing him in place.

Just do it, he told himself. Get in there!

His entry into the water was an ungainly splash, followed by a frantic kicking crawl over to Dante.

"Hey!" said Charlie when he reached Dante. "Dante!"

The big man was floating in the water, face up, eyes closed. Frantically, Charlie shook him by the shoulder.

"Dante! Wake up!"

Very slowly, Dante opened his eyes. He looked dreamy, unfocused. Quite un-Dante like. Then he blinked, and his attention centered on Charlie. With glacial calm, he raised his right hand, thumb and forefinger making an 'O.'

"I'm okay," he said.

———

Back on the boat, Dante sat heavily on the bench seat. Wound around his wrist was a hacked off piece of rope.

"Where did that come from?" asked Charlie.

"There was a diver with an R.O.V.," he said.

"What's that?" said Charlie.

"A remotely operated underwater vehicle," said Dante. "They took the chest."

Charlie's stomach dropped. "This rope was around the chest?"

"Yes. But I ran out of air before I could cut the chest free. Plus there was a diver." Dante shrugged, as if underwater combat with no oxygen tank was just a minor inconvenience.

"The dive boat!" Charlie sprang up to scan for the charter boat. It was now a distant speck motoring fast back to port. He'd missed its departure while swimming out to Dante.

"So the chest's on that boat," said Eleanor.

"Yes," said Dante.

This was all said in such a matter of fact way that Charlie wanted to shake him and shout 'you nearly died. Be more careful!' It was ridiculous to think of shaking someone Dante's size, but still.

"I think," said Bernard, "that I don't want to take you three out on the water again. We haven't even been fishing yet, and someone's nearly died."

"Here's our coast guard," said Eleanor, her lips pursed. "This is going to be a fun conversation."

Dante heaved himself to his feet. "I'm going to get changed." He stumbled into the forward cabin.

Charlie gazed after him. Dante nearly died trying to retrieve my father's remains, he thought. There must be something Charlie could do to repay him. An idea began to form in Charlie's mind.

Eleanor watched the Coast Guard approach, sunglasses shielding her from the bright sunshine.

Inspector Avery stood next to Justine as she steered the boat, her red Coast Guard jacket bright in the afternoon sun.

The coast guard pulled up alongside Bernard's craft, fenders squeezed between the two boats as they secured the stern and bow lines. Charlie seemed quite happy to remain in the bow, possibly to avoid crossing paths with Avery again.

Justine and Avery swung on board, both of them clearly adept at moving around on boats.

"I'm afraid we've hit a snag," said Eleanor.

"Seems like that kind of day," said Justine with a smile. "We went all the way to Roeback island, and either the boat in distress fixed their engine trouble and didn't tell us, or it was a prank call." Her face darkened. "There's a stiff penalty for prank calls, and if I ever find out who it was, I'll make sure they pay it."

"What is the nature of your snag?" said Avery.

"Two hours ago, Dante found Adrian's sea chest halfway down that rock formation," said Eleanor, pointing at the island. "Unfortunately, it has been taken."

Avery scowled. "If you've brought me out here on a wild goose chase..."

"Give me some credit," said Eleanor sharply. "Do you think I'd waste my time on such a transparent scheme? The chest was there an hour earlier. The Coast Guard suffered a delay due to a false distress call. Then a chartered boat anchored a hundred meters away and put up a diving flag. Dante swam down again just in time to see a diver with an R.O.V. leaving with the chest. And here we are."

Avery folded his arms and drummed his fingers on his upper arm. "Seems awfully... James Bond," he said at last.

"Believe me," said Eleanor, "I prefer to keep the theatrics on my side of the fence. This is unprecedented. And still," she said, half to herself, "it's something I ought to have foreseen."

"Eliminate the impossible," said Avery, "and what is left, however improbable, must be the truth."

Eleanor frowned. "There's a time and place to quote Sherlock Holmes."

"Who saw the chest?" said Avery.

"Just Dante," said Eleanor.

"And he is?"

"In the cabin, recovering from hypoxia," said Bernard. He'd flicked the stub of his spliff overboard when the Coast Guard vessel came into view, but the air still retained the sweet scent of Mary Jane.

Eleanor wondered briefly if Dante had managed to knife someone in addition to cutting a piece of rope free from the chest, but decided this was not the time or place to find out.

"And the boat you think was responsible for this theft?"

"Chartered from Andy at the port," said Eleanor. "I'm sure by the time we catch up with it, the chest will be long gone."

Avery checked his watch. "I will certainly check who hired a boat this morning, if only to verify your story."

"You're too kind," said Eleanor. The weight of failure settled on her shoulders, accompanied by a feeling of both exasperation and admiration. Whoever was moving against them, (and she was certain it was Ted,) was bold, clever, and worst of all, had excellent timing.

Play the long game, she told herself. Ted may have won this battle, but he has not won the war. She hoped for Charlie's sake they could get ahead of their opponent soon.

44

In which Charlie and Dante make supernatural plans

"Are you sure you're ok?" said Charlie, putting his coffee cup down.

They were sitting on deck chairs in Dante's backyard, under the spreading branches of the newly trimmed kōwhai tree.

Dante was staring into the middle distance like he was replaying a scene from the past. On the edges of Charlie's vision, a few stray ghosts drifted closer, attracted by the prospect of an interesting diversion. Charlie glowered at them. With typical ghostly insensitivity, they ignored him.

"Yes," said Dante. It appeared near drowning had not made him talkative.

"I was thinking..." Charlie chewed his bottom lip. He wasn't sure exactly how to broach this subject. But he had decided he was going to help Dante, so he carried on. "Have you been feeling a bit down lately?"

"Lately?"

"Like, over the last few years. I'm only asking," Charlie hurried on, "because when unhappy ghosts haunt a place, they tend to bring the mood down. And I thought maybe a similar thing might be happening to you."

Dante flexed his shoulders. "Are all the people I killed haunting me?"

"There were a lot of ghosts attached to you. They were behind a door, but when I was at the RSA, they came through." Charlie swallowed. "I don't know exactly how it works, but it seemed like they couldn't move on."

Dante's ghosts were a far cry from the domesticated Te Kohe ghosts, who hung around as a variety of afterlife pension plan. Charlie suspected a lot of them could move on if they wanted to, but were so comfortable in their current situation, they simply stayed.

"Why do you think they're still here?" asked Dante.

"They're not pleased about being dead," said Charlie.

"That fits. I don't remember anyone being happy to see me when I was working," said Dante.

Every so often, Charlie did move on a suffering spirit. There were a few ancient ones from pre-settler days, remnants of tribal wars and old battles. Then there were the modern ghosts, drunk driving teenagers who couldn't believe their life was over when it was just beginning, or the occasional lost soul from the geriatric hospice.

When he was a kid, Charlie had been terrified of these apparitions. There were certain parts of town he wouldn't go through. If his mum made him, he'd shut his eyes until the ghosts went away.

Then one day, he decided to not be afraid. One by one, he talked to the ghosts who seemed most unhappy, and through a process of trial and error, succeeded in sending them on.

His escapades had not gone unnoticed around town, and the reputation for weirdness he'd had in childhood came back with a vengeance. But it was worth it for the peacefulness of a town with no unquiet spirits.

Dante's ghosts were on another level.

"So you think having these ghosts hanging around is a bad thing?" said Dante.

"Unhappy ghosts suck the life out of the air," said Charlie. "They make it hard to enjoy life. They cast an air of gloom over everything. I think that if we succeed in moving them on, you'll notice the difference."

Dante nodded slowly. "I think I may have been haunted for quite some time."

"I have a plan to help your ghosts move on," said Charlie. "But it might put you in danger."

"What kind of danger?"

"Spiritual danger."

"Is that deadly?"

"I don't know. This is a new situation for me." An idea was forming in Charlie's mind. But it might not work. And if it did work, it might still be dangerous for himself and Dante.

"Charlie. I've faced deadly danger of one kind or another most of my life. If you're not sure if this is deadly or not, it's probably ok."

"Ok." Charlie blew out a breath. "We'll need to go to the end of Te Wairua road at sunset. And bring your togs."

"Togs?"

"Swimsuit."

"I don't have a swimsuit."

"Something you don't mind getting wet then."

"Ok."

45

Which proves to be a learning experience for both Dante and Charlie

It was twilight when Charlie met Dante at the end of Te Wairua road. The night fell softly, an enveloping blanket that cloaked the trees with wreaths of shadow, blending the edges of them into the night sky.

Charlie was a dim shape, standing with his hands in his pockets, waiting for Dante. He had a small satchel over his shoulder.

The sound of running water came from close by. A morepork, the small native owl, gave a mournful cry.

Dante had never spent much time in the country when he was a kid. Later, his work had sometimes taken him into dense fir forests in Eastern Europe, or jungles high in the mountains of South America.

This was different. He was here for an unknown purpose, a man without a vocation, attended on by the ghosts of the past. The night was warm, without a breath of wind, but a chill creep over Dante's skin. Uncharacteristically silent, Charlie led Dante on a path into the woods.

Under the trees, the darkness was thicker, but Dante could just make out the white of Charlie's t-shirt. The young man was sure-footed in the gloaming, seeming to know this path by heart.

The sound of the river grew gradually closer until they found themselves on its banks. The trees drew back, revealing a night sky with the first stars shining bright in the darkness.

They were at the edge of the forest. The stream flowed into a deep pool of water, shadowed by the last of the surrounding trees. At the far end of the pool, the water narrowed to a stream again before it flowed off a cliff. Looking out, Dante saw the vastness of the ocean and the last glow of the dying light over the western horizon.

He cleared his throat. "What is this place?"

"In the far north of this island, at the land's end, is a place called Piwhane, or Spirits Bay. According to legend, the spirits of the dead gather there before they depart for the next realm, leaving from an ancient pōhutukawa tree above the sea."

Charlie swept his arm around the natural amphitheatre formed by the trees, the pool, the great bowl of the sky.

"We are not at Piwhane, but this place is a land's end - the Westernmost point of this cape. It is where forest, river, sky and sea meet. Perhaps the power in this place will help move your ghosts on to the next world."

Dante had inhabited the edge of life and death many times. Often, he'd felt his own death close by, only for it to pass over and take someone else's life instead.

This place was different. There was a gathering of currents he could not see. The potential not only for life and death, but for a movement between those two far countries, as effortless and natural as breathing in and out.

Under the growing starlight, with the soft music of the stream and the low swish and rush of the waves far below, Dante felt like a tiny spark of light in a vast ocean of being.

"What do I do?" he asked.

"Become still," said Charlie. "Listen to the waters. Breathe in the air. Feel the starlight on your face. See the earth supporting all our lives. And then enter the pool. Submerge yourself in it and cross to the other shore. When you do so, you will leave your haunting spirits behind you in the waters. They will flow with the river down to the ocean and find their way home."

Charlie's voice had the rhythm of a litany, a lilting chant that was far from his usual cheerful chatter. His face was hidden in shadow, expression unreadable.

Dante shrugged off his sweatshirt and trousers, then unlaced his shoes, folding his socks inside them. He made a neat pile of clothes and stood by the edge of the pool, clad only in his boxer briefs.

"I swim across the pool and that's it? Ghosts gone?"

Charlie made no reply, so Dante breathed in, becoming focused in the way he did before a job. He stepped into the water.

It was icy cold, much colder than the ocean, the cold of snowmelt from the ranges several miles into the interior. His bare feet slid on slimy rocks as he picked his way deeper, the black cold of the waters reaching his knees and then his thighs.

With a slow out breath, he slid full length forward into the water, the chill of it hitting his chest like a mallet.

What had Charlie said? Submerge yourself.

Taking a deep breath, Dante dived under the water. There was a moment of pitch blackness, and then he opened his eyes under the water and saw them.

The dead.

In the inky darkness of the river depths, they stood, row upon row of spectres, their eyes cold and hungry.

Dante tried to push himself back up to the surface, but his body remained locked in place, heart hammering, ice constricting his veins.

The water flowed past him, or perhaps he fell through the water, a rigid ghost locked body, corpse-like with premature rigor mortis.

The dead pushed closer, and now he saw their features, men and women, but mostly men, villains all, united in condemnation of his sins. He saw their fatal wounds, the holes that bullets had carved into their flesh, the knife cuts and the strangle marks, and his own body screamed, unable to move to save his life.

Dante had often wondered how he would die. It was natural, having sent so many to their deaths, to contemplate his own. He would never have guessed at this end, but now that he was here, his awareness sharpened, focus returned. If this was his death, he was determined to miss none of it.

The rows of the dead parted, and one figure stepped forward. Dante's control shattered, his heart beat loudly in his chest. This was the one. The person whose death had been the crossing of the line he'd always walked, the reason for the end of his career.

It was of no consequence that in this matter he'd been deceived, lied to by his superiors, given false information leading to a strike that, once set in motion, he could not prevent. She was dead, and she was innocent.

The ghost was slender, her brown hair curling down to her shoulders, dark eyes watchful. She had been the pre-teen daughter of a Venezuelan drug lord, a man responsible for the deaths of dozens of innocents, and the destroyer of thousands of lives. When Dante had set the explosives, he'd been told by the men surveilling the house that it was empty of all except the target and his militia.

The truth was different. When he'd seen her young form slip between the columns of the mansion, Dante had sprinted over to delay the charge. Too late. The detonation had thrown Dante back twenty feet to sprawl in the mud, concussed, with ears that would ring for days. It killed her instantly.

There was no apology from his handlers. Just: 'this man was a high priority target. One civilian as collateral damage is acceptable.' And so he'd quit.

But quitting hadn't changed the past. Here she was, beautiful and untouched in death, until she half turned and he saw the charred and bloody mess of her back.

Dante thrashed, his muscles unlocked at last, and his head broke the surface.

In the distance, Charlie was shouting his name as he ran towards him. Dante put his arms out, the water flowing fast past him now, and realised an instant too late where he was.

He was at the far end of the pool, the end that flowed over the cliff edge and into the sea. His hands slipped on the smooth river stones, then closed on empty air, and he fell.

46

Which comes to certain conclusions

"Dante!" screamed Charlie, his voice shattering the peace of the night. "Dante!" He sprinted over to the cliff edge, heart stopping terror giving him speed.

Below, the waterfall fell into the sea, the white foam glowing white against the dark waters. Charlie knew this coast well. There was deep water where the waterfall had carved out the rock over centuries. There were also sharp rocks, and if Dante had hit one of those, he would be terribly injured, or dead.

Charlie lay full length to stare over the cliff edge. There was the falling water, the ocean waves, and nothing else.

"Shit!" Charlie ran along the cliff edge. A hundred metres north was a path down. He prayed he would get there fast enough to find Dante. And that his friend would still be alive.

After what felt like an aeon, Charlie reached the path down. He scrambled over the steep path, hanging onto the rope some thoughtful person had installed years ago.

The path along the base of the cliff was made more treacherous by the waves washing in and the water slick rock surfaces, by turns slippery with seaweed and sharp with oysters.

At last, the waterfall was there, a sheet of shimmering water crashing down into the sea.

Charlie peered into the pool at the bottom of the waterfall, chest heaving with exertion.

"Dante?"

"I'm here." A dark shape detached itself from the base of the cliff. Dante had been sitting behind the waterfall, but now he climbed around to stand on the rock next to Charlie.

Charlie stared at him, appreciating for the first time how truly ripped Dante was. But more than that, Dante's face was serene. Until the tension was gone, Charlie hadn't seen it, but now the difference was profound.

"Are you ok?" The question came out sounding hushed.

"Yes." Dante gazed at the tidal pool where the waves washed in over sharp black rocks, and the waterfall that sent sprays of white over the dark waters.

They climbed back up, Charlie puffing slightly as they neared the top of the cliff. At the river, Dante dressed in silence. When he laced his boots on, Charlie took the opportunity to do what he called 'looking twice.' It was what he'd called it as a child, and it was only years later he realised it was probably what ghost books called 'second sight.'

"Your ghosts are gone," he said.

"I know," said Dante.

Charlie wanted to ask more, but Dante's manner discouraged questions.

It was only as they walked the last stretch of road to the Buick that Dante spoke.

"Can ghosts move things? In the living world, that is?"

"It's rare," said Charlie. "Usually only if they're extremely angry - like a poltergeist. Or if they strongly want to, like Mrs Brown at the library, who reshelves books that are put in the wrong section. It takes a lot of effort."

They walked a few more paces.

"Why do you ask?" said Charlie.

"I was going to fall onto a rock," said Dante. "The big one, just in front of the waterfall. And she pushed me back into the waterfall. So I missed the rock."

"She?"

"A ghost," said Dante. "Someone I killed."

"She must have wanted you to live," said Charlie.

Dante frowned. "You said all the ghosts are gone?"

"Yes."

"For good?"

"I think so."

"I would have liked to tell her..." Dante's voice trailed off. His hand went up to the hollow of his neck, where a cord usually hung. "My necklace is gone."

"It probably fell off when you hit the water."

"No," said Dante. "She used it to pull me out of danger. She broke the cord. She took it." A half smile that was almost sad crossed his face. "I think I know what that means."

"Is it good?" asked Charlie.

Dante's smile grew. This time, it transformed his face, and Charlie realised he'd never seen him smile before. It was beautiful, and slightly terrifying.

"Yeah."

47

In which Dante takes action

Dante was silent as they drove back into town. He had much to think on, but instead of reviewing the evening's events, he simply floated, as if his consciousness were still in the sacred waters of Te Wairua.

"Do you know what Eleanor's up to tonight?" said Charlie

"She's going over Ted's finances with Avery. They're looking for any patterns of payments that might be Janice's hush money."

"Oh." Charlie gazed vacantly out of the window as they coasted down the main road. "I guess... I heard Janice's ghost has been seen around town. That's what the other ghosts say. We could look for her, but..." Charlie sighed. "We've had enough ghosts for tonight."

Dante thought as he drove. He ought to suggest an activity to take Charlie's mind off his troubles, but he'd never been in this situation before. There had been that one time he'd had to babysit an arms trafficker before handing him over to Interpol, but that scenario had significant differences. For one thing, the man had had a black bag over his head the whole time.

"How about we go back to my place and..." Dante thought hard, "check on the corpse plant."

"That's a great idea," said Charlie, a smile brightening his face. "I could show you the best way to feed the orchids and other epiphytes."

Dante turned for home, feeling quite accomplished.

Then the alarm on his watch began to beep.

"Someone's entered my house," said Dante.

"Oh..." Charlie's eyes went wide.

The next minute of driving occurred in a tense silence. Finally, they turned onto Dante's street. Dante parked a few houses back from his and automatically checked for watchers hidden in the other parked cars.

"Stay in the car," he told Charlie. "Don't call anyone, not the police, not Eleanor. Even if you hear gunshots."

"Ok." Charlie swallowed.

Dante thumbed through the current security camera footage of his house interior. No one showed up, but it could be a clever ambush.

Dante exited the car and waited for his night vision to kick in. Senses on high alert, he entered his property via the neighbour's house, peering through the back garden fence before vaulting over and landing in a crouch, sheltered from view by the flax bushes.

He waited several minutes, but no one showed. Carefully, he approached the back door. It had been professionally battered open, probably with a hydraulic door breacher. Dante moved inside, feet noiseless, his Glock 17 ready to fire.

The motion sensors in his house detected no movement, no additional heat signatures. With the calibre of criminals available in New Zealand, Dante doubted there was anyone still in the house.

However, he carefully cleared each room. Then, he went to the living room, opened the lid of his old fashioned writing desk, took out his laptop, and reviewed the security camera footage.

In black and white detail, two men entered the kitchen. They wore balaclavas and gloves, and they looked relaxed, like they already knew the house was empty. The cat poked its head out of the pantry, head tilted in curiosity as it surveyed the intruders.

One man spoke into his phone, the other approached the pantry, gloved fingers held out. The cat ducked back inside the cupboard, wary of ill intent. The man's back blocked out the camera footage, and a moment later, he emerged, the cat held by the scruff of its neck. He held at arm's length while the cat swiped angrily at the air and spat at him, teeth bared in a snarl.

The other man put away his phone, and they both left the house, the cat dangling aloft.

Ted had sent people to break into his house, and they had taken his cat. The world shifted out of focus as Dante considered the possibilities. Ninety percent of the options flitting across his mind had a two digit body count.

He studied the band on his wrist. One hundred and fourteen days, homicide free. Keep to the code. Don't break the chain.

Dante had never had a dependent before. He'd never been in the position of having someone or something he cared about threatened. All his vulnerabilities had been sawn off years ago, sanded away by constant travel, untimely loss at home, and a job that demanded no quarter. But now, unaccountably, someone had found a weak spot, and pushed it. Hard.

Dante considered calling his sponsor, John. It was impossible to know what time zone he was in, but he knew John would be okay with talking him down any hour of the day or night.

But perhaps there was another solution.

Charlie jumped when he saw Dante exit his front gate and stride up the road towards him. He slid out of the car, looking relieved.

"Charlie, do you believe that killing people is wrong?"

"What? Yes!" Then Charlie frowned. "Unless it's to protect someone. Like, If Ted tried to kill my mum, and the only way to stop him was to kill him, then I guess I'd be ok with it. I mean, I wouldn't be ok, but morally, I think it's acceptable."

It wasn't quite the black and white statement Dante was hoping for, but it would have to do.

"In that case, can you come with me to Ted's estate tonight?"

"If you want me to. Why?"

"I want you there because if not, I will likely kill everyone I meet there."

Charlie went pale. "Ok. Of course I'll come. But why are we going there?"

"Because he's taken my cat."

"What a bastard!"

Dante hadn't known Charlie felt so strongly about the cat.

"Although," said Charlie, "how do you know Ted's taken the cat to his place?"

It was a good point. "I'll check my security footage and see who came here. Then we'll go up to his house and observe the location. If I see the two people who broke in are there, we'll go in."

"And if they don't have the cat there? And how do you know there were two people?"

"They will tell me where the cat is. And there were two people."

"Okay." Charlie hunkered down in his seat. "Can we call Eleanor now?"

"No. This is just between you, me, and the people who took my cat."

Dante went over in his mind what he'd likely need for an assault on Ted's place. He remembered the security cameras, the high estate walls, the smash proof glass doors, and the top of the line alarm system.

He started up the Buick and drove it carefully into his garage. Charlie followed him into his house as if afraid to say a word. Dante left him in the kitchen and went to the secret trapdoor in the floor. It was time to assemble his tools of the trade.

A couple of hours later, Dante and Charlie lay in the bushes outside Ted's estate. They'd left the Buick a few kilometres down the road, parked behind a stand of trees. Charlie supposed it was handy, having an old car with no navigation system and therefore no record of where they'd been.

Unless someone saw it, but that was unlikely, and their parking place had been well screened from the road. Perhaps the lack of trackable tech was why Dante chose his vehicle. That, and it was stylish as anything.

Dante had given Charlie a balaclava, which itched, and a pair of black gloves, which were too big for him.

"This way we won't leave fingerprints, or be recognised on security camera footage," he'd said.

Charlie fought the urge to push the scratchy wool mask up off his face. Dante didn't seem to be aware he was wearing a balaclava. Charlie supposed this is normal work attire for him. It was a sobering thought.

Dante had carried a sports bag up the hill with them. It was filled with things Charlie had never seen before: tasers, smoke bombs, wire cutters, glass cutters, knuckle dusters, and cudgels for hitting people in the head with. Dante had checked each item carefully before packing it in the bag. Lastly, he packed a bunch of zip ties and a roll of duct tape. Charlie could guess what those were for.

Dante hadn't put guns into the bag, but that was not as much of a comfort as you'd think. Charlie had seen Dante's underarm holster with its gun, and the knives strapped to Dante's wrist, thigh and calf.

I guess he doesn't want to kill anyone, thought Charlie, but if things get dire, he might.

Since being accused of murder, Charlie felt like he was drifting ever closer to the real thing. Perhaps that was a natural result of the accusation?

"Tell me the plan again, please?"

"I'll cut the security wires on top of the fence. This will get the guards to investigate. By then, we'll be inside the perimeter."

"And the guards?"

"I'll deal with them," said Dante.

"Right…" Charlie was getting as monosyllabic as Dante, but for different reasons. "Shut up, Pete!"

Dante's head swung around, his gaze completely missing Pete Morrow, who was delivering an impassioned monologue about what a bad idea this was.

"I've made up my mind, ok?" said Charlie. "I'm doing this. Sorry, Dante. What next?"

"Then we'll get into the main house. Our first objective is the security control room. There, we'll be able to see all the cameras. Hopefully, one of them will show where the cat is."

It sounded like a wonderfully simple plan. Charlie had no idea whether these kinds of escapades went according to plan — or not. He had the feeling they usually didn't.

"If someone comes at you, and I'm not around," said Dante. "Run."

Charlie swallowed. "Ok."

"Ha!" barked Pete. "Famous last words."

"Pete is here," said Charlie.

"Can he scout ahead and tell us how many guards there are?" said Dante.

"Sure," said Charlie, glaring at Pete. "He'd be happy to help."

"Like hell I am," said Pete.

"Let's go," said Dante, swinging the bag over his shoulder.

A few minutes later, they were at the ten foot high wall that ran the perimeter of Ted's estate garden. Dante checked for security cameras, then boosted up the wall like an acrobat. He crouched on the edge of the wall, almost touching the barbed wires that ran above it.

Charlie passed the wire cutters up to him.

"As soon as I cut these wires," said Dante, "the security guards inside will be alerted. So when I do that, pass me up the gear bag, then I'll help you climb over. Ready?"

Charlie nodded.

Dante cut the wires, which sprang back on themselves, leaving a wide gap on top of the wall. Charlie imagined he could hear an alarm shrilling somewhere in the darkness, but it was probably just the adrenaline rushing through his system.

A moment later, he and Dante crouched in a clump of bushes inside of the wall.

"There's two guards coming," said Pete, and Charlie relayed this to Dante.

Dante nodded and ducked away to move towards the house. Charlie wondered if he was about to see a Bruce Lee worthy fight, with spinning kicks, lightning fast punches, and breaking bones. It turned out that was not Dante's style.

The two guards arrived in an amped up state. They shone torches at the cut wires on top of the wall. As one of them reached for his handheld radio to call for backup, Dante rose up behind them like a wrathful black shadow, a taser in each hand.

Two zaps, and the guards collapsed on the ground, shaking and spasming. Charlie grimaced. Being tasered looked horribly uncomfortable.

A minute later, the guards were zip tied and stashed under the bushes, and Dante was in possession of one of their handheld radios.

"Are you going to gag them?" asked Charlie.

Dante shook his head. "Tasered people sometimes throw up, and that could be fatal if they're gagged."

Charlie carried the bag, which was far heavier than Dante made it look, and followed him towards the brightly lit mansion. Dante put buds into his ears and listened.

"There's at least four more guards on the radio. Can you ask your ghost to locate them? And the cat, if possible."

"Sure, sure, I'll do it," grumbled Pete. "But I'm washing my hands of this if anyone ends up dead. Or in jail."

Charlie followed cautiously behind Dante as they jogged along a hedge towards the back entry of the house.

The back entry featured an enormous garage, big enough to house Ted's Hummer, Porsche, and whatever other lavish cars he owned.

Instead of being stealthy, Dante simply walked up to the small door on the side of the garage doors and looked up at the camera there.

"Two guys on their way," said Pete, poking his head through the door. "They look pissed."

"Is one of them Viktor?" asked Charlie.

But right then, someone jerked open the door Dante was leaning against. Charlie wasn't sure exactly what happened. It wasn't like a martial arts movie. It was like watching a fight where one of the fighters is on fast forward, while the other two are on normal time.

Dante dodged the fist aimed at his face and tasered the first guard. Then he shoved the man into the second guard, so that the electric taser probes heading his way from the second guard attached themselves to the first unfortunate man.

The second guard didn't have a chance to do anything more than that before he also hit the ground.

Dante stepped over them and advanced to the first bend in the corridor. He stood still, listening, then returned and zip tied the guards' feet and hands together.

He held up a hand when Charlie went to say something. "Listen."

Footsteps approached.

"One more guard's headed your way," called Pete. "I haven't found the cat yet. This place is stupidly big."

Charlie didn't see what Dante did to the next guard. He just heard a thump as the guard hit the floor. By the time he rounded the corner, Dante was zip tying him up.

Charlie gulped. "He was armed."

"It's a Glock 17," said Dante. "Ownership is tightly controlled in New Zealand. This one's probably illegal."

"It's a handgun," said Charlie. He wasn't sure why he was so taken aback. He just hadn't seen many handguns in his life. Sure, hunting rifles were a staple of farmers throughout the country.

Charlie had even read about a farmer who'd flown from Hamilton to Invercargill with his prized .270 Winchester in the overhead locker. There'd been a bit of a scene when he disembarked, but people had understood his reluctance to relegate his favourite hunting rifle to the cargo hold.

But handguns... He studied the dull grey object Dante tossed into his gear bag. Its sole purpose is to shoot people, he thought. That's how it's different.

Pete burst through a wall, looking like he'd run full pelt. Ghosts didn't need to breathe, but he looked puffed.

"There's three guards up ahead," he said. "They've set up an ambush in the main atrium room. That's just down the corridor. They have guns. And I've found your cat, but there's this huge guy guarding it."

Charlie relayed the message.

"That'll be Viktor," said Dante. He looked not exactly satisfied, but something close to it.

"Do you think we can flank the ambush?" asked Charlie.

"I can lead you, lad," said Pete. "But they're covering all the entrances into the atrium. Your friend has got them spooked. I get it. He's got me spooked, and I'm a ghost."

Charlie and Dante followed Pete through a small service corridor. At the end of the corridor, Dante took the bag Charlie had been carrying.

"Wait for me here," he said.

Out came two short clubs, knuckle dusters, and several small grey canisters. Dante popped the fuses off the cannisters and lobbed them into the main room.

There were shouts of alarm, a hissing sound, and then smoke began to billow down the corridor, accompanied by bursts of gunfire.

Dante smiled grimly and slipped on goggles and a breathing mask. Now he looked like a terrifying alien cyborg.

"Thermal imaging goggles," said Pete. "I have a feeling your friend's done this before."

Dante appeared to be counting silently, because at a signal known only to him, he started down the corridor towards the ambush, crawling army fashion.

Charlie waited, just about jumping from foot to foot with nerves. Every time a gunshot rang out, he jumped, thinking it was Dante being shot. He wanted to ask Pete what was going on, but the old ghost had gone off somewhere.

What was it Dante had said? 'I need you here so I don't kill everyone.'

But what if Dante needs my help? But even that thought didn't persuade Charlie to venture into a smoke filled room filled with an ex-assassin and a gang of machos firing blindly.

"Spot of bad news, lad," said Pete, reappearing. "These guys must have called for backup. There's a car with two more guys in it pulling up outside."

"How many people does Ted have?" said Charlie. "Was he expecting a war?"

Pete shrugged. "I can't go and warn your friend. But if you keep low to the ground, you should be ok. You can go to the corner and yell out a warning to Dante."

Charlie glanced down the corridor. The smoke bombs had filled it with an impenetrable haze, but red emergency lights shone through it like a gateway to hell. "I think that's a better option."

Charlie crawled to the end of the corridor. There was silence, then the sudden 'bang' of a gun and a thud made him jump.

"Dante!" he called. "There's two more people coming."

More silence greeted this announcement, then heavy footsteps came towards him - fast. Charlie sprang to his feet.

"Dante?"

A man emerged out of the smoke, hair wild, teeth bared. It was not Dante.

Charlie turned and ran.

48

In which Eleanor debates the relative merits of justice and morality

Eleanor took a sip of her pinot noir. It was a Romanée-Conti, considered by many connoisseurs to be the finest noir in the world. It had been a gift from a certain wealthy wine collector after she'd helped locate his kidnapped niece.

See, she thought, studying Inspector Avery, seated across the table from her. *Not all my gains are ill gotten.*

Avery had unbent far enough to take off his suit jacket and roll his shirtsleeves up. Now he looked up, his reading glasses catching the golden light of her dining room chandelier. He twirled his wineglass by the stem, inhaling the rich aroma.

"You won't be sampling this class of bouquet in prison," he said.

"All the more reason to enjoy it now," said Eleanor with an airy smile.

"You're going to disappear as soon as this is over, aren't you?"

"I've found that life is like a fine wine," said Eleanor. "It's all about savouring the experience."

Avery smiled, a thin curl of his lip that still revealed a dimple on his left cheek. "Savour this." He slid a sheet of paper across the table to Eleanor.

Eleanor slipped her reading glasses on and focused on the rows of printed figures. They didn't say much to her. Apart from the rapid calculation of probabilities, maths was not her strong suit.

"What am I looking for?" she asked.

Avery entered a string of numbers into the calculator on his phone. "Every month, Ted pays a 'social media consultant' the sum of five thousand dollars."

Eleanor raised her eyebrows. "That seems excessive. If it's for the Pepper Tree, it's the only hotel in town, and hardly needs much advertising. Ted's other holdings are all business or investor facing. Social media is not how they'd be promoted."

Avery turned a page. "Then, the Pepper Tree Hotel has a cash expenditure of around twelve thousand a month."

"That's high for a hotel of that size. It's certainly suggestive — cash is a great way to hide illegal payments."

"I suppose you would know all about that," murmured Avery, turning the page.

"You've never bent the rules, even a tiny bit, during your distinguished career?" said Eleanor.

"Only once," he said. "During my first year in the police."

"And?"

"And someone died," he said.

She sipped her pinot noir. "Do go on."

Avery shook his head slightly. "I'm here to investigate the illicit dealings of one Ted Andrews."

"But your story sounds so much more interesting."

"I'll tell you my story," said Avery, "if you tell me how you managed to reroute the Cezanne."

Eleanor half smiled. "A good magician never reveals their secrets."

"Aren't magicians old men with long white beards?"

"Sorceress? Enchantress?"

"Witch?"

"You're sitting in my dining room, perusing evidence you'd never otherwise get your over regulated hands on, and sampling one of the finest wines France has to offer. I should have served you Château de Carton instead."

"A good point," said Avery. "This wine costs around twenty grand a bottle. Whose cellar did you burgle it from?"

"The president of France, of course," said Eleanor.

"Now that's a story I'd like to hear," muttered Avery, and turned back to the financial records.

"You don't have to drink it if it offends your righteous palate."

"Not a chance." His hand curled protectively around the glass stem. "This wine is now in my custody, and," his brown eyes met hers, "once something is in my custody, that's where it stays."

Eleanor huffed in amusement. "So that's what you say in front of the mirror every morning."

"Wouldn't you like to know."

Eleanor rolled her eyes and took another sip of wine. It was exceptional. Quite worth the hijacked barge ride across the Saône River in winter, and the car chase through the Jura Mountains with her friend's niece asleep in the back seat of her Citroën DS.

"You must be aware that much of the art in galleries, museums and private collections is forged," she said.

Avery shot her a look over the top of his reading glasses. "Fifty percent, I believe."

"Oh, it's higher than that," said Eleanor. "But art forgery is a victimless crime. If a billionaire gets a special thrill from having the real deal in his vault, and the public doesn't know the difference, I fail to see the issue."

"Well, you'll have plenty of time to contemplate that philosophical conundrum from your cell in Mount Eden Corrections Facility."

"A man's reach should exceed his grasp, or what's a heaven for?" said Eleanor. "On a related topic, do you think you'll be able to use this information in the case?"

"These financial records are amazingly far from admissible. I don't want to know how you obtained them."

"Just as well, since I have no intention of telling you."

"However, if you can bring me concrete evidence of Ted's involvement in Janice's murder, I can get the SFO involved. They'll rake through every corner of his various businesses." Avery smiled thinly. "And I'll make sure they know what to look for."

"That sounds like leading the witness." Eleanor shook her head. "Just when I was regaining my faith in the New Zealand justice system."

"We won't have to lead any witnesses if we have hard evidence," said Avery. "But you don't have much time. Ted has a rock solid alibi. Everyone saw him sitting on the balcony at the time of the murder. Unless you can provide me with a better option, I'll be arresting Charlie Monday morning. Tuesday at the latest."

Eleanor momentarily closed her eyes. "You know the boy didn't do it."

Avery gave a brief, world weary smile. "Off the record? I'm nearly one hundred percent certain Charlie is innocent. But I've been wrong before, and I am an officer of the law. I'm sorry, Eleanor, but this is where I draw the line. My job is to conduct this investigation within the law."

"Ends and means," said Eleanor softly. "I suppose that's where our views diverge."

"Our court system is the best way to ensure the innocent go free and the guilty do not. If the law says Charlie is guilty, then I will do my duty."

"So Dante's off the suspect list?"

"We found a witness who saw him go into the garage at the crucial time."

Eleanor tilted her glass back, and the rich red wine filled her mouth with the essence of autumn. "How long have you been sitting on that little piece of information?"

"Some time." Avery's face gave nothing away.

Eleanor wished she could believe in a justice system that worked. But bitter experience had taught her that to get justice, you had to fight for it yourself.

"Walk me through those numbers again," she said.

Avery shuffled his chair around to sit next to her. This close, she caught the scent of aftershave and mint.

"Here," he said, pointing at a row of numbers.

Eleanor fought the urge to inhale deeply as he leaned closer. Mind on the job, she thought. Don't get distracted by the officer who plans to arrest you.

"What am I looking for?" she asked.

"It's the timing of the payments," said Avery. "There are larger lump sum payments on these dates." His finger flicked down the column to point at several amounts. "If these coincide with the timing of Janice's large purchases - cars, jewellery, and the like, it could be quite convincing."

"Timing…" Eleanor stared into space. Her mind, spinning its wheels for so long, had just gained traction. Now it raced ahead down a path she'd sensed for the last several days. "Timing!" She turned to Avery, her eyes shining.

"What is it?" His gaze flicked from her eyes down to her lips as a fierce smile lit up her face.

"I know how Ted killed Janice. It's been right in front of us from the start." She stood up and spun around like a ballet dancer, feeling the air crackle with energy. "What a sneaky bastard. I almost want him to get away with it, he's been that sneaky."

Avery sat back in his chair, eyebrows raised. "Would you care to enlighten me?"

"This calls for a celebration." Eleanor poured a stream of rich dark wine into her glass and leaned against the kitchen bench. She savoured a slow sip of liquid velvet.

"Eleanor," said Avery, his voice dropping.

Eleanor's smile deepened. Annoying Avery was an added bonus to a thoroughly enjoyable evening.

"How did Ted kill Janice?"

"It all fits," said Eleanor. "Every detail. Except…"

"Except what?"

"Except…" Eleanor deflated slightly. "You're going to say all the evidence is circumstantial. No definitive proof. No murder weapon.

Nothing that would make it a surefire thing for a jury. It's ends versus means again."

"Tell me." Avery's brows drew down.

"It's just a theory," said Eleanor. "I might even be wrong." She took another sip of wine. "What can a law abiding officer do with the evidence you have so far?"

"Don't try to change the subject."

"I can't tell you yet, Avery," said Eleanor firmly. "Besides, there's nothing you could do with my theory anyway. A good defence lawyer would pick holes in it without breaking a sweat."

"Fine," said Avery, brows still pinched together in a frown. "Keep your secrets. Here's what I can do within the law. I can subpoena Janice's financial records and start building a case against Ted. He's been off our suspect list until now, but these financial documents put him on it."

"Build a case…" Eleanor's elation at solving the murder ebbed. It was difficult to work within the confines of the law, she thought. So why bother? In the absence of definitive proof, the best approach was to get Ted to incriminate himself. But how?

"I can tell you're plotting something," said Avery.

Eleanor gave him a vapid smile straight from her society airhead act. "Who, me? Honey, the very idea!"

49

In which hostage negotiations are conducted and Dante opens the gates

Surrounded by thick smoke, facing armed men, outnumbered and outgunned, Dante was having the time of his life.

He lay on his back in the middle of the space, listening while the smoke swirled around him. The thermal imaging goggles hampered his awareness, so he turned them off. His hyper-extended senses would give him all the intel he needed to control the situation.

One man was already unconscious, zip tied in a corner, safely out of the way.

The other two were at large, but Dante had already relieved one of them of his firearm.

Dante heard Charlie call out his warning. Smoke spiraled over him and he smiled. Someone was approaching.

"I missed this," he murmured, and that was the problem with his new life. He only truly came alive when death was breathing down his neck.

A figure emerged out of the gloom and Dante exploded upwards, catching the man's gun with both hands while his forehead smashed into the man's sternum.

The man's cry of pain was cut short as Dante wrenched the gun out of his hands and pulled him close as a lover, wrist and forearm closing around the man's neck to cut off the carotid artery supply.

A few seconds later, the man slumped to the ground, unconscious. Dante zip tied the man's hands securely behind his back and did the same for his ankles and knees.

He strained his ears in the near silence. Somewhere to his left, two men were running all out away from him. He heard desperation in the sound and hoped one of the men wasn't Charlie.

If it was, he couldn't do much about it now, because here came two more men, their footsteps stealthy, approaching from his right.

Every sense extended, his body tense with energy held in check, Dante crouched low to the floor, smoke swirling around him, and waited.

―――――

Charlie rounded a corner, heart pounding like a drum in his ears. He crashed into the opposite wall and careened down the corridor.

There was a 'bang' behind him.

He shot at me, Charlie thought. The bastard shot at me while I'm running away. Well, you have invaded this home and Dante's taken out all his mates.

Charlie ignored his arguing brain and focused on staying alive.

He rounded a final bend and there were several doors to choose from.

"In here!" shouted Pete.

Charlie dashed inside and closed the door.

"Now what?" he whispered. It was all he had breath for.

Pete poked his head through the wall. "Your man's coming this way. Grab that ugly lamp and hide behind that cupboard."

Charlie did as he was told. The lamp in question was as tall as he was, a heavy iron affair with a nice heft to it.

"Hit him in the knees," advised Pete. "Head shots are a bad idea — you could accidentally kill or brain damage someone. Busted knees should heal up ok, and they take a man's mind off other things. Wait for it..." Footsteps entered the room, along with heavy breathing. Charlie didn't dare look around the corner of the wardrobe. "Wait for it..." Charlie's fingers gripped the lampshade stick. "Now!"

Charlie swung the lamp with the strength of desperation, and it cracked into the man's knees with an excruciating 'crunch.'

The man screamed and fell over, clutching his knees, gun forgotten. Charlie took this as his cue to sprint out of the room.

He ended up leaning against the wall in a windowless room far from the outside. Sweat ran down his face inside his balaclava, and Charlie resisted the urge to pull it off and wipe his face. There were probably cameras everywhere. Ted's paranoia was pathological. On reflection, it was perhaps also justified.

Up ahead was a door marked 'comms.'

"Pete?" said Charlie softly. "Can you check what's in there?"

"Right on it, son." The old ghost walked through the wall. "Oh, you're going to want to see this," came his voice from inside. "This is... whoboy."

Charlie cautiously cracked open the door. Inside, a bank of screens took up one wall, with a large desk pushed up against the wall underneath it. Someone's coffee cup was sitting by the keyboard, still half full - probably belonging to one of the guards who'd been called away from his post by their invasion.

On the bottom left screen was something that made Charlie's stomach drop. The camera showed a small, nondescript room, with various bits of kit - fishing tackle, storage boxes, etc, stacked up around the walls.

Pushed into one corner, however, was a large metal chest. It still had barnacles and bits of kelp stuck to it. Charlie recognised it from the many fishing trips he'd had on his father's boat as a child.

"That's it," he breathed. "Is there a plan of this house anywhere?"

Pete and he searched the walls and checked the desk drawers.

"Nothing," said Pete. "But it's here, no doubt about it. Do you think your friend's finished beating up Ted's security team?"

"I don't think I want to go and see," said Charlie. He noticed something else, then. A screen with a series of alerts on it.

"Look at that," he pointed at the latest text message.

"Someone's called the police?" said Pete.

"Looks like it."

The screen was flashing red, with a message that read: 'Te Kohe station alerted, callout to 175 Tūhoro Heights, reports say shots fired.'

"Hemi and the others will be on their way soon," said Charlie.

Pete shook his head. "You'll have a bit more time than usual. They'll call the Armed Offenders Squad because of the shots fired."

"Time to find this room?"

"Maybe. But," Pete scratched his jaw, "what you want is for the police to find the chest here. Which they will, if they come here and check the whole place over as a crime scene."

"Only if Ted doesn't get here first," said Charlie. Ted had managed to steal the chest out from under their noses once already.

"The Armed Offenders won't let him near the scene until they've declared it safe," said Pete. "Your best course of action is to find your friend and get the hell out of here before they turn up."

"Right." Adrenaline coursed through Charlie's body again. He thought he'd used it all up over the last few minutes of desperate running, but with the imminent arrival of the police, he'd discovered an untapped reserve.

———

Dante exited the smoke filled atrium, leaving behind the trussed up bodies of Ted's security men. There was a good air-con system here, and he expected the smoke would clear soon enough. Right now, he wanted to find his cat. Preferably with Viktor, so he could beat him to a pulp.

"Hey," crackled his handheld radio. It was Charlie. "Two things. I can see Viktor and your cat in a room with an enormous flatscreen TV."

"I know where that is," said Dante. The tour Ted had given him when he'd been hired as security and a backup fall guy had been a big mistake.

"Also, someone has called the police. Pete thinks the Armed Offenders will be here in about thirty minutes. Maybe less."

"I'll meet you back where we entered in five minutes," said Dante. Hefted the cudgels in each hand. Five minutes was all it should take.

Two minutes later, Dante kicked open the door of Ted's media room. It blew off two hinges, the remaining hinge keeping hanging at a drunken angle.

He remained outside the door, crouched low. It was never a good idea to enter a room where a hostile was prepared to meet you. But if he deployed his smoke bombs to cloak his entry, all bets were off.

Before he could deploy this tactic, a voice came from inside the room.

"My friend," said Viktor. "Truce."

Dante paused.

"I promise we just talk. If fight, we do that after."

Dante took a scope out of his gear bag and angled it to see inside the room. Inside, Viktor sat in a laz-y-boy chair, the cat on his lap.

"Ok," he said. "I'm coming in."

On seeing Dante, the cat yawned, showing white teeth and a pink tongue.

"I tell Ted this is bad idea," said Viktor. "But he never listen." His gaze flicked down to the handgun lying on the arm of his armchair. Dante thought he could beat Viktor in a quick draw, but it would be a close thing.

"You have my cat," said Dante.

"Sure. Is nice cat. I like cats." Viktor ran one massive finger down the cat's spine and it arched its back. "When shouting started, I come here. Those other guys," Viktor's grin stretched wide, "bargain bin gangsters. Run around like they are in the movies. Never been in real war."

Dante's hand felt the magnetic pull of his Glock. It would be so simple to put a bullet between Viktor's eyes. He was faster. He knew it.

Keep to the code, he thought. Viktor wants to talk. Let him.

"You think I like to talk," Viktor grinned. "Is true. But also, is police coming. I call them. Orders are to keep police away. But Ted does not pay enough for me to deal with this shit. Is finish. Ted is like that..."

he snapped his fingers. "The scorpion. Who rides across the river with the frog. Must always ruin his own plans. So. I finished. Here is your cat."

With that, Viktor stood up, leaving his gun on the armchair. He crossed the room, and placed the cat carefully in Dante's arms.

Dante transferred the cat to nestle in his left arm, leaving his right arm free to shoot with. He had to tilt his head up to look Viktor in the eyes.

Then he gave him a small nod, as one professional to another, and left.

―――

Charlie found his way back to the entrance by the garage. He was feeling nervous as a cat in a dog run. He spun around when Dante arrived, the cat cradled in one arm, its chin tucked under Dante's large bicep.

"We're going?" he said.

Dante examined the view of Ted's driveway. The night sky was dark, as were the hills, but through the high barred gates, they could see red and blue flashing lights of cop cars starting to climb the hills towards the manor.

"There's just one more thing to do," said Dante.

"Um...ok?" said Charlie. "I'd really like to be gone before the police arrive."

"It'll only take a minute," said Dante, and his teeth flashed white in the hole of the balaclava. It was not a reassuring sight.

Thirty seconds later, Charlie and Dante stood in the garage. The cat in Charlie's arms watched Pete curiously as he examined Ted's array of shiny and expensive vehicles.

"Are you sure this is a good idea?" asked Charlie.

The garage door was open, and Dante had hot-wired the Hummer. Its engine roared like an angry lion as he pumped the gas.

"Pass me that drink bottle," said Dante.

He wedged it under the accelerator pedal, and the lion roared louder.

"Stand clear," he said, but Charlie was already backing away.

It happened faster than he'd imagined. Dante sat in the driver's seat, the door open. As he shifted the Hummer into gear, he leapt clear.

The Hummer shot out of the garage, gravel spitting, and it skidded towards the gates. It hit them at sixty miles an hour, wrenching them off their hinges and ploughing onto the road.

The first corner came up fast, and the Hummer did not turn. The engine noise changed as it shot off the side of the road into the air. Then came a crash and a smashing sound as it rolled down the steep hillside.

"Why?" asked Charlie, when the noise of the Hummer rolling finally ceased. He passed the cat back to Dante, where it started purring.

"We needed to get through the gates," said Dante.

"We could have pushed the button to open them!"

"It had a security pad."

"We could have climbed over the fence where we came in!"

"I didn't kill anyone in there. Not even Viktor."

"And this made you feel better?"

Dante didn't answer. The cat's tail swished as he strolled out of the garage towards the wreckage of the gates.

Charlie sighed and looked skyward. A million stars blazed down at him, their ancient light calm and magnificent.

"There's a hiking track nearby," said Charlie. "I think I can find it. It'll get us to our car without meeting any police. Hopefully."

"Lead on," said Dante. It was hard to tell in the dark, but he sounded remarkably cheerful.

I enjoy a well kept garden and take pleasure in harvesting my fruit and veges, thought Charlie. Dante likes breaking into a mansion, kicking the collective asses of the eight armed guys there, and then sending a Hummer crashing down the hillside. I guess there's all sorts of people in the world,

They ducked off the road at the first bend, and Charlie led them down the steep slope towards the track.

He'd just stepped onto the gravelled path when the noise of sirens and the glow of flashing lights heralded the arrival of Te Kohe's finest.

I hope they find the chest soon, he thought. Even if your father's body is inside, his treacherous thoughts told him, that doesn't get you off the charge of Janice's murder.

Shut up, he thought back at his thoughts. Above him, the stars of the Southern Cross shone bright, and Orion chased Scorpio across the sky.

"I don't think Ted will try and kidnap your cat again," said Charlie.

"I don't think so either," said Dante.

They recovered the Buick, nestled behind a thick hawthorn hedge off the main road. Dante put the key in the ignition.

"Can we update Eleanor now?" said Charlie

"Yes," said Dante.

Police sirens were still wailing up in the hills. Charlie wondered what Eleanor would say about their escapade.

Dante rifled through the glove box until he found an old cassette tape with 'The King' written on the side in black felt tip faded brown with age.

"My mother liked Elvis."

It was the first time Dante had volunteered information about himself, and Charlie felt honoured.

The Buick started with a roar, and the King of Rock 'n' Roll crooned that it was now or never.

Dante tipped back his head and began to sing, in a surprisingly clear tenor:

"When I first saw you,

With your smile so tender..."

"Wow," murmured Charlie. Perhaps this was how Dante unwound after kicking ass. In the back seat, Pete began to sing along.

"I've spent a lifetime,

Waiting for the right time..."

It was true, thought Charlie. You never knew someone until you'd been on a road trip with them. With a grin, he joined in on the chorus.

"It's now or never,

Come, hold me tight..."

The Buick careened down the hairpin bends, and Charlie hoped they wouldn't run into the Armed Offenders Squad on their way up.

Perhaps he and Dante would be arrested for assault and battery. But on the other hand, whispered his optimistic side, maybe they wouldn't. Despite childhood tragedy, Charlie was naturally optimistic. This optimism had suffered during Ted's recent attempts to frame him for murder, but it was making a comeback.

A few minutes later, Elvis's promise to 'love me tender, love me true,' was cut off mid sentence as Dante turned the Buick off. They were outside Eleanor's house, and the quiet of the suburban street in the early hours of the morning felt surreal after gunfire, smoke, and police sirens.

50

In which certain things become clear to certain people

"So you got your cat back," said Eleanor. "I'm so glad."

They were in the sitting room of Dante's house, and it was seven in the morning. Eleanor had elected to accompany them there so Dante could stock up on protein shakes. She had told them how Ted murdered Janice, and then listened calmly to Charlie and Dante's recounting of the night's events while the cat lounged in Dante's lap.

Well, the recounting was mostly Charlie. Dante's only contribution was to supply the correct name when Charlie couldn't remember the make of the illegal firearms the guards had carried.

"I'd like to call Avery and check on progress," Eleanor said, standing. "We want to make sure he's secured the chest with your father's remains."

"Yes please," said Charlie.

Dante folded his arms. "They won't be able to find definitive proof we were there."

"Good to know," said Eleanor. She dialled the number. "Hello, Inspector Avery. Yes, I thought you'd be on site. Is now a good time to talk?"

She drifted away, leaving Charlie to stare into space, his head buzzing with the aftermath of the crazy night. A minute later, Eleanor returned, looking thoughtful.

"Here's the update," she said. "They've arrested the men you tied up on account of their illegal firearms. Viktor was gone by the time the police arrived."

"Do they know about us?" said Charlie.

"Avery says they're reviewing the security camera footage," said Eleanor. "Everyone is impressed with the unknown intruder's combat skills. Hemi's nephew wants to put it on a site where they post real-life fights. He says they'll make a killing."

"It was quite something," said Charlie.

Dante let the cat in his lap catch one of his fingers in its claws. It wrestled, its tail whipping around.

"I'm sorry, Charlie, but I have difficult news. The chest was empty." Eleanor's face was smooth, but her shoulders tensed.

"Oh," said Charlie. He couldn't think of anything to say. This was as bad as the chest being stolen under the sea. Perhaps even worse, because this time, Ted may have destroyed the evidence completely.

"That must have been Viktor's doing," said Dante. "I should have shot him."

"It might have been Ted," said Charlie, but his voice sounded hollow in his ears. This is how someone feels before they give up, he thought. And we were so close.

"Avery said they're going to find the contents. They'll retrieve the GPS tracking info from Ted's Hummer. This is slightly difficult because the vehicle is halfway down a steep hillside right now." She smiled slightly, then became serious. "They're also going to check the tracking from the charter boat used to steal the chest. We will find where Ted's taken the bones, Charlie."

"It's like he's playing hide and seek," said Charlie. He was abruptly furious — with Ted, with the police, with this whole town.

Eleanor looked up, a strange expression on her face. "What did you say?"

"I said—" Charlie began, but she held up a hand to stop him.

"I can almost see it...yes." Eleanor's eyes widened. "Ted *is* playing a game with us. He's playing the Shell Game." She shook her head. "What a low class..." she trailed off, then her lips curved in a wintery smile. "Do you know the secret to the Shell Game?"

"That's the game with the three shells, and the ball you hide in one of them?" said Charlie. "I thought it's impossible to win."

"It is if you think the dealer is playing fair," said Eleanor. "If you play by the rules, you'll lose every time."

"So how do you win?"

"The secret to the shell game is that the ball isn't under any of the shells. It's in the dealer's hand, and it stays there until you choose the wrong shell. Then he plants it in another shell and makes you believe it was there all along."

"And how will that help us find my father's bones?"

"Right now policemen are organising a search of the back country forest and Te Kohe Bay. But I don't think that's where Ted's hidden your father's remains."

"You think he'll keep them close at hand?" It was hard to describe Charlie's feelings right then. If Ted had been there, he was quite sure he could summon up another hex. Maybe even stronger than the last one.

"I think so," said Eleanor. "Finding them in Ted's possession should be enough to put him in jail. And before you offer, Dante, I think we'll be able to locate them without undue violence. It's all there in Ted's psychology. And... I think know how he killed Janice too. It was quite clever of him." She shook her head again. "He is a cunning weasel."

"What?" Charlie gasped. "How did he do it? Can we use this against him?"

Eleanor tapped her fingers on her knee. Charlie could see she was trying to stay calm, but her eyes sparkled with excitement.

"Have you ever heard of the saying 'hoist by your own petard?'"

"It's in Hamlet, isn't it?" said Charlie.

"Yes!" Eleanor's smile widened. "Shakespeare created the saying, but the word 'petard' is French. It was a small bomb used to blow open gates in castle sieges."

"We already laid siege to Ted's castle," said Charlie.

"If you weren't careful, a petard was liable to blow up in your face. And now, it's Ted's turn to be hoisted by his own petard," said Eleanor. "The weaselly scumbag."

A loud knocking sounded on the door. Dante's eyes flicked to his watch, and then he relaxed.

"It's Andrea from the pet shop / vet clinic / hunting store," he said, and got up to let her in, the cat still in his arms.

"Hi Dante," came Andrea's voice. "Is Eleanor there?"

"This way," said Dante.

Andrea bustled in, out of breath, her hair tied up in a large top knot. "Eleanor! You need to come with me right now!"

"What's happened?" said Eleanor.

"Ted managed to get emergency status to bulldoze your house and the others in that row!" said Andrea. "Some nonsense about ground subsidence."

Eleanor frowned. "I'm sure it's not legal to simply move the demolition date forward. Most of us haven't even finished packing up."

"That's why I'm here! Ted and his bulldozers are on site right now!" said Andrea. "They've already started digging!"

"But..." Eleanor stared into space. "How?"

"I told you," said Andrea. She crossed to link her arm with Eleanor's and tug on it, trying to get her to move. "Emergency status. I know it's dodgy, the council knows it's dodgy, things growing under rocks know it's dodgy. But it's Ted. He's bullied, bludgeoned, or blackmailed everyone into doing things his way. That's why you need to come now! If we get there in time, we can stop this. Somehow."

Abruptly, Eleanor stood. "Gentlemen, please excuse me. I'm going to rescue my house."

Charlie was already on his feet, while Dante gave the cat a careful pat and set it on the couch.

"We're coming too," said Charlie.

"Yes," said Dante.

51

In which hidden truths are revealed

Eleanor studied the bulldozers lined up, ready to chew into the row of houses. Her house was first in line, looking fragile against the huge digger wielded by a man hunched inside a greasy glass cubicle atop a grimy red machine.

Briefly, she considered lying in front of her house, or perhaps chaining herself to the white picket fence. In addition to losing her lovely house with its vintage rose garden and antique gazebo, she hated to see Ted win.

With a roar, the bulldozer kicked into gear. Eleanor stood shoulder to shoulder with the other homeowners as a digger gashed a huge slab of earth out of the bank.

A few minutes later, the bare clay of the new road was just a few metres from her house. Eleanor wondered if she should watch, or whether that would just make it more painful.

Up on the small hillock, she spotted Ted amongst a group of men in business suits and fluorescent hard hats. He caught her eye, grinned, and waved.

A hot flush of anger rose in Eleanor, which she immediately quashed. You should never let someone like Ted see he was getting to you. That was what a bastard like him lived for.

She returned his smile with one of her own, brighter, and sharper, and waved back like an ageing Jackie O. Ted looked away, his satisfaction diminished.

Seeing Ted here gave her pause. Certainly, he would be here at the scene of his great triumph, but there was something more niggling at her, trying to get her attention.

Her mind flashed to the eighty thousand dollar Hilux ute Ted had driven to the demolition site. She thought about the shell game, and how Ted had ruined his childhood bully's business and put his own in its place. He likes to flaunt his victories, she thought.

She swore under her breath. "The bastard's probably going to bury Adrian's remains under the ruins of my house." She could almost admire the pure malice, the sheer black heartedness of the gesture.

A few friends came over, faces tense. There was Fran from the RSA, Billy and Grace. She turned to Dante, who was watching the scene with narrowed eyes.

"My friends, would you like to assist me in bringing a murderer to justice and saving our houses from demolition?"

"What?" Fran started, too busy glaring at Ted to fully register Eleanor's question. Then: "too bloody right I would." She flexed her impressive forearms. "Who do you want me to thump?"

"Come this way with me," said Eleanor. "Quietly." They drifted to the back of the crowd. When Eleanor was sure Ted wasn't looking, she ducked behind a parked car. Eleanor took out her phone and dialled the Inspector, wondering exactly when his number had become quite so familiar.

The voice that picked up sounded calm as ever. "Yes?"

"I think I've located Adrian Wilson's remains. And I know how Ted killed Janice."

"And where are you?"

"In Te Kohe, about to watch my house be demolished. I'd appreciate your presence in the next few minutes."

"I'll see what I can do," said Avery.

The call cut off.

Eleanor slipped the phone back into her handbag. She hummed to herself. If Ted wanted a spectacle, then she would make sure he got one.

A few minutes later, Eleanor and her small posse of friends had worked their way around to the back of the demolition site. There were the shiny company utes, parked in a loose semicircle. The noise of the tractors and diggers was deafening. With a pang, Eleanor saw that one half of her picket fence was already ripped down, carved out of the landscape by a giant's hand.

"Would you like me to do something to the diggers?" said Dante. "I could go get my Remington 700 and shoot out the hydraulics."

"Thank you dear, but I think my way might be more permanently effective," said Eleanor. "Though I would like to ensure no one comes up this hill to interrupt us."

Eleanor peered over the tailgate of Ted's truck. The truck bed held three things. There was a statue to commemorate Adrian, an impressively ugly piece of modern art about four feet tall. It sat on a plinth, ready to be craned into position once its pedestal was made. And there was a tarpaulin laid over a pile of sand bags. All the sandbags looked entirely normal, except for one, which had been hastily duck taped closed.

"Give me a boost onto the back of the truck, will you?" Eleanor asked Fran. She immediately regretted it.

Fran boosted her so high she flew into the truck bed with height to spare, and only quick footwork prevented her from falling off the other side of the vehicle.

Ted had seen them. He and his small bevvy of burly men were turning in their direction.

Eleanor eyed Fran. "Would you and Dante stop Ted and his henchmen from getting to me before the rest of the townsfolk do?"

Fran grinned and rolled up her sleeves. Twin anchor tattoos wound up her forearms, and the anchor chains twisted as she flexed her muscles. "Let me at 'em." She headed down the hill.

Eleanor had seen one other thing, resting next to the ugly statue. An orange megaphone, useful for yelling at people on building sites, and possibly for exposing murderers. "It'd be nice to be right about this," she murmured.

Eleanor picked the megaphone up and switched it on. "Your attention, please." Eleanor's voice blasted out across the neighbourhood. "We are gathered here today to solve a mystery that has remained shrouded in secrecy for ten years. The murder of Adrian Wilson."

All the faces in the crowd turned towards Eleanor, standing on the deck of the truck on the small hill above the demolition site. His face uncertain, the man operating the digger paused.

"Keep digging!" yelled Ted. "And someone shut that woman up!"

"You'll find I'm on public property, Ted," said Eleanor.

"You're on my truck!" Ted shouted back.

"I'm glad you pointed that out," said Eleanor. "It's important to establish ownership. Now, I want to call you all to witness that right now I'm recovering a crucial piece of evidence. It's right here." She pointed at the pile of cement bags.

"Get her off of there!" shouted Ted at the henchmen to his right.

Two men started up the hill towards Eleanor. Fran stepped into the path of one of them, an evil grin on her face.

"You're not going up there," she said. "And I'll make it painful for you if you try."

"Get out of the way, sweetheart," said the man, stepping past her.

Whatever Fran did was lightning fast, but the man reeled back, both hands clutching his groin, his face gone ash white.

"Like I said," said Fran, "painful."

The second man started towards Dante, then paused. Dante stood, calm and casual, but his relaxed stance didn't seem to have fooled the man's hindbrain. He hesitated, checking over his shoulder as if hoping for reinforcements.

"I'd like all you residents up here," said Eleanor, "as witnesses."

The crowd, buoyed by that most basic of instincts, curiosity, began to drift up the small hillock from the other side.

Ted, his face red, began marching up the same path as his lackey had taken. He got to where Fran and the lackey were, the former with hands on hips, the latter still clutching his groin and making faces like a grouper fish.

Ted shoved the man at Fran and dodged around them both, breaking into a gallop as he ran up the last part of the hill.

But by then, the residents of Te Kohe surrounded the truck in a tight crowd, impossible for Ted to push through.

"Let me tell you a story," said Eleanor. "The story of Ted Andrews, a man so selfish, so greedy, so venal, that he murdered his best friend and stole everything from his grieving widow and young son."

"This is slander and libel," blared Ted.

"And then, when a similarly selfish woman found out and blackmailed him, Ted murdered her, too."

"How dare you!" snarled Ted. "Everyone saw where I was when Janice was shot."

"But that's the beauty of it," said Eleanor. "Everyone saw where you were at the time Janice appeared to have been shot. But in truth, she was shot a minute earlier. Here's how the events of the Jubilee night murder really played out."

Eleanor now had a rapt audience. Even the henchmen were listening, faces curious like passersby at a traffic pileup.

"Ted was a man with a two-fold problem. He needed to get his development done - quick - before he ran out of money and his debts caught up with him. But the woman blackmailing him - Janice - was going to take a big chunk of that payout, and he hated the thought of it. However, Janice was a smart lady. She'd laid aside a piece of incriminating evidence against Ted, and she'd told him that if she ever died under suspicious circumstances, she'd leave this item to Charlie in her will. So Ted had to remove Janice before the development went ahead. And he had to make sure that Charlie never received his package. So what did he do?"

"Shut that woman up," yelled Ted. Then he stopped and looked pale. Dante had inserted himself behind him. Eleanor thought it likely that a knife was currently pricking into Ted's back, just where his liver resided.

"It was a beautifully planned murder," she continued. "On the Pepper Tree Hotel balcony, Ted seated Janice at the end of the top row, and himself at the front row, where it was plausible that a bullet hitting Janice in the head could graze his arm. Then, when the fireworks started, he went to the pantry in the West wing of the Pepper Tree Hotel. He broke the window pane, and then, using a contraption we found in the dump, he fired a bullet so it grazed his arm. Then, he returned to the fireworks. As he passed Janice, he shot her in the side of the head using a handgun, and the fireworks hid the sound of the shot. Finally, he returned to his seat, hiding the gun in the holster in his unnecessarily bulky dinner jacket. The fireworks ended, Ted detonated the small explosive over the pantry window with a signal from his cellphone, and yelled that he'd been shot. Everyone assumed that the sound of the explosive was the gunshot, and Janice had just been murdered."

"This is preposterous," blustered Ted. "This is a fairy tale dreamed up by a meddling woman trying to keep her gardener out of jail."

"I kept wondering why the public murder," said Eleanor. "Then I realised. It was the perfect way to clear yourself, kill Janice, and make sure Charlie was framed for murder. With him in jail, it would be a simple matter to intercept the package sent by the person executing Janice's will. Getting desperate, you even tried to burn down Charlie's house with him inside it. But as well as trying to solve Janice's murder, we kept uncovering evidence of the original murder. And so you stole the chest with Adrian Wilson's remains in it."

"You're delusional," said Ted. "I have a chest, but it's something I found while diving years ago."

"You know the key to winning the shell game?" said Eleanor.

"What?" said Ted.

"It's not about which shell the ball is hidden under," said Eleanor. "Because anyone who understands how it's played knows that as soon as the game begins, the ball goes into the dealer's hand, so he can put it wherever he wants."

"She's gone mad," said Ted. "Someone, please shut her up."

"Adrian's remains were in the sea chest," said Eleanor. "And you wanted us to think they'd been buried somewhere out in the woods, where we could waste hours of police time searching for them. But they never left your possession." Her gaze was cold as ice. "It must have made you so proud, thinking how you fooled us all. How pleased you would be to bury the bones deep in the one place they'd never be found - in the wreckage of my home, under the brand new road. In fact, you were planning to bury them today, while the police searched your home and the surrounding land for signs of freshly moved earth. Dante, do you have a knife I could borrow?"

Dante materialised another knife and passed it handle first up to Eleanor.

"Now look here," blustered Ted. "Everything on that truck is my private property, and if you touch any of it, I'll have you arrested."

"Once again, I'm glad you've established ownership." Eleanor moved the knife over each bag of cement, but she wasn't looking at the bags. She was watching Ted's face.

When she hovered the knife over the last bag with the duct tape, Ted's eyes gave an involuntary flicker. With a swift cut, Eleanor sliced the bag along its length.

Sand slid out. But it was just sand, nothing more.

Ted smirked. "Not much of a grand reveal m'dear. Now, I suggest you be a good girl and hop down off my truck before I get you arrested for property damage."

Eleanor froze while her brain raced like a hare with the hounds hot on its heels. Her gaze alighted on the astonishingly ugly statue to commemorate Adrian Wilson. *Ted likes to flaunt his victories.*

In for a penny, in for a pound, she thought, and looked straight at Dante. "Get everyone back," she said, and threw her weight against the statue.

Dante shoved backwards, pulling a struggling Ted, now nearly incoherent with rage.

The statue rocked on its plinth, teetered for one agonising moment, then tipped off the truck as the crowd scattered.

There was a smash as the statue hit the ground. Shards of ceramic and sand exploded across the dark earth.

Eleanor gave a deep sigh, and the crowd gave an audible groan. There, lying amongst the sand and broken statue pieces, were bones, yellowed by time and the seawater.

Eleanor put down the megaphone and addressed Ted directly. "You, Ted Andrews, are an utter bastard. You were going to hide the bones of the man you murdered in his memorial. What a supremely venomous thing to do."

At the back of the crowd, a calm voice said, "Please step aside. Police coming through."

Inspector Avery, Hemi and Rosie pushed their way through the reluctant crowd, uniforms freshly pressed, faces grim.

"Inspector Avery," said Eleanor. "On the ground here you will find the remains of Adrian Wilson, murdered by Ted Andrews ten years ago. Dental records will confirm his identity."

"That's nothing to do with me!" snarled Ted. "That woman planted them there. She's trying to frame me!"

"Ted Andrews," said Avery, "you are under arrest for the murder of Adrian Wilson and Janice Enderby. You have the right to remain silent. You do not have to say anything unless you wish to do so. Anything you do say may be recorded and used as evidence. You have the right to consult and instruct a lawyer without delay and in private." He raised his voice. "Everyone else, this is now an active crime scene. Please move back to the road."

"You can't do this!" shouted Ted, as Hemi clamped one large hand around his upper arm. "I own this town!"

"You'll end up owning nothing but your life sentence," said Eleanor.

"I'm the victim here," cried Ted. "You've all been against me from the start! I had to make my own way from day one! I was just trying to get my fair share!"

"I suggest you exercise the right to remain silent," said Hemi, his face stern. "Come on. It's time to go."

Ted seemed about to protest again, then he looked at an empty space in the crowd, his mouth opening in silent horror. He looked, Eleanor thought, like a man who'd just seen a ghost.

"Get me out of here!" Ted rasped. He tried to back away from whatever it was he'd seen, but the bulk of Hemi was as immovable as a tree.

"Watch it, mate," said Hemi.

"Just go away! Leave me alone!" Ted held up his hands as if trying to ward off an attack, and his eyes were wide with terror. "Ok, ok! I did it! I killed Janice, and Adrian, and... just get her away!"

It seemed Janice's ghost had finally made an appearance. Eleanor scanned the crowd for Charlie, wondering what he'd see Janice doing.

"I'm not sure who you think is trying to get you," said Avery, "but your confession has been duly noted. Let's go."

Eleanor watched Ted being marched away. She searched the crowd once more for Charlie, but he was nowhere to be seen.

52

In which old memories surface

Pete and Charlie watched in great satisfaction as Eleanor's crime reveal played out. But as Ted said, 'I was just getting my fair share,' Pete gave a gasp.

"Pete, what is it?" said Charlie softly. He turned away from the scene to see Pete clutching his chest, looking pale, which, for a ghost, meant he'd turn chalk white.

Charlie stood, at a loss for how to help Pete as the crowd looked on at Ted's ruin.

"Pete," whispered Charlie. "What's happening to you?"

"I remember," rasped Pete. "I remember... everything."

"Come this way," said Charlie. "Please. Pete! Can you make it?" He ignored the strange looks people were giving him and beckoned Pete up the road, towards the little church and cemetery. Pete's ghost would be stronger there in the protective circle of the graves and the quiet resting place of his bones.

Inside the graveyard, Pete slumped against an oak tree trunk. His breath was laboured, and if he hadn't already been dead, Charlie would have feared he was having a heart attack.

It seemed foolish to try to help him over to the bench - after all, he was incorporeal. Charlie tried anyway, his hands guiding the old ghost's shoulders, only a slight chill where his living flesh met Pete's spirit.

Pete sank onto the bench with a sigh. His head tipped back, and he sat there, resting.

"Charlie, I remember how I died," he said at last. "I remember why I'm still here, after all these years."

"You want to talk about it?" said Charlie.

"Of course I do," Pete snorted. "I'm not one of your modern fragile butterflies. I just... needed to catch my breath, is all."

Charlie forbore to say that Pete hadn't breathed for ten years.

"It was what Ted said that brought it all back," said Pete. "Just now, when he said 'I was just getting my fair share.' It was exactly what he said the night he killed me."

Charlie stilled, then he was on his feet, heart pounding.

"Easy lad," said Pete. "The man's already going down for two murders. Making it three's not going to make a lot of difference."

"What happened?" said Charlie.

"After Adrian found out Ted's dodgy dealings, he created a family trust," said Pete. "He made me the executor. The trust was there to ensure Delia and you got his assets if he died. By then, Ted had already inserted the fake will into Adrian's documents, but it would have never held up in court if the trust deed had come to light. The trust already contained all of Adrian's assets."

"How did Ted find out about the trust?" said Charlie.

"Janice," said Pete. "At that time, Adrian's lawyer Leonard was hardly paying attention. He was half-drunk most of the time, and Janice was running the show. She must have told Ted about the trust, because two days after Adrian's death, he showed up at my place like he was in mourning. My house had already been broken into and searched, and I was already suspicious, but not suspicious enough. Ted had brought around my favourite whiskey. He said we had to drink a toast to Adrian."

"Poison?" said Charlie.

"My heart started to hammer, faster and faster, and a pain spread down my left arm. Ted, that bastard, said he'd give me the antidote if I told him where I'd hidden my copy of the trust deed. I guess Janice had kept her copy as blackmail collateral, and he needed to make sure my copy never came to light."

"And did you?"

Pete shook his head. "Ted would have let me die as soon as I told him. He's that species of snake. Also, screw him. No way was I backing down. So I played the cards I had. I told him nothing, and I died."

Charlie sat down and let his head fall into his hands. "Sometimes, I wish I was more like Dante."

"A reformed assassin?"

"Just an assassin."

"And I didn't remember how I died until now," said Pete. "Is that normal?"

"It happens," said Charlie. "That's why ghosts aren't usually that great at solving their own murder."

Pete leaned back in his chair. A small smile formed on his face, and he looked more relaxed than he had in days. "We have to go to Dante's place."

"Why's that?"

"I remember where I hid the trust deed."

———

Eleanor took Avery's offered hand as she prepared to hop down from the back of the truck. She gasped as he tugged her slightly off balance, catching her in his arms to set her down on the ground with a little more force than was strictly necessary.

His voice said in her ear, "I see you've decided to take the law into your own hands again."

"You were late, Inspector," said Eleanor. "And besides, my house was about to get demolished."

The inspector stepped back and surveyed the scene.

"I always thought small town crimes would be fairly pedestrian," he said. "I'm revising my estimation."

Eleanor was silent. The inspector followed her gaze to the carved out hillside, where a quarter of her garden had been destroyed, scooped clean out of existence and deposited in an untidy wreckage to one side of the road site.

"I'm sure we can get everything reinstated as it was," he said gently. "We'll probably find quite a few of the council members will come forward and admit to being intimidated into even considering this. There'll likely be a big fine taken out of Ted's estate to pay to repair the damage."

Eleanor folded her arms over her chest. The rush of excitement that always came from high stakes theatrics was fading, leaving her cold.

"I suppose so," she said. But she doubted her ancient roses, ripped from the ground and buried in rubble, would appreciate the eventual reign of justice.

53

In which the buried secrets are unearthed

Charlie waited, Pete by his side, as Dante unlocked the greenhouse. They made their way to the corpse plant pot and stood looking down at the brown soil.

"All this time," said Charlie. "I've been looking after this plant, waiting for it to flower. And it was here all along?"

"Adrian thought it would be fun to leave you a time capsule," said Pete. "You were such a gardening nut, even as a kid. Maureen Davison had just acquired the corpse plant, and you loved spending time in this greenhouse. I just put my copy of the deed in there as an afterthought. Something to look at on your 21st, when you were going to be gifted some shares. Neither of us thought we wouldn't be around to tell you about it, or that the lawyer wouldn't do his job. Adrian never even got around to telling Delia before he died."

Silently, Dante handed Charlie a small trowel.

"Here goes," said Charlie. Part of him was afraid that somehow Ted had gotten here too and removed his father's parting words. But on the second exploratory dig of the trowel, the blade struck metal.

Carefully, Charlie cleared the soil around a small aluminium tin. He levered it clear. It was wrapped in duct tape and when he shook it, it was packed full of something heavy.

"The trust deed is inside?" he said.

"And something special from your father, just for you," said Pete. The old ghost drew in a deep breath, as if testing the air, and a smile deepened the wrinkles on his face. "Well, I think that's about it for me." He looked over Charlie's shoulder at a scene visible only to him. "You know what, Charlie? That over there looks like just the place I'd like to go."

Pete was already fading as he took a step into infinity and disappeared from view.

Charlie wiped his eyes. He was fairly sure this was the last time he'd ever see his godfather Pete.

Inside Dante's house, Charlie laid the box on the kitchen bench and wiped the earth away. Dante took out a lethally sharp knife from his knife block and slid it around the tin lid, removing the duct tape.

A heavy package was nestled tightly inside the box, wrapped in three ziplock bags. There was an envelope with 'Adrian Wilson Family Trust Deed' typed on the outside, and a DVD in an unmarked case. 'For Charlie,' was written on the dvd in black vivid. Charlie recognised his dad's handwriting, and a lump formed in his throat.

Dante slit open the ziplock bags and teased the envelope and dvd case out. The two objects lay on the table. To Charlie's eyes they were heavy with significance, a Schrodinger's cat of information, literally buried for ten years, representing a fork in the road of his life.

He wondered what was in the trust deed, but even more, he wanted to watch the dvd. And he didn't want to watch it. Because then he would know what was in it, and it would be the last new thing he ever learned about his father.

"I think I'll watch this later," he said, sliding the dvd towards himself.

Dante nodded.

"I can take the trust deed to the police station," he offered. "Seems like it would be important to this case."

Charlie wanted to talk to his mother, he wanted to go for a walk in the bush, a swim in the sea, and he wanted to crawl into the deepest, darkest place he knew and never come out.

He gripped the dvd in both hands. "Thanks again, Dante."

54

In which satisfactory outcomes are reached

That evening, Charlie and Dante stood in Eleanor's front garden, surveying the replanted roses they'd rescued from the pile of earth where they'd be dumped. Charlie had carefully pruned them back, given them extra compost, gallons of water, and a sprinkling of Fran's special rooting compound.

Dante had had a quiet word with the road construction team, and Eleanor's front yard had been reinstated that day. There were still men working on her white picket fence, and it looked like they'd be finished soon.

Dante hefted the spade, unconsciously assessing its weapon potential. He thought it would work quite well as an instrument of blunt trauma. However, he did concede that it also worked well for digging in roses. "You think they'll be ok?" He pointed the spade at the replanted row of roses.

"By the end of summer, they'll be taking over the front garden en masse," said Charlie with supreme confidence. "I don't know what

Fran puts in her rooting compound, but it's basically voodoo steroids for plants. By April, I'll be trimming them back every week."

Eleanor's voice sounded from the back garden. "Tea's ready."

In the back garden, Eleanor had set out a pot of tea, cheesecake, and three cut crystal glasses filled with ice, a clear liquid, and a slice of lemon.

"I said tea," she said, eyes crinkling, "but I meant G&T. This mix has Fran's botanicals in it, so I take no responsibility for any side effects."

Dante sat in a wicker chair under the gazebo, the flowering wisteria dripping purple petals all around.

"The tea needs time to steep," said Eleanor. "So we may as well get into the good stuff."

"I haven't had a G&T before," said Charlie.

"Today's a good day to start," said Eleanor, passing him the glass. She raised her own vessel. "To truth, justice, and peace for those who've left this world behind."

"To justice," said Dante.

"To dad," said Charlie, his voice hoarse.

The silence that followed was companionable. Dante didn't have anything to say. Eleanor and Charlie seemed lost in their own thoughts.

Dante was only a tiny bit surprised when, with a lithe hop, the cat landed on the deck of the gazebo, slipping between two turned wooden balusters. It gave a small 'prrr' and leapt into Dante's lap, alighting so softly he hardly felt it.

"Your cat knows where to find you," said Eleanor approvingly.

"Umm, Dante," said Charlie. "You know that cat's on its seventh life, right?"

Dante stroked the cat between its ears, and its purring rumbled to a crescendo. "That's a thing?"

"Yes," said Charlie. "And cats can see ghosts. As far as I know, they're the only animals that can. Well, some dogs can smell ghosts, but I don't think they see them."

"Strange to think they could be all around us now," mused Eleanor. She took a sip of her G&T. "Are they, Charlie?"

Charlie shook his head. "Ghosts are great gossips. Any ghosts awake at this hour are probably over at the police station, watching Ted get read his rights."

"And your father?" said Eleanor. "Though you don't have to say anything if you don't want to."

Charlie shifted in his seat. "I haven't seen him. I don't think he's stuck here, though. He only came back when I got into trouble."

Eleanor reached across and patted his arm. "We're here for you."

"Thank you," said Charlie.

The cat purred like a small and satisfied tractor and stuck its claws into Dante's pants.

"Finally tracked you all down," came a voice. Inspector Avery strode down the garden path, still immaculately dressed, as if he hadn't spent the day directing the flood of forensics, uniformed officers, and other personnel who'd descended on both Ted's demolition site and his house.

He pulled up a seat at the table uninvited, creasing his perfectly pressed trousers as he sat.

"I've come to let you know they found Janice's package for you, Charlie. It was in Ted's safe. He'd intercepted it at the post office after your house was burned."

"Oh," said Charlie. "Good."

"It was a copy of your father's trust deed," said Avery. "He'd left his half of the hotel to your mother and you. I expect the whole business will revert to you both once the dust settles after Ted's trial."

"How about an apology for arresting Charlie?" said Eleanor.

Avery eyed her. "How about an apology for breaking and entering a private property, and vandalising a custom Hummer?"

"I have no idea what you mean," said Eleanor. "Do you, Dante?"

"No," said Dante. He stroked the cat, feeling back muscles flex under its silky fur.

"How's Ted doing?" asked Eleanor.

Avery smiled thinly. "He's clammed up now, but it won't do him much good. His original confession is admissible, as it was made after he'd been read his rights."

"How fortunate," said Eleanor.

"This isn't a drawing room," said Avery, "but I'm sure you'd like to do a full rundown of Ted's crime. Purely for my benefit, of course."

"Certainly," said Eleanor, beaming. She gestured like someone holding a cigarette, though her hands were now empty. "I noticed Ted was overheated throughout dinner. All the other guests had taken off their jackets, but not Ted. He needed to keep his on, to hide the fact he was armed. The device we found at the dump was necessary for Ted to shoot himself accurately, and from a distance that would leave no powder burns. And he had to do it just before he murdered Janice. The wound had to be fresh, otherwise Doctor Galway might notice the blood had already started to clot."

"That all fits," said Avery.

"After shooting himself, Ted covered the bullet buried in the wall with wood filler. That's the bullet I found."

"I had a word to forensics about missing that," said Avery.

"Ted then either threw the device in the skip bin on the way back, or put it in a wastepaper bin, knowing the staff would clear everything later. Your forensics team was looking for the murder weapon, not an unknown device, and so they didn't pick it up."

"A point docked from forensics," murmured Avery.

"Back on the dark balcony, Ted had seated Janice at the end of the row, in a corner with the deepest shadows. Ted walked by and shoots her in the side of the head. Again, the distance is enough to prevent power burns. It's an easy shot though — far easier than shooting her from the pantry window. All you'd need to take that shot is strong nerves, and the narcissist's absolute belief that what they want is the only thing that matters."

"Ted waits till the fireworks are ended, then activates the small incendiary device he's put on the pantry window hood," said Avery.

"It explodes, making a sharp bang like a gunshot," said Eleanor. "Ted yells he's been shot, and a lovely alibi is created in front of sixty people."

Avery gave a deep sigh and rested his elbow on the table. "It all fits. Every detail. You know, you're rather clever."

"And?" said Eleanor.

"And you and your friends solved a murder case. Thank you."

"You're welcome." Eleanor smiled and sipped her G&T.

"I won't stay," said Avery, standing. "Lots of paperwork. I hope to get back to Auckland tomorrow." His gaze sought Eleanor's, communicating something Dante didn't understand. Then he turned to Dante. "You, sir, I hope never to see again."

"Likewise," said Dante.

"Charlie, I'm sorry about your father," said Avery. "I'll do my best to make sure your family gets back everything you're owed as quickly and easily as possible."

"Thanks." Charlie had been bright red ever since Avery had mentioned breaking and entering, but he smiled and bobbed his head.

They all watched the inspector leave.

"Do you think Delia will take over the hotel?" asked Eleanor.

"She's always wanted to," said Charlie.

Dante was glad the almond croissants would remain of a high standard.

"Mum knows you don't like visitors much, Dante," said Charlie, "so she wanted me to tell you thank you for all your help."

Dante appreciated this. His opinion of Delia, already high, rose a few more notches.

"I imagine there'll be a good chunk of money coming to you from Ted's estate, Charlie," said Eleanor. "Not that Ted has a lot of money left with all his debts, but there should be enough to pay off your mum's mortgage and get your own place if you want it."

"Mum said it's a good result," said Charlie.

Dante studied the young man. Charlie didn't look happy, exactly, though Dante supposed that was a result of not having dispatched his father's murderer himself. However, the young man held himself differently. It was a subtle change, but Dante was good at reading bodies. Charlie seemed both lighter, as if he'd let go of something, and more grounded.

"I've talked to Noah, the investor who was here on Jubilee Night," said Eleanor. She smiled in satisfaction. "He's going to buy up what's left of Ted's holdings. And he doesn't want to knock anything down. He's into historical preservation. Also, he wants his watch back." Her smile widened. "Nice how things can come back to bite those who deserve it." Her smile grew pensive, and Dante wondered what was on her mind. "All in all, a satisfactory outcome," she said at last.

Dante surveyed the garden and wondered what the human equivalent was of rooting compound — something that would cause a person to become attached to a particular place. Perhaps, he reflected, the compound involved solving a murder mystery with two new friends, one of whom saw ghosts. And a cat.

"Yes," he said.

55

In which Charlie says goodbye

Back in his family home, still smelling of smoke and charred timber, Charlie sat on the couch, the DVD case cradled in his hands. His mother was still staying with her cousin, and he hadn't yet told her about the dvd.

This was unusual for Charlie. Generally, he told Delia everything, and this was helped by the fact that he never did anything he would want to hide. But this last message from his father was his, and while he did plan to share it with his mother, he wanted to watch it by himself the first time. That way, it would feel like it was just his dad and him.

Charlie opened the DVD case and knelt down by the TV cabinet. While she'd made the switch to Netflix several years ago, Charlie's mother still owned a DVD player. It was dusty from disuse, but it started the first time Charlie switched it on, making unidentified mechanical noises as the DVD drawer slid out of the machine.

Charlie placed the DVD in the holder and watched it slide back into the player. He had a sudden fear that it might not play. Maybe it hadn't been encoded properly when his father made it?

He sat back on the couch and pressed 'play' on the remote. The few seconds it the player took to get started felt like several years, but then, there was his father.

On the screen, Adrian Wilson was sitting in his office at the Pepper Tree Hotel. Charlie hadn't been there for ten years, but he knew it well. It was where he used to wait sometimes after school when his mum was busy. His dad used to let him read the Yates Gardening Guides, looking for exotic plants to put in their garden.

His dad looked at the camera, brows faintly creased as he checked it was recording. Adrian Wilson had the same hazel eyes as his son, and brown hair with a hint of red in it.

On screen, Charlie's father took off his reading glasses, rubbed his eyes, then put them back on again. To Charlie's adult gaze, he looked tired. But then his father smiled, straight at the camera, and an answering warm glow lit in Charlie's chest. That was the father he remembered.

Adrian cleared his throat and began. "If you're listening to this, son, then I've died. I don't think there's an elegant way to say that, so I'll just say it. These things happen. Death and taxes, the only two certainties." His wry smile faded. "And I want to say I'm so sorry. Because I want to be there for all the milestones of your life: the first time you shave, your end of year ball, (or do they call it a disco these days?) your first date, your first car, all the firsts. And all the seconds, and thirds, and thereafter."

"But if you're listening to this, then I'm so sorry, son. It means I've kicked the bucket, and I won't be around any longer. Hopefully, we've had a good innings together, and you're in a strong place.

"But no matter how long we've had, please know that I'll always love you. Don't tell your mother, but being a father has been the best thing I've ever done. Of course, marrying her was the second best." Adrian's grin reappeared, and an answering smile curved Charlie's lips in reply, even though his face was wet with tears.

Adrian looked serious again. "Now there are a few business things I want you to know about. Firstly, Ted was your legal guardian, but I've recently uncovered some financial misdeeds of his. So I've transferred all that over to Pete. It's all in a family trust I've drawn up. Delia's been stressed lately, so I haven't told her all this yet. But I will, as soon as all the paperwork is finalised. It's what she'd want, too.

"It's all arranged so if her and I were to cark it, Pete will look after things until you're twenty one. He said he's put the trust deed somewhere safe, but he's a bit forgetful sometimes, so I'll make sure Delia knows where it is too. I'm buying Ted out of his share of the hotel, and on your twenty-first, a portion of those shares will come to you as a 'welcome to adulthood' present."

His father scratched his chin in a heartbreakingly familiar gesture.

"Now we've got the legal stuff over with, here's some life advice." His father leaned forward, eyes twinkling. "Floss every day. I know it seems boring, but you gotta look after those teeth. You're not a shark, you only get two sets of 'em."

Adrian held up two fingers. "Second, listen to your mother. It's going to be tough with just the two of you, so look after her, and she'll look after you, and you'll both be alright.

"Lastly, and I left this till last in case I need to cut the tape short for emotional reasons. I love you, son. Always know that. It's been so good getting to know you, and I'm so proud of you."

Adrian stopped and a loud sniff punctuated the silence. Charlie half laughed through his tears. He'd always known he'd gotten his easily activated tear ducts from his father.

"Son," continued Adrian, "that stuff you told me about seeing ghosts? I believe you. It's what makes you special, and I hope you'll accept it for what it is: a gift. I know you'll use it wisely."

"I'll be seeing you around, kiddo. Bye for now."

Charlie's father reached towards the camera and the screen went black as he switched off the recording.

"Seems like only yesterday I made that."

Charlie looked to his right.

Adrian Wilson was sitting next to him on the couch, a silvery light glowing around the edges of him, the couch cushions visible through his ghostly form.

"Dad!" Charlie swiped a hand across his eyes. He tried to pull himself together. "Hi."

"Hi, son." Adrian squeezed his eyes into a half happy, half sad smile. "I meant every word on that tape. I'm so sorry I missed the last ten years. But son? You look good." His father's gaze swept Charlie from head to toe. "You've grown into a man I'm proud to call my son."

"Dad." Charlie had to resist the urge to throw his arms around his dad. He knew from experience this didn't work well with ghosts. You ended up feeling like you'd stepped into a freezer. Questions crowded his mind, and he plucked one at random. "You know about Ted?"

"Yeah, sure," said Adrian easily. "Looks like I was right to cut him out of my legal affairs. You and your mum should be set now he's out of the picture."

"Aren't you mad at him?"

"Ted? No." Adrian shrugged. "Funny thing, death. It gives you a new perspective on life. I'm sad I missed you growing up, but I'm not mad at Ted. He's facing the consequences of his actions now, and they're not pretty, believe me. Not now, and not in the hereafter."

"Why are you here now?" said Charlie. "Why not when I was a kid and had just lost you? I would have done anything to see you then."

"Yeah, I know," said his dad quietly. "It would have been nice the first few times, and then what? You'd have stopped living, Charlie. You'd have had two feet in the afterlife, rather than just one. Life is for the living, and..." he spread transparent hands, "I died."

"Where have you been, then?" Charlie winced. He sounded like a surly teenager.

Adrian smiled, an expression Charlie knew from the countless days and nights of his childhood. "I was on the other side. Not stuck between, like those poor souls you help. I was beyond." His smile shone. "It's beautiful. Quite different from anything I can describe in words... But then I knew you were in trouble, so I came back."

"And you couldn't just tell me where the trust deed was hidden, and saved us all a helluva lot of trouble?" Charlie was losing the battle against his inner sulky teenager.

"Son." Adrian tried to look serious, but his face was luminous with affection. "Trouble is what life is for. And it's hard to describe how different things are, after life. It took me a while to find my way back into this world, to remember how it works, to get the hang of time and space again. And by then, it turned out you and your friends already had things pretty well in hand." He laid one ghostly hand on Charlie's shoulder, and it wasn't cold. It was featherlight, with the faintest warm glow. "Charlie. You done good."

"Dad..." Charlie wanted to hug his dad and bury his face in his shirt, like when he was a kid. But he was probably as tall as his dad now, and infinitely more solid. And he also wanted to ask a million questions, like 'can I see you again,' and 'why do you have to go now?' but he already knew the answers he got wouldn't be the ones he wanted. Instead, he just said, "I'll miss you."

"Not too much," said Adrian. "Live life the best you can. Give your mother my love." He started to fade. "And, son? Remember to floss."

"Bye, dad," choked Charlie, and he was alone in the room.

56

In which Dante attends his weekly AA meeting

"You look different," said John.

"I think I am," said Dante.

John's eyebrows drew together, a delicate crease appearing on his high forehead. "Do you want to talk about it?"

"I had a moment..." Dante drew a breath. "I nearly died, and then I saw..." He hesitated. It was hard to put into words the pearl-like perfection of the moments after he'd fallen down the waterfall. Moments when he'd cared enormously about being alive, and at the same time could have died that instant and been utterly content. "...I saw everything. How it all connects. I don't think I could stay there. But coming through it, I feel different."

"I see," said John.

"Death is part of life," said Dante. "They're the same thing, if you look at them from the other side."

"I understand where you're coming from, and I agree in a philosophical sense," said John. "However, in a practical sense, I'd prefer you kept to the code. If you want to remain part of this group, that is."

"Ok," said Dante.

"Yeah," said Frankie. "Keep to the code, man. Or we'll all come and find ya."

57

In which Eleanor receives an invitation

Eleanor had stored the documents in a vintage leather messenger bag. Quite possibly, it had held similarly sensitive documents during WWII, since it was a gift from an old friend who had been in MI6.

Inspector Avery was waiting at the corner table of Eleanor's favourite cocktail lounge, located in the centre of Auckland. He was wearing an expensively well-cut dark grey suit. Somehow, whatever he wore, he couldn't seem to shake the 'officer of the law' vibe.

Eleanor shrugged internally. Maybe that was what he was going for.

She made her way through the tables, feeling the consequential weight of the documents in the bag far more than their actual weight.

A certain malaise was gathering in the area of her heart. Once she gave the inspector the documents, she doubted her arrest would be immediate. In the interim, she could perhaps leave the country under another of her passports. Or a friend's superyacht.

But at a deeper level, she felt weighed down, too melancholy to fly. She liked having a home, and friends who weren't in the business, and a garden that bloomed all year round.

With a smile, she sat opposite the inspector. He had already ordered a drink - a Manhattan. She wondered if that was a subtle dig at her natural habitat.

She beckoned a waiter over and ordered an espresso martini. For old time's sake.

"Cheers," she said, raising the cocktail to her lips.

With a smile, he mirrored her movement.

"Well, Inspector Avery," she said. "Let me be the first to congratulate you on solving three cases - Janice Enderby's murder, Adrian Wilson's murder, and an art heist from several years ago. I'm sure this will put a nice grace note on your illustrious career." She handed over the messenger case.

"Please, call me Marcus," said Inspector Avery.

"I suppose since you're about to arrest me, there's no point standing on ceremony, Marcus," said Eleanor. More than half of her espresso martini was already gone. She signalled the waiter to bring her another.

Marcus fished a pair of reading glasses out of his breast pocket and began examining the document, skimming through them with a practised eye.

"What do you plan to do after this meeting?" he said without looking up.

"Go dancing," said Eleanor. "There's a lovely club just two blocks up. They have a live band and play Latin, tango, ballroom and jazz - all the classics. And not to worry, I've put my address on the card there," she indicated the inside flap of the bag. "So you know where to find me."

"Hmmm." said Marcus. He took an idle sip of his Manhattan and leafed through a few more pages.

Eleanor set aside her empty cocktail glass and started on the second one. She didn't intend to go home tonight until it was morning. She'd always believed it was a good idea to see the dawn when you're about to start a new chapter of life.

The waiter set a plate of hors d'oeuvres down on the table - scallops, sashimi, and elegant pastries reminiscent of Paris.

Eleanor savoured a pastry as she scanned the drinks menu. There was time for perhaps one more cocktail before she left for the club. She wondered if Marcus intended to pick up the tab at the same time as she decided there was no way she was going to pay. She was already paying more than her fair share.

"I didn't know you could abseil and pick locks," said Marcus.

"Two skills every lady should cultivate."

He flicked a glance over her black evening gown. "You won't get a chance to wear that for the next few years. I believe the current uniform in most prisons is bottle green."

"It's said that manners maketh the man," said Eleanor. "And clothes do not make the woman."

"What's going to happen to your garden while you're gone?"

"Oh, I expect Charlie will look after it for me. It'll probably prosper marvellously."

Marcus regarded her impassively for a moment, then went back to reading the documents. Eleanor tapped her shoe. Already, her feet were preparing for the dance floor later tonight.

"Well." Marcus folded the glasses back into their case and disappeared them back into his jacket. "This all appears to be in order. Quite a thorough set of evidence."

"Would you like me to walk you through it?" said Eleanor with a pointed smile. "In case you've missed anything."

"I don't think that will be necessary," said Marcus. He carefully returned the documents to their case and slid it back to her across the table.

She stared at him.

"As you said, an in-depth summation of the case. It thoroughly implicates you at every level of the theft," said Marcus. He appeared to be enjoying himself. "Even though you had to have had at least one accomplice, it seems you've fabricated a way around that. And might I commend you on the Cezanne forgery. It seems to have fooled all our authenticators. Although, under the circumstances, it was easier for them to go along with the narrative you took such trouble to create."

Eleanor frowned, her fingers tightening on the soft leather of the messenger bag. "I agree. But why am I the one holding the documents?"

Marcus smiled a warm smile, sharp as a knife. "I wanted to see if you'd keep your end of the bargain."

"To see whether there's honour among thieves?" Eleanor was not certain whether she was furious, relieved, amused, or a combination of all three. Against all expectations, it seemed she'd been played.

"Quite," agreed Marcus. "And, having kept your side of our deal so rigorously, I'm prepared to let this go, and let you go. On one condition."

"And that is?" Eleanor's danger radar went back up to full capacity.

"I hear there's a place just a couple of blocks from here. Where a live band plays music suitable for dancing. So." He gave a slight inclination of his head. On the chair where he'd put his coat, there was a black fedora hat. "I have one question for you."

Eleanor noticed the small scar on the left side of his chin and the five o'clock shade on his jawline where he'd missed a small patch shaving this morning. The heaviness that had weighed her down since she'd compiled these documents was disappearing like absinthe in a flame.

Marcus's brown eyes met hers. "May I take you dancing?"

Her mouth curved upwards. "Why yes," she said. "You may."

58

In which Dante encounters Society

It was three weeks after the events of the Jubilee Murder, and things had returned more or less to normal.

Dante had managed to dodge all the invitations and social engagements that came his way once Ted had been arrested and a highly edited account of his part in the solving of the case had circulated the town.

But then, the corpse plant had sent a tiny pale shoot up into the dappled sunlight of the greenhouse. And suddenly Dante was a celebrity again.

As Charlie predicted, the Botanical Society, by some strange osmosis, had found out. Then the Friends of the Cemetery, the Lions Foundation, and all the horticulturally minded groups in Te Kohe (which seemed to be all of them) also knew.

They all wanted to drop by and see this floral wonder. Dante had seriously contemplated disappearing into the Urewera Ranges for a year, or maybe joining an expedition to Antarctica.

But Eleanor had swooped in, as Charlie had promised, and funnelled the town's curiosity into one afternoon.

"It's just three hours, dear," she'd told Dante. "Even you can manage that without shooting anyone."

"Just make sure none of them comes into my house," said Dante. "Or touches my cat."

Dante wasn't sure when 'the cat' had turned into 'my cat,' but it had happened, as smoothly as a feline stretching out in a patch of sun.

"Your cat will be fine," said Eleanor. "All the various Te Kohe societies like cats."

Now it was the day. Dante had spent the morning pounding his punching bag until a big dent marred one side. Then he cleaned all his firearms, polished his body armour, and sharpened all his knives.

This occupied his time until 2pm, when Eleanor, Andrea and Charlie arrived to set out a large table in the front yard filled with disposable cups, homemade lemonade, and assorted cakes and slices.

Andrea's presence puzzled Dante until he remembered she was part of the Te Kohe Botanical Society.

"Yes dear, I'm sure that's why she's here," said Eleanor with a smile when he informed her of this. "Now go and help her put up the marquee."

It was, Dante reflected, not as bad as he'd thought it would be. There was a crowd of people in his garden, that was true. But they kept to an orderly line as they trooped in to view the corpse plant, and most likely none of them had weapons. (Eleanor had vetoed his proposal to have a metal scanner at the front gate.)

He and Charlie had put in extra hours of gardening that week, and there was not a leaf out of place. Dante had quite enjoyed sharpening the chainsaw blades. He had a new appreciation of the combat potential of gardening implements.

And inside his greenhouse, the corpse plant bloomed, an enormous, strange, lewd flower, ten feet in height, with a violet frill like an Elizabethan lady, and a stamen like a protruding tongue.

It smelt of decomposing corpses, an odour Dante was disturbingly familiar with. But no one seemed to mind. There were many photos taken in front of the plant (Dante declined to be in any of them) and many handshakes and 'congratulations,' as if Dante had personally caused the plant to bloom.

People were... friendly. That was it. There was a friendly atmosphere throughout Dante's home.

Again, these were words Dante had never considered could ever apply to him. But there it was.

"Well done," murmured Eleanor, passing him a glass filled with a clear liquid.

Dante took a sip and discovered it had been spiked with something decidedly alcoholic.

"Grace made an adult only version of the lemonade," said Eleanor. "About 45% proof, I'd say."

Dante thought about what to say next. Nothing came to mind.

"You're doing just fine, dear," said Eleanor, patting his arm. "And everyone's behaving themselves. Though I'll have to make sure Mr Whittaker and Bernard don't get to talking. They always argue about the best way to prune roses. As if either of them knew more than Charlie. But I don't want them coming to blows on this lovely occasion."

"Thank you for organising this," said Dante.

"We're friends now," said Eleanor, her green eyes direct. "Any help I can give you, I will."

"Likewise," said Dante, and marvelled at how the words both had weight, and made him feel lighter.

It was midnight in Te Kohe, and Dante lay deep in a dreamless sleep, the cat curled up in the crook of his arm. Several streets over, Eleanor slept, a patch of moonlight slipping through a slit in the curtains to cast a silver glow on her face.

In his childhood home, Charlie dreamed the dream of a person who can talk to spirits.

He walked through a field of golden lilies, where each flower shone like the sun. The lilies glowed brighter as he smiled and waved their gilded petals as he passed.

And in Dante's greenhouse, under the light of the full moon, the corpse plant began to release its pollen into the night air.

The ghost of Mrs Davison studied the cloud of dust, brushing over the leaves and drifting out through the vents in the roof of the greenhouse.

She exchanged a glance with Charlotte Evans, deceased 1955, and through a strange series of circumstances, Botanical Society president from 1940 to 1959.

"Well, that's torn it," said Mrs Davison. "I don't think Charlie knows about what's going to happen next."

"So much for a quiet and peaceful summer," said Charlotte. She cracked her knuckles. "I guess there's time to prepare for what's coming."

"I suppose…" said Mrs Davison. Her old eyes saw through the glass of the greenhouse into another realm entirely. She sighed. "I hope so."

AUTHOR'S NOTE

I started writing this book when my twin son and daughter were about a week old.

There is something about being woken every 2-3 hours through the night that inclines the mind to murder. Writing a cozy mystery seemed like a healthier outlet for that impulse :)

I also had a huge wave of nostalgia for the New Zealand of my childhood. It was a land full of pristine beaches, mellow Sunday afternoons, and magical forests.

That country still exists, of course, but perhaps it is only accessed through the eyes of a child.

On the Town of Te Kohe

This is a fictional town. All the references to Maori history are fictional, as are the tribe names.

Te Kohe is populated by fictional people. If you think a character might be based on you, and it's a likeable character, kapai. It probably was.

If you think one of the more villainous characters was based on you, then no, absolutely not. Though you might want to try being a little nicer :)

On the inspiration front, I'd like to recommend to you all 'Hicksville' by Dylan Horrocks, and the Moomin books by Tove Jansson. Both of these writers achieved the indefinable mix of comfort, mystery and adventure that I was aiming for.

As a mystery writer, I owe a great debt to Agatha Christie, who created the inimitable Hercule Poirot, David Suchet who embodied him, and of course Sir Arthur Conan Doyle.

Whether or not this story was a two pipe problem, I hope you enjoyed it.

For more information (and some other neat stories,) go to:

www.ShadowKingdomBooks.com

Made in the USA
Monee, IL
25 March 2025